About the Author

I have been a fan of crime fiction for many years, but I was tired of reading about older detectives who start the story off damaged. With the love of true crime among people my age I was surprised that no one had thought of writing about a younger detective. I couldn't wait for the detective story that I wanted to be written, which has resulted in 'Cult', the first story of DC Ashley Fenway.

I live in North Wales and work in the financial sector in Manchester. I live and breathe football and for my sins I support Crystal Palace.

Cult

Jon Day

Cult

Olympia Publishers
London

www.olympiapublishers.com
OLYMPIA PAPERBACK EDITION

A CIP catalogue record for this title is
available from the British Library.

ISBN: 978-1-78830-597-6

This is a work of fiction.
Names, characters, places and incidents originate from the writer's imagination.
Any resemblance to actual persons, living or dead, is purely coincidental.

First Published in 2020

Olympia Publishers
Tallis House
2 Tallis Street
London
EC4Y 0AB

Printed in Great Britain

Dedication

Dedicated to Nana Pat and Gramps, for telling me my voice mattered.

Chapter 1

Good to see my taxes going on making sure kids have a place to do crack safely... #smh #whatstheworldcomingto?

New Mayor team starting as they mean to go on by throwing money at shit and seeing what sticks. #outwiththeoldinwiththeold

Daughter just had her phone stolen by some gippo on a moped. #wildwestouttherefolks

Looks like this new Labour council wants to raid my pay packet, time to make bonuses more appealing. #onestepahead

This city is going to the dogs, needs something to change it round.

One murder a year is too much but having three a week is a scandal. #getagrip

Heading to @GMP headquarters today for some big announcement. #99problems

The murmurs of the assembled press filled the room; reporters conversing about their private lives, other stories their rivals were printing and about the story they were here to report on. Photographers prepping their cameras, bloggers, news stations; everyone was being assembled for the announcement that they were gathered for.

The door to the press room opened and the Police and Crime Commissioner for Manchester, the Chief Constable and the newly-elected Mayor of Manchester walked out. As they walked up to the erected pulpit some journalists placed their recorders on the pulpit. The cameras started clicking and the scribble of pen on paper filled the air. The Commissioner, who was leading the announcement, took centre stage while the Mayor and Chief Constable flanked him.

The Commissioner's name was Glen Mayer, a former businessman that had been elected to office with the promise of cleaning up the crime that was plaguing Manchester's streets. Mayer was a former head teacher with short, military-style, grey hair, a trim physique and a stern gaze that always made you feel that you were being constantly watched.

"Ladies and gentlemen of the press, thank you for coming." He shuffled his papers and looked out at the sea of reporters.

"As you are aware, I was given the task by this great city of cleaning up the streets with regards to the gang violence, gun crime and violent sexual attacks that have been associated with Manchester in the past few years." He sipped on a glass of water that was on the side of the pulpit and continued.

"With the help of the Mayor and the Chief of Police we have made great strides in reducing crime and educating people on what it means to be part of a better community." A few journalists looked up at him with raised eyebrows.

"I'm not going to say that the decrease is dramatic, because it isn't," Mayer said, his hands gripping on the sides of the pulpit. "There is more that can be done, that will be done; starting with what we are here to announce today.

"Manchester and its surrounding boroughs have the bravest police force in the country, but even they need help. Help with the cases that are the things of fiction and television drama. We are devising a new task force that will benefit not only us but the surrounding area. Starting next week, we are creating the MMC, otherwise known as Manchester Major Crimes Unit."

More scribbling from the journalists.

"The MMC will deal with every major crime that comes its way, whether it be murders, kidnappings and robberies; they will deal with these heinous acts, and more to the point they will solve the crime committed."

A couple of journalists made sceptical faces.

"I want to assure all of you that this isn't some gimmick. This new unit will operate out of a state-of-the-art facility in Manchester's City Tower with all the bells and whistles that is needed for a department like this. And before you all get your knickers in a twist, this money has been allocated in the budget for the year.

"So today, I want to tell you, the press and the public that we aim to make Manchester the safest city in the country. This is only the first in a new raft of initiatives to cut down on crime but also poverty, drugs, gangs and the causes of why people turn to the other side of the law."

The speech got more head nods, and more notes taken.

"This is the rise of a new dawn for Manchester!"

***

Donald McArthur was sat behind his desk in Longsight police station. On his desk were the files of the detectives that he wanted to bring into his new team for the new Major Crimes Unit. The office was dark, barely lit by an old desk lamp. He ran a hand through his thick, grey hair and took a sip of his coffee.

It had been a long and arduous process to pick out the team. A couple were easy picks while some of them needed some convincing; even he himself needed convincing to join this new team. Ever since his transfer from Glasgow he just wanted to stay as a DCI, but because of his team's continuous success he was asked to head up his own team for the MMC. His wife twisted his arm and here he was.

"Late night Donald?" Detective Chief Superintendent Cartwright was at the mouth of his office. He too was joining the MMC as the head detective.

"Just sorting through the names," Donald said, patting the neat pile of files on his desk. "I have one more space, and I have no idea who to allocate it to." Cartwright smiled and walked into the office. He sat in the chair opposite McArthur.

"So, who are the potentials?" McArthur leaned down and pulled some more files onto the desk, clearing the members with relative ease. Cartwright pulled out a pack of cigarettes.

"Do you mind?" He offered one to McArthur who shook his head.

"Wife told me to give up if I wanted to see the grandkids married," McArthur explained. "Eight, six, five and four." He shook his head. "At least it's an excuse to go down to Eastbourne once a year."

Cartwright picked up one of the files.

"I know a few of them have already picked names for their teams, have you got one?"

"The official name is Manchester Major Crimes Unit Thirty-Two," McArthur said. "I think just to piss of AC I'm going to call us MC32." Cartwright laughed.

"That'll really piss 'em off," he said. They both started to look through the files of people on the desk, chatting as they went and reminiscing. "What about this one?" Cartwright picked up a file that was on his unread pile. McArthur frowned as Cartwright opened it up. He frowned too.

"Ashley Fenway, twenty-four years old, Metropolitan CID." He flicked through the file. "You might want to give this one a miss," he said, throwing it onto the out pile. McArthur frowned. He gulped down the rest of his coffee and asked for it. Cartwright handed it over, while McArthur leaned back in his chair and flicked through the file.

"Ashley Fenway, born in Lancashire, 10th February 1993. Head girl at both secondary school and college. Won the Lancashire County Girls hockey cup, North England Cup and captain of her school, her district and her county and the North of England. Has a double first in psychology and sociology from the University of Edinburgh, as well as a first in criminology from Manchester University which she did as a PC." McArthur was intrigued.

"Joined Manchester Metropolitan in 2014 with a personal recommendation from DCI McCallum of Edinburgh CID," McArthur smiled.

"She must have done something to have impressed him," McArthur mused.

"Yeah, three guesses how."

"Prolific PC," McArthur said going through Ashley's arrest record. "Has two special commendations but along with that a suspension for flouting the odd rule. Fast tracked to Metro CID under the wing of DS David Hughes."

"That's Carter's division," Cartwright said having a drag from his cigarette. "They're on the cusp of a killer at the moment."

"Is that Fenway on the case?" McArthur asked. Cartwright nodded.

"That's how I know she's trouble. Carter needed me to have a word with her about intimidating a potential suspect. She's adamant that they have their man."

"Potential hot head," Cartwright nodded.

"Maybe in a few years, but now?" He gave McArthur a knowing look. McArthur understood. That was Cartwright's subtle way of telling him not to go for her.

But the more he read about this girl the more he was impressed. Cartwright said that she was trouble, but he saw a tenacious streak.

Chapter 2

"Right, don't do anything stupid." Ashley shifted down and accelerated past the car in front by going onto the wrong side of the road. It was a quick in and out manoeuvre but got blares of horns from an oncoming car. Ashley was still watching the Passat in front that was weaving in and out of traffic.

Inside the car was Steve Marler, a youth centre worker who had been the main suspect in the murder inquiry of three teenagers that were all at the cut-off point of the club's age policy; all sexually assaulted and murdered by strangulation with the assailant facing them. After a couple of near misses and a department under pressure with the new Major Crimes Unit coming in, they needed a result.

The orders of Ashley's DCI, DCI Carter, were to monitor Marler; because he was, in Carter's words, "A slimy bugger," and wait for him to make a mistake. Well, that was for DS Hughes to monitor him. Ashley on the other hand was told to stay away after making the accusation but with no hard evidence to back it up.

Marler made a sharp left that was taking him out to a less built up area. Ashley had to make the turn quickly, testing the BMW's brakes as she swung round and sped down towards a disused industrial area. Without any cars in the near vicinity, Ashley sped up, trying to overtake.

Marler though swung left and went into the courtyard of an old warehouse. Ashley braked sharply, went full lock and screeched to a halt, but thankfully facing in the right direction. Ashley sped down toward the warehouse.

Marler had tried to drive out but saw Ashley's BMW descending on him. Marler abandoned the car and ran off towards the warehouse. Ashley stepped out of the car and slammed the door quickly shut. She quickly tightened the ponytail that housed her dark brown hair and ran off towards the warehouse.

Run.

Why did they always run? she asked herself.

Ashley saw the dark figure of Marler shoulder-barge the door open and slip in a gap. If he could fit in then Ashley would definitely be able to.

Ashley pushed the door open and squeezed through into the warehouse. Ashley had a quick look around. From what she could see, and it wasn't a lot, this was the only way in and out. Ashley got her torch out and looked around to see if there was anything, she could use to barricade the door. Ashley found an old piece of welding rod and rammed it through the chain holding the doors together and the handle. She looked around the warehouse; an old welding factory. She could hear Marler moving around but was unable to determine where he was, her brown eyes scanning around the dark silhouettes of the warehouse machines.

Ashley moved forward slowly, her torch lighting up the abandoned projects. The sound of metal on concrete filled the warehouse. Ashley shone her torch towards the source of the sound.

"You've got nowhere to run Steven," Ashley called out. "I know you were the one who killed those girls."

Nothing. Ashley could hear his footsteps on the metal grates further down the warehouse. Ashley looked down at her torch. If she kept this on, Marler would see any time she got close. She looked round, moving back and bumping into some chains dangling from a freight rail.

Ashley grabbed the chains and bound her torch to them. She gently pushed it away, so it mimicked the torch moving further down the warehouse.

She set off and walked quickly towards the sound, keeping low so her shadow didn't alert him. Ashley crouched behind a machine, scanning the grates where she heard Marler. The shadows though betrayed nothing. Ashley pulled a pained face. For her plan to work she needed some sort of contact with Marler.

Movement.

Ashley's eyes darted to the movement and went forward on her haunches, her eyes still locked on the movement. Marler had made his way to the door. He tried to open it, but the bar Ashley used was wedged tight between the handle and the chains. Marler tried to un-lodge it but it was wedged in tight. He looked around frantically. He saw the torch with its sparse light moving further away.

Marler looked at the second floor of the warehouse where there were large windows with a metal walkway. Marler went to run to the stairs towards the second floor. Ashley though, sprang into action. She got down low and tackled Marler into some drums. Ashley tried to keep him on the floor but was easily brushed aside by Marler.

But the plan was in motion. Marler got to the metal staircase taking two at a time. Ashley got to her feet and went after him. Marler got to the top of the staircase. He kicked hard which made the rusted metal come loose and fall. Ashley slid to a stop and somersaulted out of the way as it crashed to the floor. Ashley looked up, Marler was running across the metal walkway on the other side of the building to the fire escape. He got there but it wouldn't open.

"You killed those girls Steven Marler!" Ashley called out. There was a pause as Marler stopped fighting with the door.

"Yes, I killed those poor girls." He started pacing, trying to find another way out. "They all needed to be spared, from the pain of growing up, where evil boys will want to corrupt them and… and defile them." Ashley was disgusted.

"So, you defiled them yourself!" she shouted back. "You thought that it would be better if you raped them!" Marler was bawling; a show of the pathetic boy he truly was.

"I didn't rape them!" he shouted. "They wanted me to."

"You've just admitted killing them, Steven Marler," Ashley said still trying to find a way up. "For god's sake, they were just children!" She got back to the haulage rail. She grabbed the chain and began to climb up.

"But they were going to leave…" The tears evident in his voice. "They… they were going to."

"Go on to great things before you killed them." Ashley pulled herself to the top of the rail. She made her way carefully to the metal walkway

16

Marler was on and climbed over. She took in a gulp of air, but she smelt smoke. She looked over and saw a small fire on the floor. The drums were full of old oil; when she'd tackled him, it had spilt over the floor. When the stairs hit the floor, a spark must have caught.

Ashley turned to run across the metal walkway to where Steven Marler was now running away from her. A triple murderer and rapist now at the end of his rope. He tried the door again but to no avail. He saw Ashley advancing. He took one look at the window leading outside and made his mind up.

"No!" Marler though ran and jumped out of the window. The glass shattered in slow motion as he jumped through. Ashley could see the Manchester skyline in the distance of the broken window, but it was brought to earth with the shattering crunch of Steven Marler. The fire was now spreading across the ground floor. If she couldn't find a way out: best case — she lost her case, worst — her life. Ashley kicked the fire escape door, but it was wedged shut. Ashley kicked it hard again and it moved slightly.

"Good, good!" Ashley looked down to see the fire spreading. Knowing how much old machinery was in here, if one went the rest would blow up like dominoes. Ashley kicked again and the door splintered open.

Ashley took a step back and unleashed one more kick. The lock broke and she fell forward onto the metal railings outside. She groaned and winced at the pain, but when she looked up, she saw Marler's lifeless body surrounded by glass.

"Shit." Ashley started to make her way down the metal staircase.

Ashley jumped off the staircase and onto the gravel below. She winced at the pain and looked back at the building that was engulfed in flames. Her priority though was Marler. She stumbled over, holding her ribs which throbbed with pain and pulled Marler further away from the fire. After what felt like an eternity of pulling, she let him down far away from the fire. She checked his pulse.

She checked the other side of his neck.

She placed her ear to his chest.

"Oh no you don't." She huffed as she started chest compressions. "Come on you son of a bitch!" She gave him mouth to mouth.

"You have to pay for what you put those girls through!" She pounded his chest. She balled her fist and pounded his chest again.

"Don't, die, on, me!" She pounded him hard and he spluttered into life. He coughed and tried to move but the broken bones he'd suffered in his fall restricted his movement. Ashley coughed but felt pleased with herself and sat down on the ground.

"You... you should have let me die," he whispered. The plan.

"And why's that?" Ashley asked out of breath.

"You... you still have nothing on me," he sneered. "And now, beating up a potential suspect." He laughed lightly.

"You're screwed."

"Not very classy for someone's last free words." Ashley reached inside Marler's jacket, pulled out a smart phone in a heavy casing and pressed a button. Marler stopped grinning.

"What's? What's that?" He asked, slightly scared.

"Oh, this?" Ashley held it up while sitting next to him, looking at the fire. "When we grappled earlier, I planted this on you," she explained. "Amazing what people say when they think no one's recording." She rewound the recording back and pressed play.

"You killed those girls Steven Marler!"

"Yes, I killed those poor girls. They all needed to be spared, from the pain of growing up, where evil boys will want to corrupt them and... and defile them."

Marler frowned.

"I want my solicitor." Ashley heard fire engines in the distance.

"Why don't we get you an ambulance first, eh?" Ashley patted his broken leg which made Marler cry out in pain.

"Sorry. Oh, and one more thing." Marler turned to her.

"Steven Marler, I'm arresting you for the murder and rape of Hollie Tyson, Chelsea Kinnock and Tamsin Cox. You don't have to say anything in your defence, however anything you do say can and will be used as evidence against you in a court of law. Do you understand?"

Marler didn't reply.

"Marvellous," Ashley said, pulling her own phone out which now had a cracked screen. She was still able to call 999 though.

"999, which service to you require?"

"Yeah, all of them," Ashley replied.

"All of them?" The responder asked, perplexed.

"Yes, I have a suspect that's thrown himself out of a burning building and has multiple broken bones and injuries; so that's fire, ambulance and the police because he's a suspect in an ongoing murder inquiry."

"Sorry, who are you?" Ashley sighed and ran a hand through her hair.

"I'm Detective Constable Ashley Fenway." The building blew up again. Ashley looked at it and shrugged.

"And an ambulance for myself would be nice too."

***

There was something very therapeutic about fire. The way it danced, with no inhibitions, sensual and crazy all rolled into one; and like her, it always danced better at night.

Ashley was sat in the back of an ambulance with only a badly grazed arm and bruised ribs for her trouble. She had been sat down on the gurney but was now sitting on the edge of the van with her shock blanket around her shoulders. Marler was on his way to hospital. The paramedics said he should be OK and ready for formal questioning the next day; it was mainly the shock that had stopped his heart.

Ashley looked up from the rim of her cup at the burning warehouse. The fire crews had decided that it was better to let it burn down rather than waste water putting out the flames. She went to take another sip, but the cup was empty.

"Dammit." She placed the cup down and continued to look at the flames.

"Fancy another?" Ashley looked to her right to see a man walk from behind the van. He was a good-looking man in his fifties, well-built with light hair. He too was looking at the fire, his long coat fluttering in the wind. He was holding two cups of Starbucks.

"I said, fancy another?" He held out one of the cups. His Scottish accent had a soothing tone to it.

"Thanks." Ashley took it and took a sip. She made a face at the taste; black. Ashley took her coffee white. "But I prefer tea."

"Huh, most coppers prefer coffee," the man replied; his gaze transfixed on the fire. Ashley looked back up at him.

"I'm not most coppers."

"Indeed, you're not, DC Fenway." Ashley stopped drinking and looked up at him.

"What do you want?"

"My name is Donald McArthur."

"I know who you are. Detective Chief Inspector McArthur," Ashley replied. "I asked what you wanted?" McArthur laughed. He took a sip of his coffee.

"Tell me DC Fenway, what do you know about the new MMC?" Ashley thought for a moment, still watching the fire. She rotated her shoulder.

"I've read the news." She took a sip of her coffee and winced again. "It's an overzealous, boys' club," Ashley said, looking back to the flames. McArthur smiled.

"I can't argue with that," McArthur replied. "Listen, I'm putting together a team for the MMC, DC Fenway. I've had the files of countless detectives thrust on my desk."

"And what makes me the lucky one?" McArthur pulled out his phone and his glasses, he unlocked it and scrolled through it.

"That I found yours by accident." McArthur replied looking down at the file. "Your superiors say that you are rash, impulsive and can be rebellious against authority."

"Not the CV of an MMC detective," Ashley quipped, taking another sip.

"You're right, it isn't." Ashley shrugged

"Which is exactly why I want you on my team." Ashley looked back at him.

"Sir?" McArthur took a sip from his cup but continued to stare at the burning building.

"That rash streak, that take no shit attitude is something this city lacks," McArthur explained. "In my opinion it's something it's lost. This new department is dealing with the very dark and depraved individuals,

20

and I need somebody on my team who is sometimes going to bend the rules to do what needs to be done."

"And you think I'm that person?"

"Your DCI told you not to go after Marler tonight and yet you caught him," McArthur said, taking another sip from the cup. "I doubt your partner knows that you did either?"

"No, no he did not," Ashley said, looking down at the floor.

"Why?"

"Because he wouldn't approve." Their conversation was stopped by the wailing of sirens in the distance. McArthur looked over at Ashley.

"Because he was supposed to be tailing Marler tonight," Ashley said, now looking down at her cup. McArthur chuckled to himself at the police marked Vauxhall that came through to the courtyard of the warehouse. Inside were two men, the man in the passenger seat instantly got out of the car before it stopped and slammed the door shut.

He strode over towards the ambulance that Ashley was in. His name was Darren Carter, her current DCI, his bullish features and small eyes bored into her.

"What the fuck are you playing at Fenway?" He scowled. "I told you that Marler was off limits! Not to antagonise him or contact him in any way! I have DS Hughes telling me that he can't find Marler anywhere, only to get a phone call from my DCS telling me that he's in the hospital!" He stopped in front of Ashley who glared back at him.

"Care to explain since you were the one who put him there?"

"He jumped."

"Don't get smart with me!" Carter whispered viciously. "You'll be lucky if there's a case left after the stunt you just pulled. I hope you have the same balls to tell the families that you let the only suspect we have get off scot free!"

Ashley didn't say anything at first. She nodded and reached into her jeans pocket and pulled out a mobile phone. She scrolled through and pressed play on the recording.

"You killed those girls Steven Marler!"

"Yes, I killed those poor girls. They all needed to be spared, from the pain of growing up, where evil boys will want to corrupt them and… and defile them."

21

"So, you defiled them yourself! You thought that it would be better if you raped them!"

"I didn't rape them! They wanted me to."

"You've just admitted killing them, Steven Marler! For god's sake, they were just children!"

"But they were going to leave... They... they were going to."

"Go on to great things before you killed them"

Ashley stopped the recording and held the phone out for him.

"By all means, show them. I'm sure that they'll be heartbroken."

Carter looked on surprised at her. Ashley nodded for him to take the phone. Carter took the phone off her gingerly. McArthur smirked to himself as Carter walked away. His face angry at the fact Ashley had bested him.

"You OK?" Ashley looked up at DS David Hughes, the detective who had taken her under his wing when she first moved to Manchester. He was a kind man with thinning, blonde hair and calm, blue eyes.

"I'm fine, Dave," Ashley said, looking down at her grazed arm. "Sorry about all this," she said, pointing back to the burning building behind them.

"Don't worry about that," he said. "From what I heard it'll mean he'll be locked up for a while." Ashley breathed out heavily.

"Thanks for the coffee," she said. Hughes was only now alerted to the presence of McArthur, who nodded.

"My pleasure," he said. "DCI McArthur." He held his hand out to Hughes who shook it.

"DS Hughes. Why did you get her coffee? She drinks tea." Ashley got on her feet and pushed Hughes back.

"David, stop it!"

"Stop calling me David."

"There's nothing untoward if that's what you're wondering," McArthur explained. "I just wanted to have a chat with DC Fenway." He reached into his long coat and pulled out a card.

"Have a think about it," he said, offering it to her. "Just let me know ASAP, otherwise I'd have to start sifting through all those files on my desk again." Ashley smiled slightly and took the card.

"Thanks. I'll think on it." McArthur turned and walked away from the ambulance towards his car. Ashley looked down at the card. The MMC, the new super department that was going to encompass Manchester and surrounding areas for all major crimes, or what was deemed a major crime. But she'd worked hard to become a detective with Dave ever since she joined the force, she'd only just got the transfer to his team six months ago. Was now the right time to go... what if the chance never came again?

"Are you sure you didn't bump your head?" Dave asked.

"No." Ashley's concentration was solely on the card in her hand. Just as she finished, Carter came over with a disgruntled look on his face.

"I don't think your recording will be enough to prosecute but we can use it to scare a watertight confession out of him. That and with the other evidence we found it should be enough to get him convicted." He swallowed hard.

"You did well tonight Fenway," he said, through gritted teeth.

"Thanks sir," her attention still on the card. Carter was waiting for a more smart-arsed reply. He just grunted.

"Hughes, take me home."

"Yes sir. I guess I'll see you tomorrow?"

"Yeah." Ashley got up and hugged him. "Take care." Hughes walked off with Carter, leaving Ashley on her own. She looked at the warehouse fire which was now dying down. This was now or never.

***

Ashley parked up in the underground carpark and sighed. A hot shower would do her the world of good. She closed the door of her 1 Series BMW and walked to the lift in the middle of the car park. While waiting for the lift she reached into her jacket and pulled out the card McArthur had given her.

PING!

Ashley walked into the lift and pressed the button for the fifth floor. When the lift got to her floor she got out and walked right towards her apartment. She walked down the corridor which was pitch black save for the moonlight coming in from the windows.

She got her keys out and opened the door with ease and turned the light on.

The apartment was all open plan with the front door opening to a kitchen, dining room, living room combo which spread across the whole of the apartment.

Ashley undid the laces of her boots and walked left into her kitchen which was separated by a low wall. She turned her radio on, got her phone out and saw that she had two messages. She opened the voice mails and played them on speaker while she went about her jobs.

"Hello Ashley, it's your mum."

"Damn." Ashley was supposed to phone her tonight. She opened the fridge and pulled out a smoothie.

"I don't know if you forgot that it was catch up night, but knowing your work load it wouldn't surprise me if you're out." She sounded disappointed. Ashley undid the top of her smoothie and started drinking.

"Hopefully with a young, gentleman caller." Ashley rolled her eyes. *"But you wouldn't tell me if you were. Everyone's OK, your sister, Jamie and I are going to a wedding fair over the weekend and your brother had his open day at university. If you get a chance phone me, if not I'll catch you next week. Look after yourself, love you, bye."* Ashley finished her drink and wiped her mouth with her sleeve.

She loaded the next message and pressed play.

"Hey, Ashley... It's Mike..." Ashley groaned. She walked to her bedroom which was on the right of the living room.

"Listen... I was wondering if you fancied meeting up again? I had a great time last week."

"Glad you did," Ashley said, as she walked into her bedroom.

"If you want to give me a bell, I'd like to meet up again. Bye." Ashley rummaged through her chest of draws and pulled out a t-shirt and some pyjama bottoms. She stripped down and walked into the en-suite.

She spent a while under the hot water; she instantly winced as it hit her graze and bruised ribs. She looked down at her graze and ran her hand over it. Ashley cleaned off the soot on her skin as well as the rubble in her hair. All the while though she was thinking about the card in her coat pocket; about the MMC. A chance to deal with major crimes every day, not just when she was lucky enough to stumble across one.

After her shower she changed, poured herself a glass of wine and sat down in her living room which looked out on the canal and Manchester skyline. She rubbed some Vaseline over the graze and wrapped some bandaging over it.

When she finished, she threw the card on the table and continued to stare at it while tapping the rim of her glass. She took a large gulp, picked up her phone and dialled the number. It was answered on the fifth ring.

"Hello?"

"Hi, DCI McArthur? It's Ashley Fenway," she said, cursing herself for her piss-poor opening.

"DC Fenway," he said, tiredly. "Now what makes you call me at one in the morning?"

"Oh." Ashley turned and looked at the clock. "Shit, sorry," she said, wincing. "Look, I was thinking about your offer for the MMC."

"Oh, and?" She gulped.

"I'm in," she rushed.

"Excellent. I'll make the arrangements with DCI Carter," he said. "Now, will you let me go to sleep?"

"Oh yeah, yeah, sorry," Ashley fumbled. "I'll see you soon then."

"You will, DC Fenway. Good night."

Ashley hung up. She breathed out and smiled to herself. She finished the rest of her wine in one and walked back to her bedroom. She placed her phone on charge and got in under the maroon sheets. She winced as she applied too much pressure on her arm and got herself comfortable.

PING!

Ashley looked over at the phone. She rolled over and looked who the message was from.

Dan: *Hey u, hope your well. Fancy some fun this week?*

Ashley unlocked her phone and opened her messages, most of which were from work or the occasional one from her family.

Hey u, hope your well. Fancy some fun this week?

That would be so nice, but I don't know what's
happening with work. I'll let you know.

She sent the message off. Almost immediately the little dots appeared showing a message was being typed out.

Busy saving the world detective?

***Something like that, might want to get the Herald
tomorrow.***

Front page?

Not me but my DCI will be

Shame, I think you'd look sexy in that small bowler hat. ;)

You think I look good in anything

*Well show me what you're wearing now and we'll
call it even.*

You'd love that wouldn't u.

Come on, don't make me beg.

Well you do look sexier when u beg.

Ashley smirked to herself and sent it off. All that was sent back was a winking face. Ashley placed her phone back on the side table.

Chapter 3

Ashley walked into Manchester Metropolitan police station rubbing her head; late nights chasing murderers and escaping burning buildings were catching up with her. Despite being early in the morning it was still busy, an anti-austerity march in the city centre had gone bad with some anarchists deciding it was the perfect place for a punch up.

She cast an eye over on one boy who didn't look older than eighteen. As soon as he clocked Ashley casting an unimpressed eye over him his mouth gaped.

She jogged up the two flights of grey stairs to her team's office. She passed the incident room that still had the case work for the Marler case on the white boards. She walked into the office for her team, Dave was already there like he always was, filing paperwork. She took her jacket off and looked around.

DS Jones and DC Cuthbert, the other two members of the team were probably having breakfast at some seedy, greasy-spoon while she could make out DCI Carter in his office.

"He wants to see you." Ashley looked over at Hughes who didn't look up from his paperwork.

"Don't suppose he was happy, was he?" Ashley asked.

"Quite the opposite."

The door to Carter's office swung open. Carter, his bullish eyes falling on Ashley, narrowing at the sight of her.

"Fenway. My office." He walked back in with the door slamming firmly behind him. Ashley looked down at the floor and breathed out. She opened the door and walked into the office. Carter was finishing writing a statement. Ashley waited patiently, folding her arms across her chest, resisting the urge to tap her foot to show her impatience.

"Marler confessed," Carter said, not looking up at her. "Sang like a bird after we played him that recording, not to mention a goldmine of evidence in his car. His lawyer thought that he might be able to get Marler off, saying the recording was under duress. But after this morning, he's going down for life for sure." An underwhelming feeling of 'is that it?' flowed through Ashley.

"So… that's it, job well done?"

"Seems that way," Carter said, still not looking up. Ashley frowned. In the short time that she knew DCI Carter she never knew him to congratulate her on just doing her job. He must have known about her joining the MMC.

"With respect, sir," she said through almost gritted teeth. "You wouldn't just call me in here to say job well done." Carter exhaled loudly through his nose. It reminded Ashley of a boar readying itself for a charge. He didn't say anything at first. He threw his pen on his desk and leaned back, folding his arms across his chest.

"I got this phone call earlier." He looked up at Ashley. "The Chief Constable has sanctioned your release from this department to the new Major Crimes Unit." Ashley nodded.

"I got asked last night, and after a lot of thought I think it's the right thing to do." Carter thought for a moment.

"I don't understand you. You pestered me for months to take you on, changing your shifts so you came to our crime scenes, always canvasing out cases." He looked down at the Costa coffee cup on his desk. "Bloody finding out what coffee I drink. How did you find that out by the way?"

"I followed you." Carter shook his head.

"See, you're a natural," he said. He got up and walked to his window that overlooked central Manchester. "Before you say anything, no, I'm not bitter. Well, maybe a little." He ran a hand as well as he could through his short hair. "I'm just upset that we're losing a bloody good detective."

That surprised her.

"Sir —" He held his hand up for her to stop talking.

"You have one week to leave a good impression," he said turning back. "All the best." It certainly surprised Ashley that Carter thought she was a good detective. It didn't mean she should be any less humble in his praise.

"Thank you, sir," Ashley said.

"Now get out, you still have to write your statement for last night. I can only wonder just how long it's gonna be." Ashley smiled to herself and nodded. She walked out of the office and sat at her desk. Ashley let out a huge sigh, resting her hands behind her head.

"Went well then?" Ashley looked up at Dave.

"You could say that," she replied, taking another deep breath.

"Not being suspended?" Ashley shook her head.

"No. He's sanctioned my release to the MMC."

"The MMC?" Dave asked, walking to her desk. Ashley was starting to write her report into the chase last night.

"When did they ask you?"

"Last night," Ashley said, looking up at him. "That's what DCI McArthur was doing when you turned up." She went back to typing.

"And you accepted?"

"Why not?" Ashley replied, not looking up from the screen. "This is a great opportunity." She could tell from Dave's silence that he didn't think so.

"I don't think it will last," he said. "It'll crash and burn like every other major unit they've tried to roll out."

"Then I'll make it work," Ashley said, looking up at him with a smile. Ashley went back to typing. "Anything to prove you wrong." Dave laughed to himself.

"Well in that case, Sharon told me to ask you if you fancied coming out for dinner tonight. It can double up as a congratulation dinner too. Up for it?"

"I finish hockey at nine."

"Great, half nine it is."

***

"Come on! Run the channels!" Ashley looked up and saw Kimberly making a great run down the line. Ashley got the ball out in front of her and stroked the ball across the astro-turf pitch. As soon as the ball left her stick Ashley sprinted forward into the space being vacated by the defence going to close-down Kimberly. Kim controlled the ball and looked up.

"Kim!" Ashley shouted. "Kim!" It happened in a flash, but it all seemed to happen in slow motion. Kim looked up and saw Ashley pointing at the space with her stick. Kim played the ball in low, but a little bit quicker than Ashley would have wanted. Ashley though adjusted her footing and swept the stick across the ground.

She connected with the ball, using the extra pace and it swept across the keeper and smashed into the net. Ashley fist pumped and her teammates came up and congratulated her. A sharp blow on a whistle made them look to the side-line.

"OK girls, good practise." Karen the coach said, clapping her hands. "Get the cones in, come on, hustle, hustle!" Ashley helped collect the cones in while chatting to some of her teammates.

She played for Didsbury Northern Hockey Club. They were a good side; of course, the coach was thrilled when Ashley turned up for a training session and ran the show. She was thrust straight into the first team to some of the other girls' annoyance, but over the years they had come to appreciate her skill. The team were third last year and currently sitting four points behind the league leaders.

"Right, big game against Alderley Edge on Saturday," Karen said. "I'll text you all the details; be at the tennis club for two."

She walked back to her car with her two friends from the club. The two wingers: Di, raven haired, blue eyes with white skin which earned her the nickname Snowy and Eliza. Her brother had a thing for Eliza. She was almost as tall as Ashley, light brown skin and frizzy, brown hair which she often wore in an afro but now was pulled back into a ponytail.

"We so need to go out," Eliza said. "That last guy I took home was so shit I made my shopping list in my head."

"It's because, you always take home fuckboys," Di said. "Just go for a nice guy."

"Too boring."

"They are not." Eliza looked to Ashley.

"Ash, back me up," she said, with imploring eyes.

"Sorry, have to back Eliza on that," Ashley said, taking a swig from her bottle. "The majority anyway." Di waved her hand dismissively.

"That's why you two are still single. Too picky."

"And yet me and Ash always have male admirers," Eliza said, putting her arm round Ashley's shoulder, which made her laugh.

"The difference being that you act on it," Ashley said.

"You took that Mike home with you," Di pointed out.

"Yeah, didn't I regret it?" Ashley said. She said her goodbyes and walked over to her car, opened the boot and put her stick and bag in the boot of the car.

Ashley got in and looked at a group of three girls chatting to one another. Ashley started the car and pulled away.

***

If there was one thing Ashley hated doing more than paperwork it was doing make up. Her sister always had a natural affinity for this sort of thing but she on the other hand wasn't as graceful. She'd picked up a couple of tips, so she was always able to get away with the bare minimum.

After changing into some jeans and a smart top her mum had sent her for her birthday, she made her way out.

She walked past the new block of apartments that had been slowly been going up over the last year or so and went to the Northern Quarter.

The Northern Quarter of Manchester was the new, vibrant hub of what people were calling the 'New Manchester'. Trendy bars favourited by smart, young workers with low lighting and exotic tastes. Ashley found it weird that of all the places in Manchester she could have settled: Didsbury, Salford, and Castlefield, yet she had settled best in the city centre. Ashley had never thought herself as a city person but in the last couple of years that she'd been here she was always discovering something new. Ashley's mum had commented on it when her parents came to visit her.

"You always know the best places to go," she commented. "And you always know somewhere new when we do come." Ashley smiled to herself as she walked past a packed bar, to the restaurant she was meeting Dave at.

It was a strange friendship, her and Dave. When Ashley first joined the police, she didn't really know anyone. She had joined the local hockey club and 'knew' people, but no one she thought she would be able to confide in.

Her first murder case though she met Dave, who was the first responding detective, so she had to relay the crime scene to him. Over the years though Ashley had struck a friendship with him and his family, seeing them more so than her own.

Ashley reached the food hall and walked to Mogli's, the street Indian cuisine restaurant. Ashley walked upstairs to the top floor where Dave and his family were already seated. His wife, Sharon, was an unassuming middle-aged woman with brown hair and a kind face. His teenage son, Ollie, who had something of a crush on Ashley, was fourteen.

"Ashley dear." Sharon came over and hugged Ashley. "So glad you made it."

"Thank you, Sharon," Ashley replied. She saw a bottle of Budweiser at her place at the table.

"Danielle is running late so she should be here in a moment," Sharon explained.

"That's fine," Ashley said, sitting down next to the empty chair at the table opposite Ollie. He was smartly dressed for the occasion, his brown hair shaved at the sides and gelled at the top. He shuffled nervously while Ashley took a swig from her bottle.

"How's school going with you Ollie?" He cleared his throat.

"Fine, thank you." His voice was deeper, a ploy to make him seem older. Ashley smiled to herself. "Yeah, I've taken my options so... Uhm..."

"Looking forward to it?" Ashley asked. "I remember doing my options."

"What did you do?"

"History, Electronics, P.E and they did a sociology course with the local college, so I did that," Ashley said. As she finished Danielle showed up.

Danielle was Dave's daughter. She was twenty years old and was in her last year of university in the city. She also worked at the local, down the road from Ashley's place. She was good looking and knew it too; long, wavy, blonde hair with dark blue eyes. She was naturally pretty with soft curves that her clothes always seemed to compliment.

"Hi everyone," she said in a bright voice, as she sat down next to Ashley. "Bloody traffic was murder, some idiot thought he could beat a lorry to the lights."

"What happened to the idiot?" Ashley asked.

"Well, I wouldn't want to be the one who has to explain why my new Porsche is now a cube." Ashley laughed while the waiter came with their menus.

"Dani dear, where's Tom?" Sharon asked. Tom was Danielle's boyfriend of four years.

"He got held up with football. He won't be back till late and he apologises for not being able to make it."

"Well then, in that case." Sharon held up her drink. "I think congratulations are in order now everyone's here. To Ashley, congratulations on your promotion to the new…" She looked to Dave to help her out.

"Manchester Major Crimes." Sharon nodded. "To Ashley."

"To Ashley!" Ashley smiled and had a drink. The food was nice, the laughter flowed, and it felt weird to Ashley how Dave's family had taken her as one of their own. Not that she was estranged from her own family, but Ashley aspired to something greater than the farm she had grown up on. Her mum and dad were the third generation to look after it while her younger brother was being groomed to look after it after them. Her older sister was still a waitress, (wait, head of service operations; she did hate it when Ashley called her a waitress), at the local country club where she met her husband to be, no doubt ready to turn out little ones and be a devoted housewife.

Ashley though, wanted to experience the wider world. She was the first person in her family to go to university; her mum had wanted her to stay local, but she went to Edinburgh to put some distance between her and the life she was leaving behind. Her decision to join the police surprised her mum who tried to talk her out of it. It was her dad who had supported her moving to Manchester to make a name for herself.

They came to visit occasionally, but Ashley was more her own woman now. Surrounding herself with hockey, MMA and her work.

"So." Danielle leaned over towards Ashley. "What is it you're gonna be doing in this new super unit?" Danielle had been the first real female friend Ashley had made in Manchester so they were quite close, plus Ashley knew she could confide in her any personal issues.

"I'm not sure," Ashley replied, honestly. "I think I'll be dealing with crimes that are high priority and ones that haven't been solved yet."

"So, you're basically The Avengers of Manchester police."

"Like the TV show?" Ashley asked. Danielle laughed and touched her shoulder.

"Yes Ash."

"Sure, why not then? Are you still coming over on Sunday?" Danielle nodded while she took a sip of her white wine and lemonade.

"Yeah, I finish at Jimmy's around twelve." Ashley nodded.

"Well, I guess the countdown to the MMC begins."

***

"What constitutes a major crime?" The TV anchor tapped her pen on her desk.

"Nearly a month after this supposedly super crime fighting unit was established and it's been reduced to the proverbial rescuing of cats from trees. Its new headquarters in the middle of Manchester has cost taxpayers north of ten million pounds to fund and equip. It hasn't dealt with anything that I personally would consider a 'Major Crime'. What are we getting for our money? What do we think ladies?" The anchor, a smart looking woman in her fifties looked at the rest of the women that made up the panel of the show.

An older woman in her sixties replied. "To me it sounds like a huge government waste of money that could have gone on the NHS." There was a smattering of applause from the audience.

34

"The hype for this new police force is a farce quite frankly. There was nothing wrong with the old Serious Crimes Unit in Manchester, so it looks more like a re-branding."

"But old major crimes divisions are still intact."

"Then what are they actually doing?"

"According to the Mayor of Manchester the unit is helping to tie up all existing Major Crimes in Manchester and surrounding boroughs. Very few major crimes have actually happened at this point since its inception."

"Hardly; there are three murders a week in Manchester at the current rate, surely gangland activity should be high on the agenda?"

An old model in her thirties, looking worse for wear after a few bad surgeries picked up a newspaper.

"I think the real issue has been brought up in The Guardian by Melisa De Luna," she said, opening the broadsheet to a two-page article.

"Only twenty percent of this new department, which I might remind you encompasses Manchester and the surrounding areas, are women." There was a huge gasp from the panellists and the audience.

"Only twenty?" The lead anchor asked. The old model nodded.

"To make matters worse, almost all of them are behind the scenes jobs: admin, HR, support and canteen staff; very few actual female police officers."

"This is 2017, this is totally unacceptable," the lead anchor said, disgusted. "How many rapes and sexual attacks are not being investigated because an all-male department doesn't constitute it as a major crime?" There was a 'hear, hear', from the audience.

"I think the Manchester Police and Crime Commissioner should come in here and explain these facts!" There was a loud applause from the audience.

***

The rain drizzled down on the street outside the hotel. He pulled his collar up from the wind, taking one last final check that he wasn't followed. Satisfied, he walked into the hotel lobby. Plain looking with floral vine wallpaper with a large sofa seating area which were covered in maroon cushions. He looked around again, everywhere he'd been looking for days there had been... the... object of his desires.

Young, petite, innocent.

He looked both left and right. A few of his friends had been caught in stings similar to this, something that was seemingly too good to be true. But he had been careful, every step done behind the mask, but he had spoken to the agent. They'd been sympathetic to him but he knew deep down he disgusted them. He disgusted everyone. No sane person could like and respect a man like him, for the things he wanted; but he was too desperate to care what they thought of him — it had been too long.

He walked to the receptionist's desk. She was young, blonde, pretty and perfect to be the face of this hotel branch. She smiled politely at him as he got to the counter.

"Hi, I have a reservation." He tried not to sound nervous. One shifty look and the whole thing was up in smoke.

"Can I ask what name it's under sir?"

"Nicholas." The code the name they had agreed on.

"Ah yes, room 245?" She asked. He nodded. It must be the one. She smiled, turned to get the key off the hook and handed it to him.

"There you are," she said in a cheerful voice. "If you're free maybe you could answer this questionnaire." He didn't have time for all the small talk. He wanted to get out of here, and quick.

"Sorry, I can't right now," he said, fiddling with the key going to walk away. "Maybe later."

"If you need anything just call the front de —"

"I will, thank you!" He didn't mean to be tetchy; she was only doing her job, but he was on edge. It had been years since he could partake in these desires.

He took the lift to the second floor, shuffling nervously in both anticipation and fear. When it stopped, he walked out quickly into the corridor not looking up in case there were cameras about. He got to room 245 and opened the door quietly. He made his way into the hotel room. It was plain and basic; perfect. He drew the curtains, got everything he needed ready and then sat on the bed.

Months of talking, planning and fantasising had come down to this one moment. He was here for something darker, much more depraved and frowned upon in real life. It wasn't like the old days, where people like him would know how to get the things they needed.

He thought the internet would make it easier but it was a double-edged sword. "It made things easier in a way, but it also made it easier for you to get caught.". Proof, evidence, it was all stored on a computer and could be used against him. In the old days there was only the evidence you kept but now it was easier to organise things like this. No more hiding in dark alleys to sort out details or silly masks at old manor houses.

PING!

He checked his phone. The messages he had been waiting for. He got off the bed and walked to the door and opened it.

"Hello," he said, turning to invite them in. "We can —" Before he could finish, he was hit over the head.

***

When he came to the room was dark. The only sound he could hear was the rain gently patter on the window. He tried to get up but felt his arms strain against something. He looked up. In the shadows of the room he saw his hand tied up.

"Oh god…"

"He won't save you now." He strained, trying to hear where the voice was coming from but it was no use.

"Are you going to kill me?" He asked. There was a pause.

"Yes," was the reply. He took a deep breath.

"What are you waiting for?" Another pause.

"I wanted you to be awake." He nodded.

"Can I at least see who's taking my life?" The figure walked in front of him. He let out a breath. "You've grown…" He nodded, "But they will find you."

"'They' are next on my list because I'm making sure they never hurt another innocent person again."

"Will it be quick?" They paused.

"No. You don't deserve it to be."

The knife came down swiftly. He spluttered on his own blood. Then, the knife slashed across his neck, spraying blood over the room.

Chapter 4

The more things change, the more they stay the same.

Ashley had thought that a lot recently over the last month or so. The new Major Crimes Unit had spent the last month mopping up old cases for other forces. Same old shit. New surroundings. The more things change.

Not many people know this, but most murders are domestics gone wrong. Wife having affair, husband finds out, husband takes meat cleaver to wife's head while children are watching. The more they stay the same.

Her new team were a colourful bunch. There was DCI McArthur who ran the team. DI Parland, an older detective in his late forties with greying, brown hair and an avid triathlon runner. DS Murphy, a Manchester boy through and through, grew up a stone's throw away from Old Trafford and supported Manchester United through thick and thin, though he would never make it as a pro. He was older, black, with a kind face. Out of all her new team Ashley liked him the most.

DS Armstrong, a cocky boy from the new establishment and an avid city fan, clashed with Murphy in that regard; well-built and thought that he was god's gift to women. Ashley had run into him in the past as a PC, he left a lasting impression, not for the right reason. The more things change.

"Oi, Fenway, cuppa please love."

"All right Ash, fancy going out for a drink after we go through these?"

"How does a good-looking girl like you not have a boyfriend?"

The more they stay the same.

***

06:23am

Ashley's phone vibrated on the bedside table. She looked over at the side table bleary eyed at the clock. She wasn't due to go to the gym for another few minutes. She angled her phone up and saw McArthur's number. She sighed picked it up and swiped.

"Fenway," she said, groggily.

"Fenway, we have a murder." Ashley pushed herself up on the bed.

"Sir?"

"Male, mid-fifties, slashed neck."

It may have felt wrong, but Ashley felt a flutter in her stomach. From feeling half asleep she was now fully alert and already out of bed, getting ready.

"Whereabouts Sir?"

"Outskirts of the Arndale — The Cambrian hotel. Do you know it?"

"Yes Sir," Ashley said, holding her phone to her shoulder while pulling her trousers on. "I'm in the Northern Quarter, I'll be there in ten." She winced at the time frame she had given herself.

"Excellent. I'm en route, I'll meet you there." The phone went dead.

"Shit."

Ashley rushed around to get ready. She quickly sprayed some deodorant on and pulled on the first smart shirt she could find and buttoned it up quickly. She stumbled across the living room, pulling her suit jacket on and rushed to tie up her boots. Police standard, she could never work in heels. She walked past the mirror and saw a glimpse of her tired reflection. Her skin looked pale and there were small bags under her eyes from late nights, studying case notes and other extracurricular activities. Should she do something with her make up?

"Fuck it." She jogged to the door and locked it behind her. She jogged down the corridor and took the stairs down. She had to go through the three separate security doors and finally slipped out into the morning drizzle of Manchester. The sky was still dark, but the morning purple and oranges were fighting through the darkness.

Ashley ran down Newton Street into the heart of the Northern Quarter; it seemed weird to see it so desolate and quiet. The only people about and awake were the homeless who were set up in their tents and hauled up in doorways to get away from the rain. She looked up at the new block of flats which was slowly starting to take shape. The face of Will Oatley, a local property magnate on the boards in front of it.

Oatley Developments. Tomorrow's housing crisis solved today!

Ashley pulled her jacket round her and carried on.

***

The outside of the hotel was surrounded by police cars with the blue lights on which reflected everywhere. Ashley jogged to a stop. The hotel itself was unremarkable with a bland and boring exterior, a building that would be easily missed if you drove past it. Ashley flashed her identification. The PC lifted the tape and Ashley walked into the lobby where most of the hotel staff where congregated.

From the looks on their faces it was a bad one. Uniforms were standing guard but not asking questions. Frustrated, Ashley walked over to one of the uniforms who looked half asleep.

"Who's the senior detective here?" She asked. The uniform suddenly sprang into life, standing up straight.

"Uhm… you are… Mam."

"Mam?" Ashley said raising her eyebrow. "Has DCI McArthur arrived?"

"No… Sir?" He asked unsure.

"Detective is fine," Ashley said, shaking her head. She looked around. Only the staff were downstairs, where were the guests?

"Guests?"

"In their rooms, orders of DCI McArthur," the uniform answered. Smart. But if she was the killer she would have left straight after the deed; chances were the murderer was long gone. She looked around and saw an old-style CCTV camera.

"CCTV?" Ashley pointed up to it.

"Being gathered now."

"Where's the body?"

"Second floor… Detective," he said, not looking down at her.

"Thanks." Ashley walked to the back of the lobby and pushed the door open to take the stairs. She jogged up the carpeted stairs, opening the door to the second floor. SOCO were already combing the corridor for clues. Ashley heard the shutter of the camera from further down the hall. A man, not much older than Ashley came over in his blue overall and face mask. He nodded at Ashley to confirm who she was.

"DC Ashley Fenway," Ashley said, flashing her identification.

"You'll need these." The SOCO handed her some blue overalls, shoe covers and a hair net.

"Thanks."

"Are you sure you should be here, you look ill." Ashley looked up at the SOCO officer and narrowed her eyes at him.

"Excuse me?" The question was long and drawn out, giving the SOCO a chance to retract the statement.

"You look tired." The SOCO walked away leaving Ashley with her pile of overalls. Ashley swore under her breath and got changed. If she had taken a couple of minutes to do something with her appearance, she wouldn't have had that. Ashley pulled the hairnet over her ponytail and walked slowly down the corridor. When she reached the door, she pulled it back to see exactly what she was dealing with.

The bed had been pulled into the centre of the room with the victim, naked, tied on the bed with most of his throat hanging out. In the early days Ashley would need a moment to compose herself before continuing. Instead she knocked on the door. The pathologist, who Ashley knew as Dr Cramer was inspecting the body. He was in his late forties with short, brown hair and a thick, brown and ginger beard. He looked down his glasses and waved her in.

"Ah Dona —" He looked up and saw Ashley walking in. His brow furrowed.

"Oh, I was expecting DCI McArthur," he said, going back to the body.

"DC Fenway," Ashley said, flashing her ID. Cramer didn't look back at her, just letting out a small 'Ah', while going back to the body in hand.

"Any idea who our vic is?" Ashley asked.

"No." Cramer replied softly, not even bothering to look back at her. Ashley could feel herself getting irritated

"Time of death?"

"I'm working on it," Cramer replied, in the same soft voice while taking swabs from the body. Ashley had to bite the inside of her mouth to stop herself snapping at him. She went to walk forward.

"Be careful where you're standing. I don't want you contaminating anything." Ashley looked back over her shoulder at Cramer. She let out a disgusted sound under her breath and shook her head. She walked to the foot of the bed while a SOCO took a photo of the man. He was tied to the bed by his wrists and ankles. Sex game gone wrong?

Ashley knelt, inspecting the ties. Tough knots to break free of, the bruising around the legs showed he tried to put up a fight, or just strained against his bonds. Ashley opened her note pad and started to make notes. She looked back to inspect the blood spatter around the walls. The cut on the neck must have been clean to have this much splatter, the side of the walls were stained with blood.

There was another knock on the door. Ashley looked up to see McArthur at the door wearing his long coat, with only the shoe protectors. Why didn't he have to wear these ridiculous overalls?

"Martin." He walked over to Cramer. Cramer looked up and nodded.

"Donald, always a pleasure." McArthur looked over at Ashley.

"Fenway."

"Sir." McArthur looked down at the body, the cogs working in his mind as he took in the scene before him.

"Any idea on our vic?" Cramer got to his feet.

"Your victim is male, early fifties, no ID and no wallet." Ashley turned back to Cramer.

"Cause of death?" She asked.

"OK, I was getting there," Cramer said, defensively. Ashley resisted the urge to roll her eyes. "Victim was stabbed in the neck with a large object, won't be sure on what 'til I get him in and do an autopsy. But most likely a knife." Ashley was still at the foot of the bed looking at the ties.

"Has CCTV been looked at yet?"

"Hotel is gathering it now Sir," Ashley said. She turned back to the back wall. Her gaze was on the blood spatter. Ashley looked round the side of the room where the blood was more prominent. She turned back to the foot of the bed where the blood spatter was lighter. Cramer and McArthur were still talking while Ashley took down notes.

"Sir, I think you shou —"

"Guv." Armstrong walked into the room, minus overalls. He let out a low whistle with his hands in his pockets.

"What a fucking mess." His eyes rested on Ashley.

"Geeze Fenway, you look like crap and all." Ashley looked up at him.

"Not all of us can worry about our make-up. I've got murders to solve."

"Ohhhh, didn't catch anything on the prowl the other night," Armstrong said, as he strolled in. "Although you know the offer is always there Fenway." Ashley shook her head.

"Bite me Armstrong."

"Only if you ask nicely."

"Kids." McArthur raised his eyebrow. "We've got a murder to solve."

"Yes, Sir."

"All right Guv." Armstrong walked to the bed and looked at the ties. Ashley ignored him as he made his own observations.

"Anything on the vic?"

"Nothing yet, where's Parland and Murphy?"

"Murphy is downstairs, Parland was right behind me," Armstrong replied. McArthur nodded.

"What do you think?" Armstrong looked at McArthur with a strange glance. "Well come on, you're supposed to be detectives, what do you think happened?"

Armstrong pulled a strained face. Ashley went to answer, but Armstrong cut in before a word could come out of her mouth.

"Reckon the guys been a little too heavy handed with a prossie," Armstrong said, putting his hands in his pockets. "Tried to short-change her, throat slashed and she made a runner."

"Well done Armstrong. Your powers of observation really do you justice." Ashley didn't look up to see the reaction of her comment. Instead she got off her haunches.

"Really?"

"No," Ashley replied dryly. "I'd say this was too staged to be a random killing. Based on the severity of the cut I'd say this was personal."

"The severity?" Cramer said almost laughing. "We won't know the severity until after the autopsy."

"Well look at it." Ashley pointed her pen to the entrance wound. "If it was an accident there would only be the entrance wound, they would panic and scarper. If it was frenzied there would be more across his body. But look." She pointed her pen at the bare torso. "Nothing. This was planned, and they knew what they were doing. Were there any footprints?"

"Nothing we could find," Cramer said, irritated. He glanced sideways to McArthur and nodded towards the door.

"Sir." Parland came around, again, no overalls for him. He scanned the room as well. "Looks nasty."

"Yeah, looks like someone did a number on this guy," McArthur replied. He looked around at the team. "Everyone outside, we'll let you finish off in here." Everyone filed outside while SOCO moved the body away.

"Right, hotel is in lock-down until further notice." Everyone had to take off their shoe protectors while Ashley had to take off her overalls.

"Parland, you and I are going to talk to the staff. See if anyone recognised our vic" McArthur turned to Armstrong, Murphy and Fenway. "Murphy, Armstrong, you two get the CCTV footage, go back to base, start combing through the footage and recent missing persons profiles. We need to find out who this guy is, what was he into."

"Bondage by the looks of it."

"Well no shit, Sherlock," McArthur replied. "*Who* was he paying for this, does his wife know, was she the one who did this, what else did he like doing?" Ashley waited patiently for McArthur to allocate her a job.

"Fenway, I want you to head the door-to-door enquiries with uniforms, see if you can find anything out specifically from the people on this floor". Ashley felt the blood boil in the pit of her stomach. The rest of the team went off to do their jobs while Ashley was left by herself, her hand balled up into a fist. Sometimes she felt like a glorified PC.

"Yes Sir," Ashley replied, through gritted teeth.

Ashley waited for McArthur to walk down the stairs to the lobby and went through some of the notes she'd jotted down.

Ashley tapped her pen on the note pad. The blood spatter was something that had intrigued her in the crime scene. The spatter was more prominent on the sides of the wall but not the back. Ashley pictured the crime scene in her mind, a visualising technique to picture how the crime scene unfolded.

John Doe was on the bed tied up, hoping for the time of his life. Assailant, male or female TBC, attacks him with a kitchen knife. From what Ashley saw of the body the blow was from above. So, the murderer was straddling him, then attacked. It could be one person, but this was premeditated not random. She was sure of it.

Ashley walked to the first room, 246, the room next door and knocked. A middle-aged man opened the door. He was balding and overweight, with an angry stare that bored into Ashley.

"What's going on here? Who are you?" the man exclaimed.

"Sir, I'm Detective Constable Ashley Fenway —"

"We've been stuck in here all morning and no one has told us why!" He continued. "What's gone on that warrants us being kept in our rooms like animals?" Ashley waited patiently for him to stop his ranting. It was something every police officer had to learn; take a rant without replying, no matter how much they annoy you.

"Sir, if you'll let me finish."

"You coppers, are all the same, you know that? Think you can keep people in their rooms without any due course, I know my rights!" Ashley looked down at the floor and smiled to herself.

"And what's being done about the smell from next door? Smells like a pig sty!" He raged.

"Why am I even listening to you people, what's stopping me from leaving right now?"

"Because if you do, you'd be our number one suspect in a murder enquiry," Ashley said, looking up. The man's face was dumbstruck.

"Wh-what?"

"Sir, the man in the room next to you has been murdered. We're trying to establish what happened." The man almost shrank. His demeanour changed from angry and confrontational to quiet and meek.

"Right, right..."

"Did you hear anything suspicious at all between three and seven yesterday afternoon?"

"No, I was out. You see I'm here on business," he explained.

"You were out all day?" Ashley asked, jotting it down. "What time was that?"

"Well I had to go early to the office at half eight, bloody northern lot can't do anything right."

"Is that so?" Ashley muttered under her breath, writing wanker on her notepad and underlining it. "What time did you get back?"

"It was late, not until nine."

"And you can confirm that?" Ashley asked. The man nodded.

"Yeah... my, my business can back it up."

"Did you meet the person next door at all?" Ashley asked. "No passing in the halls, anything like that?" He shook his head.

"No, nothing at all," he said, shaking his head.

"Can I just take your name, please?"

"Cowan, Darren Cowan." Ashley wrote the name down.

"You don't think they could have been after me could you." Ashley went to reply but was so dumbstruck by the question that she couldn't answer him straight away. She blinked and shook her head.

"No... Sir." She scribbled something down in her note pad. "This, this seems like it was pre-meditated." Delusional.

"Thank you for your time." He hastily closed the door. When it hit the latch, Ashley let out a long breath.

"Wow," she mouthed, as she walked to the next room. She knocked on the door, waiting for the response. The door opened. A short, petite woman wearing only a dressing gown answered it. Her long, blonde hair and dark eyes made Ashley lose her breath for a second.

"Oh, hi, are you with the hotel?" She asked, with a smile and slight Spanish accent. Even her smile was infectious.

"No, no," Ashley said, looking down at her note pad. "I'm Detective Constable Ashley Fenway."

A man's voice floated from inside the room. "Who is it darling?"

"The police, love," the woman said, looking back over her shoulder. A man now came to the door. He too was wearing a dressing gown.

"Hi, what's this all about?" He asked.

"The man next door to you has been murdered," Ashley explained. The shock came over their faces, the man held the woman tight to him.

"I just need to ask you some questions about yesterday afternoon."

"Of course."

"Where were you both between three and seven yesterday evening?"

"We were here," the woman said, lightly embarrassed, or nervous? Ashley felt a knot in her stomach. Brilliant. The husband nodded as well causing Ashley to think that she might have a solid lead.

"What were you doing?" Both parties went red with embarrassment.

"We were... here," the man said. "Together." Ashley nodded knowingly and made another note.

"And you didn't hear anything? Anything at all?" Ashley asked hopefully. Both the man and woman shook their heads.

"Oh god I feel so bad," the woman said. "I mean... what if we could have helped that poor man."

"Don't blame yourselves," Ashley said, closing her notebook. She put on her sweetest smile, trying not to let her annoyance bubble at the surface. "Have you seen anyone suspicious around the hotel?" The man looked down at the floor, a classic sign of knowing something.

"Sir?" No time to be subtle about this. He looked up at Ashley who held eye contact with him. He shifted uncomfortably.

"Yeah... I..." The woman now looked at her husband.

"I went out to get some food yesterday. I saw this guy hanging around this floor." Ashley felt a jolt of excitement go through her.

"When was this?"

"I don't know, about one-ish," he said unsure.

"How was he acting suspicious, Mr?" Ashley asked.

"Oh... Pennington, he was... lurking around this floor," the man replied. "We've gone out for food and he's always there, watching us. I don't know, it just seems unnerving."

"Yeah, there is that guy." Mrs Pennington hugged herself a little more. "We'd go out for dinner and he was always there, watching us."

"Do you know what room he's in?" Ashley asked, making a note. Garden variety weirdo, probably not the killer, probably some sex pest who got off on hearing other people doing it. If he was watching the

Pennington's room, then maybe he might have been watching the victim's inadvertently.

"No, sorry, he might not even be on this floor for all I know, we just try to avoid him," the husband said.

"Can you describe him please?" Husband and wife looked at each other, trying to figure out who should go first.

Mr Pennington started. "He isn't tall, about five six, seven."

"He's quite slim as well," Mrs Pennington added. "But he wears this baggy hoodie so I'm not really sure." Ashley made the notes.

"What about facial features, anything that could make him stand out?"

"He looks very… Buggy," Mrs Pennington said, shaking her shoulders. "You know, those eyes…" Ashley knew what she meant.

"I know what you mean. What sort of hair does he have?"

"It's blonde, you know, thin and wispy." Mr Pennington said. "He just… looks like a weirdo." Ashley made a note of looking up known sex pests from the area who fitted the description.

"I don't suppose you've seen or heard from him today, have you?" Ashley asked, hoping they'd make her life a little easier.

"We haven't exactly taken note of that," Mr Pennington said, looking down at the floor. "We just try and ignore him."

"No problem. Thank you for your time." Ashley took their details in case they needed to talk again, and he closed the door on her. It wasn't much but it was a start. Ashley walked to the nearest uniform and told him to relay the message that if anyone found a man fitting a description the Pennington's had described, to contact her.

Ashley made her way down the rooms, asking about room 245, but no one seemed to know anything about who was in the room. Ashley though did have more luck about the bug-eyed man. He was seen by other people on the floor, loitering about for the last couple of days. Uniforms on the other floors confirmed that this bug-eyed man had been seen around but hadn't been questioned yet.

Could have been a local voyeur, might not be staying in the hotel. At least it was a lead, hopefully something the others hadn't been able to get.

"And you're sure you saw a man like that."

"Yeah… I came out ready to go on the town and he was scuttling away, like he was listening in. I have an eleven-year-old in there." The woman at the end of the hall Ashley was questioning, was called Ms Pemberton. She had long, flowing, blonde hair and smart features. Her daughter, who Ashley could see in the room, was hiding in the bathroom for the most part.

"So just to recap, you never saw anyone coming in or out of room 245?" Ashley asked. "And you saw this bug-eyed man over the last few days." Ms Pemberton nodded. "We should have a sketch artist coming up to take a description soon." Ms Pemberton gave Ashley her details and she closed the door.

"Fenway." Ashley looked down the corridor and saw Parland coming towards her. "Guv wanted to know if you found anything else about this bug man." He wasn't looking at her, but at his note pad.

"No, nothing yet. Apart from that people on this floor and the third floor have seen him skulking around. Apparently listening against doors."

"Weirdo then," Parland summarised. Ashley sighed.

"Seems so. What did you and the Guv find out from the staff?"

"Room was booked under an alias. No shock. Don't know what people expect from a hotel that you can book by the hour," Parland said, going through his notes. "According to the receptionist it was booked to a James Nicholas, male voice."

"Armstrong's theory on a prossie seems legit," Ashley said, making a note of her own. Parland shrugged.

"Guv's still questioning the staff, plus we have CCTV to go through so it might get a hit. Pretty hard to get a room key in a hotel without someone seeing you. What about up here?"

"No one's seen any comings and goings from the room," Ashley explained. "No CCTV in the corridors. The guy next to the room was out when the murder took place, couple in the other room next to him were too busy having sex to hear anything," Ashley said, looking back down the hallway. Parland laughed.

"Good old British public," Parland said. "You can always rely on them for the details." Ashley wasn't listening. She saw someone walk towards the staircase. He was wearing a black hoodie with the hood pulled up. No one had given the OK for the lock down to be lifted.

"Sir." Ashley moved away from Parland. "Sir!" He looked down the hallway at Ashley. She could see thin, wispy, blonde hair with… bug-like eyes. Ashley walked quicker towards him.

"Sir, what are you doing? The hotel is in lock down!" Parland was now coming up behind her. The bug-eyed man froze. He looked back at the staircase, but Ashley was now running towards him.

"Stop! Police!" He looked around as a uniform came from the staircase door. He ran over to the laundry shoot. He pulled it open and with his slight frame he crawled into the drop-down.

"Shit." Ashley and Parland got to the shoot. It wasn't that big, but Ashley was confident that she could fit down it.

"No one can fit down there," Parland said, angrily.

"You can't." Ashley looked over at him. "I can." Parland looked confused over at her.

"What are you?" Before he could finish Ashley was climbing into the shoot.

"FENWAY!"

Ashley dropped down the shoot. She wasn't sure how far it went down so used her elbows and boots to control the descent. The shoot was dark with the only light a bright, white light from the bottom. As the light got closer, she tucked her arms in and dropped through. The first thing she saw briefly was lots of people looking at a staircase that led out of the laundry room. Ashley landed on a pile of sheets. She scrambled quickly to her feet and pulled herself over the vat she landed in. She ran over to the one door leading to the staircase.

Ashley yanked the door open and sprinted up the staircase, taking two at a time. Ashley reached the top and saw a fire-exit door to her right, that was flapping in the wind. She ran towards it and pushed it open, running into the loading bay of the hotel. On the corner of the street she could see a black hoodie hunched over for breath. He looked up at the bang of the door and ran off again down the alley towards the main road.

Ashley cursed under her breath. She sprinted down the alley the hoodie went down, and onto the main road. He was quick but Ashley was hopeful that she was fitter, physically. He was running towards the zebra crossing on the main road. He pushed past a group of people waiting to cross.

A car blasted its horn, slammed on the brakes and the hoodie avoided it. He weaved past the crowd on the central platform and ran across the other side. The car had stopped right across the crossing. Ashley shouted for people to move; they all moved back leaving Ashley with a run-up. She slid across the bonnet of the car. The crowd waiting to cross gasped at Ashley's graceful landing and pushing off all in one movement. She weaved in and out of the crowd of people and all the stationary traffic. If only they fucking stopped to catch the guy.

Ashley looked ahead and saw the hoodie running towards the city centre. Ashley had lost a lot of ground from hurdling cars and running past people, so she had to sprint towards him.

The hoodie darted down an alley; Ashley stopped abruptly at the mouth. She sprinted down the narrow walkway, hurdling some loose rubbish to the other side.

She reached a set of stairs and saw the hoodie at the bottom. He had now run down another passage. Ashley jumped down the stairs, using the railings as supports. She jumped down the last six steps. Ashley landed hard on the floor, falling on one knee. Ashley looked up and saw the hoodie struggling to climb over a mesh fence further down.

Ashley grunted, pushed herself off and sprinted down towards him. As she bore down on him, he pushed himself over.

Ashley jumped up, grabbed hold of the fence and started to climb up. When she got to the top, she pushed herself up and swung her leg over the rim. Ashley sat on the top of the fence and dropped down onto the ground.

Ashley pushed off again. She ran to the edge of the alley into another street that was slowly filling up with people. Thankfully the looks of a lot of affronted people told her that her prey had come down here. She ran after him, weaving in and out of the crowd. She looked up and saw the black hoodie running away from her, looking back to see where she was. Ashley smiled to herself and quickened her pace.

He obviously must have seen her because he quickened himself, although it wasn't much faster. Ashley went onto the road to power past people running slowly on the pavement. The hoodie saw what she was doing and ran right across the road again. He weaved in and out of the traffic and went down another alley.

He must have thought that he could lose Ashley in the small back roads but Ashley had made a point of knowing all these side streets. He was heading towards the Arndale. Ashley had to make the right turn across the traffic with a few beeping car horns. She ran down the alley to another loading area where a van was parked. Ashley side stepped it and ran into another side street to Shambles Square. She jogged into Exchange square which was full of people.

"Bollocks." All she could see were people in black on their way to work, but the crowd was so dense that she couldn't see the man in the black hoodie. She jogged forward, trying to crane her neck to see across the crowd. She looked around the square almost turning around in circles. She lost him…

Ashley swore loudly, but a flicker of black made her turn her head. Jogging towards the Arndale Ashley craned her neck. He looked back, the bug-eyes. Ashley smiled to herself and ran towards him. She ran through the crowd, side stepping and dodging in the small spaces. The hoodie saw her and started to run away again. Ashley jumped up the steps where people were sitting having their morning coffee.

He was slowing. He may have been good at running away from the scene as a voyeur but not so fast as to run away from her. His steps were laboured, and it looked like he was running with a stitch. He looked back and saw Ashley sprinting towards him. He pulled down a display cabinet, its merchandise crashing to the floor, spreading like a pool of blood on the floor.

Ashley hurdled over the obstacle with ease. He pulled another display to the floor which Ashley jumped over. Ashley landed on the floor and sprinted away from the destruction behind her. The hoodie ran up Market Street.

Ashley was gaining ground fast. The people around her were only a blur as her tunnel vision zoned in on him. He was slowing down rapidly. He stopped to catch his breath, resting his hands on his knees. Ashley was slowing down herself. A horn blasted out.

A tram was going towards the hoodie. Ashley sprinted towards him. He was like a rabbit in the headlights. Ashley jumped across the rails, rugby tackling him to the ground as the tram thundered by. Ashley was quicker to react. She pinned him to the ground and cuffed him.

"You're under arrest," Ashley said, pinning her arm into his back. She looked up. There were people videoing her making the arrest.

"Great," Ashley muttered under her breath. She pulled him up by the handcuffs. "Sir, you are under arrest on suspicion of murder. You do not have to say anything but it may harm your defence if you do not mention when questioned, something which you later rely on in court. Anything you do say may be given in evidence." She looked around to see people videoing her on their phones. Ashley got her phone out and dialled McArthur's number.

"Fenway," he said, in a surprise tone. "Last I heard you were chasing a suspect through the streets."

"Caught him," Ashley said, getting her breath back. "I need someone to come pick us up."

Chapter 5

The office that Ashley was working in now was a million miles away from her old office in the Metropolitan unit. Sleek new computers with matching furniture, windows that let in lots of light and clean, warm incident rooms; a billion miles away from Metro. She spent the last month here helping to tie up ongoing investigations but now this was her team's first major crime.

The MMC took up twelve floors of the building with her team's office space on the 12th floor, along with three other MMC teams. Ashley walked from the corridor into the office area where her team was based. There were a few murmurs from the other teams as she walked to her desk.

"There she is, the bionic woman." Ashley looked over at one at the other teams who were pointing at her.

"What are you on about?" Ashley asked.

"Haven't you seen the news?" One of the civilian staff unmuted the TV hung up on the wall which had BBC News running. Ashley walked closer to the TV.

"The new Manchester Major Crimes Unit has come under fire in recent weeks for its huge cost and point of purpose, but it seems that it is going in the right direction. Witnesses saw a member of the elite crime fighting unit chasing a suspect through the streets of Manchester this morning."

"Damn." The TV feed cut to Ashley chasing the suspect through the streets of Manchester. Most of the footage was caught on mobile phones but it clearly showed Ashley. The report finished with Ashley rugby-tackling the suspect out of the way of an ongoing tram.

"It's all over Twitter and Facebook," one of the other detectives said. "Bit of good press and all that. DC Fenway, the face of Manchester Major Crimes." He mocked with the other detectives.

"Chief Super is gonna want you in something a little more low-cut than that, if he's going to show you off," he said, pointing to Ashley's top. Ashley folded her arms across her chest.

"Or maybe he wants to show off an officer that doesn't get out of breath going to Krispy Kreme." She walked over to her desk and got her phone out. One WhatsApp message from her brother.

Matty: *Just seen you on the news Sis. Keep kicking ass!*

Ashley smiled to herself, placed her phone on her desk and looked out the window down on the tram station and the street food vendors. Ashley went back to her computer. She checked her e-mail and thankfully there was nothing relating to her chase in there. She started to type her arrest report before McArthur got back.

Twenty minutes later and a few renditions of the Bionic Man theme tune later, the rest of her team came sauntering back through. McArthur came in with a bag of McDonalds and started to bark out instructions on what he wanted done.

"Fenway, my office please." Ashley got her arrest report and went to McArthur's office that was at the back of the room. He opened the door for her then went to his chair. He pulled out a Double Sausage and Egg McMuffin for himself and slid Ashley a bacon one.

"I didn't know which one you would want. I decided for bacon because most coppers go for sausage."

"Bad time to tell you that I prefer sausage," Ashley said. "But thanks anyway." She picked it up.

"Don't worry, that joke was made too."

"Of course it was," Ashley said.

"So, who's our suspect?" McArthur asked, as he took a bite of his muffin.

"Giles Fawnley, twenty-nine years old," Ashley said, getting her note book out. "He's in the system for voyeurism and indecent exposure. Just an all-round sex pest." McArthur frowned.

"I don't see him for the murder," he said round his muffin.

"Neither do I Sir, but I was thinking that he could shed some light on the room. He might have seen if someone had gone into our vic's room." McArthur nodded.

"Good idea. I also had the liberty of having all the statements from the guests in the hotel finished by uniform and placed on your desk for you to cross reference with the ones you already have."

"Thanks Sir," Ashley said.

"Have you ever done an interrogation before?" McArthur asked.

"I've sat in on a few but never led one," Ashley replied.

"Well this is a perfect opportunity for you to lead one," McArthur said. "He'll probably wet himself that a girl is actually talking to him instead of reporting him."

"So, it'll be an easy one," Ashley said, disappointed.

"We all have to start somewhere Fenway." McArthur rolled the wrapper up and threw it in the bin. "I've also had a request from the Chief Constable for you to do a meet and greet with some news station over what happened this morning."

"You've got to be joking."

"Afraid not Fenway, the department has been getting some bad press recently, he thinks that you going down a laundry shoot, running through the street, then saving a suspect's life is the real deal in policing terms. Proactive policing, he calls it."

"Well fuck that," Ashley said. McArthur smiled

"In that case then, shall we go interview Mr Fawnley?"

***

Ashley and McArthur walked down to the interview room where Giles Fawnley was sitting nervously with his solicitor. Ashley and McArthur sat down opposite them. The recording started by blaring out an unbearable noise

"This is DCI Donald McArthur seeing this interview, at Manchester Major Crimes HQ City Tower, 13th November 2017 at 09:30am, of Giles Fawnley with..."

"DC Ashley Fenway..."

"Fred Dickinson."

Ashley took out her notebook and flicked through the pages.

"Mr Fawnley, we have reports from the people staying at The Cambrian Hotel that you have been seen loitering around some of the rooms." Dickinson looked annoyed and whispered in Fawley's ear. Fawnley shuffled nervously. He looked up at Ashley and quickly down at the table.

"Yes," he whispered, timidly.

"Mr Fawnley are you aware that Major Crimes have been investigating a murder that occurred at the hotel yesterday, between the hours of three and seven o'clock yesterday evening?"

"Are you formally charging my client?" Dickinson asked.

"No," Ashley said, looking at him. "Not yet." She looked back at Giles. "Doesn't look good though. Running from a scene. Loitering on the same floor. Imagine how a jury is going to look at that."

"Have you got any evidence to back up this claim?"

"Only a matter of time before we do. You see these things are all about progression, Giles," Ashley said, leaning forward.

"First it's porn. Then indecent exposure, then indecent assaults, rape, then murder. Let's see, how far up the scale are you?" She looked over and saw Giles squirming in his seat. Perfect. Ashley smirked to herself.

"Your client is basically the biggest sex pest this side of the Northern Quarter. It would be at least a couple of years before he steps up to indecent assault, if he had the stones to. We don't think he carried this out. He isn't smart enough, but, if he co-operates with this investigation then we will turn a blind eye to this bout of voyeurism."

Dickinson leaned over and whispered in Fawnley's ear; Fawnley nodded.

"My client is willing to co-operate in whatever way he can," Dickinson said. Ashley wanted more of a challenge, but she should have been grateful that he was opening up so easily.

"OK Giles, we know that you were listening in on rooms of the Cambrian hotel. The one we're interested in is room two forty-five. Now, did you watch the room at all?" Ashley asked. Giles nodded.

"The witness has nodded to indicate an answer," McArthur said, folding his arms. "But for future reference he will, from now on, answer

57

questions put forward by myself and DC Fenway with clear answers. Is that understood?"

"Yes," Fawnley said, quietly.

"So, answer DC Fenway's question." Fawnley looked up.

"Yes," he said again.

"And what did you see?" Fawnley didn't say anything at first. His hands were shaking nervously on the table.

"Giles, I know you don't want to hurt anyone, but we need to know if you saw anything. So please, tell us everything you know, and you can be on your way." Giles took in a large gulp of air.

"I listened on the door in the morning but there wasn't anything going on." McArthur tapped Ashley on the shoulder and leaned in.

"Receptionist says that the room was booked into at twenty to three." Ashley nodded.

"What time was this around?" Ashley asked making a note.

"About eleven…"

"And there was nothing going on inside?" Ashley asked.

"I… moved onto the next room where…"

"No need to elaborate," Ashley said, knowing which room he'd gone to. "Did you keep eyes on the room at all? Did you go back at all between those times?"

"I went back up to the upper floors," Giles said. "I didn't go back for the rest of the day."

"So, you saw nothing, no one coming in or out?" Ashley asked.

"I'm sorry. I don't know any more than that." Ashley ran a hand through her hair and looked over at McArthur. He shook his head, indicating that there wasn't any more information to be had from him. Ashley reached over to the tape recorder.

"Interview terminated."

***

"Don't worry Fenway. We'll get another lead when the post-mortem comes through," McArthur said, as they walked back to the office. They stopped by a coffee machine which McArthur put some money into.

"I thought we had a lead," Ashley said, leaning against the wall looking up at the ceiling.

"You never know we might still do," McArthur said. He looked over at Ashley who was looking up at the ceiling.

"No one ever solves a murder in the first interview," McArthur said. "Even the domestics. Fawnley isn't our guy, we knew that, we just tried to get something from him."

"And we got nothing."

"We got confirmation that the time of death matches up," McArthur said, blowing steam away from his coffee. "Get started on those witness statements, see if there are any discrepancies. Let's find that new lead."

"Yes Sir," Ashley said, a little deflated.

"Fenway." Ashley turned around.

"You did well. I didn't see anyone else get after him like that," he said, picking his cup up and walking with her.

"I'm surprised it took that long to catch him," Ashley said, as they reached the door. "He's quicker than he looks." Ashley pushed the door open and they walked into the office.

"So, how was the sex pest?" Armstrong asked as they walked over.

"Asking why you don't call that much," Ashley said, sitting down, which earned a laugh from the other detectives.

"So, he's not our guy?" Parland asked.

"He's not our guy," Ashley said, turning around in her chair. "I've been tasked with looking through these." Ashley patted the pile of witness statements. Ashley's desk phone went off, she leaned over and picked it up.

"Fenway."

"Hi, is this DC Fenway?" It was a woman's voice with what Ashley called a phone voice. Overly airy and nice, to give a false sense of doom.

"Since you called my phone directly, I think you know the answer," Ashley said. The voice faltered into a nervous laugh.

"Yes… right. I'm secretary of Chief Constable Bowden. He wants to know what time you're free to do an interview with the local press about what happened earlier today." Ashley pulled a face and span round in her chair.

"An interview?" Ashley asked. She placed a finger in her ear to drown out the talking in the office. McArthur was allocating jobs.

"Yes, about the chase. The Chief Constable really wants some good publicity."

"Look, I'm really busy," Ashley said, looking at the paperwork.

"The Chief Constable will sanction time."

"Yeah, sounds great, let's make it sometime next week," Ashley said, before placing the phone down and shaking her head.

"Murphy, check the missing persons list, let's see if our guy has been reported missing or not," McArthur said. "I have uniforms going through the witness statements and see if they match up, they'll just discount any passages that relate to Fawnley."

He turned to Ashley.

"Fenway, I've forwarded CCTV to you, go through it and see if anyone was following our guy." Ashley nodded and logged onto her computer. Other people started to file out of the room while Ashley opened the e-mail with the CCTV files for The Cambrian Hotel.

Ashley opened it up and looked down at the times that their guy came in. The room was checked into at twenty to three. She opened the file for the lobby camera.

Ashley played it, her eyes scanning the screen. At 14:38 she played it at normal speed which showed their guy walk into the hotel. He looked instantly twitchy as he walked in; constantly looking over his shoulder. He walked to the desk and chatted to the receptionist before picking up the key and walking out of the lobby.

Ashley rewound the tape and played it again. She wasn't looking at him but people around him, were there any people looking at him? Following him? Ashley tapped her pen on the desk, watching the footage repeatedly. It was like any other person coming to and from the hotel. Maybe if she could see where he came from.

Just as she was about to get up, the phones around the office rang.

She waited for her phone to ring and picked it up.

"MMC, DC Fenway speaking."

"Hi, this is Chloe from the coroner's office. We've had a match on the DNA database for your John Doe this morning."

"Do you have a name?" Ashley asked, readying her notebook.

"Yes, his name is Gordon Ferrets. Born 05/06/1962."

"Are you sure?"

"One hundred per cent," she replied. "OK, thanks. Any word on how long the autopsy will take?"

"We should be done in a couple of hours." She ended the call.

"Thanks," Ashley said, placing the phone down. Ashley brought up the police database and typed in the name Gordon Ferrets, along with his date of birth.

As soon as his mugshot appeared Ashley knew it was him. He had hard, sharp features with slicked-back, black hair with a small curl at the front of his hair. Ashley looked at what he was in the system for.

Aggravated assault.

Breach of restraining order

Drunk and disorderly offences.

The aggravated assault was against a man who accused him of being a paedophile when Ferrets worked as a football scout.

His ex-wife had a restraining order placed against him after the said assault. He had become emotionally abusive and physically violent towards her. That was three years ago.

The drunk and disorderly offences were scattered between the three years since. The report had the name of his ex-wife while also showing that he had a daughter as well. Tracy Ferrets.

Ashley placed the name into the system and one only came up. She clicked onto the file and saw the resemblance straight away.

She was in the system as well for drunk and disorderly offences and GBH.

Ashley got up from her seat and knocked on DCI McArthur's door.

"Come in." Ashley opened the door.

"Sir, we've got an ID on our John Doe."

"And?"

"His name is Gordon Ferrets, he's in the system for a restraining order breach, assault and public order offences."

"Good, do we have an address?"

"A flat in Didsbury. He also has a daughter in the area as well," Ashley said. McArthur nodded and got to his feet while grabbing his coat.

"Good work," he said, walking towards her. Ashley moved to the side to let him pass. He was walking to her computer and Ashley followed and sat down while McArthur looked over her shoulder.

"Well it's a start," McArthur muttered under his breath.

Chapter 6

Blues and twos over at @cambrianhotel this morning, mate there said they found some guy tied to his bed. #WTF #badmonday #extraservice

Did y'all see that girl chase that guy through Manchester this morning? Girl was a MACHINE!!!!! #whatshersecret? #timetodocrossfit?

Whatever that girl's hairspray is I NEED IT!!!! #flawless #anythingyoucandoshecandobetter

Just seen some girl tackle a guy out of the way of a tram this morning! @Englandrugby would've been proud of it!!! #girlpower!!!!

That girl on the news was fit as!!!!! #thethingsIwoulddotoher

@GMP can you lend a homie a number for that girl chasing that guy this morning? #askingforafriend

In America police brutality is some fat guy pounding your ass. In the UK you have fitties rugby tackling you to the ground and putting you in handcuffs... #wrongcountry #kinky #harderplease

Ashley was sat in the office waiting for the financials of Gordon Ferrets to come through, his phone record sitting on her desk along with his police file.

Gordon Ferrets, fifty-nine years old. Born and raised in the Manchester area, worked as a scout for both Manchester clubs and did part-time PE teaching. He then set up his own private football academy which provided sports training to under-privileged schools and communities which was part-financed by local government. All that from a quick Google search.

What it also brought up was local news articles that accused him of being a paedophile, although he was acquitted and sued the paper for liable; but the smears had done their job and his academy was shut down.

McArthur had taken the team to Ferrets house while she was tasked with painting the picture of what they were dealing with.

As far as she could make out, this Ferrets was a guy trying to do the right thing, but it seems mistrust in the public conscious, especially since the Rochdale scandal and the youth football abuse scandal, people were more aware of these sorts of things; and it cost him his work, his marriage.

Ashley opened Google again and looked at his marriage. His ex-wife was Tammy Ferrets, lived in Manchester and divorced five years ago after the smear campaign. She also took a restraining order against him after he bombarded her with messages and texts.

She was currently living with another man in North Wales. Ashley found her on Facebook and was able to get a mobile phone number from her profile. She wrote it down, making a note to phone it later. Ashley then looked up his daughter, Tracy.

Again, born and raised in Manchester but unlike her mother she stayed around and supported her father. She had Facebook too and had more photos of her father on there. Ashley made a note of her mobile number too. Someone would have to go around and break the news to her.

Just as she finished, an e-mail came through with the financials. Ashley opened them up and sighed at their length.

"Great, I need tea," Ashley said, locking the computer and walking to the kitchen. She was waiting for the kettle to boil when she looked over at a TV which was showing The Cambrian with the police swarmed outside. At least they didn't have a name yet, but with everything like this it was only a matter of time.

Ashley sat back down and opened the financial records which were for one bank account dating back to the late seventies. Ashley had also found the account for the Sports Academy too and had it sent over.

Ashley started to go through the lines of transactions, trying first to find a pattern — things that people paid for every week, every month.

Rent, mortgage.

Utilities, insurance.

Car payments.

Food shopping.

Drawing money out for disposable income (because everyone draws money out, whether it's a tenner or two hundred.)

Once the patterns are established, then the other things become clearer. Ashley had done this enough times so she had a system for it. His rent out was highlighted in red with his utilities in blue and constant withdrawals in green, with his incomings in yellow.

Judging by his financials he was still living off the winnings from his liable claim with no real, steady income.

There were a few odd transactions that were going out to something, but Ashley didn't know what. A Tillerson 2071 Limited. Ashley searched the name in Google and it came up on Companies House as an incorporated, limited company.

Ashley clicked on it and saw it was registered in Castlefield. Ashley checked their filings. On their latest annual accounts it proved that it was a holding company. Ashley looked further down the document and saw that they held the shares of lots of companies. When Ashley finished counting it was over two hundred with no indication on what sort of industry, they were in.

Not even her tea could distract her from the fact that while her team were shaking down suspects, she was here trying to piece paperwork together. The sooner she became a DS the better.

She checked the business account for the sport academy, the account went inactive in 2012. Again, finding the pattern.

Salaries.

Payments in from clients.

Rent.

Stationery.

Travelling expenses.

Taxes.

Accountancy.

Once all the usual things were accounted for Ashley looked at the other comings and goings. The academy was getting large grants and donations from local government up until five months before it was dissolved.

He seemed well off once upon a time ago, but his finances now showed a man who was now living on past glories. The more she thought about it, maybe it was a disgruntled parent that wanted revenge.

Ashley started to look into the claims against him. The only things in the public domain were local newspaper articles about him and the academy. The main source of news was from the Manchester Evening News. Ashley looked them up, found a phone number for the news desk and dialled it on her office phone.

The phone continued to ring, and Ashley swung idly in her chair from side to side. Finally, a woman answered the phone.

"Hello, Manchester Evening News." She sounded young, probably an intern.

"Hi, this is DC Ashley Fenway with the Manchester Major Crimes Unit, I was hoping to speak to the editor."

"Concerning what?" The receptionist asked.

"Concerning one of your stories."

"We check all of our sources, Detective." Ashley pulled a disparaging face.

"It's about a past story, one Gordon Ferrets and the sports academy he ran."

"Surely everything's in the pieces we published," she replied.

"You clearly haven't been working there too long," Ashley snapped back. "Trust me, your editor will want to talk to me." After a disgruntled sound, there was a pause from the other end as she was put on hold for a minute or two.

"Hello, I'm Sam Lingard, Editor."

"Hi Mr Lingard. I'm DC Fenway."

"The girl on the desk already explained who you are love," Lingard said, tiredly. "What is this about Ferrets, does he want to sue for harassment too?"

"He can't do that, he's dead," Ashley said.

"Damn... How can I help?"

"You ran the story about Gordon Ferrets. Correct?"

"Don't I know it?" Lingard muttered. "Yeah, we had some strong sources that proved what he was up to, but none of them wanted to testify in court to put him away."

"Why didn't they?" Ashley asked.

"No idea," Lingard replied. "I think Ferrets might have leaned on them; he had friends in the council with his academy."

"Thanks, but I wanted to know about the people who accused Ferrets of being a paedophile," Ashley clarified. "Maybe one of them wanted revenge."

"I can see that," Lingard said, wearily. "I'll gather a list, and have it sent over to you. I'm not sure a lot of them will be too sad that he's gone."

"So, they'll be co-operative?" Ashley asked.

"Don't count on it."

"What do you mean by that?"

"Listen detective. A lot of the people who were wronged by him were low income families, people who are looking to win the lotto or X-Factor rather than work a day for a wage. They hold a strict sense of morals that don't spread to people like Ferrets."

"Are you saying they won't speak to us?" Ashley asked.

"Those morals don't stretch to police either, especially with the Rochdale scandal still hanging over you." Ashley hated it when the public brought that up.

"Listen, can I take your number in case I need to ask you anymore questions. I don't fancy having to talk to the intern on the desk.

"I don't think she wants to talk to you either," Lingard said. She thanked him for his time and left her e-mail address and phone number with him.

Ashley leaned back in her chair, trying to figure out what Lingard had said to her about the people that Ferrets supposedly played on. Just as she finished thinking about it her phone started going off. Ashley checked and saw that it was McArthur.

"Fenway."

"Hey. How's his financials looking?"

"Pretty piss poor," Ashley said. "He was raking it in with his academy business."

"But?" McArthur asked.

"In 2011 he was accused of being a paedophile by a group of ex-recipients of his sports training. Business fell and his academy was dissolved a year later."

"Good, good, that explains the trophies and pictures. What else, a wife?"

"Ex-wife," Ashley clarified. "Broke up not long after the accusations. But when he was cleared in court, he tried to win her back, took it to the nth degree, she filed a restraining order, he broke it."

"Where's the ex-wife now?"

"Living in North Wales. I have a phone number for her."

"Good, can you phone her? At least rule her out."

"Will do," Ashley said. "I also spoke to the Manchester Evening News. They were the ones who broke the story about him and they're sending me a list of people who gave evidence to the paper."

"We'll sort through those tomorrow," McArthur said. "So, if his academy went under, how was he living?"

"He was living off the settlement he won from the liable case against the paper. He might have been doing odd jobs on the side, I don't know."

"Well we found a diary in his house. I've sent a uniform to bring it in to you, can you make a timeline of his day? Uniform are also dropping off his laptop to the computer lab too."

"OK," Ashley said, writing it down.

"Any anomalies in his financials?"

"He made a payment to a Tillerson 2071 Limited, which is a holding company with over two hundred subsidiaries. I don't know what the link is, but I'll keep looking into it."

"You do that." Ashley bit her lip.

"What about your end?" She asked.

"House turned up a few papers and this diary along with his laptop. No sign of his phone though."

"What about the autopsy?" Ashley asked.

"Me and Armstrong are on our way there now. Parland and Murphy are on their way to speak to the deceased's daughter, and we have uniform canvassing the area for character witnesses."

"Convene tomorrow?"

"That's the plan," McArthur said. "Main thing though, go through that diary and trace his last movements so we have something for tomorrow."

"Yes Sir." He ended the call. Ashley slumped back in her chair and looked at the mounting paperwork on her desk. Sometimes she felt like a glorified PA, for someone who didn't even know their own schedule.

Ashley picked the phone up and rang the number for Ferrets ex-wife. It rang and rang 'til it went to answer phone.

"Hi, this is Tammy, I can't come to the phone 'cause I'm too bizzaay by the poolio! Leave me a message and I'll get back to you on Wednesday!" Ashley ended the call before the beep. She didn't know what was worse, that someone actually had a message like that or that a fifty-year-old woman had one like that.

Instead, she phoned North Wales Police and left a message with them to talk to her when she got back next week. As alibi's go it was pretty good.

Ashley checked her e-mail and saw that Lingard had got back to her. Ashley checked the list — just random names she knew nothing about, but at least Lingard gave their addresses too. That was one less thing to worry about.

Ashley walked over to the front of the room where the board was. She updated it with what they knew. More so on why people would kill him, the paedophile scandal was a big one; but hopefully this diary they were sending would shed some more light on him. In the meantime, she looked at the phone records.

For the most part the only person he phoned was his daughters' number, with the odd takeaway phoned every now and again.

"Why would anyone want to kill someone so boring?" Ashley said to herself.

"Uhm, is there an Ashley Fenway in here?" Ashley turned around in her chair and saw a uniform wandering around.

"I'm Ashley Fenway," Ashley said, waving her hand. The uniform clocked her. He took a deep breath and tried to discreetly ruffle his hair as he walked over to her.

Ashley took a moment to study him: average height, niceish hair, OK to look at. She did have to admire his confidence though.

"Uhm, DCI McArthur asked me to give this to you." He thrust the diary towards Ashley. He was deliberately trying to appear taller and he had lowered his voice slightly. Ashley smiled to herself and took it from his hands.

"Thanks."

"Do you need help with it?" He asked. Ashley looked back at him.

"It's OK, I can read," Ashley said, placing the diary down on the desk. He was still at her desk. Why was he still at her desk?

"Can I help you with anything?" Ashley asked as politely as she could without sounding rude. He faltered. A little confidence Ashley thought to herself, start something, follow it through.

"Uhm… no." Ashley picked up the diary.

"Bye…"

"Oh, yeah, bye." The uniform walked off as Ashley opened the diary. He tried to afford another look round but quickly walked to the lift at the end of the room. Ashley shook her head and flicked to the back of the diary to see if anything had been written in it. Nothing.

Ashley went to today's date and looked at what he had planned for today.

MM 11:00.

LB 15:00.

An appointment, Ashley thought. For what though? Ashley flicked back through the diary and found more appointments with different people, with their initials marking who it was. Ashley flipped back to the week previously and saw that he had a few appointments. The majority were peoples' initials, but he also had sections scribbled out with kids scrawled over it. His grandkids maybe, Ashley mused.

She looked back to the day he died and looked at the appointment for LB. It came across the time he died. Ashley walked over to the board and put the initials LB on the board and wrote down the time. She circled it and wrote time of death with a large question mark.

Ashley sat down on the edge of the desk and looked at the board. He must have been up to something. Ashley wondered where to go next. She might be able to track down some of the names. Ashley walked back to her desk, brought up the electoral roll, looked at the house Ferrets was living in and saw he was the only occupant.

If someone was starting a new business, they would probably start with neighbours. Ashley looked at the initials of the neighbours and tried to place them.

Ashley wrote down the initials on a piece of paper and cross referenced them with the names on the screen. Ashley looked around the houses that surrounded his. Most of them seemed to be younger people. If he was helping around the house then balance of probability told her that this person had to be older. Well, that and none of the initials matched up. Ashley leaned back in the chair.

"OK, that doesn't work," she said, her eyes following the street to the other side of the road. Ashley narrowed her eyes and looked at the house directly opposite his. "A… Maria Mellors." Ashley checked her birth date. She was old, lived alone, maybe he did some odd jobs for her, and her initials made the list. Word of mouth spread fast.

Ashley made a note of her name to talk to her at some point. Hopefully, there was more information about his movements on his laptop, but IT Forensics would call when they were done.

***

Ashley was making a small profile of the names that Lingard gave her. All low-income families like Lingard had told her. They all had sons that Ferrets had at his sports academy, who were now grown up. Ashley had also been able to find the civil case that they had brought forward against him.

But Ferrets had the benefit of a good lawyer, in fact the Deputy Mayor, Harold Donaldson who cleared him of any wrong-doing.

Through more digging she found an old court document about his ex-wife's restraining order.

Manipulative, controlling, conniving.

"Wow," Ashley said, while scrolling through the description of him. She printed it off and started to add it to the board.

Her desk phone started ringing. Ashley picked it up.

"DC Fenway." Ashley sat on her chair and put her feet up on the desk.

"Just come back from the autopsy," McArthur said. They were in a car. "Victim was stabbed in the neck with a knife, possibly a kitchen one and had his throat sliced."

"Right." Ashley put the phone to her ear, held it up with her shoulder and wrote it down on the board.

"Any defence wounds?" Ashley asked.

"None. Seems like he was tied up voluntarily," McArthur said. "But there is a large blunt-force wound to the back of the head as well. Enough to put him out so maybe he was assaulted and then tied up."

"Next of kin?"

"Next of kin has identified the body too. Where are we with the laptop and diary?"

"Diary shows that he had appointments with people, maybe neighbours to do something."

"Maybe Murphy and Parland could shed light on it. What about the laptop?"

"Won't get a full analysis till the morning," Ashley said.

"OK, we're on our way back to look at the autopsy report. Cramer should be e-mailing it over. How far have you got with that list?"

"Haven't even started it," Ashley said. "Besides, we'll need to split up, there's too much ground to cover."

"Agreed. Have a look through the autopsy report. See if anything stands out to you."

"Yes Sir." He ended the call. Just as he did, Ashley heard an e-mail come in with the autopsy report. Ashley sent it to print. As the pages came out, she looked at the some of the facts from the body. When it finished, she gathered it up, walked to her desk and started to read it.

The time of death was between three and seven yesterday; matches up with his appointment in his diary. Ashley wrote that down on the board and went back to the report.

The initial cut was brought down with great force, most likely a male, considering the force of impact and the subsequent slash. Instrument was a large, sharp object, most likely a knife. Subject was tied down using a reef knot, a knot used for camping. Ashley recognised it from her own camping days.

Ashley wrote down on the board that their killer probably had some sort of outdoor experience. Cause of death wasn't the cut and slash itself, but the blood loss.

Ashley flicked through the toxicology report which showed that he had a small amount of cocaine in his system as well. He was also on medication for blood pressure and a form of anti-depressants.

She was still flicking through the report when McArthur and Armstrong walked in. Armstrong sat at his desk while McArthur looked at the board.

"Daughter said she'll come in tomorrow to answer some questions and SOCO said they'd have the results from the hotel room tomorrow too. Seems like we can't do much till then." That was all Ashley needed to hear.

"Bright and early tomorrow then?" She asked. McArthur nodded.

"I need to talk to the DCS, keep him informed. Also the Chief Constable is looking for you."

"Me?"

"Yeah, still wants you in front of the camera," McArthur said. "And before you do." He cut off Ashley's reply. "It's got back to me, and he's right, the department could do with some good press. All you have to do is stand and wave and talk about all the good work we want to do."

"I couldn't think of anything worse," Ashley said.

"That's the spirit," Armstrong said. "If you get more of that cleavage out you might make it to DS by the end of all this."

"Armstrong, unless you want to find my fist on your jaw I would shut up," Ashley said, picking up her gym bag. "And trust me, I have quite the right hook."

Chapter 7

"Come on Ash, show me that right hook!" Ashley punched the pad and then ducked the other. She kneed up and kicked out.

"Whoa! Slow down girl."

"Sorry, rough day," Ashley replied, breathlessly.

"Go on let's see that combo again." Ashley repeated it, her muscles aching and sweat falling down her brow. Ashley repeated the combo and threw in a sneaky left which was easily caught.

When Ashley first moved to Edinburgh, she was hit on a night out by a drunk woman. Having to walk around with a black eye for a week wasn't the nicest thing in the world so a friend got her into Tae Kwon Do. She had got quite good at it and had been a black belt for nearly eighteen months after carrying on her training in Manchester.

The Dojo was a studio in the Northern Quarter; people walked past it every day and would be none the wiser. The Dojo was run by Clarence and his wife Chloe. After she got her black belt, which she really enjoyed, she asked to come back to train, do some more.

At the moment, Clarence had been teaching her MMA for the last year or so and if she said so herself, she was OK at it.

"OK, girl," he said. "What's got into you?"

"I've spent all day staring at screens and paper and I need to let some steam off."

"Wasn't that chase enough for you?" Clarence asked. Ashley punched the pad particularly hard.

"How did you know about that?" Ashley asked, slightly out of breath.

"It was on the news," Clarence said. "You do parkour on the side?"

"Hardly," Ashley said, ducking Clarence's hit and then punching him twice quickly to the chest. Clarence laughed and backed off.

"Well done girl," he said, taking his pads off. "I think you've had enough for today." Ashley's aching shoulders agreed.

"Yeah, I think so too," she said, taking her gloves off. Clarence came over and patted her on the shoulder.

"You're getting better," Clarence said. "But next week you have to keep up on your Tae Kwon Do. Got it?"

"Yeah." Ashley swigged some water from her bottle as they walked to the changing rooms. "I'm practicing."

"Good, Chlo will see you next week at this time instead," Clarence said, as they walked into the changing room which showed its age. Ashley waited by her locker while Clarence stood next her.

"Are things OK with work?" Clarence asked, as Ashley pulled her bag out of the locker.

"I told you. It's fine," Ashley said. "Just a little frustrating at the moment." Clarence nodded sympathetically.

"Keep at it," he said, lightly punching her shoulder. "They're lucky to have you."

Ashley said her goodbyes, sat down in the changing area and took a swig from her bottle. She started to undo the tape on her wrists and hands. After that was done, she had another swig of her drink and wiped the sweat from her brow. Ashley swung her bag over her shoulder and walked down the worn and battered stairs, outside into the cold Manchester night.

Ashley fished her headphones out of her bag's side pocket and swore when she saw them all tangled up. How? They weren't even in there for long. Ashley walked down one of the alleys while someone from across the street clocked her doing so.

He looked to make sure no one was following her inside the alley. He pulled his hood up and walked across the street, following Ashley into the alley. From his pocket he pulled out a switch knife and flicked it open.

"Oi, you!" He shouted. Ashley turned around and saw him with the knife in his hand, twirling the blade around in his fingers.

"Phone, purse, any jewellery, that sort of thing," he said, walking towards her. Ashley quirked an eyebrow and looked down at his blade.

"Are you deaf bitch? Phone, now!" Ashley looked up at him.

"You didn't just see where I came out of, did you?" Ashley said.

"I don't care where you came out of sweet cheeks," he said. "Get your stuff out or I'm gonna shank you!"

"Right, sure you are," Ashley muttered under her breath while turning around and putting her hand into her bag.

He walked up behind Ashley; she looked discreetly over her shoulder.

"Well…" he said. "You're quite a looker in the light." Ashley could smell the cigarette smoke on his breath.

"So, you play nice and I'll let you keep these looks." He moved the knife closer to her face with his hand next to her mouth.

"So, your phone."

"Right…" Ashley turned her head slightly and bit into the guys hand. Ashley turned sharply, she ducked but landed a punch into the guys diaphragm. "Here!" He breathed out winded but threw his hand blindly at her with the knife in it. Ashley grabbed his arm, twisted his wrist and with her other arm elbowed his ribs. She kicked his groin really hard. Ashley kicked the back of his knee.

He fell to his knees and cried out in pain. Ashley straightened her hair.

"I just came out of a fighting dojo," she said, straightening her bag as he whimpered on the floor. "Think about that next time you try to rob a girl round here." He fell onto his front and curled up in a ball on the floor. Ashley shook her head and walked on down the alley while trying to untangle her headphones.

Robbers, always an occupational hazard.

Ashley decided to walk on the main roads after that, she really didn't fancy getting mugged again. Most people like her who were out at this sort of time were just trying to get home before the bitter cold set in. Ashley saw the rows of homeless people now huddling under the alcoves of shop entrances to keep warm.

Ashley went into Morrisons, bought a few things and continued the walk back to her apartment. Ashley got back without any other mugging attempts and let herself into her apartment.

Her mum had talked to her about maybe getting a roommate, so she didn't always come home to an empty house. The idea was tempting; she had a roommate when she was at university but there was a new liberation at living on her own. There were still days she came home and wished that she had someone to talk to about her day, but she had the freedom to do what she wanted without worrying about anyone else.

Ashley locked the door, walked into her kitchen and turned her wireless radio on; a gift from her father for when she worked out in the fields on her parent's farm, because 'You can't trust everything with a plug.' It survived three years in Edinburgh, three so far in Manchester and three back home.

Ashley was unloading her shopping when the local news started. It was talking about the body that was found in the Cambrian. That is something that always felt odd, when your work is on the radio. But it soon faded away into a piece on how kids were spending too much time on a new video game.

Ashley had a protein shake then went to have a shower, letting the warm water soak her aching body, particularly on her back. Today had taken a heavy toll on her.

She changed into some pyjamas and checked her phone. She had some messages from a few guys who had decided to randomly contact her, but she had one from Dan.

Dan: *Saw your moves on Twitter earlier. Are you that flexible in everything you do?*

Ashley smirked to herself and got into bed.

Maybe, you'll have to come round and find out.

Don't tempt me.

Ashley put her phone on charge and made herself comfortable under the duvet.

***

06:30 AM

Beep.

Beep.

Beep.

The alarm from her phone woke Ashley up instantly. She rolled over, shut the alarm off and was out of bed and getting changed for the gym while putting her work clothes in a bag. She walked into the kitchen.

Two glasses of cold water to speed up metabolism.

A banana for afters.

She put her gym bag over her shoulder, got her keys from the side and closed the door; she made her way down to her car and drove to the gym.

Her gym was on the edge of the main road into Manchester from the ring road. It had been her gym since she moved to Manchester, quick and easy to get to from her apartment and then a direct route to her new work.

Cardio.

Core.

Upper body.

The bag.

When *It's My Life* (No Doubt not Talk Talk) finished on Spotify, she took her MMA gloves off and went to the changing rooms. After a quick shower and change she was on her way to The City Tower. Hopefully she would have a fuller day than yesterday; well, chasing a suspect was a good way to start the morning.

Ashley parked up in the car park, made her way to the stairs and walked up to the office.

She walked in, turned the lights on and the TV to the BBC news channel. Ashley sat down, got the banana out of her bag and started to peel it as she turned on her computer.

She looked at the board at Gordon Ferrets, hopefully they would be able to add more to it by the end of the day.

When her computer loaded, she checked her e-mails. She had a copy of SOCO's report from the hotel room and corridor along with the CCTV from the hotel throughout the day. Ashley decided to make up a porridge and a tea. She took a sachet out of her draw and went to the kitchen.

Bing.

Ashley got her phone out and saw a message from Dan. She smiled to herself and boiled the kettle

Hey you, how you been?

Good thanks, works been busy though.

Mine to 🙁

Maybe we should go out and let off some steam.

Can't working lates and we have some gigs on,
maybe you should come?

Can't, need all the sleep I can get at the moment.

We really suck at this.

It's work, I'll let you know when I'm free.

The kettle boiled and Ashley poured boiling water into her bowl and mug. Ashley sat back down at her desk and started to read through the SOCO report. According to them there were two sets of footprints found on the carpet on the room, one male with shoes on and one possible male with no shoes on, but the depth and foot size ruled out the same person.

DNA was next to useless with only Ferret's and the cleaners' found in the room. So, gloves, possibly. Ashley started to break up the names of the parents who would have had a vendetta against him, so they could all start to question them. All they had were names and addresses, so she would put it down to the uniform pool so they could pick up stragglers.

Ashley gave herself the ones that were close to where Ferrets lived so she could go to neighbours too. Hopefully she could find something the others had missed the other day.

After her porridge was finished and the lists had been broken up, she placed the DVDs of the Cambrian's security in her computer and started to watch the feed of the lobby, from the day Ferrets died.

She watched Ferrets walk into the lobby, even then he looked jittery, constantly looking over his shoulders. Was he waiting for someone, or was someone waiting for him? He got his key and walked out of the lobby. Ashley made a note of the time he walked out and loaded the video for the lifts and staircases.

Ferrets walked straight to the staircase.

"Because there's cameras in the lifts," Ashley said. She continued to watch the lobby to see if anyone followed him. But it looked more like a normal day in a hotel lobby. So, either the killer was already checked in or they were more discreet.

Ashley looked up and saw McArthur coming into the office.

"Morning Fenway," he said. Ashley looked up.

"Morning Sir," she replied.

"Anything new come in?" McArthur asked.

"SOCO's full report has come through."

"And?"

Ashley explained to him the footprints found at the scene, and the lack of DNA in the room.

"I've finished looking at the list of people who filed claims against our vic, and split them up," Ashley said, patting the piles. "Something we can do today. Rule out a few people."

"OK, tell everyone I'll brief them when they come in so we can get a clear picture of what we all know." He walked towards his office. He stopped before the pane of the door.

"Fenway, could you please chase up IT and see what was on his computer as well?" He walked into his office and closed the door. Ashley ran a hand through her hair and rang up the computer lab which went to answerphone. Ashley left a message and went back to watching the CCTV.

Parland came in next and turned his computer on.

"Morning, find anything useful yesterday?"

"List of people who might want him dead," Ashley said. "He was taken to court because people thought he might be a paedophile but was acquitted. These are the lists of people." Ashley held up the four lists.

"Nice lists."

"One here with your name on it," Ashley said. "What did his neighbours have to say?" Parland flicked back through his notepad.

"Big shock, why would anyone do this, was this about his you know what's?" Parland put his notebook down.

"Did he do anything for them?" Ashley asked.

"Like what?"

"Odd jobs, gardening, things like that?" Parland looked back through the notes.

"No mention of it," he said. "All his neighbours said that he kept himself to himself and there was no commercial vehicle at the premises."

"Lay low after a paedophile scandal, sounds very smart to me," Ashley said. "SOCO came back though, no other DNA in the room apart from our vic's and the cleaners'."

"Joy, oh joy." Ashley nodded. Murphy then came in, said hello to her and went over with Parland what they learned yesterday. A few minutes later Armstrong rocked up looking a little worse for wear.

"Morning all," he said, cheerfully. There were a few grumbled hellos. Ashley didn't do anything as she was preparing everything, she found from yesterday to present to them later.

"Have you all woken up on the wrong side of the bed?" Armstrong asked, sitting at his desk.

"We're busy," Murphy said. "Guv's gonna go through the evidence to see what we know now."

"Guy got killed by a prossie or an ex-wife, guarantee it," Armstrong said.

"Except his ex-wife is in Zante," Ashley said. "Phoned her." She said, to the bemused looks. "And looking at his financials he didn't have enough to hire a prossie, well, unless he goes to the same place you do," she said, looking over at Armstrong.

"Well he wouldn't pay by plastic, would he?" Armstrong said, with a laugh. "Unless they do swipe." He said to the laughter of everyone else. Even Ashley had to turn her lip up at that.

"Well, he didn't draw out lots of cash either," she said. "And CCTV isn't showing anyone following him."

"Receptionist was sure no one asked about his room either," Parland interjected.

"Telephone records don't show him making any calls," Ashley added. "And there was no burner phone found at the scene."

"Killer might have taken it," Armstrong said.

"Or the killer was already there, pre-planned rendezvous?" Murphy offered.

"We'll need his computer back before we can confirm that," Parland said. "Otherwise it could just be a random murder."

"It seems like too much hassle though," Armstrong said. "To kill one random person walking into a hotel, I mean, why was he even there?"

The question caused an eerie silence. For everything they did know, they still didn't know the answer to the fundamental question, why was Ferrets even there on that day? Hopefully his laptop would provide some answers to this.

McArthur came out of his office to break the silence.

"Morning everyone," he said, as he walked to the front. "Right, let's get a clearer picture of our guy." He tapped the board.

"Gordon Ferrets, fifty-nine years old, found stabbed and tied up in a cheap hotel room. What do we know, Fenway?" Ashley looked up.

"You were the one looking into this, tell us about him." Ashley took a deep breath to prepare herself.

"OK, Ferrets owned a sports academy which provided free PE to local schools, deprived groups, worked primarily in the Sounds Edge area, things like that," Ashley said. "He also worked as a scout for both United and City, to find players."

"So, what happened? There's a lot of money in that," Armstrong said.

"Two years ago, a civil suit was brought against him by a group of people claiming to have been abused by him while under his care," Ashley explained. "It was costly, but he cleared his name, but the publicity from it in the local area tainted him; he was living off the settlement because he couldn't get any work."

"Poor guy," Murphy said.

"Could be one of the people who lost the case?" Parland mused.

"We'll get to that later," McArthur said. "Ashley, continue."

"Financials showed only the amenities while phone records only showed him talking to his daughter."

"Nothing out of the ordinary?" McArthur asked. Ashley pulled the list over.

"There were payments to a Tillerson 2071 Limited which is an operating holding company, but they have shares in hundreds of companies, so I don't know which one it's going to."

"No luck finding the link?"

"No but I'll keep looking."

"Right, what about his neighbours?" McArthur said, looking over at Parland and Murphy. Ashley got her notepad out.

"Neighbours were quite shocked to be honest," Parland said, consulting his own notes. "He'd recently moved to the area and everyone thought he was a nice bloke."

"Part of the community?"

"Not really, kept himself to himself," Murphy said, looking in his own book. "People saw him walking out and about but mostly stayed in his flat."

"Well, where did he go out and about to?"

"No idea. There are some shops along from a bus stop, maybe he went on one?" Parland said.

"Good point. Fenway, can you chase that up?" Ashley smiled to herself and wrote it down. The perfect chance to talk to neighbours too.

"So, any confirmation on how he died?" Parland asked. "What sort of weapon are we looking for?"

"Cramer says it was a knife, a small blade, probably between three and five inches. He died from the blood loss from the initial wound and slash. Toxicology showed a trace amount of cocaine in his system as well but nothing else."

"From what we know these are the questions we need to answer today." McArthur picked a pen up and went to the board.

"Why was he at the hotel?

"What was he doing when he was out and about?"

"And what is his daily routine?" Ashley's desk phone went off; she peeled her eyes away to see it was the computer lab.

"Fenway," she said, quietly.

"Ashley's already got us a lead. The Manchester Evening news have sent over a list of people who put the civil suit against Ferrets together. I've been able to get uniform to provide us with some extra bodies to track the ones further afield but here's a list of people that I want us to look at by the end of the day. So, if we can at least clear two out of the three on the board it'll be a good day."

"You're sure about that?" Ashley said. She looked up at the boards to see everyone still talking, while the lab confirmed everything, they just told her.

"Thanks, can you send the full analysis over... thanks." She ended the call.

"Sir." She said interrupting. "Computer analysis came back."

"And?"

"They found porn on it."

Armstrong laughed. "News flash Fenway. Every man's computer has porn on it," he said, easily. Ashley rolled her eyes.

"Child porn," she finished. There was a deadly silence around the room.

"You're sure?"

"Lab's confirmed it and sent the analysis over," Ashley said, looking at the report in her e-mails. "He really was a nonce." McArthur nodded and tapped the board.

"All the more reason for someone to kill him," McArthur said. "I have to go see the DCS and Chief Constable and let them know of our progress. In the meantime, you know what we have to do — go back out there and find me a suspect. At least one person on the list has some sort of grudge against him. Also, in light of this info that he was a nonce, go back and question everyone you did yesterday about him, see if someone knew on the side," McArthur handed out the lists to everyone and walked out.

"This looks like a wasted day, Armstrong said.

"The killer might be on there," Ashley said, getting up.

"Ha, unlikely love," he replied, getting to his feet. "I bet you my pension none of these geezers did it, they're not smart enough."

"Who said they had to be smart?" Parland asked, taking his own list and going with Armstrong. Ashley ignored them and picked up her list along with Ferrets' diary.

"It's more than they found yesterday," Murphy said, getting his coat and smiling warmly at her. "Come on, we can get a head start." Ashley got her coat and keys and followed Murphy.

"What car do you drive?"

"BMW."

"Nice, what kind?"

"1 Series, 61 Reg."

"Sweet, we'll take your car," he said.

"What car have you got?" Ashley asked raising an eyebrow.

"Zafira. Family run around," Murphy said. "0-60 eventually." Ashley nodded.

"Let's take my car," Ashley said, putting her keys in her pocket.

Chapter 8

"Nice, very nice," Murphy said, as they walked towards her car. "I always wanted a beamer." He continued as Ashley unlocked it.

"Why didn't you?" Ashley asked while opening the door.

"Kids," Murphy said, getting in to. "The wife wanted something safer."

"What did you have before?"

"MX-5," Murphy said nodding, reminiscing in his head about the car. "Jamiliea though said the Zafira had this safety rating and this and that." The car fired into life and the radio came on. Murphy peered at the station and laughed.

"How old are you?" He asked.

"Twenty-four," Ashley replied, as they drove out. "Why?"

"You're twenty-four and you listen to Radio Two," he said.

"Hey, I like it," Ashley said, defensively.

"But it's for old people. My mum listens to Radio Two."

"She's a woman of fine taste then, unlike her son." Murphy laughed.

"She wouldn't argue with that."

"My mum and dad listen to it," Ashley said, finding the need to explain herself. "They always had it on back home and I just... carried it on." They joined traffic leaving the city centre.

"Radio One," Murphy said.

"How old are you?"

"Thirty-six."

"You're way too old to be listening to that," Ashley said. Murphy laughed and looked around her car.

"So, how does a twenty-four-year-old have a car like this?" He asked.

"I repaired it," Ashley answered.

"You repaired it?" Murphy said, not quite believing it. Ashley nodded.

"A neighbour of my parents, their son died abroad. He'd left the car behind and they wanted rid of it, so I bought it because my car was on its last legs, and I'd just joined the police, so I had some more money in."

"What did it need doing to it?"

"New brakes, an engine tune-up and some electronics," Ashley said. Murphy thought for a moment.

"Don't take this the wrong way but… where did you learn to do that?"

"I grew up on a farm with a few dodgy tractors," Ashley said, with a smile. "You had to learn how to fix them or you were screwed."

"I can change the oil and that's about it," Murphy said, getting the list out of his pocket.

"So, why were you so keen to have this one then?" He asked.

"Because it's the one with people close to where Ferrets lived," Ashley explained. "I want to know a little more about him."

"Me and Parland went over nearly the whole estate, we didn't find anything useful." Ashley patted the diary in her breast pocket.

"I have a hunch."

"A hunch," Murphy said. "You have, a hunch."

"Yeah," Ashley said, defensively.

"This isn't like the TV shows, Fenway," Murphy said. "You need to explain yourself when you have a hunch." Ashley breathed out.

"I… I think that he may have been doing odd jobs for neighbours. There's a series of initials in the book with some of them pencilled in at regular times. It would explain why he wasn't withdrawing enough cash to fund his lifestyle."

Murphy nodded.

"People said he kept himself to himself. They also said that he was quite new to the area."

"There must be something, his financials didn't really add up," Ashley said.

"And you think he's been doing some work on the side."

85

"It's the only thing I can think of. Maybe his neighbours saw where he was going."

"Yeah, don't count on that," Murphy said. "People round the estate aren't that forthcoming to us." That was the second time in as many days she'd heard that.

As Ashley drove in, she saw what people meant. The houses were a dull grey and were semi-detached from one another with unruly hedges in front of them with them, all in various states of disrepair.

As they drove through Ashley could see people stopping their conversations and looking at her car as she drove past. A group of kids as well, who she thought should be in school, were riding on their bikes but slowed as they saw it go past.

"If I knew we were coming here I would have insisted on taking your car," Ashley said. She parked up in a small carpark which had a newsagent, bookies, café, Bargain Booze and a taxi rank. Ashley and Murphy got out with Ashley making sure she locked her car.

"If we come back to find this on bricks, you're buying me new tyres," Ashley said, pointing at him.

"You decided to come here, so no," Murphy said, checking the list.

"Founders Avenue is just down there; a Carey Sutherland is on the list. Maybe we should go down there first." Ashley nodded and they made their way. Ashley though, could see people looking at them as they walked.

"Do you know this place well?" Ashley asked.

"I grew up on the next estate along, I had a few mates that lived down here," Murphy explained, as they walked down a side street to Founders that was in unison, with the one they had just come from.

"So, you know these mean streets."

"Different times," Murphy said, looking at the list. "It used to be a place where everyone knew everyone. Now with immigrants coming in and taking up housing, you can see what they think about that." He pointed to a house with 'Go Home' written in red spray paint across the door.

"They get behind certain causes round here, that's one of them," he said.

86

"Did you get anything like that?" Ashley asked. Murphy shook his head.

"Racism isn't only about what you look like, it's what you sound like too," he said, looking down at the list. He stopped outside number thirty-five which had a large, overgrown bush and a rusted gate. Murphy opened it and it groaned loudly. Inside the grass areas either side were overgrown and had weeds littered across them, along with a few empty beer cans.

Murphy knocked on the door. At first there was nothing. Murphy looked at Fenway and nodded at the window. Ashley went to check and saw a TV on, with what looked like a figure sitting in an armchair.

"Someone home?" Murphy asked. Ashley nodded. Murphy knocked on the door more loudly and Ashley walked over towards the door. They heard a groan and the shuffling of someone behind the door. After a few fumbled attempts the door was opened by an overweight man wearing a stained vest that was white once upon a time, who had a beer can in his hand.

"What do you want?" He barked.

"Are you Carey Sutherland?" Murphy asked.

"Who wants to know?" He shot back. Ashley never understood why people said, 'Who wants to know?' they might as well just say yes.

"Sir I'm DS Murphy, this is DC Fenway." Both flashed their ID's. "We wanted to talk to you about a civil suit you were part of a few years ago."

"What about it?" He snapped.

"Sir, where were you between three and seven on Sunday the twelfth?"

"I was... here," Sutherland said, not understanding the link. "What does this have to do about my court case?"

"It was against Gordon Ferrets, wasn't it?" Murphy asked. His already harsh features hardened.

"I want nothing to do with that nonce," he said. "He's a bastard and he ruined my life!"

"He's dead," Murphy said.

"Good," Sutherland spat. Ashley was taken aback that someone could say that after hearing someone had died.

"Where were you between three and seven on Sunday?" Murphy asked again.

"I was here." Sutherland pulled his tracksuit leg up to show an ankle tag. "You can check with my parole officer. I was here all day." Sutherland dropped his tracksuit.

"How did he die?"

"He was stabbed," Ashley said. "We're going through all the people who were part of the civil case." Sutherland smiled.

"Looks like it's all our lucky day," he said. "And his luck ran out."

"Luck?" Ashley asked. Sutherland laughed.

"He was always getting away with it, there were rumours about him for years. How he got off I will never know, but hey, what goes around comes around. People like him and Will Oatley always get found out in the end."

"Did you know he lived not far from here?" Ashley asked.

"No, but I wish I did. I'd have saved the guy who did it a problem," Sutherland said. "There are a few people who would have."

"Who brought this case against him?" Ashley asked. Sutherland shrugged his shoulders.

"No idea," he replied. "All I know is that there were quite a few people. How they found him not guilty I'll never know."

"Well, thank you for your time," Ashley said.

"No, thank you," Sutherland replied with a smile while backing into the doorway. "You've made my year. Maybe you should go after that twat of a mayor next!" He slammed the door shut.

"This is going to be a long day isn't it?" Ashley said, turning back. Murphy nodded and crossed Sutherlands name off the list, indicating he had an alibi.

"We'll have to check with his parole officer just to cross the Is," Murphy said, looking at the list again. "There are a few more names to go through but I can do those." He pointed down the road.

"Ferrets lives the next street along. It bends round into a cul de sac. There should be a uniform outside it."

"Thanks. I'll call you when I'm done." Ashley started to make her way down the road. Her gaze falling on the rows of houses where some people took pride in their homes and others who didn't at all. Some houses had boards in the windows and some had graffiti on the front with various slogans.

Ashley followed the road to the next street and followed it down to the cul de sac. His house stood out like a sore thumb with police tape along the front and a uniform stood outside, who looked bored out of his skin. Ashley made her way over to him. He was young, black with frizzy hair underneath his hat.

"DC Fenway," she said.

"PC Thomas. Don't suppose you have a cuppa, do you?"

"No such luck," Ashley replied. "Just following up on a lead."

"Well, I hope you solve it quick cause I hate standing out here all day," Thomas said, rubbing his hands together. Ashley smiled sympathetically.

"How well do you know the neighbours?" Ashley asked.

"Not that well," Thomas said. "They hardly come out."

"Were you part of canvassing?"

"Yeah, they were more unhelpful then."

"I know, I had to wade through it all," Ashley said. "Were there any elderly people in the canvassing?"

"Not on mine, why?" Ashley pulled Ferrets diary out and went through it. "There is a list of initials and I wondered if it had anything to do with his neighbours." Thomas had a look.

"Doesn't ring any bells," he said. "You can have a talk to some of them."

"Thanks," Ashley said, walking to his neighbours. Not only did they not match up initials or know anything else, but they all said the same thing. He kept himself to himself, went out but they didn't know where, nice man and no they didn't know any of the initials.

After visiting seven houses Ashley had to conclude that she had hit a dead end. She sat down on the curb, got her notebook out and looked through it. The initials obviously meant something else so she would have to have another look at that.

It would be helpful if she could figure out where he had been going. She got her phone out and called Murphy.

"Hello Ash, how's the hunch?"

"Dead," she said. "Listen, doesn't Ferrets daughter live around here?"

"Yeah, why do you ask?"

"I want to ask her a few questions," Ashley said. "Maybe she knows more about her dad's routine."

"Not a bad shout, I don't think Armstrong would have asked that many questions about it," he agreed.

"Do you remember where it is?" Ashley asked.

"I'll text it over to you. She still might have family bereavement officers with her."

"I'll be so lucky," Ashley said. "Thanks."

Ashley looked up at the overcast sky, just relishing the slight breeze on her face and the peace of this suburban life. Her phone buzzed, she put the street name in and started to walk over to it while thinking over what questions she should ask.

She saw the house, turned the maps app off and strolled over. If she had been walking past it, she would have missed it.

Ashley walked up to the door and knocked. After a couple of seconds, the door opened and one of the bereavement officers looked at her.

"Yes?" Ashley flashed her ID.

"I need to talk to Tracy," Ashley said. "Just need to ask her a couple more questions." The officer on the other side of the door looked behind her.

"OK, come in," she said, stepping aside and letting her through. The front door opened into a dark and cramped corridor. Ashley followed the officer to the end which opened into a kitchen where Tracy Ferrets sat.

She looked older and more dishevelled than her Facebook photos. It was obvious from her complexion that there had been tears as well.

"Hello Tracy, my name is DC Ashley Fenway." Ashley opened her ID. "I'm with DCI McArthur's team that's investigating your father's murder."

"That was quick." Ashley looked at the bereavement officer who shared her bemused look.

"I'm sorry but, what do you mean by quick?"

"My dad's murder, you've solved it."

"No... not yet." Tracy sank the drink in front of her.

"Then why are you still here? Why aren't you out there looking for the bastard who did this!" She slammed the glass down on the table. The bereavement officer recoiled slightly while Ashley stood firm.

"We're following up on some promising lines of enquiry," Ashley said. "But I need to ask you some more questions." The angry outburst from a moment before collapsed into a sullen meekness.

"... Yeah, I'll..." She swallowed back tears. Ashley sat down opposite her and got her note pad out.

"We're trying to piece together your dad's movements. His neighbours say that he went out of his house, but we don't know where. Did he ever tell you?" Tracy shook her head.

"No friends he visited or errands he ran?" Tracy shook her head.

"He kept a low profile after what happened with that court case. He didn't do anything wrong, but everyone thought he was guilty anyway."

"When did you two move here?" Ashley asked.

"Not long after that court thing. It wasn't safe for me or my kids," Tracy said. "We both decided to come here. Start afresh."

"Was he doing any sort of work?" Ashley asked. Tracy shook her head.

"He was living off the money he won off that case," Tracy said. "Not sure what else he could do apart from football." Ashley nodded.

"I just feel so lost..." Tracy said shaking her head. "There seems to be so much I didn't know about him." Ashley felt a big weight come over her, she didn't know that her dad was a paedophile.

"Is there anything else you can tell us, anything about him at all you might have remembered?" Tracy shook her head.

"Just one last thing before I go." Ashley pulled the diary out of her pocket.

"It's your dad's," she said, sliding it over to Tracy. She picked it up and started to look through it. "Do any of the initials mean anything to you?" Ashley watched Tracy's face as she flicked through it, searching for any flicker of emotion.

"Nothing, sorry." Tracy threw it back towards Ashley. Ashley sighed. There was nothing more to be had here.

"OK, thank you for your time," Ashley said, getting up. "We'll keep you informed of our progress," Ashley said.

"Do you have anyone for it?" Tracy asked.

"We're still making enquiries," Ashley said. "We're looking through the list of people who were part of the civil suit against your dad." Tracy nodded her approval.

"What about when they tried to kidnap him?"

"Sorry?" Ashley said.

"A few years back someone tried to kidnap him. That's what he said anyway."

"Did he ever say who?" Ashley asked. "That sounds quite serious." Tracy shrugged.

"I don't know," she said, in a deflated tone. Ashley looked at the bereavement officer and nodded to the living room. Ashley went there and waited for her to follow. Ashley looked around the living room which had a Sky box plus an XBOX and a PlayStation with various toys scattered around two worn leather sofas.

The officer came in.

"How has she been?" Ashley asked.

"She's been drinking the pain away," the officer said. "And smoking like a chimney. In my experience, not well."

"How about the kids?"

"Secondary in her mind at the moment. I think I might get social services to come in if things don't improve."

"Is she sober at the moment?" Ashley asked looking back at the kitchen, at Tracy slumped on the table.

"Well, I had to use the spare key to get in. She was passed out on the sofa." She pointed to the sofa; Ashley could see Tracy's imprint on the leather.

"She's still having coffee."

"I might need to come back to question her when she has her bearings." Ashley said. "How long are you assigned to her for?"

"'Til the end of the day, technically."

"Ashley."

"Sharon." The two women shook hands. Ashley got her card out.

"If she sobers up, call me." Sharon nodded as Ashley walked out the door. She got her phone out and rang Murphy.

"How's the list going?" Ashley asked.

"Not that good. We have more alibis to check and more happy people. When I joined the police, I wanted to spread good news, telling someone a person died wasn't on that list. How was the daughter?"

"Drunk," Ashley said. "She's still grieving, didn't know anything about what her dad was up to during the day. How much have you done of the list?"

"Just one more: Tim Williams."

"I'm going to head back to the car, as long as it's not on bricks," Ashley quipped.

"I'll meet you there." Ashley ended the call and walked back to the car with her hands in her jacket pocket, thinking about what Gordon Ferrets did during the day.

Ashley saw her car in sight and thought about maybe having a bottle of water. As Ashley walked into the shop, she saw a CCTV cam on the front of the shop looking out at the car park.

Ashley picked up her water and went to go and pay. The man behind the till was Asian and totting up the total of the woman in front of her. Ashley looked up at the CCTV monitor by the till. The monitor showed various cameras around the shop and the one outside.

Ashley looked at the one outside. It was showing the carpark and the bus stop on the opposite side of the road. Ferrets didn't have a car anymore so how did he get around? There was no car at the scene, and it didn't come up in searches. It would explain how he got to Manchester, and there was no other bus stops around.

Ashley paid for her water and went outside. She walked over the road to the bus stop and checked where it was going. There were two that came down, the Castlefield line and the Metro line. Ashley tapped the glass.

Maybe this would shed some light on where he went. Ashley turned back and saw Murphy walking to her car. Ashley walked over to him.

"You OK?" Murphy asked.

"Is this the only bus stop going in and out of this estate?"

"Yeah, was always a ball ache," Murphy replied.

"Maybe not," Ashley said, looking over at the shop.

"Ferrets didn't have a car so he would have had to get the bus to wherever he was going," Ashley said, looking at Murphy. "The shop across the road has CCTV. Maybe we can see where he was going."

"Worth a shout," Murphy said, as they walked back into the shop. Thankfully there wasn't anyone else in there.

"Hi," Murphy said, showing the owner his badge. "Does that CCTV record?" The man nodded.

"Good," Murphy said, pocketing his ID. "Me and my partner here need a copy of it for the week."

Chapter 9

"Well come on, what did you find?" Armstrong said, looking over at Ashley's desk. The shop owner had reluctantly given her and Murphy the CCTV. Ashley wasn't sure why he was so tetchy about it.

"A lead... maybe," Ashley said. It was a longshot, but this was how most criminals were caught. She had a photo of the bus timetable up on her computer screen as well, trying to pinpoint what time Ferrets would leave.

The quality of the CCTV camera was good at short distance but not that great over a long distance. Ashley thought she saw a couple of people that looked like him but again she couldn't be sure if it was him.

The bus timetable said that if someone left that that bus stop at two, they would have got into Manchester bus station at 14:35. More than enough time to get to The Cambrian from the bus station. Ashley was looking at the bus that came across at the time and saw a group of people at the station, still not being sure if Ferrets was amongst them.

They got on the bus and set off. Ashley wasn't impressed; she was hoping for a clearer picture. Maybe if she was lucky then Ferrets would have got off at the bus station.

Ashley looked up the number for the bus station and thought about phoning, but it would be easier to walk over and speak to security directly. Ashley grabbed her keys and phone and went to go out.

"Not got that lead?" Armstrong asked.

"What exactly are you doing?" Ashley asked.

"Getting my own," Armstrong replied. "Someone can't be sure of their movements so I'm looking into it."

"Good to see you're finally being useful," Ashley said, as she walked out. Ashley took the stairs down to the lobby and walked out into the car park. Ashley got her phone out and put in the directions to the bus station.

The weather was still overcast which gave Manchester it's grim northern status. It was the same with Edinburgh, in the sun it looked a little worn, and in the winter, more than a little rough.

She sighed and made her way to the bus station which had just undergone a major renovation. With it being the early afternoon, it wasn't that busy. Ashley walked up and down the bus stops trying to find out where the number fifty-two stopped off at. She must have looked weird doing this, but they didn't print the stops on the website.

After scanning a couple of them she found stop seven which the number fifty-two was on. Ashley looked up and saw a security camera which was pointing at the stop.

Ashley turned around and a little further down the rows of stops, saw another camera which would show if Ferrets went the other way.

Ashley walked over to the security terminal which was a small booth being manned by an overweight security guard, who had his gut overhanging his trousers which were fit to burst. In Ashley's mind he couldn't catch a cold let alone a criminal. He was busy tucking into a Greggs sausage roll with the flakes of pastry falling onto his round gut.

Ashley tapped on the window. The security guard held up one finger to indicate to wait while he finished his snack. Ashley raised her eyebrow in disbelief and he shoved the rest of it into his mouth and looked up at her.

"How can I help you love?" He asked. Ashley held her ID against the glass; he leaned forward on the already straining desk chair and squinted his eyes at it.

"Oh, what can I help you with?"

"I need CCTV for Sunday the twelfth" Ashley said. "It's to do with an ongoing murder enquiry." Ashley added before the guard could ask her.

"Err... OK, I think IT deal with the CCTV." Ashley looked down at a phone that was on his desk.

"Well, could you phone them for me? Time is of the essence here," Ashley said. The guard picked the receiver up and looked dumbly down at the numbers. He was mumbling to himself and put in a few numbers.

Ashley rolled her eyes, folded her arms across her chest and tapped her foot impatiently as he finally made a call.

"Hi, yeah it's Stuart from security, I have police here wanting to look at CCTV from Monday. Yeah, something about a murder. OK, I'll tell her." He put the phone and looked up at Ashley.

"There should be someone coming down to help you now."

"When?"

The guard looked up at Ashley and shrugged.

"I don't know, when they get here, I guess." Ashley pursed her lips, shook her head and looked down at her phone thinking that if she was a DI or higher it would be in her hand now. After a couple of minutes, a man came up towards her in an ill-fitting shirt which looked baggy round his wiry frame, and with a pair of round spectacles.

"Are you the police officer?" He asked. Ashley didn't have the energy to correct him.

"Yes, DC Fenway," Ashley said, introducing herself. "I was hoping to look at your CCTV footage from Sunday," Ashley said. "It's to do with an ongoing murder enquiry."

"Yes." He laughed a little nervously. He led Ashley into a small office in the heart of the building. When he opened the door, what greeted Ashley was a small room with hardly any lights but with three or four old, retro TV screens.

"Here we are; the controls are there in front of you and the old tapes on the side."

Before Ashley could ask the questions she wanted to, the man closed the door behind her. Ashley looked around the small room when one of the stacked DVDs fell from its side to its front.

"Right, better get started," Ashley said, flicking the light on. The light in the room was coming from a bulb which was on its last legs. Ashley sat down and looked at the screens. She was looking for the camera that looked on bus stop seven: camera 3b, and the one further down — 4a.

Ashley got up and looked around at all the stacks of DVDs. It didn't look as though it was kept in any sort of order. Ashley ran her hands down her cheeks. All her books and DVDs were kept in alphabetical order back in her apartment; this was doing her love of order no good at all.

They were kept in CD cases with a date at the top but they weren't in order. After a few minutes of sorting out Ashley finally found the cameras she was looking for as well as the date. She sat back down at the monitor and put the DVD into the player.

The grainy screen starting to splutter into life before flashing black. Ashley looked around and smacked the screen. It whined but sprang into life and showed the walkway Ashley had been looking for. Ashley smiled to herself and started to watch; she fast forwarded just after half two. She watched closely as the buses started to come in with a wave of passengers coming out. Ashley squinted at the screen. It was way too small and grainy to see anything on this.

Ashley got all the DVDs she needed and made a note of the ones she took, although she was certain that they wouldn't miss them. She made her way out and went back to the security booth where the guard was eating a jam doughnut.

Ashley rapped the glass with her knuckles which made him scoff.

"Wha!"

"I made a list of the days I've had to take," Ashley said, handing the list over.

"Can't you tell Mike?" He asked, "I'm busy."

"Right…" Ashley said, shaking her head and walking away.

***

Ashley put the DVDs into the dual player, brought up the split screens and pressed play. The HD screens in the tower showed it in crisp quality. Ashley watched the passengers come off.

From her psychology days she remembered that people who are nervous do one of two things; they are either too eager, or too passive. So, she was looking for him to be coming off the bus first or be the last one off. Ashley looked over at a picture of the clothes that Ferrets was wearing.

She looked at the screen again. A slew of students came off the bus first, followed by a few old men and women. Then finally, Gordon

Ferrets thanked the driver and got off. Although he had been the last person off, he powered past some of the other people on the bus and headed up towards the south exit which was further away from the Cambrian. Ashley paused the video and checked the time stamp. She placed the time into the other videos and watch as Ferrets walked down to the south exit.

Ashley followed him as he walked straight out to the entrance. Ashley checked the outside camera and saw him look around before heading across the road and then back round towards the Cambrian. Ashley closed the bus station footage and consulted the map of Manchester in the incident room.

The map had all the CCTV cameras under Manchester Council control, that the police had unlimited access to. Ashley checked the camera number (D34) she was looking for and placed a red tack on there to show Ferrets route. Ashley fed in the time stamp Ferrets walked out and checked the camera and sure enough he was there coming out of the bus station.

"Good, we have a route." Ashley followed his movements along the CCTV route to the Cambrian. Ashley had planned his route and left post-it notes on the board for the time frame. The last camera on the route showed Ferrets walk in. Ashley rubbed the bridge of her nose and looked at the screen. She leaned over to turn it off, when something caught her attention.

There was someone in a black hoodie walking towards the hotel. He made a note on a piece of paper and turned away. Ashley rewound it and looked at it again. Without a shadow of a doubt there had been someone following him. Why hadn't she seen him though on the other tapes?

"Well that was a waste of time," Armstrong said, as he walked into the office along with Parland and Murphy.

"Almost everyone on the list has an alibi."

"Couldn't you account for anyone?" Ashley asked.

"Yeah, one Kate Marsh, a Tommy Wainwright and Tim Williams," he said. "They could be in the wind or moved on, might have to check the electoral roll," he said, sitting down forcefully.

Ashley though now realised that she hadn't been watching this too long. After Ferrets went past the camera's line of sight this hooded figure came in afterwards. He must have known the camera's position and time. This was a professional, whoever they were.

"What have you got Fenway?" Parland asked.

"Someone stalking him," Ashley said.

"What?" All three came around to her computer. "So, here's Ferrets walking down Santon Avenue." Ashley showed them. "And he walks on." She pointed back to the first camera and the hooded man walked behind him.

"Do we see his face at all?" Parland asked hopefully.

"A partial," Ashley said, pointing to the camera outside the Cambrian. After he made the note he turned, and Ashley paused. He had fair hair and what looked like stubble.

"This looks good," Parland said. "When did he start following Ferrets?"

"Not that far after the bus station," Ashley said. "Maybe it's a route he did frequently."

"Neighbours said he went out," Parland added. "Maybe this is our killer. What's the time stamp on that?" He asked, pointing to the partial photo.

"Two thirty-nine," Ashley said. She looked over at the timeline made up on the chart. "It lines up." They looked down at the partial.

"We need to find out where this guy went," Parland said. "Fenway, can you track his movements back through the city?"

"I'll do my best," Ashley said, getting out a green tack for their suspect.

"You do that, print off the partial facial, we might be able to get it out on the socials for home time," Parland said.

"Maybe we should aggressively start looking for Wainwright and Williams," Murphy said. "They're the only two not accounted for."

"What about Marsh?" Ashley asked. "Women can put on fake beards to."

"This isn't the Life of Brian, Fenway; this is a murder case," Parland said. "We need to look at the balance of probability." Balance of probability was that it was one of the two men, even Ashley had to concede that.

"OK."

"Once you've finished tracking our suspect can you see where he goes off to?" Armstrong piped up. Ashley swallowed and nodded.

"Right."

"Armstrong with me, we're going to track down Wainwright. Murphy, you do the same for Williams."

"Sure thing," Murphy said, sitting back at his computer and typing something while Armstrong and Murphy walked out.

"Good work, Ashley," she muttered under her breath. She brought the tapes up and started to play them back, searching for the hooded man following Ferrets. Ashley placed the green tack next to the red one to see where the following began. She had lost track of time, her focus only disturbed when Murphy got up and walked out, probably had a lead on Tim Williams.

From the CCTV it looked like he was being followed from Piccadilly Gardens; that was the last any of the CCTV cameras saw him in the area. Ashley swore under her breath. That meant he could have arrived from any direction.

She looked at the CCTV camera which showed Ferrets walking into the hotel. She saw the man in the hood watch him and make a note of the hotel. He walked away towards the Oldham Road. Ashley continued to follow him. He walked across the Rochdale Road down to the train tracks. She lost sight of him there. Ashley consulted the map and saw there was another camera near the exit that went towards the A665. Ashley brought up Google maps; by her estimation it should take around ten minutes.

Ashley fast-forwarded the tape which looked over a church. Twelve minutes later he came over the footbridge and stood at the bus stop. Ashley checked the map ahead, there was only a couple more cameras before he was out of the city limit.

"Come on, pull your hood down," Ashley muttered under her breath. She fast forwarded again and slowed down when a bus came.

He got on the number 135 bus. Just before he got on, he pulled his hood down. Ashley tried to pause it, but he pulled it down just as he got on board. Ashley sighed and ran a hand through her hair.

The bus started to pull away. Ashley made a note of the licence plate. She could see if the bus had CCTV. Her phone buzzed and she looked at it. Tuesday… hockey training.

She looked at the clock; half six in the evening. She had half an hour. Ashley got up and looked at all the empty desks and then outside at the dark sky.

Where did the time go?

She looked at all the progress she had made. The bus depot wouldn't be open now but she could go down there first thing in the morning. Ashley searched for the depot and made a note of the address.

She placed the last tacks on the board for the man in the hood. He was heading north towards Cheetam Hill. Maybe he lived or worked up there. Ashley needed to see where he got off the bus.

***

"Dammit! No, follow the run!" Karen shouted. She blew on the whistle and everyone groaned to a stop, including Ashley who took her mouth guard out.

"We know that bitch makes the run through the middle!" Karen shouted, walking into a massive hole left open in the middle of the midfield. They were playing West Kirby on Sunday and they had an ex-England international on their books who tore them apart last time. As a centre it was Ashley's job to stop her.

"One pass gets in here and we're fucked! Ashley!" She rounded on Ashley. "Why is there such a gaping hole here?"

"I had to go over to cover the wing," Ashley said, pointing to a small group of them.

"But she likes hanging in here," Karen said, pointing round herself.

"You have to be sitting in here waiting for her." Ashley ran a hand through her hair.

"Surely though if I stop the ball from getting to her then she can't do anything, she'll have to come closer to me."

"She doesn't work like that though," Karen shot back. "Trust your team mates to win the ball back and then you're there to be passed to."

"And have their best tackler on me," Ashley argued.

"Enough; do that play again and make sure it's right." She started walking back to the side-line.

Ashley shook her head, put her mouth guard in and walked back to where Karen wanted her to be. Ashley had enough confidence in her own ability to mark this player; Karen though was scared out of her mind. This was negative tactics. They should play their game and worry about anything else afterward. Her trail of thought was lost when Karen blew sharply on the whistle.

"These dummy runs are important ladies!" Karen shouted. "You need to know exactly where she's going and familiarise yourself with it!" Ashley set herself and the play started again.

The ball came out of the defence, to the winger who played it up. Ashley resisted all her years of training and stayed inside. Ashley was marking Rachel, who was the other centre. She had been given the instruction to stay infield as well.

Ashley thought it was more laziness rather than tactical noose to not go and support the team. If she was being forced to do this, she was going to do this her way. She moved further back so the other centre was in front of her rather than behind. That way, Ashley could keep an eye on her and run across her if necessary.

The ball went down to the by-line and Rachel darted across. Ashley though saw it first and was hot on her heels. When the ball went in Ashley put her stick across Rachel and took the ball away from her. Rachel cursed under her breath, but Ashley was already away and striding across the astro-turf, looking left to right to see who was up with her and leaving Rachel behind with each stride.

But of course, since they had been told to hang back to double up on the wings, the wingers weren't getting up quickly.

The whistle blew again, and Karen started spewing about how good that play was. Ashley turned to look back and saw Rachel scowling at her before looking back.

Rachel was the undisputed first choice centre when Ashley arrived, but now she was on the edge of the team, thinking that she could force Ashley out; although plays like the one Ashley just did, didn't put her in a good light.

"Excellent ladies," Karen said, clapping her hands. "That's what we want to happen!"

"We'll be fucked if they decided to play down the wings," Ashley muttered to herself.

"Right, again, remember we don't practice 'til we get it right. We practice 'til we can't get it wrong." The rest of the session went smoothly enough. It was mostly practising for Sunday and working on shape and set plays.

Ashley was chatting idly to Eliza and Di, talking about the game. They had been on different teams in training since they were doing attack vs defence but on Sunday they would be on the same team.

"We just need to make sure that we get up the pitch quicker when you get the ball," Di said.

"But we'll be knackered though." Eliza chipped in.

"Do it in shifts then," Ashley suggested. "When I get the ball, whoever's closest make the run forward. The other then make the late run across the back of the D." Ashley took a swig of her drink. "Then, me and the other half-back can let it roll."

"As much as I hate doing this, having a walkthrough for a game is really good." Eliza said, as they reached her car.

"Why's that?" Ashley asked.

"At least it's not alien to us then," Eliza said. "At least we could have planned in case anything went wrong." Ashley quirked an eyebrow.

"Excuse me, I have to go," Ashley said, walking away. "I'll see you on Thursday!" Eliza and Di looked at her funny as she jogged away. Ashley jogged to her car, chucked her stuff in the back. She swigged her drink. Dummy runs. She had an idea.

***

The Cambrian wasn't normally busy, but even now it was deserted. The receptionist was idly twirling her pen on the empty booking sheet when the door opened. She looked up to see a brown-haired woman in hockey gear striding down with a thin layer of sweat on her skin, which showed off her lean muscles.

"Hi." She pulled out a police warrant card and showed her. Now she recognised her. "I need some videos from you."

Chapter 10

Beep.

  Beep.

  Beep.

Ashley opened her eyes. She turned over and touched her phone when she saw she had a message. She rubbed her eyes and checked.

Mum: *Hi love, tried to ring but you were busy, please call me. Love Mum xxx*

"Dammit," Ashley said, running a hand through her hair. She told herself she would phone her mum later.

Ashley pushed the duvet away, got changed into her gym gear and packed her work clothes. Ashley walked into the kitchen, got a smoothie out of the fridge and looked at the list she made for herself.

Bus depot.

Tracking suspects movements.

Look over Cambrian CCTV for last week; did they do a dummy run?

Ashley downed the rest of her drink and threw it into the bin.

"Swish," she said, closing the door behind her.

Cardio.

Core.

Arms.

The bag.

Ashley punched the bag hard one last time and looked up at the clock. If she wanted to get to the bus depot before it opened, she had to get going now. After a shower and a change of clothes she was driving up towards the depot.

The depot was a large storage yard on an industrial estate outside of Manchester. The sky was a murky grey, as Ashley pulled up next to a metal fence with all the buses lined up on the other side.

Ashley made sure that the CCTV from The Cambrian was still on the front seat and got out of the car.

Ashley walked by the metallic gate and could hear laughing from a small out-building.

Ashley walked over to an office which had the door open and let herself into a small waiting area which was in a generic cream colour, with a waiting desk and door at the back. Ashley looked at the walls which had famed photos of a portly man in a suit and his wife by a fleet of buses. Next to it was a newspaper article with the same photo of them in a local paper. The photos were worn and faded from sunlight, but everyone was happy.

Ashley walked up to a small desk in the room and looked for a bell but didn't see any. Ashley looked around at the back door but in the end settled with banging on the desk. The laughter stopped and then the shuffling of feet.

A woman came to the door. She was old with curly hair and tattoos on her arms.

"Are you OK love? We're not open for another ten minutes."

"I'm fine," Ashley said, getting her ID out. "DC Ashley Fenway, Manchester Major Crimes Unit."

"Oh… how can I help you detective?"

"Do your buses have CCTV?" Ashley asked, putting her ID away.

"Uhm… some of them do," she said. "I'm not sure, you're better off asking Nicky, he's the owner."

"Could you get him for me?" Ashley asked. "We're trying to track someone, and time is of the essence here."

"Of course," she said, going out the back. Ashley went back to looking at some of the photos of famous people who had been on their buses. Famous though was scraping the bottom of the barrel. Ashley didn't have a clue who these people were.

"Nicky!" She shouted. "Nicky love! Someone here to see you."

"We didn't find any phones Bev!" A voice shouted back.

"No Nicky love, it's the police." There was silence and then a young man came into the room.

"That's my old man," he said, pointing to the two portly figures Ashley was looking at. "He started this business about thirty years ago."

"You must be Nicky," Ashley said. "DC Fenway."

"Bev said about CCTV for the buses."

"Yes." Ashley pulled out the still of the 135 bus and showed it to him. "Does this bus have CCTV?" He looked at the photo.

"Yeah, it does, but it gets sent to the council for their centralised database."

"Don't you have any hard copies here?" Ashley asked. Nicky shook his head.

"We're not licensed to keep sensitive information on site," Nicky said. "The council have this new smart transfer camera. It records a continuous loop for the entire trip and resets when it comes to the bus station and the video transfers over.

"So, it's at the bus station?" Ashley said, not really wanting to go back to that soulless place. Thankfully he chuckled and shook his head.

"No, they wouldn't keep it there, it's only the transfer point. The data is in Manchester City Hall, it was part of the charter all the bus companies signed up for."

"Thank god," Ashley muttered under her breath. "Thank you for your time, you've been a big help." He smiled warmly at her and Ashley walked back out into the gloomy day. Ashley got in her car and put the council building postcode in.

Google maps showed it being about a half an hour drive and wasn't that far away from where she lived.

Ashley put her seat belt on and drove away, hoping that there was someone there early enough. She then remembered that McArthur wanted them all in early in the morning, plus she could get some groundwork on what was in the Cheetham Hill area, or what was around that area.

Ashley pulled into the City Tower car park and made her way up to the office. As usual she was the first one in. She sat down and looked at the map of Manchester she had set up the previous night.

Ashley sat down and loaded up Google maps and looked at the 135bus route and where it ended up in Bury. The possibilities for this were too large to speculate, there could be any number of reasons a man would come here.

Ashley ran a hand through her hair and looked around. There wasn't much to do until the others came in and compared notes. Ashley looked back at her phone and saw her mum's message. She swiped her phone to call her.

"Hello."

"Hey Mum."

"Hello dear, I wasn't expecting you to call this early."

"I have some time before I start work," Ashley yawned. "Plus, I had a late night, last night."

"Gentleman caller?" Ashley laughed.

"No, work," she said, looking at the green tack which stopped at the bus stop. "Lost track of time."

"How are you going to meet someone if you work all the hours god sends?" Her mum asked.

"It's not the be all and end all," Ashley said. "I just... lost track of time," she replied, lamely. "How are you and Dad?" She asked, getting up and walking to the kitchen to make a tea.

"Oh, we're good," her mum said. "Your sister though is driving me up the wall with this wedding." Ashley nodded. Her sister loved to be organised with things like this, but she could be very overbearing. Ashley put the kettle on.

"I thought she would, hence why I've stayed out of it," Ashley said, preparing her mug.

"You are supposed to be a bridesmaid," her mum reminded her.

"I told you I would turn up at the last dress fitting," Ashley said.

"Well that might be a bit away," her mum said, quietly. "She wants it done at Tatten Hall."

"OK, and?"

"Well they're fully booked from April to August this year and next year." Ashley laughed lightly and looked up at the office ceiling.

"She wasn't happy," Ashley said, turning as the kettle finished boiling.

"She had her heart set on it," her mum said. "She's seriously considering waiting two years."

"Mum, it's Abs, she's always been a diva when she never got her way," Ashley said, stirring the milk in. "Couldn't she get married somewhere else?"

"Well everyone said that, but she wants it to be there and I can't convince her to change her mind," her mum sighed. "She was seriously thinking about asking you to dig up some dirt on one of the other couples who booked it." Ashley smiled and shook her head.

"At least she thinks of me," Ashley said, having a sip.

"Could you have a word with her?" Her mum asked hopefully. Ashley laughed.

"If she's not listening to you, she won't listen to me," Ashley said, walking to her desk. "It might mean I'm invited to the next dress fitting."

"It's next week." Ashley laughed

"I was joking, but why though, she hasn't even set a date? Even then it could be years away."

"She's your sister."

"Your daughter."

"And I love her very much."

"As you should but... Jesus there must be limits."

"Trust me, it applies to all three of you," her mum said. "But I think her friends are starting to get miffed with her as well."

"With weekly weigh-ins it must feel like weight watchers," Ashley joked.

"Your dad made that same joke." Ashley smirked. "Peas in a pod you two," she said. "How's the hockey?"

"Good, good so far," Ashley said. "I have a game on Sunday, another must-win so I need to bring the A-game."

"I know you will, good luck, and how's work?" Work was always the sore subject between them. Her mum didn't like Ashley working for the police and was against the idea of her being a detective. But stubbornness ran in the family.

"Good, we have our first case."

"That's good," her mum replied with forced interest. "What is it exactly?"

"A murder," Ashley said, waiting for the response.

"Oh," her mum said lightly. "That's… nice."

"Well not for him," Ashley said. She looked up and saw Murphy and Parland coming in. "Listen Mum I have to go, love you and send my love to Dad and Libby, OK?"

"OK sweetheart, we'll speak soon. Love you."

"Love you too, bye." Ashley ended the call and took another sip.

"Morning Ash."

"Morning Herschel."

"No luck tracking our guy?" Parland asked.

"He got on the bus between Bury and Manchester," Ashley said. "I went to their depot to get a copy but they're all stored on a database at the council.

"Not everyone is an early riser like you," Parland said, sitting down.

"I'll make my way there after this is done," Ashley said.

"Better bring bagels for them, everyone knows they don't start work 'til ten," Murphy told her.

Ashley finished her sip and placed her mug down.

"They will for me," she said, nodding.

"Any luck tracking the others from the list?"

"Can't get hold of Williams," Murphy said. "But the other guy Wainwright was back at home, he confirmed his movements."

"Where was he?"

"AA convention," Parland said. "Six months sober."

"Kate Marsh's in the wind though," Parland said. "Seems to have vanished off the face of the earth."

"Maybe some of them want to do that," Ashley said. "Get away from it all." Parland and Murphy nodded.

"Morning all," Armstrong said as he came in. "Any luck with that guy Ash?"

"Only my friends call me Ash."

"Aren't I a friend?"

"DC Fenway is fine," Ashley told him. The door to McArthur's office opened and he came in.

"Morning everyone," he said, getting to the front of the room. "We made good progress yesterday. Fenway has got us one promising lead so

110

far." He patted the picture on the board of the guy who was following Ferrets on the bus.

"Have we got any clue on who this guy is?"

"None so far," Ashley said. "I went to the bus depot this morning. They don't have hard copies of CCTV. It gets sent to the council via the bus station."

"So, are you going to chase that up?"

"Right after this."

"Good work," McArthur said. "As soon as we get a clear shot of this guy, I want it plastered everywhere. What about people on the list?"

"We have alibis for all but two of them," Parland said. "Tim Williams who we can't seem to get a hold of, and Kate Marsh who's disappeared off the face of the earth."

"If nothing comes of this, we'll put a shout out for her as well," McArthur said. "I want though to find this Tim Williams. I want him found today. Got it."

"Sure, thing Guv," Parland said, getting up.

"Fenway, see that we find out who this guy is," he said, patting the board.

"Yes Sir."

"But before you do that, PR have been on to me; they want you down there now to interview you."

"Sir, do I have to?" Ashley asked.

"Afraid so. Just get it over and done with now. Rip the plaster off as it were."

"Or the wax in your case," Armstrong piped up.

"I don't remember anyone asking your opinion," Ashley said, getting to her feet.

"Just putting it out there."

Ashley made her way to the press room where the PR representative was waiting for her. As soon as she saw Ashley, she beamed a set of teeth that looked brighter than Ashley's future.

"You must be DC Fenway," she said in an airy voice and shaking her hand.

"Yeah," Ashley said. "Can we do this quickly only I have places to be."

"Yes, of course, you're very busy catching the crims as they say." She finished with a laugh which Ashley wasn't sure if she should respond to.

"Well let's get you in make-up and then we can rock and roll." She said with another laugh.

"Yes." Ashley stretched out, wondering if this woman had a screw loose.

Ashley was ushered into the side room which had a couple of mirrors and a make-up selection her sister would be envious of.

"Well, why don't you sit down and let's get to work," The PR woman said, sitting Ashley down in front of a vanity mirror.

"Nothing too… over the top," Ashley said.

"I wouldn't dream of it dear, only a little touch up here and there. But you would look lovely with some eye shadow."

"No thanks. I'm a detective, not on the pull," Ashley said. The woman looked a little taken aback by Ashley's remark, but Ashley just didn't care, she wanted this over and done with. The process was as painful as Ashley thought it would be, with this woman trying to make her into a catwalk model rather than a police officer. She had to a couple of times say no to things.

"You do realise you're going to be in front of a camera dear."

"To talk about doing my job which I will be going back to after this is done," Ashley said.

"Suit yourself dear, I think we're done here anyway." Ashley thankfully got out of the room and went to the actual press room. A gleaming white room with a high-rise table for people to sit at during a major investigation and a slew of chairs in front of it for the media.

The social media team was there along with a news crew and a couple of journalists who were already talking to Assistant Chief Constable Delany.

Delany had been groomed for positions of power ever since he joined, never spending more than a year in a role 'til he got to this. He also had a less-than sterling reputation from other women officers, hence the nick name, 'Wandering'.

Just by watching him Ashley could see that he liked having the limelight on him; it was all about him. Maybe this would be easier than she thought if he did all the talking. Though taking another look, it looked as if he was wearing more make up than her.

"Ah, here she is DC Fenway," he said, beckoning her over. Ashley walked over and shook his hand, his other coming round to the small of her back, turning her round to the cameras which were flashing away.

"Absolutely tremendous police work," he said. "We're lucky to have someone like you on our side."

"Thank you, Sir," Ashley said, supressing the rage of wanting to slap his hand away. They sat down on the edge of the raised platform.

"Let's make it look more like an informal chat," one of the social media team had said. Ashley sat on the ledge and faced Delany. He was in his fifties with silver hair, which was gelled back; to the uninitiated they would say that he was a silver fox. Ashley though left a good distance between them. After being told which camera to look into the interview started.

"So, DC Fenway, have you seen the footage of you chasing your suspect yet?"

"Uhm… bits and pieces, not all the way through," Ashley replied.

"Well we have a few clips for you to look at." Ashley was shown a screen where she saw herself slide over the bonnet of a car and chase Fawnley through the streets. The last clip was her rugby-tackling him out of the way of the tram.

"So, what did you think of that?"

"It's…" She didn't really know what to say. "It's just doing my job, to be honest. I'm sure anyone of my team would have done that."

"DC Fenway is right," Delany cut in. "We view ourselves as one team, which shows the core teamwork that my officers' pride themselves in."

As she suspected it was mainly all about him which she didn't really mind. She was only called upon to back up what he was saying and as they had all said, look pretty for the camera.

After it had finished Ashley went back upstairs, stopping off at a toilet to wash her face before going back to sit at her desk.

"How was it?" Murphy asked.

"Like pulling teeth," Ashley said, sitting down.

"For you or them?"

"Probably both," Ashley said. "What the hell are you supposed to say in situations like that?"

"How good we all are."

"Well yes," Ashley shot back, annoyed. "What about how catching a criminal made you feel? How did you feel after catching someone?"

"Not gonna lie, it felt good."

"Well I'm not going to go up there and say that I was wet chasing a guy through Manchester," Ashley said. "Jesus my mum's going to see that."

"Good or bad?"

"Ashley, you should smile more," Ashley said, in a mocking tone. "At least look as though you want to be there." She shook her head. "I'm not going to hear the end of it."

"Did Delany keep his hands to himself?"

"For the most part," Ashley said, thinking about that hand on her back which made her shiver. "I think with cameras watching he didn't want to risk it." She grabbed her coat and bag.

***

When did being an @England fan become as painful as being a @CPFC fan? #canonlyoneofubeshitpls

My BF legit thinks I like rugby... #wholikesshortshorts #Ilikeshortshorts

Just watched @Bosch, get on it people!

Archie Cook to @ManUtd, that display for England shows that he's the sort of player Utd need. #Shit #Wifesfitthough

Ashley drove into the city centre to the council building and parked up outside, putting her police permit in the windshield. The council building was perhaps the grandest building in Manchester with large, stone columns outside and limestone stairs up to a pair of large oak doors. Ashley walked in and went up to the front desk where a young receptionist yawned as she approached.

"Morning," Ashley said. She slipped her ID into her hand. "I'd like to speak to your head of IT please," she said, showing the receptionist her ID. "It's to do with the City Bus CCTV."

"Of course, I'll phone Mister Smythes." She phoned up and a couple of minutes later Mr Smythes came down. A thin but well-dressed man in his forties came up and shook her hand. He led her down to the viewing room.

"I didn't know the bus CCTV came here," Ashley said.

"Not many people do," Smythes replied. "We found it was easier than all the CCTV being spread out at lots of different hubs."

"Wish I knew that yesterday," Ashley muttered, as they reached an office with a frosted door with IT in the glass. They walked into the office which was empty.

"Are you the only one here?" Ashley asked.

"We have flexible hours for our staff. Most of them don't start 'til ten." Ashley tried to supress a grin. Smythes sat down at his desk.

"Do you know which bus you're looking for?"

"The number 135," she said, getting her phone out. "Manchester to Bury."

"OK…" Smythes typed on the computer. "Do you know what time?"

"I have the license plate of the bus I want," Ashley said. Smythes nodded unconvincingly.

"Well that's a start," he said, looking at Ashley's phone. "What day did you need?"

"Monday the thirteenth."

"OK, I have all the CCTV for that day," he said, showing her the files. Ashley got her phone out and consulted the timetable.

"I need these three," she said, pointing at three files.

"You can use this computer, I'm going to get myself a coffee, do you want one?"

"No thanks. Actually, can you send them over to me?" She asked, wanting to get back to the office and try there.

"Of course." He put them together and sent them off.

"Happy hunting."

***

115

Ashley sat down at her desk. Only Murphy was around, typing away. Ashley put the CCTV on and watched the bus go along the road, at people getting on or off. The other screen she had was the one of the bus stop the guy got on.

Ashley's eyes flickered between the screens; she watched the guy go over the bridge and up to the church. Ashley flickered over to the other screen and saw the bus coming up to the stop. Ashley watched as he came off the bus and pulled his hood down just as he went on. Ashley flicked back over and paused.

He had longish, dark hair and stubble. Since the camera was quite new it captured his face, when he looked for a seat before paying.

"Yes," Ashley whispered, with a pumped fist.

"Herschel!" Ashley shouted. "Here's our guy." Murphy came over and Ashley pointed at him.

"He looks familiar," Murphy said. "Get this printed off and I'll have it sent out on the socials." Ashley sent it to the printer and sent an e-mail to the media relations team.

"I've put your number on that so you can field the questions," Ashley said. "I have to see where this guy's going."

Ashley opened Google, brought up the bus route and placed a tack on where this guy got on by the church. Ashley brought the stops up on her screen and followed. She kept an eye on where their suspect was going. Finally, he got up and walked off the bus. Ashley checked the time stamp against the bus timetable.

He was getting off at Cheetam Hill Road. Ashley pressed pause and leaned back in her chair. Cheetam Hill. What was in Cheetam Hill?

Ashley consulted Google maps and looked; there was only shops and residential areas. So, this person lived there? There wasn't any CCTV in that area. Ashley put Cheetam Hill into Google; nothing of progress came up.

"Why can't they just turn themselves in?" Ashley said to herself.

"No luck finding out where he was going?" Murphy asked.

"He got off in Cheetam Hill," Ashley said. "Is there anything in Cheetam Hill?"

"Not really," Murphy said. "He might live there." Ashley frowned and looked at the screen of him coming off.

"Maybe…" Ashley got off her chair and grabbed her coat.

"Where are you going?" Murphy asked.

"Cheetam Hill," Ashley said, putting her coat on, pushing her ponytail over the collar. "I'm going to see what's there."

"Good luck to you," Murphy said, as Ashley walked out.

Chapter 11

Ashley drove into Cheetam Hill, a modest residential area with a mixture of lower- and middle-class residents. She passed the shopping centre and went up towards the bus stop their man got off at. Ashley found a parking space on a side street and walked to the bus stop their man got off at.

There was nothing remarkable about it, a normal bus stop surrounded by rows of terraced houses. Nowhere with CCTV. Ashley bit her lip in thought. He must have come up here, where else would he go? Ashley got her phone out, searched for Cheetam Hill in Google maps and turned on the points of interest.

Mostly shops with a shopping park down the road, a few pubs and a couple of parks as well. She decided on a more pragmatic approach, she took the photo of him and started to knock on the doors of people around the bus stop. A lot of people didn't answer the door, presumably at work Ashley thought, but there were some who didn't come to the door.

Those who did were more interested in questioning Ashley on things outside her control, rather than helping her.

"Can you tell those kids to stop loitering outside my house in the mornings!" One old woman shouted at her. Ashley turned her head and saw her house was opposite the bus stop. Ashley sighed deflated.

"Mam, they're taking the bus to school," Ashley said, trying to keep a measured voice.

"Well they're all outside, laughing, being loud and loitering around my house. Can you tell them to move further down the road?"

"I'm sorry mam but that's not really in my remit," Ashley said.

"Well I pay your wages officer, so you better do as I —"

"Have you seen this man?" Ashley asked abruptly, holding up the photo. The woman peered at it.

"No, I can't say I have." Finally.

"OK thanks for all your help," Ashley said, walking back down the path and back onto Cheetam Hill Road.

As she walked past where the number 135 stopped off, a couple of people went on and it then pulled away. Ashley walked to the bus stop which was adorned with a perfume advert. She looked at the timetable which showed the time the bus left and what time it should arrive in Bury.

Ashley crossed the road and looked at the other timetable which showed the same. Ashley looked at the times. The bus left Cheetam Hill and would take nearly thirty-five minutes for the bus to get back to the city of Manchester.

"Plenty of time to come back," Ashley said. Time of death was between three and seven. Ashley took a photo of the timetable and walked across the road. Maybe this guy followed Ferrets to the hotel to make sure he was there, went back to get his tools and went back.

Ashley put her hands in her pockets and thought it over. Why come back here though... why go through the trouble of tracking Ferrets to the hotel and then leave him? Unless he wasn't going to kill him. Maybe he was being watched.

Ashley looked around but couldn't see any CCTV cameras.

Why though, would someone stalk Ferrets only to stop when he went to the hotel? Ashley thought back to the sort of man he was. An ex-football coach and scout who was a suspected paedophile, later proven to be true with lots of grudges that people held against him. So, who would follow him...?

"Vigilantes," Ashley said, muttering under her breath. She sat down on a bench, got her phone out and searched for vigilante groups in Manchester. Most of the results were of newspaper articles of groups confronting paedophiles. Ashley scrolled through the pages; most of the groups didn't have an address, probably out of fear of reprisals.

Ashley had a feeling she was on the right track with this. Maybe he was being stalked by a vigilante group.

***

119

Ashley made her way back to the tower where it was only herself and Parland on their side of the office. It was coming up to five in the afternoon, hopefully the others were out there trying to shake down some leads.

"Any luck finding our man?" Parland asked.

"No, there was no CCTV in the area and people don't recognise him from the photo," Ashley said to him.

"But I have an idea about why he was stalking Ferrets." Ashley sat down and started her computer.

"OK, please, go on," Parland said, folding his arms, waiting for her response.

"Maybe he was being stalked by a vigilante gang," Ashley said. Parland leaned back in his chair and thought it over in his head.

"That would explain why he went away from the hotel rather than go inside," Parland mused. "Maybe they were stalking him to ambush him." Ashley nodded.

"And whoever was stalking him might know who killed him." Ashley pointed at him and nodded without looking up from the screen.

"So, what are you doing then?"

"Finding out more about these groups," Ashley said. "They have to be operating somewhere."

"Do you reckon they do meet and greets?" Parland asked. Ashley ignored him, opened Google and looked up some of the well-known vigilante groups. She opened the Facebook and Twitter pages of them and read through them.

There were posts and videos of various people's entrapments and calls to arms against the army of perverts in the world. Ashley ran a hand through her hair and continued to go through the pages. She tried to narrow down the search to groups that operated in the Manchester area.

Dark Justice did a few stings in Manchester along with Guardians of the North and Soul Survivors. Ashley checked their social media pages but there was no way of contacting them over the phone nor an address. Ashley tried their websites too; they made enough boasts about the work they did but again no way of contacting them.

Ashley was searching Google for phone numbers for them, but they were careful and there was no trace of them on the net. Maybe she was thinking too large.

Ferrets was more local, he probably abused boys in the local area rather than on a national scale. He wasn't that technologically conscious so wouldn't prowl the dark net or social media and come to their attention.

She went back onto Google. Looking more so for local vigilante groups that operated solely in Manchester and the surrounding area. After trawling through numerous newspaper articles, websites and blogs it looked like she found one.

The Child Protection Group, which only seemed to operate in Manchester and surrounding area. They had sealed the conviction of a paedophile only last year. They had a website which Ashley visited, it too was modelled much like Dark Justice, no addresses or contact numbers; the only contact info was an e-mail address.

Her concentration was interrupted when Armstrong and Murphy came into the office.

"How did it go with his ex-business partners?" Parland asked.

"Not well," Armstrong said. "They were pissed at him for never spending any money to expand the academy; well we know why now."

"Alibis?"

"Tight," Murphy said, flicking through his notes. "We talked to all the people he worked with in the council, but they were surprised that he was murdered. Will probably want to distance themselves if they find out he actually was a nonce."

"What about the schools?" Parland asked.

"Same, all very sorry he died but nothing they could do to help," Armstrong said. "The more I think about it, maybe the killer is on that list."

"What about our stalker, Fenway?" Armstrong asked.

"No ID yet," Ashley said. "But we do know that he got off in Cheetam Hill." She tapped on the board. "I went there earlier to the stop he got off at and there's no CCTV in the area and no one from round there saw him."

"Just another face in the crowd, that's the problem with stalkers," Murphy said.

"So, all we have is this Tim Williams," Parland said, getting to his feet. "And we don't know a hundred per cent if he's involved with it," Parland sighed.

"Right, all of you go home, come back with one fresh look at this. We'll go over everything again to see if we missed anything."

Ashley checked her phone; good time as well, she felt like she could do with a drink.

***

Jimmy's, a rock bar in the centre of Manchester; blink and you'd walk past it. But since Danielle worked there Ashley started going in there to have a drink and a catch up while she worked on the bar.

After dropping her car off and changing, Ashley walked down the stairs into the bar. She walked to the back where Danielle was at the bar wiping it down. She looked up and saw Ashley.

"Hey stranger," she said, as Ashley sat down at the stool.

"What can I get you?"

"I'll have a Bud thanks," Ashley said.

"How are things?" Danielle bent down and got the bottle out of the fridge.

"Good, got our first proper case."

"Nice, what did you get?" She popped the top off.

"A murder," Ashley said, paying with contactless.

"Oh good, you like murders." She slid it over, she frowned. "Should I be saying that?" Ashley laughed lightly.

"Not sure, but yes, it's a good one. It's the one they found at the Cambrian."

"Oh yeah, dad was ranting about that," Danielle said, with a smile. "So, what's the deal with it?" Ashley took a sip of her beer.

"Guy's been found in a hotel room tied to a bed with a slashed neck," Ashley said, putting her beer down. "No signs of forced entry and he was hit on the back of the head which knocked him out."

"Sounds like a sex game gone wrong," Danielle replied.

"More than likely, but I don't think so," Ashley said, thinking it over. "The severity of the cut tells me that this is personal."

"Was it a mess?" Ashley nodded. "Bummer, we had some guy split his head open here at the weekend. Not the same but still."

"Was it a random one?"

"No, his ex, saw him chatting to another girl and got her stiletto." Danielle mimicked what happened with her hands.

"She wouldn't be able to do that shot again if she tried." Ashley laughed. "Which brings me onto this." Danielle got her phone out, after a couple of swipes she showed Ashley the video of her running down the street.

"Get that out of my face," Ashley said, to Danielle's laughing.

"That was amazing," Danielle said, closing it down. "Twitter loved it. Maybe you should go into social media, some guys really want your number after that."

"What?" Danielle showed Ashley some of the tweets, her face distorting at some of the things being said. "Fuck me."

"I think most of the guys do."

"Well there's a line," Ashley said. She looked up at Danielle who was smirking at her.

"Don't, I had to do PR today for it," Ashley groaned and slumped on her hand which was holding her head up.

"Did you know that the police have a make-up girl? Because I didn't," Ashley said, taking another drink.

"She must have had a field day with you," Danielle said, with a grin. Ashley shook her head.

"My boss had more make up on than I did," Ashley told her. "Though he made it all about him so got me out of saying anything."

"I'll keep an eye out for that tomorrow," Danielle said. "I can't wait to see what your mum's gonna say."

"I think I can," Ashley said, swirling the bottle and downing it.

"Do you have a gig on tonight?" Ashley asked.

"Some student band if you're interested."

"Not really," Ashley said, getting up. "Nice to chat, I'll text you soon."

"Yeah, you take care," Danielle said. "Try not to chase someone on the way home." Ashley waved her hand dismissively and went for the door.

"If you do, at least make sure they're cute!"

Chapter 12

Just seen that police woman from the news on ITV talking about that chase. #DCFenway #didIleavethestoveon?

@ITV Do men ever shut up? #Lethertalk #DCFenway

@ITV That eye roll from DC Fenway is every woman when a man talks. #purestsite

She's pretty, but that #DCFenway has the personality of a stale potato. #ITV #beautyisonlyskindeep #Stillwouldthough

She didn't look comfortable doing that interview, some people are like that though. Just let her do her job instead. #gladshesonourside

DC Fenway takes no shit from nobody. #DCFenway #Mykindofgal

See, this is why women having the vote was a bad idea! #getbackinthekitchen

I like DC Fenway but not this new MMC shit.

***

"Morning." Ashley waved at the elderly man and smiled at him before going into the gym which was already coming to life. Ashley swiped in; since she had training later, she decided not to work herself too hard.

Cardio.

Squats.

Arms.

Bike.

Sauna.

Ashley poured some water on the coals and sat back as the warmth engulfed her. She was going over in her mind what she was missing from this murder.

The most logical reasoning at the moment was that it was someone he knew, maybe someone who he abused, if he did abuse; maybe he just liked looking at it. But there was this civil case against him as well which made the possibility of him abusing significantly higher.

Aim for the day was to find out if this stalker was part of Dark Justice or the CPG. Ashley had a look at their websites yesterday but nothing that suggested an address.

Ashley could feel the sweat pouring from her pores; maybe she should skip work and spend the day in the sauna. She looked up at the clock and saw that it was time to go. Just as she got up, she heard some people outside the sauna. She opened the door. Two of the regular body builders were busy taking a pre-shower before going in.

As Ashley towelled herself off one of them hit the other on the arm and nodded over towards her. Ashley just wanted to get out of there now and went to the door leading to the women's changing room.

"You can tell she squats," one of them said, as the door closed behind her. Ashley looked down at her bum.

"Damn right you can," she said, walking towards the showers.

***

Ashley turned the lights on for the office, the beams coming on as Ashley walked in. She turned the TV on which showed that Archie Cooke, a Manchester United centre back was supposedly subject of a bid from Real Madrid. A photo of him came up on screen; tall, dark blonde hair with a sharp and chiselled chin with a thick stubble. Ashley nodded her approval.

No doubt Murphy would have an opinion on it. Ashley turned her computer on. She looked around her desk and saw the CCTV she picked up from the Cambrian for the last week. Now was as good as any time to watch it.

She loaded it into the computer then headed to the kitchen to get herself some tea and make up some porridge. After that she sat down at her computer and opened the CCTV viewer. Ashley loaded the lobby camera for last Sunday and had it playing at 5x normal speed. She was gulping her tea while watching.

The people on the screens were either weary travellers with nowhere else to go or regulars with women of the night. Ashley didn't recognise anyone, apart from Giles Fawnley who was milling around; not this stalker nor anyone on the floor the deceased was found on.

The door to the office was opening intermittently with other members of the team coming through. Ashley was on Monday morning, watching a man's suitcase fall open in the middle of the lobby. She smiled to herself and stopped, she went back to searching for contact information for the CPG.

She was about to write an e-mail to them when she noticed something in the small print.

The Weston Foundation is a registered charity in the United Kingdom.

Ashley frowned; The Weston Foundation. Ashley opened a new tab and Googled it. Nothing else on it apart from The Child Protection Group website, but if it was a registered charity it might be on Companies' House. Ashley opened the search page for Companies' House and put in The Weston Foundation.

It came up, but it said that it was regulated by the Charities Commission.

"Got ya." Ashley went to the Charitie Commission's page. The name of the trustee was Simon Weston and it gave an address. Ashley put the address into Google maps. When it came up...

"Cheetam Hill," Ashley said, her stomach fluttering with success. Ferrets was being stalked out by the Child Protection Group. Maybe they considered him a threat. Maybe he was an active abuser again...

Her phone pinged. Ashley pulled it out and saw it was from her mum.

Mum: *You could at least smile when they're interviewing you. Anyway, I'm very proud of you, love you xxx.*

"Fucks sake."

Ashley got to her feet and grabbed her coat.

Chapter 13

Ashley checked Google maps to make sure she was on the right street. The road was a residential one with cars parked either side of it. Ashley parked in the first available space and got out of her car. She checked her phone again to see what number she was looking for.

Ashley walked down the row of houses 'til she came to the right one. She wasn't sure what a vigilante group would look like, but she didn't think that it would be hiding in plain sight. Ashley opened the gate and walked down the garden path to the front door.

The curtains were closed across the windows, both first floor and ground. Ashley thought that was odd because it was the middle of the day. Ashley pushed on the doorbell and waited to see a rustle in the curtains or something, but nothing happened.

Ashley knocked loudly. Maybe they were on a bust. Just as she was about to turn away, she heard what felt like a heavy lock. Ashley turned back and looked at the door. There was another large clang which sounded like another lock. Ashley watched the door intently and it opened, but only partly. There was a small chain across the latch.

"Yes?"

"Is this The Child Protection Group?" Ashley asked. She walked up to the crack in the door and saw a beady blue eye behind glasses staring back at her.

"Who wants to know?"

"My name is Detective Constable Ashley Fenway," Ashley said, reaching inside for her ID. "I just want to ask you some questions."

"Give me your ID." Ashley quirked an eyebrow.

"Excuse me?"

"Your ID. Can I see it?" Ashley held her ID out in front of her. A chubby hand came out through the gap in the door and snatched it from her.

"Hey!"

"I'm checking your credentials." Ashley looked on, confused, at the door. She heard murmuring from the other side of the door. About a minute later Ashley heard the chain unlatch. The door opened and Ashley took a step back.

The man standing before her must have been around five feet. He was overweight with his belly showing underneath a blue polo shirt and shorts. He had short hair and flaky, blotchy skin.

"Sorry Detective Constable," he said, holding up her ID. "We have lots of people come here imitating police."

"That's OK," Ashley said, not believing it herself. "I take it you're the Child Protection Group."

"Yes. My name is Simon Weston," he said, pushing his glasses up his nose. "How did you find us?" He asked sceptically.

"You take donations under a charity name," Ashley said. "That's registered with the Charities Commission and that gave me this address." Weston nodded.

"Very clever," he grumbled, hiding his admiration. "How can I help you detective?" Ashley looked around.

"Maybe we should go inside," Ashley said. "This isn't the sort of thing we want to do in public." Simon looked back.

"Of course." Simon walked back into the house and Ashley followed, still marvelling at the ridiculous height difference.

"How long have you been operational?" Ashley asked, as she walked through.

"About five years," Simon said, closing the door. Ashley looked around the house. There was hardly any light coming in; from the looks of it the décor of the house was green, with a wooden staircase in the hallway.

"In that time, we've helped secure convictions for over twenty abusers."

Ashley turned around to see how many locks there were on the door. Simon pulled a box from the side of the corridor. He stood up on it and did up what looked like seven locks on the door, then the small chain at the top.

"That's a good return rate," Ashley said.

"It's not just a passion project with us," Simon said, placing the stool back. "We take this very seriously." He waddled in front of Ashley to walk her through the house. Simon waddled into the next room where there were seven computers all linked up. From what Ashley knew of computers they were top of the line models with new screens and equipment.

"A lot of these vigilante groups as you know, are in it for the ratings on YouTube and Twitter. They're not really about making this world safer." Ashley saw that there were two other people in the room.

An overweight woman with buck teeth, matted hair, glasses and blotchy skin like Simon, was typing away on a keyboard. Next to her was a man who Ashley thought was part-stick insect with thin limbs, features and greasy, long hair. He too was typing away.

"They just want their five minutes of fame." Simon sat down behind his own computer. Ashley looked to the walls and saw boards with people's faces on them with the words 'suspects'. "We here at the CPG are committed to protecting children from exploitation. So, how can we help you detective?"

"I saw you on YouTube," Ashley said. "You must care about ratings in some form too."

"We like to keep a profile," Simon said, in a measured tone. "It's how we garner investment."

"Is this sponsored?" Ashley asked. Simon shook his head.

"We do other work," Simon explained. "For concerned parents, to check if their children are safe. PI work to look over evidence and research. There's money in outsourcing IT work."

"I take it you're not incorporated," Ashley said, opening her notebook. "Really doesn't seem like child protection is the passion project."

"This work helps us pay the bills DC Fenway," Simon said, with a slight narrowing of his eyes. "Our main goal is and always will be protecting children."

"Seems like you can make more money with outsourcing IT," Ashley countered. "Why do this?" Simon beckoned Ashley in closer.

"Because we've all been victims of these scumbags here," Simon whispered. Ashley nodded and leaned back.

"I'm sorry," Ashley said. "I didn't know."

"It's OK detective," Simon said. "We act as a support group for one another."

"How many of you are there?"

"Too many," Simon mused. He looked up at Ashley's quirked expression. "The number of victims. I was trying to be -."

"Profound?" Simon nodded.

"Something like that," Simon replied. "There are nine of us. We try and help each other." Ashley nodded.

"I wanted to ask you about the people you are currently watching," Ashley said. "And have watched."

"Oh, well rest assured you'll get all information for any paedophiles we gather enough evidence to convict," Simon explained. Ashley placed the file she was holding on the table.

"OK." Ashley picked out Gordon Ferrets photo and showed it to him. Simon's jaw physically set. "Do you know this guy?"

"Yeah. We know him. That's Gordon Ferrets." Good, Ashley thought.

"How do you know him?"

"I don't," Simon said, looking up at Ashley. "One of our members. Tim, that's his abuser."

"How do you know?" Ashley asked.

"He told us," Simon replied. "One of the things you need to do to join, is face up to what happened to you and accept it. Naming your abuser is a first step."

"Were you following him?"

"Tim was," Simon explained, pointing at one of the boards. Ashley walked over to it. On it was Gordon Ferrets, his age, height, place of residence, along with what looked like covert photos of him. Ashley sighed. She didn't want this to look like a gold mine, but it was. It would give means, and motive. It was becoming more and more likely that Tim was the guy stalking Ferrets the day he died. Ashley pulled her phone out and took a picture of the board.

"Is he dead?"

"Yes," Ashley said. "What's Tim's full name?"

"You don't think Tim killed him, do you?"

"He has quite the obsession. He had motive," Ashley shrugged. "Plus, we have a person following Ferrets to the hotel he died at and getting a bus here. It doesn't look good." Simon looked on blankly and the other two looked round as well.

"We just want to speak to him so we can rule him out," Ashley said. "I'm sure he has a reasonable explanation. What does he do?"

"He heads our surveillance," Simon explained, his voice light. "He's good at it too. You lot could give him a job," he added, weakly. Ashley hummed and continued to look at the board. In the corner was a picture of Ferrets outside the Cambrian with Sunday's date around it and a question mark.

"If he didn't, then he might help us find out who killed him."

"He might not," Simon said. Ashley turned her head.

"Excuse me?"

"He really hated Ferrets," Simon said, shaking his head. "He might even be pleased he's gone. He might not even help you."

"He's vengeful," Ashley mused. It fitted the MO. "What's his full name?" Simon sighed.

"Tim Williams," he said. This just got better and better.

"Do you have an address, anything like that?" Simon opened a desk and pulled out a piece of paper and handed it to her. It looked like an application form. It had an address, but one of the sections said other occupations. His was filled in with labourer.

"Where else does he work?" Ashley asked.

"I don't know that." Ashley gripped her phone.

"Thank you for all your help," Ashley said. She reached into her wallet and pulled out a twenty-pound note and placed it on the table.

"What's this for?"

"A donation," Ashley explained. "I'm a fan. Can you… let me out?"

"Of course, of course," Simon said, waddling to the door.

After being let out and thanking them again, Ashley walked to her car and got in. She phoned the office. Parland answered.

"Manchester Major Crimes, DI Parland speaking."

"It's Fenway," Ashley said. "Can you run a name for me?"

"Sure, ex-boyfriend?"

"Ha-ha," Ashley deadpanned.

"Potential boyfriend?"

"Jesus, you sound like my mother. It'll be undertakers if you carry on like that," Ashley said, tapping her dashboard impatiently.

"OK, name?"

"Tim Williams," Ashley said. "Full name might be Timothy." She waited while Parland typed in the name.

"We got a match. Tim Williams."

"What's he in the system for?" Ashley asked.

"Common assault, intimidation, petty theft, burglary, ABH. He's a real tearaway." Ashley thought it over for a moment.

"Can you put me through to McArthur?"

"Is he a person of interest?"

"Could be if you put me through," Ashley said. Parland grumbled and the line bleeped to indicate she was on hold.

"McArthur."

"Sir, I have a lead," Ashley said, trying to suppress the enthusiasm in her voice. "The name is Tim Williams."

"So Parland told me. What does he have to do with our vic?"

"He was one of the children Ferrets abused. He works for the Child Protection Group as surveillance. He was the one we saw stalking Ferrets to the Cambrian."

"Right, bring him in. Good work Fenway. I'll sent Parland to meet you."

"I'll send the address to him."

Chapter 14

The house Tim lived in was on the same estate as Tracy Ferrets but around the other side. Ashley parked up and thought about waiting for Parland. She wasn't too sure how he would react to be talking about Ferrets. She decided to wait and five minutes later Parland turned up and parked behind her. Ashley got out of the car and walked over to him.

"How did you get this address?" Parland asked.

"From the CPG," Ashley said. "I wasn't sure if I should go up and talk to him myself."

"I remember him from this assault. Very angry lad. This sort of explains it."

"How so?" Ashley asked.

"You see it with some of them. Pent up frustration, unable to channel the anger about what happened to them and they lash out. But you know what boys are like, don't want to talk about it."

They walked up towards the house which had the same dull, grey complexion as Tracy Ferrets. Ashley knocked on the door only to be greeted by the bark of a dog.

"Toby, shut up!" It was a woman's voice. Ashley looked over at Parland who smirked to himself. Through the frosted glass Ashley could see someone walking towards the door with the dog still barking. The woman undid the chain and opened it. She was still in pyjamas with her dark hair up in a bun. She looked Ashley and Parland up and down.

"What do you want?"

"Hi, I'm DC Fenway with Manchester Major Crimes Unit and this is DI Parland." Ashley got her ID out of her pocket and flashed it as did Parland.

"Is Tim Williams in?"

"Whatever it is he didn't do nuffin', right," the woman said heatedly. "You lot comin' round 'ere, accusing 'im of all sorts, he's changed now."

"He's not in trouble, we just want a word with him about something," Parland said.

"Yeah, 'bout what?"

"We want to know about what he does for the Child Protection Group," Ashley said. "Some of their work has come up in a case and we want to talk to him." The woman shifted uncomfortably.

"I'm sorry, what's your name?" Ashley asked.

"Carrie," she said, shortly.

"Look, Carrie, we just want to ask him some questions. If he does then he can come home. If not, then it might have to get messy."

"Is that a threat?" Carrie asked heatedly.

"No. What it means is that if you don't tell us then he could be in more trouble," Parland explained. "Think about it, Carrie. I know Tim's been on the straight and narrow for the last year or so, his name had just come up in this investigation and we want to clear it up."

Carrie looked at the two of them and then looked down at her feet. Her gaze shifting nervously. "He has worked hard," she muttered, under her breath.

"We know. Is he out working today?" Ashley asked.

"He works for some scaffolding firm," Carrie said now, leaning against the pane of her front door.

"Don't suppose you know the name of it?" Parland asked. Carrie muttered something to herself and went back inside. Ashley and Parland exchanged glances and Carrie came back with a card.

"Here," she said. "I'm not sure where they're working at the moment." Parland took the card.

"We'll give it a try," Parland said. The door swiftly slammed in their faces. Parland and Ashley looked down at the card.

"Well, great," Parland said as they walked down the path. "That's helpful."

"Give it here." Ashley took the card and took out her phone. She dialled the number and waited.

"Hello, Scales Scaffolding."

"Hi, I was wondering if you could help me, my chimney's become misaligned. The builder gave me your number to organise something." Parland quirked an eyebrow at Ashley's sudden higher octave voice. Ashley shook her head and waited.

"I'd like to help you, luv," the guy said. "But we have a big project on now."

"Where is it? You might be close to me."

"Uhm, it's the new construction by Newton Street."

"Oh, that's a shame," Ashley said. "Well thanks, bye!" Ashley tapped her phone.

"I know where it is," she said, putting her phone away. "Just follow me." Parland was still looking at her with a quirked eyebrow.

"What?"

"Nothing." Ashley knew what was wrong

"Using my feminine charm to get a lead isn't a bad thing."

"Equality."

"Yes Parland, because I would love to see you use your charm," Ashley said, with a coy smile while opening her door.

"Worked on my wife."

"And lovely she is too, but would it have won Dave, the scaffolder?"

"Probably not."

"You're right, probably not," Ashley said, getting into her car. "I'll meet you there."

Chapter 15

Ashley and Parland pulled up outside the construction site that Ashley went past every morning. When she moved here it was nothing more than a pile of rubble but now, they were building a block of modern apartments which Ashley had tentatively looked into.

Ashley opened the door of her car and with Parland, walked up to the site.

"Do you reckon we need hard hats?" Parland asked.

"Well I got my boots," Ashley said, as they reached the door. Ashley pushed it open and her and Parland walked in. The forecourt was filled with workman in high-vis jackets working in the hollow shell of the new complex.

"Hey! Hey!" Instantly the foreman came over to Ashley and Parland waving his arms. He was portly with a bushy moustache. "You can't be on here without a hard hat! Jesus Christ, who do you think you are?"

"DI Parland and DC Fenway, Manchester Major Crimes," Parland said, flashing his ID which Fenway did too.

"We're looking for a Tim Williams, he works for Scales Scaffolding," Ashley finished. "Is he here?"

"What's this about?" The foreman asked suspiciously.

"It's about a case," deadpanned Parland. "His girlfriend told us he was here." It was obvious to the Foreman he wasn't getting anything more.

"I'll check the time sheets," he said, waddling back to the unit that was his office. Ashley and Parland followed him slowly across the court. Now she could see eyes boring into them. More so that she was suddenly the only woman on the site, but to her surprise it was Parland who looked the nervier out of the two of them.

"Don't worry, the catcalls nowadays are very creative," Ashley reassured him. Parland didn't look too impressed.

"He is here, should be up on the top floor."

"Can you call him down?" Parland asked. The foreman mumbled something under his breath, pulled his phone out and called someone.

"Hey, Mick, it's Gavin, can you send your boy Tim down. Thanks."

"Should be down in a minute," he said. Ashley looked up at the top of the building and saw someone making their way to an external lift.

A couple of minutes later Tim came towards the foreman's office. He was starkly different from the weedy teenager Ashley saw in the profile picture; he was more fleshed out with a thick beard and longish hair, that was styled back at the sides.

"Tim Williams?" Ashley asked. He instantly tensed, it was as if her and Parland had a huge neon police sign over their head. Tim looked round.

"Don't do it Tim." Parland warned, while walking towards him. Tim though was already backtracking, his head turning towards an exit.

"No!" Tim threw his hard hat to the ground and sprinted off. Parland looked round at Ashley who was looking at him.

"Equality, I got the first one," she said. "I'll go around the back." Parland grunted and ran after Tim. Ashley put her hands in her jacket pockets and walked to the building site door.

Parland was chasing Tim through the ground floor of the site. Most of the other builders stopped what they were doing to watch Tim hurdling over the stray beams and concrete bags with Parland chasing after him, cursing under his breath.

Tim hurdled over a stack of beams and ran up a staircase to the next floor. Parland ran around it and made his way up.

Ashley was walking round the construction wall, looking up as Tim was giving Parland the run around.

Tim weaved his way through the first floor with Parland lagging behind him. Tim looked over his shoulder and went up another staircase, as the external lift went past. Parland stopped and swore under his breath and carried on.

Ashley walked to the back of the construction site and saw a road leading away. Ashley looked up at the complex and walked down the road.

Back on the site Tim got to the third floor and was now running across the concrete floor; he saw the external lift and ran in just as Parland got to the top floor, but before he could go down, the lift was taking him up.

Tim tried to stop it, but the lift went up. Parland huffed and went to run up the next floor. When the lift got there Tim sprinted out, knocking over the builder who was waiting. He was taking a risk and ran up to the last floor.

Ashley walked down the street that led away from the site and saw a road leading off to the side. Ashley peered down the side and saw a couple of building materials that had been thrown out.

Tim realised now that there was nowhere to go. He skidded to a stop and looked around the site which offered no other way out. Parland came up from the partially made staircase.

"Tim, there's nowhere left to run," Parland said, walking towards him. Tim was backtracking, looking over his shoulder and around him nervously. "Look, we just want you to answer some questions."

"Whatever it was, I didn't do it!" Tim snapped back. "I know how you lot work!"

"You're the one running," Parland pointed out. "Why would an innocent man run?"

"Because I know what you lot do to guys like me," Tim said.

Back on the side street Ashley was looking at two planks of wood. One was eight by four while the other was a four by four. Ashley picked them up, comparing the two of them.

"It doesn't have to end messy," Parland said. "Surrender and let me and my partner ask you the questions we wanted to."

"I am not going to jail again!" Tim said. He was now by the shaft of the external lift. He looked down.

"Tim, there is nowhere left to run," Parland said, warningly.

"I can think of one way," Tim said. Parland's brow furrowed in confusion.

"What?" Tim turned around. "NO!" Tim jumped down. Parland ran to the edge of the lift and saw Tim was on top of the external lift going down.

"Fucks sake."

When the lift got to the first floor, he jumped from the top of the lift onto a lorry filled with dirt. He jumped up from the lorry to the construction wall. He slammed into the side of it. He was able to clamber over it and dropped onto the road the other side.

"Son of a —" Parland got his phone out and phoned Ashley while running back down the staircases.

"Fenway."

"He's heading towards you," Parland said, panting.

"What, didn't you catch him?" Ashley asked.

"Can you see him?" Ashley looked around the corner of the side street and saw him running towards her.

"I see him." Ashley cut Parland off. She picked up the four by four wood and practised a swing. She looked around the corner again and readied herself. Just as he was about to come out, Ashley swung out with the piece of wood. It hit him in the stomach and made him keel over.

"Oh my god, are you all right?" Ashley asked. Tim could only groan as he curled up in the foetal position while holding his stomach. Ashley rolled him onto his back using her boot.

"Sorry, I have a terrible swing, I was never that good at rounders," she said. As Tim rolled onto his back he groaned again. Ashley frowned and cocked her head slightly.

"I really don't want to do this. Tim Williams you are under arrest, you don't have to say anything in your defence, however anything you do say can and will be used as evidence against you in a court of law. Do you understand?"

"Ow."

"I'll take that," Ashley said, getting her handcuffs out. "Come on, on your feet."

"I need a minute," Tim said, trying to get his breath back.

"You can have a minute on your front then." Tim scowled at her but rolled over meekly. Ashley kneeled and handcuffed him.

"That hurt," Tim said, as he got to his feet.

"Well you had three chances to surrender yourself from what I heard," Ashley said, walking back towards her and Parland's car. "We just wanted a chat. You didn't have to give us the run around and now you're under arrest." Tim didn't say anything; from the top of the street Parland came around.

"You got him then," he said, panting.

"She hit me with a piece of wood!" Tim shouted.

"Sure, she did," Parland said, looking over at Ashley.

"How comes he came my way?"

"Spiderman here jumped over the construction wall from the top of a truck," Parland explained. "Nifty moves mate, did they teach you that at surveillance school?"

"I want a lawyer," Tim replied.

"Sure, you do," Parland said. "Can you believe this guy?"

"Can't you do parkour from doing triathlons?"

"No."

"How you do triathlons I'll never know," Ashley said.

"He does triathlons?" Tim asked. Ashley smirked at Parland who took him off Ashley's hands.

"Come on you," Parland said, leading him towards his car.

***

Parland was taking Tim to booking so Ashley walked up to the office to type up the arrest report. She walked into the office and walked to the board. She wrote down Tim's name on the board as a branch off Gordon Ferrets', with a question mark next to it.

"Well done Fenway, another good collar," Murphy said, as she sat down.

"Yeah," she said, in a drawn-out voice, her eyes still focused on the board.

"You don't see him for it?" Murphy asked.

"He was abused by Ferrets," Ashley explained. She got her phone out and emailed the photo she took of the board in the CPG to her work computer and printed it off.

140

"Where's the murder weapon?" Ashley asked, placing the photo on the board.

"Guv's got people going through his house. We have a profile of the knife and we'll find it there," Murphy explained. Ashley shook her head.

"I still don't see it," Ashley said. "He was working hard to turn his life around. Why risk it all? Look." Murphy got to his feet and stood next to Ashley.

"That is very good, covert work," Ashley said. "Tim was building a case against Ferrets, he wanted to see him go down. Why snap and murder him?"

"Says in his file he's had a problem with drugs in the past, maybe a psychosis thing?" Ashley shook her head. McArthur then came in.

"He's really kicking off down there now," McArthur said. "He can sleep it off, in the meantime we need to get our case together for tomorrow." Ashley sighed. It meant another long night.

"We have SOCO at his house and people at the Child Protection Group to get his work from there. Fenway, I want you to look back through his movements and see what time he goes back to his house."

"Yes Sir," Ashley said, deflated.

It had been a long night. Ashley's eyes were tired from staring at the screens for so long, but she had her pattern and the tapes and photos. She closed her computer down and pulled her coat on. She picked her file up and walked over to Murphy.

"Here's Williams making his way home, before the time of death; photos are marked as well."

"You are a superstar, thanks Ash."

"No problem."

"Going home?" Murphy asked.

"I have hockey and girl's night," Ashley said.

"Make sure it's not a heavy one."

"You don't know the girls," Ashley said, see you in the morning.

141

Chapter 16

Beep

   Beep

   Beep

Ashley opened her eyes, instantly rubbed them and spread her arms above her head. Her mouth was a little dry from the wine she had drunk last night. Ashley turned her alarm off and got out of bed. She looked at her phone.

Her friends' Tinder project with her phone was a resounding success on their end. Ashley flicked through some of the matches, not really her thing though. In her opinion things like Tinder took the thrill out of the chase of dating. Or maybe it was just her that liked a challenge.

She deleted Tinder and went to have a shower.

***

Cardio.

Arms.

Core.

Weights.

Ashley hated doing dead weights, but it made her bum look fantastic. She did the step and stopped. That was enough for the day. Ashley put the dumbbells back on the rack. She looked over and saw one of the other girls quickly going back to her work out.

Ashley smirked to herself, swigging on her water on the way out.

***

Ashley walked into the office, turning on the computer, getting tea and porridge then catching up on her paperwork before anyone else came. The agenda of the day was simple; talk to Williams and get him to confess. The team was being stretched in finding evidence and prepping for the interview. Ashley had spent the morning going over Tim Williams' movements to see if there was anything she missed. But that's what tea was for.

"Who's taking point on the questioning?" Ashley asked, going back to her desk with her fifth mug in her hand.

"Me and Parland," Murphy said. Ashley logged back into her computer and started to type up her report on the arrest.

"Can I look in?" Ashley asked.

"Sure," Murphy said, as his phone started to ring. He picked it up.

"Murphy." He listened for a moment. "Right... have you checked everywhere?" There was a pause. "You're sure?" Another pause.

"OK, no it's OK we can get it out of him. OK thanks."

"Search on the house came back, nothing matching the profile of the knife," Murphy said. "I was hoping to use that against him." Ashley shrugged.

"I wouldn't try to antagonise him," Ashley said. "He doesn't trust the police."

"He shouldn't commit crime then," Murphy said, walking away. Ashley sighed, looked at Murphy and shook her head.

***

After writing up her statement, Ashley walked down to the interrogation room where Tim was being held. She typed in the number to the door and walked into the viewing area, where she could see Tim and his solicitor sitting beyond the glass. McArthur was in the room too and nodded curtly as Ashley entered.

"Do you think we have enough to charge him?" He asked. Ashley shrugged her shoulders.

"I don't think so. Murphy seems intent though," Ashley said, folding her arms across her chest. "Maybe he knows something I don't."

"Maybe something to do with that CPG."

"That's what Murphy said," Ashley mused. "Even if they were, they wouldn't know. I think we should ask for a copy of their systems in case they're holding out on us."

"Do you think they'll give it up willingly?" McArthur asked.

"They say they'll help the police, but I think a warrant might be needed just in case," Ashley said. The door to the interrogation room opened. Parland and Murphy entered in silence and sat down across from Tim and the Solicitor. Even on the other side of the glass that unbearable noise that the tape machine made cut through her.

"This is Detective Inspector Andrew Parland, seeing this interview at Manchester Major Crimes HQ, City Tower on the 17th November 2017 at 10:00am, of Tim Williams with..."

"Detective Sergeant Herschel Murphy..."

"And Connor Mason."

Parland shuffled his papers and looked up at Tim who was still staring ahead at the back wall like they weren't even there. Parland took out a piece of paper from the file.

"Mr Williams. Do you know what this is?" He asked pushing it towards him. Ashley craned her neck. It was the photo she took of the board at the CPG. Tim still looked forward. His eyes focused then looked down at the photo.

He reached out and touched it. Taking his time to study it. Parland and Murphy looked at one another.

"Mr Williams?" Tim's hand stopped over the photo.

"No comment," he said.

"Mr Williams, we know that this is your board at the Child Protection Group," Murphy explained. No reaction at all from him.

"Do you know the name of the man in these photos?" Parland asked, pointing to Ferrets. Ashley saw his jaw physically set at the sight of him.

"No comment," he said again. Parland and Murphy looked at each other.

"Mr Williams, you saying no comment to all our questions only makes you look bad," Murphy said. "We know this is your board. Why were you looking at Gordon Ferrets?"

"No comment," Tim said.

"Mate, help us out." Parland looked over at his solicitor.

"My client is entitled to do this, Detective Inspector," he said. "The onus is on you to provide the evidence." Murphy got out the photos of his stalking.

"We are giving the suspect a copy of file B1," Murphy said, sliding it over. "If you open B1 to photograph AF1, you can see Gordon Ferrets getting off the number 52 bus at Manchester bus station on the 12th of November. Photo AF2 shows this hooded figure following him from the bus station." Murphy sprayed out the photos of the hoodie stalking Ferrets up to the hotel.

"For the tape, we are showing Mr Williams photos AF3 to AF20 of this figure following Mr Ferrets to the Cambrian Hotel, on the afternoon that Mr Ferrets died."

Ashley looked at Tim's face which was now frowning at her handiwork. Murphy too was looking at his reaction.

"Mr Ferrets goes inside at twenty-five to three on the 12th November," Murphy explained. "Mr Williams, where were you at this time?"

"No comment," he said.

"You can't possibly think this is my client," Mason said, with a laugh. "You can't see his face at all in any of your photos."

"True, but we took the liberty of following this person," Murphy said, nodding to Parland who took out another folder.

"For the tape we are showing Mr Williams photos AF21 to AF50 which shows this hooded figure going to a bus stop. At this bus stop the hooded figure gets onto the number 135 bus to Bury. As you can see the figure pulls his hood down as he gets onto the bus."

"Again, still can't prove it's my client."

"Well, this bus has CCTV. So, we found the tape." Parland got out another photo. "This is photo AF51 which shows a picture of Mr Williams on the bus and paying for a ticket." Murphy looked at Tim.

"Why were you stalking Gordon Ferrets?"

"No comment."

"Well. We followed you on this bus. We are now showing Mr Williams photos AF52 to AF65 which show him getting off the bus at Cheetam Hill where the Child Protection Group is located. Gordon

Ferrets was found dead the next morning. How convenient that you were tailing him, and he died the next morning."

Tim didn't say a word, but he could see his solicitor looking a bit shifty, looking up at Williams who was still quite calm.

"Do you have CCTV of my client going back?" Mason asked. Murphy smiled.

"Photo's AF66 to AF98 show Mr Williams getting back on the bus and going back to the city centre and then back to the Cambrian," Murphy said. "He then goes to the bus station and takes one back home."

"But the more we're looking into this we find that this wasn't the first time you stalked Ferrets, was it?" Parland asked.

"We're now showing Mr Williams photo files C1, D1 and E1 which show him following Gordon Ferrets on numerous occasions."

"We have your boss, Mr Weston, confirming you work at the Child Protection Group in Cheetam Hill, we have you stalking Gordon Ferrets to his place of death on the day he died and the days leading up to it. Not to mention a John Hinckley-style board of our victim, who you seem to have a personal connection with." Tim's hand gripped into a fist.

"Now what do you say to that? Because a jury would say probable cause."

"No comm—"

"Excuse me," Mason interjected. "Do you mind if I have a quick word with my client?"

"By all means," Murphy said. He and Parland put the pictures away and walked out.

"Looks like we have the lawyer rattled at least," McArthur said. As he said that the door opened, and Armstrong came in.

"How does his alibi stack up?" McArthur asked.

"He's clean."

"What?" McArthur took the file Armstrong had in his hand.

"He was at home at the time of the murder with his girlfriend; they ordered a film on Amazon Prime and ordered a takeaway. Both of which his girlfriend can back up."

"Shit," McArthur said, looking up. "Maybe he's an accomplice."

"He'd just say 'no comment'," Ashley said. She really wanted to know what was being said between Williams and his lawyer.

Chapter 17

"He's a tough one," Murphy said, walking into the observation room with Parland behind him. He slammed the file on the desk while Parland closed the door. McArthur was waiting for them while Ashley was still looking at Tim, who was talking to his lawyer.

"He doesn't want to talk about Ferrets," Parland said. "We have enough to charge him for the murder of Ferrets."

"No, we don't," McArthur said. He handed Murphy the alibi. Murphy read through it and swore. Parland held his hand out and Murphy handed it to him to read through.

"Fuck," Parland sighed.

"If he doesn't talk about Ferrets, we could make it admissible."

"It's watertight," Ashley said, not looking back at them. "Any lawyer would shoot it down. What we have is circumstantial."

"What about CCTV?"

"He doesn't show up on it," McArthur said, running a hand through his hair. "Unless he sneaks through the back and out again; were they looking for the wrong guy?"

"He's stalked Ferrets though," Murphy said. "He has a motive!"

"But no opportunity," McArthur mused.

Ashley was still staring at him while her teammates were arguing behind her. Maybe there was another way to get him to open up. While the other were talking she took her chance. Murphy looked around the small room.

"Were the hell, is Fenway?"

Chapter 18

Ashley slipped into the room and closed the door behind her.

"Is this going to take any longer?" Tim's solicitor asked. "My client has been here for nearly twenty-four hours." Tim looked up. When he saw Ashley, he instantly recognised her.

"This is the last sitting I promise," Ashley said, walking towards them.

"Didn't your friends fancy another go?" He asked smugly. "Do they even know you're here?"

"Of course not, I'm a DC," Ashley said, sitting in front of them. She stared them down, her eyes flicking to the two of them. Both shifted nervously.

"Are you going to…" He pointed to the tape recorder.

"I wanted to talk to your client off the record first if that's OK?" He smirked to himself.

"And why would he want to do that?"

"Because unlike my idiot co-workers he knows I'm not to be trifled with," Ashley said, looking at Tim. Behind the glass Murphy and Parland awkwardly looked at one another while McArthur smiled to himself.

Tim was now subconsciously rubbing his front where Ashley had hit him just a few hours previously. His lawyer had picked up on it.

"Was she the one? Were you the one who assaulted my client!"

"He was evading arrest," Ashley pointed out flatly. "Of course, if he was innocent, he wouldn't have run."

"Do you have any proof that he's not innocent?" He asked with a smug smile. Ashley smiled to herself.

"No. But the fact that Gordon Ferrets is dead, a man that your client knows well, has stalked for the last few weeks and has made a very detailed itinerary of his movements…" Tim looked down while his lawyer was visibly angry.

"Which reminds me, since this is all off the record, how did you get all this?" He pointed at the photo of Tim's board on Ferrets.

"I visited the Child Protection Group." Ashley explained. She looked over at Tim. "Simon Weston told me about your… past with Gordon Ferrets." Tim looked down at his knees.

"Are you threatening my client?" He asked.

"We wanted to talk to you about this," Ashley said, placing her fingertips on the photo. "My stupid colleagues didn't follow my advice on how to approach the subject." She looked over at the recorder. "I just want to talk to you. Face to face, no recordings, no lawyers." She looked at Mason with a piercing stare.

"Listen, you'll be lucky if we come away with single digit complaints after my client's treatment!"

"Leave us," Tim said quietly. His lawyer looked at him with a shocked look.

"Look, I wouldn't recommend this. They could manipulate you."

"Just let me talk to her," he said. "If I need you, I'll shout," Tim said. He looked over at Ashley.

"Can I have a moment with my client?" He asked as politely as possible. Ashley smiled sweetly.

"Sure," she said, folding her arms across her chest. He bit his tongue and spoke to him from behind his hand furiously, with Tim trying to make a point to him. His lawyer looked over at Ashley and said something else. After a few moments he straightened his jacket and got up.

"For the record, I think this is a bad idea," he said, walking past the table.

"Tell it to the coffee machine, it loves a rant," Ashley said, turning in her seat. He smiled weakly and closed the door behind him. Ashley opened the file and rearranged the papers she had brought in with her.

"Sorry about hitting you with the four by four," Ashley said. "I'm more into hockey than rounders."

"You got me good," Tim grimaced. "Shouldn't have run." He rubbed his front. "How did you know I'd go around the back?"

149

"Balance of probability," Ashley said. "If you'd gone out the front I would have been screwed." Tim laughed to himself.

"I'll remember that next time."

"There won't be a next time," Ashley said.

"Yes, of course."

"You went to see Simon?" Tim asked. Ashley looked up at him.

"I did, he's a nice man," Ashley said.

"How did you find him?" Tim asked. Ashley shrugged her shoulders.

"A hunch," Ashley said. "I saw a piece on the news about Dark Justice, and I thought that there might be a link." Tim nodded.

"How did you find them?"

"The Charities Commission," she said. "They use the CPG as a trade-as name. The Commission gives an address." Tim nodded. "How did you find them?"

"I tailed them from a meet," he said.

"Why did you?" Ashley asked.

"I wanted to help," Tim replied. "I was sick of being such a fuck up, I had got clean, I had Carrie. I wanted to make up for all the stupid shit I'd done in my life." Tim hunched his shoulders. "It was personal." Ashley nodded.

"How did they take it at first? You asking to join them."

"Simon wasn't keen," Tim admitted. "I don't know much about computers and I had a history." Ashley leaned forward.

"What made him change his mind?" Tim swallowed hard.

"I knew how to track people. I learnt it from my…" He looked at Ashley.

"I get it," she said. "He took you in." Tim nodded. "How long have you been doing it for?"

"About a year; I watched other nonces and did some private stuff." Ashley nodded. She pointed at the photo board.

"What was this?" Tim gripped his fists.

"I wanted to get him," Tim said. "He ruined my life. If it wasn't for him then…" He tried to compose himself. He took a couple of deep breaths.

"Take your time," Ashley said.

150

"If it wasn't for him, I would have had a normal life," he said. Ashley nodded sympathetically.

"He told me that I could play for united or city, have my pick, that they'd be fawning over me and throwing more money at me than I knew what to do with it," Tim said. "Of course I listened, I liked him, my parents liked him, he was the one that was going to make me a footballer."

"Living the dream," Ashley said. Tim nodded.

"But… he would give me lifts to training. My dad couldn't get the time off so he would take me." Ashley noticed his hand shaking.

"It's OK," Ashley said, placing a hand on his.

"It was all my fault."

"No," Ashley said, shaking her head. "No, no of course not."

"If I hadn't been so good then maybe…"

"Tim. Tim look at me." Tim looked up at Ashley. "You did nothing wrong. It was him OK, it was all him."

"Why me though? Why me? Why the countless others?" The million-pound question, Ashley thought.

"Because he was a sick man," said Ashley.

"I told Simon, I told him I wanted to kill him," Tim explained. "I really did. But he…" Tim smiled and nodded.

"He told me that made us no better than them. If I wanted justice, I had to make the law see." He pulled the photo towards him.

"He was clever, I tailed that bastard for months and he did nothing. I thought that he would try something with his grandkids but no. Nothing."

"I followed him to his dingy pub, to…" His face contorted to anger, his fist visibly shaking. "Watching football matches." Ashley nodded sympathetically.

"Was there anywhere else he would go?" Ashley asked. Tim looked at the board.

"Yeah, he used to go to this old pawn shop in the city centre every so often," Tim said. "I knew he was on hard times after football let him go." Ashley nodded.

"Where was that?" Ashley asked.

"I don't remember the name, but it was in the city centre, by the sorting office."

"You're sure?" Tim nodded.

"Is it wrong that I'm happy he's dead?" Tim asked. The question caught Ashley by surprise. The she looked over at Tim whose stare was fixed on Ferrets picture. His fingertips moving over the eyes of his fallen tormenter. "All I've thought about is him dying and now it's happened I…"

"What is it?"

"It's anticlimactic," he said, pushing the picture away. "After everything that's happened." Ashley quickly put it into the folder.

"We don't always get what we want," Ashley said, getting to her feet. "Thank you for your time." She went to walk out.

"Why are you trying to find them?" He asked. Ashley looked back. "The guy whose done this, why are you looking for him?"

"Because there's a daughter and her kids out there without a father and grandfather," Ashley said. "You may have your justice, but they don't."

"You should be giving him a medal," Tim said, as Ashley closed the door.

Chapter 19

Another footballers house broken into, you would have thought they'd had better security. #allmoneynobrains

Government making a shit show of #Brexit. Send Will @OatleyDPLC, guy can sell ice to Eskimo's #Manchestersfinest

Just picked up my lovely wedding photos from @Whikleypho. They are 100% certified gorgeous!!! #Happybride #memories

Ashley sat down at her desk, she picked her phone up, phoned officer dispatch and asked a uniform to confirm that Tim's alibi held up. Even though it hadn't been confirmed yet, she walked up to the board and put a red cross on Tim Williams's photo.

She sat down again and looked at the board. Great, their one good lead was now a dead end with nothing.

Parland, Murphy and McArthur came back through.

"I really thought it was him," Murphy said, sitting down. "He has all the things we're looking for."

"It wasn't enough," McArthur said. "Where are we on his alibi?"

"I've sent uniform out to confirm it," Ashley said, fiddling with a pen. "But I think he's telling the truth. He was trying to build a case against Ferrets."

"Well, I want surveillance on him for a couple of days," Parland interjected. "You might think he's telling the truth Fenway, but he could be lying through his teeth." He had a point Ashley thought.

"I'll sort that out," McArthur said. "What else do we have to go on after this?"

"Kate Marsh," Ashley said. "She's the only person from the list not accounted for."

"If you can find her, find her," McArthur said. "But Cramer seems certain that we are looking for a man."

"So, what do we do now?" Murphy asked.

"We have to look back on everything. See if there is anything we missed," McArthur said, looking at the board. "There must be someone who knows why?"

"Maybe there isn't a why," Parland said. "Maybe this was random."

"No, it was too staged to be random," Ashley said. "We all saw the room; this was planned. Maybe the answer is in his computers, maybe that pawn shop Tim was talking about."

"What do you think he was doing there?" Murphy asked.

"Ashley, phone up IT and see if they can go through his computer again to find anything about this pawn shop or anything else. Death threats, anything like that," McArthur asked. Ashley nodded.

"I'll do that now," Ashley said, picking the phone up.

"OK, look over it one last time and try and find a new lead, besides, it's late, and we've been working flat out. Tomorrow and Monday we can track down Kate Marsh and look at this pawn exchange as well," McArthur said. "I'll inform the DCS and we can get this show on the road." McArthur walked away as Ashley waited for someone to pick up her call.

"I still don't like it," Parland said, getting his coat. Just as he spoke, IT went to answer phone and Ashley left a message.

"Why can't people just turn themselves in?" Parland asked.

"Why what time is it?" Ashley asked, again losing track.

"It's half five on a Friday which means pub," Armstrong said.

"Fuck," Ashley muttered, closing her browser.

"I second that," Parland said, getting his coat on. "I'll meet you down there."

"Hot date Fenway?" Parland asked, noting her rush.

"No, I have dinner plans," Ashley said getting her coat. "I'll see you tomorrow."

Chapter 20

Ashley pulled up outside Dave's house; she pulled the visor down and made sure she looked presentable at least. She got out of the car and walked up to the house.

Dave lived in Didsbury which wasn't too far away from her hockey team. The house was in a nice, residential part of the district; a detached house with a lovely, green, front lawn and his Mondeo estate in the drive, with Sharon's Mini parked next to it. Ashley knocked on the door and it was instantly answered.

"Ashley," Sharon said, showing her inside. The entrance hall was a light beige colour which was adorned with pictures of the Hughes. Ashley briefly made eye contact with one of them before looking away and taking her shoes off.

"Sorry I'm late," Ashley said.

"Oh no need to apologise," Sharon said, as they walked down the hall. "Experience has taught me how to keep a dinner warm." Sharon and Ashley walked into the dining room, which was to Ashley's right, with a set of French doors where the table was set.

"Is Dave by the pond?" Ashley asked.

"Yes, can you get him in, and I'll serve dinner up?" Ashley slid the door open into the garden which was Dave's pride and joy. A neatly trimmed lawn with flowerbeds and trees. On the higher level was a greenhouse and to the left of that was his Koi pond with a bench big enough for two.

Dave was sat there, like Ashley still in work clothes throwing fish food into the pond. She remembered him telling her when she first became a police officer that she would need something to detach herself from the job. Something that made her think about or forget the day she was having.

"You OK?" Ashley asked, sitting next to him. Dave nodded mutely.

"Carter's been pissed with you lot," Dave said. "Thought that murder at the Cambrian should have been ours."

"Major crimes now," Ashley said, looking at the Koi Carp swimming around in circles, much like her day. "It's still the same though. Same shit, different name." Dave nodded mutely again.

"What was it today?" Ashley asked.

"She's only a kid, nineteen and two kids from this lowlife," Dave said. "We get a phone call every few months that he battered her again, and today the cycle repeated when she went back to him." He threw the rest of the food into the pond.

"I don't understand, how can someone be so weak?" Dave asked.

"Maybe she has nowhere else to go," Ashley offered.

"Mum and Dad said they'd put them up," Dave said. "I…"

"We can't save everyone," Ashley said, taking his hand. "Some people might not want to be saved." Dave nodded and they both looked at the Koi.

"Any new ones?" Ashley asked.

"No, Tywin was the last one," he said, pointing to a large fish swimming away. "Sharon said I'll have to give some up if I want anymore." Ashley laughed.

"Come on, she said dinner was ready," Ashley said, standing up.

***

The dinner was lovely; home-cooked Thai green curry with rice and prawn crackers. They had laughed well into the night. It had been nice to think about anything but work for a few hours, but when people aren't talking about work…

"So, Ashley… when are you going to bring a nice young man round?" Sharon asked.

"You can't ask Ashley that, you're not her mother," Dave said. Ashley laughed.

"What, it's a reasonable question," Sharon said, in a tipsy state. "She's young and…" She motioned at Ashley. "Let's face it, you're gorgeous, you must beat the men away with a stick."

"You do sound like my mum," Ashley said, round a laugh

"But there is someone," Sharon said.

"She didn't say anything like that," Dave retorted.

"I do listen to you, you know. When you drone on about what people say when they avoid a question." She pointed at Ashley. "Classic case." Ashley smiled and shook her head. Sharon got her there.

"So, Ashley, is there a young man in your life?"

"Nothing concrete," Ashley replied, evenly.

"She's a lady of leisure," Dave clarified.

"Well you're young and attitudes have changed so much since we were young," Sharon said. "You should have fun."

"Why don't I clear the table?" Dave said going to get up.

"No, no. You two sit, you've had long days. Why don't you go into the living room?" Ashley shook her head as they made their way in.

"Sorry about that, I know how much you hate talking about your love life."

"It's fine, really," Ashley said, as they walked into the living room which was lit up by two lamps. She sat down next to Dave on the sofa.

"It's like speaking to my own, except you don't have someone going on about the biological clock," Ashley said.

"I bet that's annoying."

"It is when you're trying to have a good time," Ashley said; she looked vacantly around the room. Dave picked up on it.

"So…" Ashley looked at him and shrugged.

"So, what?" Dave shrugged his shoulders with a questioning gaze.

"Are you going to tell me what's bothering you about your case or…"

"There's nothing bothering me about it."

"Sure, there is. You've been trying to switch off all night but can't; which means there's something that's confusing you," Ashley smiled to herself sardonically and shook her head.

"And here I thought I was hard to read."

"To other people maybe. Come on, what's bothering you?" Ashley leaned forward.

"Man, dead in a hotel room, tied to the bed, one slash mark across his neck," Ashley said. "On his way to said hotel he was stalked by a man he used to abuse as a child. He though, has a clean alibi, which begs the question. How did a killer get into a hotel, commit a murder and walk out scot free?"

Dave thought for a moment; Ashley could see the cogs in his mind turning and turning. He shrugged. Clearly, he had less of a clue then she did.

"They walked in and then out."

"Yeah, but how?"

"Killer was smarter than you thought. Most modern hotels have CCTV in the halls, key cards and things like that. The Cambrian doesn't, still uses actual keys."

"Why not kill them at home though? At their home?"

"What did the guy do?"

"He was a football scout," Ashley said. "But was living off a settlement suit after being called a paedophile. He had to move to a new neighbourhood."

"Oh, that explains it." Ashley quirked her eyebrow.

"What? How?"

"He probably didn't want anyone looking at the house, drawing attention to himself. People like him are always under scrutiny, no matter where they move. Maybe the killer insisted on it." He looked at Ashley's confused expression.

"The hotel tells you that it's pre-planned, so what you have to do is look through his computer to find out why he was there." Ashley went to answer but didn't. They didn't know why he was there.

"Maybe it was random."

"No, the links you've put together so far show that this wasn't random." Ashley thought again.

"Revenge killing," She said.

"More than likely," Dave agreed.

"Why would he go?"

"Maybe he hated what his life had become," Dave said. "Some people become remorseful and destitute." Ashley nodded.

"We already considered people surrounding his civil suit and they all have alibis."

"Maybe this is just the tip of the iceberg," Dave said. "You find the conversation between the killer and the victim and you'll know." Ashley had a scrupulous look on her face.

"And they pay you to be a detective?" Ashley asked seriously.

"Probably more than you because I've seen it all before." Ashley frowned at him.

"I could have told myself that."

Ashley's phone buzzing disturbed the silence. She pulled it out of her pocket and saw that it was from Dan.

Dan: *Hey Beautiful, in the quarter tonight?*

"Work?" Dave asked.

"Friend," Ashley said. "Asking if I'm free."

"Male friend?" Ashley hit his shoulder.

"Maybe," she said. "But I don't talk about my love life so…" Dave held his hands up in surrender as Ashley messaged back.

Hey Beautiful, in the quarter tonight?

Not thinking about it…

You can try and convince me though.

"You know what I think?"

"What?" Ashley asked running her hands across her face.

"Maybe you should go have a night out," Dave said. "Not a late one mind you, but something to take your mind off this." Ashley nodded to herself.

"I have my Koi. You have that club of yours," Dave said. "Go on." Ashley smiled and hugged him.

"Thanks for dinner, and the advice," she said.

"Anytime," Dave replied, patting her on the back. "Go on, you'll crack this case tomorrow." Ashley smiled and made her way back to her car.

Ping.

Ashley checked her phone.

Dan: *How about we cut the small talk and I come to yours?*

Was Ashley that easy?

I'll slip into something comfortable then.

She mulled it over and apparently she was, because she sent it off.

Chapter 21

Stan looked uncomfortably out of the window of his house. Through the net curtain and dark street, the shadows from the streetlights betrayed nothing. Stan closed the curtains and started to pace across the living room, a thrill building in his stomach. It had been so long since he had been able to feel this thrill. Ever since the networks downfall he hadn't been able to feel like this.

Maybe Will was right, maybe he did need to branch out; but it wasn't easy for him like it was for people like Will, Gordon and Harold who had the resources for a network. For him it was more difficult, but he always got his favours for his own network.

The internet had been a wonder in that regard; he didn't have to rely on phone messages, letters and blind luck. No, now the internet made buying his pleasures easier than ever before, but it was like films; sure, they still looked good on screen, but there was nothing like having it in your hand.

Stan waddled back to his computer and opened the chats between himself and his prey for the night. According to the agent the girl would be a willing participant, she should be happy with the amount of money he was paying for the privilege, but it had been so long…

Stan went back over the conversations on his computer, the details of what he was going to do to her. Something in the back of his head told him that she was looking forward to it. Did he have time to?

Before Stan could finish the thought, there was a knock on the front door. This was it — what he was waiting for. Stan got up from his chair and set the webcam to record on his command.

He walked down the stairs, his bulky frame making the stairs creek with each step. He unlocked the door but kept the chain on. Stan opened the door and saw the agent. They were just as their photo promised. He closed the door and unlocked it.

The front door burst open sending him sprawling back, he felt something hard across his head, and his world went black.

***

Stan woke up with a start and groaned as the pain from the blow to his head spread through his body. He went to get up, but his arm strained against some rope. His breathing increased and he started to panic. God, how was he going to explain this to his mum?

"You're awake. Finally." Stan tried to look down the end of his bed, but his gut was blocking his view.

"We had a deal." Stan gritted out while straining against his bonds.

"For a child?" There was a cold laughter, but he couldn't see where it was coming from. "You're still one sick pup, aren't you?"

"Look, I have money. You know I have money." There was a pause, everyone had a price.

"I don't want money," the voice said again. "Money can't bring back what you took from me." Stan started to panic again and struggle against the bonds. He could hear footsteps coming towards him.

"Please, please, I, I'll do anything," Stan blubbered. He could see a figure now walking round the back of the bed.

"A little too late for that." The last thing Stan saw was the glint of the knife as it came down.

Chapter 22

Beep.

Beep.

Beep.

Ashley's hand reached out and turned her alarm off which was hurting her head. She pulled the duvet back and sat on the edge of the bed, yawning and stretching.

Ping.

Ashley reached over to her phone; hopefully it wasn't work. She really wanted to play today. She smiled when she saw that it was Eliza in the hockey group chat.

Eliza: *Come on Bitches! It's game day!*

That was the motivation Ashley needed. She got out of bed and went about preparing herself for the game.

She needed this today. After Tim Williams they hadn't made much more progress beyond surveillance, which Ashley had done a bit of, so the weekend had been a welcome reprieve. She rummaged around her floor and picked up a t-shirt which she checked.

"That..." Ashley threw it on the bed and messaged Dan.

You left your t-shirt here yesterday.

Ashley started cleaning up her room, sorting her clothes out for the week and getting her washing on.

Ping.

Ashley checked her phone.

Dan: *Can you send me a picture of you in it?*

Ashley laughed.

No, I got hockey, and no photos of that either.
Use your imagination.

Oh I am.

Ashley threw her phone on the bed and got her dirty clothing.

Warm Weetabix with bananas, sugar, milk and a cup of tea. She was sitting at her small kitchen table while watching a Sunday morning debate programme. It was a rare occurrence, having breakfast at home, usually she had something at the station after the gym.

On the programme she was watching (The Monnargan Moment) there was a smattering of applause from the audience and the camera focused on the host, a professional woman in her mid-thirties wearing a smart suit. Her name was Vicky Monnargan, a television host with her own daytime show. With a smug smirk she appealed for calm from the audience.

"My next guest has been given the seemingly impossible task of helping to turn around Manchester, where gang violence and petty crime has been steadily on the rise, but he says that there are green shoots. Welcome my next guest, Manchester Deputy Mayor Donaldson!" A suave, older man came onto the stage to applause, shook hands with Monnargan and sat on the green sofa.

"Welcome."

"Thank you for having me," Donaldson said, with an easy smile.

"Well, you and Mayor Buchannan seem to have given yourselves mission impossible," Monnargan said. "At the current rate there is still three murders a week in Manchester and over sixty per cent of robberies go unsolved. How are people supposed to feel safe?"

"Well, I'm glad you brought those statistics Vicky, because me and Mike think that they are unacceptable figures and are numbers which are a consequence of successive Tory cuts to the police service, where the bottom line is of more concern than the bread line."

The audience applauded with a few whoops thrown in for good measure. Monnargan appealed for silence which she got.

"But police spending is at its highest for over a decade and yet there is hardly an increase of officers on the street where people want them."

"That's throwing fire," Donaldson replied, in the same calm tone. "We know that causing a decrease in crime is a root and stem problem. While others are targeting the stems, we are pouring money into the roots of crime and stopping that at source. People in poorer areas are seeing more officers in their neighbourhoods, but more importantly they are seeing a more diverse pool of officers that they can relate to and trust."

"All very good but I have statistics here which show that police spending is being spent more on padding the salaries, pension pots and bonuses of your little pal Glenn Mayer and other senior offices in Greater Manchester and Metropolitan police forces." There was a little falter on his face. "And let's not get started on the new Major Crimes Unit."

"The problem has been that a lot of people have tried to do what we are doing and stop when the bumps in the road appear," Donaldson said, the same bravado intact. "Tackling these problems requires a strong will to see it through to the end. So, although there are these bumps in the road now, in the long term it will be a smoother road."

"I doubt people living in a constant state of violence would see this as a 'bump' would you?" Monnargan asked.

"Part of our plan is to get people who have the money and influence in this city to help as well. The Manchester clubs, pillars of our community are doing more outreach projects to give children an alternative to gang violence with football, and other sports. Will Oatley has been building more affordable housing to make home ownership a reality rather than a pipe dream. He is also pouring more of his own money into local community centres so people can take pride in their communities and work to make it a better place."

There was another applause for him which was stronger than before.

"But that is the future, what is happening now?" Monnargan asked. "People want some short-term results. What about the three murders a week ratio? Or how about three people stabbed every week on our streets. Surely some sort of stop and search powers would be useful?"

"Vicky, everyone knows that stop and search was a tool used to oppress and unfairly target minorities." Another smattering of applause.

"I don't know what it would do apart from drive our communities apart with more mistrust, when what we want is more people coming together. I think the prejudices in our society are the main reason for this perfect storm of crime as it were."

"Well I couldn't agree more," Monnargan said. "Did you know that black on white crime is at its highest rate in twenty years?"

"No, but —"

"How about talk of another grooming gang with Pakistani and Indian men grooming white girls with drink and drugs operating in Manchester suburbs? Or the increase of moped gangs in the city centre? The rise of far-right extremism? Or, do we talk about the spike in gang culture and knife crime?"

"Well obviously there is still work to be done. I'm not trying to pin the blame on crime being an only white problem."

"I didn't say it was an only white problem."

"Everyone is a victim of crime at some point in their life, and all they want is for the system to work; for too long in our city the system has been broken. Our plan is to change the perception of Manchester and make working for your community more appealing than gang culture. As an ex-prosecutor for this city and as a private lawyer I saw the need to give young people a chance, but also a place to go to find themselves."

There was another round of applause from the audience which Donaldson thanked them for.

"Since we're talking about crime in Manchester, let's talk about the new Major Crime Unit or MMC as it's being affectionately known. Over fifteen million pounds has been spent on this new unit which I suppose is one of your plans for tackling crime now."

"We asked the police what it was they wanted to try and get crime down. Instead of every station having some sort of flying squad which were ill-equipped to deal with Major Crimes they wanted a series of teams stationed around the area which could respond to a major incident quickly and effectively, which is what we have authorised them to do. The Tower base in the middle of Manchester is state of the art with its HOLMES capabilities and an onsite IT analysis centre which cuts waiting times drastically. We hope these ideas will become standard for all Major Crime Units across the country in the future."

"This though seems more like a large vanity project than it is about bringing down crime," Monnargan said.

"We'd prefer to judge this unit in the next eighteen months to two years," Donaldson said. "I'm sure yourselves and the people of Manchester will see that it is worth the money we have invested into it."

After changing and packing her hockey gear, Ashley made her way down to the leisure centre in Didsbury. The sky was a dark grey with the feel of rain in the air. Ashley parked up and took her gear and stick out of the boot.

***

"How are things at work?" Eliza asked.

"Busy," Ashley replied, as they took shots waiting for the last people to turn up. "I need this today to let off a bit of steam." She moved the ball in front of her and smacked it with the stick, sending it low into the corner, smacking off the bottom of the goal. Eliza raised an eyebrow.

"No kidding," she said, looking at the small pile of balls already nestled in the net.

"How about you?" Ashley asked looking back at her. "How's the business analyst business?"

"Clearly not as stressful as what you do," Eliza said, looking at the balls.

"Just a rough week," Ashley said, as she and Eliza went over and collected the balls.

"Apparently Rachel was slagging you off after training according to Di," Eliza said.

"You would have thought after two years she'd get over it or move," Ashley replied. Eliza shook her head.

"She's persistent I'll give her that." They looked over at Rachel who was staring at them while her clique of friends were shooting in a goal at the side.

"We should have grown out of this," Ashley said. "Petty jealousy."

"Some people never do," Eliza said, picking the balls up. "And it's not just the girls, my brother's the worst for it."

"Anyone would have thought that we're a team." Eliza smiled and patted her on the back.

"Yeah, they would."

As they were doing so the coach for the opposition came into the car park. Both Ashley and Eliza looked up at the women coming off the bus.

"We can take them," Ashley said. As she said that their centre came off. Ashley remembered her well.

About as tall as her, dark black skin with her dark hair in a bun. Former under 19s England player and three England caps, but let go for poor attitude.

"She ran rings round us last time," Eliza said. "Glad we have you today." Ashley smiled. She did love a challenge.

"Come on, let's warm up."

***

For reasons now lost on her she always prepared the same way for matches, the same breakfast, shooting before the proper warm up and changing into the team kit. She trained in a separate kit before changing; it used to cause her mum no end of grief with the washing.

Karen was at the front of the changing room with the tactics board with positions on.

"Right, Di, Eliza, remember you have to tuck into midfield to cover up since Ash is going to be dealing with Demelza in the centre." Ashley pulled her shorts on, applied her shin pads, tape and socks.

"Ash, remember, you have to hang in the middle, that's where Demelza likes to do her work."

"Yep," Ashley said, now putting her under armour on.

"This is going to be a tough game," Karen said, pacing up and down the changing room. Ashley was doing the last part of her routine which was retying the grip on her stick.

"But we can beat them, I've given you the game plan to beat them, all you have to do is go out there and do it. Come on girls."

Ashley picked her stick up and followed her team out of the changing rooms to the pitch where the other team were waiting for them. Ashley lined up on her patch of the pitch and bounced up and down on the spot, stretching her back then touching her toes, she raised her stick over her head and shook her hips to loosen herself. She looked up at this Demelza who was twisting her waist.

"This is going to be a long game," Ashley said to herself, as the game started.

***

Anyone who thinks that the locker room talk is solely sweaty men talking about football and women in derogatory terms has never been in a female sports team locker room. Of course, it would be a teenage boys dream, lots of women walking round in stages of undress, talking about things that would make grown men blush.

Ashley was sitting in just a towel on the bench with Eliza and Di either side of her.

"Gonna find me some man tonight!" Eliza said, rubbing her damp hair with her towel.

"Shaking off the black book?" Ashley asked.

"Nah, big win, that means new man. You girls in?"

"Love to," Di said. "Might join you in the new man game too."

"Wing woman sorted, what about you Ash? Girl of the game performance like that deserves a night out," Eliza said.

"And the first round," Di reasoned.

"Yeah, don't forget that too," Eliza agreed. Ashley sighed and flopped back on the bench.

"I'm supposed to be in work early tomorrow."

"Not a large one. We find some nice guys, go home, hop on the good foot then do the bad thing," Eliza said, with a wicked grin. Ashley looked at Di.

"Are you seriously into this?"

"Well it's that or wine at my house, we both know what happens then," Di replied.

"You know what, you're right," Ashley said. "The drinking and having a good time, not the man part, especially so close to a workday. Meet you in Apotheca?"

"Ha, sure," Eliza said. "But I bet you'll find someone to make you feel good." Ashley smiled, no doubt. Just as she finished Karen came in. She closed the door and punched the air which made them all cheer and clap.

"Well done ladies," Karen said, after calming everyone down. "That puts us in a really good position for the rest of the season. Ashley."

Ashley looked up.

"I don't think that bitch knew what hit her!" The rest of the team laughed as Eliza rubbed her hair.

"But seriously ladies, well done, go home, do... whatever it is you do and come back Tuesday. Onward!" The team went back to getting changed. Ashley stood up and dropped her towel.

"Girl you have got to warn me before you do something like that," Eliza said, looking at Ashley up and down.

"Why?" Ashley asked, putting her bra on. Eliza raised an eyebrow and looked her up and down again.

"My bro' will be disappointed," Ashley said, pulling her jeans on with a smile.

"Eliza, Jesus," Di said, throwing a towel at Eliza's head as Ashley pulled her shoes on.

"Apotheca at ten?" Ashley asked, pulling her top on, pushing her hair over the collar.

Chapter 23

Another good performance from our Ladies 1st team, beating @PendleForestHoc 4–1. Good performances all round #GOTG was Number 10 Ashley Fenway #upthenorthern

Is your child at risk playing on Overwatch? Probably kills their brain cells but TV did that to us anyway. #newgenerationsameexcuses

Another part of her hockey routine was to phone her brother and tell him about the game. It was mutually beneficial. She would talk to him about hockey and he would talk to her about his football game he had over the weekend.

Her brother Matty was six years younger than her but in a strange way she was closer to him than her older sister, where there was only a two-year age gap. He was currently studying business management at Nottingham University and had got in because he was good at football.

"It's not every day you can say you bested an ex-England international," Matt said. Ashley was stood in front of the mirror doing her hair, she was due to meet Eliza and Di in half an hour or so.

"You're right, it's not," Ashley said. "What I didn't want to do was change the way I play."

"Do you want to lose with your ego intact?" Matt asked. "Good players know when to play for the team."

"When was the last time you took one for the team?" Ashley asked. "And no, taking a grenade for your friends doesn't count." He laughed.

"No, because the teams I've played for usually win." Ashley couldn't believe he had the cheek to say that.

"You're such a little shit," she said, adding a slight curl to her hair. "How many ex-international midfielders have you bested again?" He laughed.

"There's still time," Matt said. "What are you doing to celebrate?"

"Going out with Eliza and Di," Ashley said. "And no, I'm not putting a good word into Eliza for you."

"A good sister would."

"No, that would make me a great sister," Ashley said, pulling her pyjama bottoms off. "And I know what your reputation's like."

"That would make you a great sister," Matt said. "How's work?"

"A ball-ache," Ashley said, pulling her dress up. "Man gets killed in a hotel room with enemies galore, but no one has all of means, motive and opportunity, and our best suspect has a watertight alibi."

"Maybe it was random." A flash of the crime scene swept Ashley's mind; the blood on the walls, the throat of Gordon Ferrets hanging out over his body. Too cold and too precise to be anything but vindictive.

"… It wasn't random," Ashley said, looking at herself in the mirror. "Boss wants us to go through all of it tomorrow to find another suspect." She sat down on the bed, picked her shoes up and put them on.

"Enough about my work. How's Uni going?"

"It's going fine," he said. "You know, working hard."

"Good. You should phone mum; she's worried about you."

"Same to you."

"I'm older, she trusts me. She's worried you're getting into trouble."

"I'm fine Ash," Matt said. "I know I can call you if anything bad happens."

"Good. Sorry to love you and leave you but I'm heading out and I can't wait to see Eliza in the dress she's wearing."

"You see, I don't know if you're joking or not," Matt said, seriously.

"Just teasing, love you and remember to phone mum."

"Will do, see ya soon sis. Bye."

"Bye." Ashley ended the call and looked at herself in the mirror. "Remember, you have work in the morning, just a couple."

***

Ashley loved the Northern Quarter and she loved the nightlife. Edinburgh was good, the Quarter though was better. Vibrant bars that catered for all tastes and always able to find a good time. After a quick

171

shower and change she was out among the hundreds having the same idea as her.

Ashley walked to Apotheca where Di and Eliza were waiting for her at the bar, chatting away.

"There she is," Eliza said, handing Ashley a beer bottle. "Since you said you were working you wouldn't be on the hard stuff."

"True," Ashley said, taking a swig. She could see why her brother had a thing for her; her dress was more than complimentary to her figure and her brown skin and frizzy afro.

"My brother says 'hi' by the way."

"Isn't he a bit young for her?" Di asked.

"It was teasing, Ash."

"Tell him that," Ashley said, noticing Eliza's gaze shifting.

"She has her prey in sight," Ashley commented, then took a drink.

"Three of them," Di said. Ashley looked across, sure enough three guys with pints talking about something.

"I want the dark one," Eliza said, now going back to her drink. Ashley took the chance to look at the dark one. Tall, good looking, slight tan, shaved stubble.

"Which means Di has dibs on the ginger one," Ashley said, looking at Di; even in the dark light she could see her blush.

"I'm not that easy."

"To sleep with, no," Ashley admitted. "To read however."

"Well we left you with blondie," Di retorted. The tone of her voice told Ashley that wasn't a good thing. She looked over again and saw a very wiry guy. Very not her type.

"Bollocks."

"Should have got here earlier," Di said, taking a sip of her wine.

"No, you guys can do better," Ashley said, not relishing the thought of talking to the guy and then cutting him out.

"I think Eliza has other ideas." Before Ashley could stop her, Eliza had gone over and started talking to them.

"Please be married," Ashley muttered under her breath. Despite her praying they came over to talk to them. Eliza started talking to the dark one, Di, the ginger and Ashley with...

"Earl?"

"Yeah, Earl." Who called their kid Earl? Ashley wondered.

"So, what do you do Earl?" Ashley asked, trying to be polite. Her friends were obviously having more stimulating conversations.

Ashley took her phone out of her purse discreetly and messaged Dan to come out.

"I work as a project manager," he said nodding, as if he was trying to impress her. Ashley soon regretted asking that question because then it was all about him. His job, his boss, his friends, his family. The idiots who he had to work with. Ashley might have taken an interest if it wasn't so boring. He hadn't even asked her what she did for a living yet.

"Ash, toilet, coming?"

"Yes," Ashley said quickly, following her friends to the toilet.

"Dean thinks we should go to a club," Eliza said, dreamily into the mirror.

"Oh, does he," Ashley said, darkly while checking her hair.

"Stop being such a prude, take him back to yours have some fun and turf him."

"Not my style… now," Ashley said.

"Well at least come to the club and talk to him till we seal the deal," Di said.

"Fine," Ashley said getting her phone out and checking her messages; she saw a message from Dan.

I'm out if you are.

Good, I'll let you know where we go. You can come save me then.

They went back, Ashley having to stomach talking to Earl. Thankfully Eliza started to steer them out. Earl was complaining about how long he'd have to wait for Saturday or something.

Ashley though wasn't, she'd be lucky if she had a day off until this time next week. Ashley checked her phone.

Dan: *I'll be out in about an hour. Think you can hold out that long?*

They made their way out into the street to go to her usual haunt.

Nightcore.

It was in the middle of Deansgate Lock between ARK and Revolution. Ashley could see it in sight and smiled. She stumbled across this place by accident one night with her hockey team when she first moved here. Now, it was her favourite.

The queue for the club wasn't that long. Above the open mouth of the club was the name in neon lights with the end of the H and bottom flick of the C framing the name underneath, like the old Atari sign. They waited patiently in line and got to the front where the mouth of the club opened out to a cloakroom and the opening of the staircase down to the club itself.

The rest of them paid with Ashley at the back with Earl. He went before her and paid for himself and waited for her.

"You go on, I'll be a sec," Ashley told him, looking for some change. Earl didn't wait and went inside.

Ashley paid and walked into the mouth when her phone buzzed. Dan wasn't due to be out for another hour.

Ashley got her phone out and saw that it was McArthur. She sighed.

"Sorry, can I take this?" She asked the bouncer who nodded. Ashley moved to the street and answered.

"Fenway."

"You out and about?" McArthur asked. Ashley looked up at the night sky.

"Yeah…" Ashley said, drawing it out, watching the stars twinkling. "Why?"

"We have another body."

Chapter 24

Ashley was only half pleased when she got the phone call telling her that there was another victim, only half. After rushing home and getting changed she was out of her apartment. The phone call said that this man was killed and found the same way as their first victim, which is why the MMC had been called in.

Ashley was now driving to a suburb that she didn't believe could belong in Manchester. She could see the blues and twos of the police cars down the road. Ashley pulled up, stepped out of the car and checked her phone which had a message from Dan, which was only a sad face emoji and one from Eliza.

Bitch, what the fuck? You can't just bail like that. Earl is wondering where you are?

Sorry, dead body came up, can't pass that up.

She saw Eliza typing out her response.

Just had to explain to him what you do for a living.

He doesn't know whether to be scared or aroused.

Ashley made a face. What a creep. She knew she hated the name Earl.

If he's aroused, then he's going to be the next dead body.

You seriously need dick.

Maybe next week.

Ashley shut her door and locked it, walking towards the perimeter.

The officer on the perimeter was about to ask Ashley who she was when she flashed her identification and was let through. All the neighbours were stood around the perimeter in their pyjamas looking up at the house. Ashley walked up the garden path to the house when she noticed a man sitting on the grass. He was dressed all in black with a blank look on his face.

Ashley thought it was odd, but she got to the scene logger who was on the door. She was an Indian woman in overalls who was writing in a large book.

"Evening, name and rank?" She asked.

"Ashley Fenway, Detective Constable," she said, handing over her ID.

"Major Crimes?" Ashley nodded.

"Who's he?" Ashley asked, pointing to the man on the grass. The woman looked over at him.

"Would you believe it? He was going to rob this house when he found our vic upstairs," she said. "Funny old world isn't it?"

"Very, is there anyone else from Major Crimes here yet?" Ashley asked. The scene logger looked back in her notes.

"Yes, a DS Armstrong turned up about fifteen minutes before you." Ashley looked round at the uniformed officers that were just standing around. Why weren't a couple of them at least asking the neighbours questions?

"Are you going inside?" She asked.

"Yes, in a sec. I just need to do something first." Ashley walked to the edge of the perimeter and beckoned one of the uniforms over.

"DC Fenway, has anyone started talking to the neighbours yet about what they know?" Ashley asked.

"I've asked a couple of people," he said. "The house belongs to a Joyce Kettings; she lives with her son, Stan."

"Good start, anything else?"

"Uhm…" The uniform flicked through his notes. "One neighbour said that she is on holiday with a friend in Norway."

"Right… Have you started canvassing?"

"Not yet."

"Didn't Armstrong get the bowl rolling?" Ashley asked. The uniform shook his head.

"Right, I want you to ask all these people what they know about this house," Ashley said, pointing at it. "Who lives here, has there been anything strange over the last couple of days. Also, start getting statements from the neighbours. We may as well make use of them while they're up." The uniform was making notes.

"Anything else?"

"Ask them if they've seen strange men, women, cars, vans loitering around the place, I want to know, and when DCI McArthur gets here, I want you to relay it to him as well."

"Yes Ma'am."

"No."

"Excuse me?"

"Not Ma'am, Mam, Sir, just Detective."

"Yes... Detective."

"Thanks." Ashley went back to the mouth of the house and started to change into the SOCO scrubs. She walked into the house which was being lit by powerful lights while SOCOs went about their work. The hallway was decorated with fluffy, pink carpet and floral wallpaper with SOCOs dusting the place for fingerprints. Ashley looked back at the scene logger.

"Where's the body?" She came to the door.

"Up the stairs, first on the right, you can't miss it," she said. Ashley thanked her and went up the stairs. On the walls were old-style photos. One was of what looked like a young Joyce Kettings who was in a pretty floral dress with a handsome man in uniform. Probably Stan Kettings' dad. There were a few more photos of the happy couple along with a small baby. The timeline of the family went up, with a toddler Stan to the landing.

Ashley was looking at this happy family when the sound of a camera shutter drew her back to reality. She walked slowly across more fluffy carpet to the first room on the right. Ashley tentatively pushed the door open. It was the same bloodbath as the first one. There was a man lying on the bed in the same pose as Gordon Ferrets with his throat slashed and blood spurted onto the wall, with the blood falling over the victims protruding gut.

Cramer was busy inspecting the body while his assistant photographed the scene. Armstrong was in the room looking down at the body.

"Detective Fenway," Cramer said, in his light voice as he looked down at the body.

"Doctor," Ashley replied.

"Fenway, I didn't think you'd turn up," Armstrong said with a cocky smirk.

"I wasn't busy," Ashley said. "Besides, why didn't you start getting statements together?"

"I wanted to see the body," he replied easily.

"It's not like it's going anywhere."

"I knew someone would pick it up," he said, shrugging his shoulders. Ashley shook her head in disbelief.

"So, do you even know who's house we're in?"

"No."

"Do you even know whose body you're even looking at?"

"Not a clue." Ashley shook her head.

Ashley pointed up to the ceiling. "We are in Joyce Kettings house, she's currently on holiday in Norway." She pointed to the bed.

"She lives here with her son Stan, who fits the profile of the deceased. And here you are walking into their house without the slightest care as to who they are."

"Jesus, Fenway, don't get pissy about it," Armstrong replied, with a slight laugh. Ashley shook her head.

"How did you make DS?"

"Detectives, we have a murder to solve," Cramer said, rubbing his temple. Armstrong smiled smugly and went back to observing. Ashley got her notebook out and started to inspect the body for herself. She walked to the feet at the end of the bed and noted the bruising around the joints. The knots as well, were the same as the first victim.

"Is there a time of death yet?" Ashley asked hopefully.

"Nothing concrete," Cramer said. "I'll know more when I complete the autopsy, but I can say it's been more than twenty-four hours."

"They look like they were killed in the same way," Ashley mused. "With the same knife?"

"I can't be sure but yes, it looks likely," Cramer said. "And the knots look consistent with how the first victim was found." Ashley nodded, got to her feet and looked around the room.

It was strange how different this room was to the rest of the house. The walls were covered with posters of old vintage movies with a dark painted wall underneath. Over in the corner was a modern looking desktop computer with a bookcase to the side, which had an assortment of CDs and DVDs.

Ashley walked over and browsed some of the titles. Most of the films she had never heard of while the CDs were mostly blank. Ashley looked up at some of the posters above the PC. They were of conspiracy theories such as Roswell and Nine Eleven.

Everything from the room so far screamed that he was a loner. Not a worry to anybody. So, what was it that made someone want to kill him so brutally and in such a way as this? Ashley noticed a notebook on the side of the desk. Ashley picked it up and read the first page which was full of code, sequences of numbers and letters that didn't make sense. Ashley put it down. What connection, if any did this guy have to Gordon Ferrets?

The sound of another person entering the room made Ashley turn around. McArthur walked into the room. "Armstrong, Fenway."

He looked down at the body and frowned.

"Who's our vic?" He asked. Ashley was just about to speak when Armstrong cut across her.

"It's not confirmed yet, but we think it's Stan Kettings," Armstrong said. "House belongs to Joyce Kettings, she's on holiday in Norway now." Ashley shook her head and continued to make notes on the desk layout.

"Good, what else do we know?"

"It looks like this guy was killed in the same way as our other vic," Armstrong said. "Have we found any footprints?"

"Not yet, DS Armstrong," Cramer said. "We'll know more after the autopsy and the sweep of the house."

"How soon can we get it done?"

"I'll have it done for tomorrow," Cramer said. McArthur nodded. He walked over to Ashley who was making notes on the layout of the DVDS he had; alphabetical.

"A computer nerd," McArthur said, looking at the desktop. "Any work uniforms? Anything like that?"

"Nothing like that, but I think that he could work in computers, this looks very sophisticated," Ashley said, looking at it.

"We'll leave you to it." McArthur turned to Armstrong and beckoned the two of them out into the hall.

"You know, I didn't want to believe when I was told about this, but it looks bad," McArthur said, walking down the stairs with Armstrong and Ashley in tow. "But we'll take this in our stride."

"So, what do we do now?" Ashley asked.

"Wait for the evidence to come in tomorrow morning," McArthur said, coming out of the house so they were on the front lawn. "I've told the scene commander to have everything they've found tonight to be on our desks in the morning."

"We're having statements taken from the neighbours as well," Ashley said. "See if they've seen anything useful."

"Good idea," McArthur said, looking at the flashing lights. "We also need to contact the foreign office, see if they can get hold of Joyce Kettings, see if she is in Norway or doing one of those cruises." Ashley finished making notes.

"What about the media?"

"Give them the usual gist about appealing for information but nothing more," he said. "We can't have this turn into a cluster fuck."

"Yes Sir," Ashley said, underlining the note she just made. "Is there anything else?" Ashley asked. McArthur turned and looked up at the sky.

"Let's have a word with our burglar friend," he said, looking over at the man sitting on the grass. Ashley nodded and they walked towards him. He was still sitting on the grass staring out into space with a foil blanket round his shoulders.

"Sir?" It took him a moment, but he looked up at Ashley and McArthur.

"Sir, my name is DC Fenway, and this is DCI McArthur. We have some questions to ask you." He nodded.

"What's your name son?" McArthur asked. The burglar took his balaclava off.

"Ewan," he said, blankly.

"Right, Ewan. Why this house?" McArthur asked.

"What?"

"Why this house?" McArthur asked. "There are thousands of homes in Manchester that are easier to steal from, why this one?"

Even with his shock, Ashley could see a falter. She looked over at McArthur who had a small curl on the edge of his mouth that told Ashley that he had seen it too.

"I just did, OK?" he said, defensively.

"I'm not buying it," McArthur, said shaking his head. He looked at Ashley. "Are you buying it?"

"Not at all," Ashley replied. "You don't seem smart enough."

"Hey, what's she playing at!"

"Forgive DC Fenway, she was head girl at school," McArthur replied. "Me, I grew up in Glasgow, I know how difficult it is to break into a house." Ashley looked at him out of the corner of her eye.

"Look at it from our view. See the only person who would know that no one was home would be the killer." Ewan went white and started to get up.

"Wait, I didn't." McArthur put a hand up for silence. Ewan stopped talking and sat back down.

"Tell me how you knew this house was free to be burgled and we can eliminate you as a suspect," McArthur reasoned.

"I got a tip from one of my sources," Ewan said. "They said the owner was away on holiday, old lock and windows. Dead easy in and out job."

"But when you went upstairs you found the body?" Ewan nodded.

"Why did you call an ambulance?" Ashley asked. Ewan shrugged before answering.

"No one deserves to be left like that," he said, staring off into the middle distance. "I was going to run before you lot showed up but…"

"That's fine." McArthur turned to a uniform and summoned him over with his hand.

"Please take this man in to give a full statement," he said. "Then charge him with breaking and entering."

"Eh?"

"It's just a formality," McArthur reassured him. "Since you've been so helpful, we might, you know, look past it." Ewan nodded and got to his feet and allowed himself to be led away.

McArthur beckoned the uniform in closer. "Keep him in overnight, let's make him sweat," he whispered.

"Yes Sir." The uniform helped Ewan to his feet and led him away.

"Cheers mate," Ewan said to McArthur.

"Oh, and Ewan." Ewan looked back. "If I find you burgling again, I won't be so lenient." Ewan nodded and was led away. Ashley frowned slightly.

"Sir?"

"Sometimes Fenway we must, grease the wheel as it were," he said.

"But we still don't know why he was burgling this house though."

"We'll know by the morning," McArthur said. "He's in shock now. Tomorrow he'll sing like a bird."

"I'll take your word," Ashley said. "I'll call the home office. See you in the morning."

Chapter 25

It hardly felt like Ashley had slept at all. The alarm on her bedside table was vibrating loudly, waking her up. She rolled over to the other side of the bed, turned it off and got out of bed, taking her phone out of the charger. Ashley walked into the kitchen, took a smoothie out of the fridge and looked out of the window.

Manchester was still silent and unmoving in the darkness. Ashley downed her smoothie and placed it in recycling; she changed into her gym gear, shoving her work clothes into a bag and made her way out of her apartment. She locked the door, pulled her phone out and rang her work phone.

She knew it was going to answer phone but when it went to the machine, she started to leave a list of all the things she needed to do that morning when she got in.

"And lastly don't forget to chase up Gordon Ferrets ex-wife if we haven't heard from her," Ashley finished, around a yawn as she let herself out of the building and into the carpark.

She got into her car and drove off towards the gym.

Cardio.

Arms.

Core.

The Bag.

Ashley was punching the bag, with her music blocking out the outside world. Not that there was a lot of people in the gym. Ashley did a combo on the bag, breathing heavily, then wiping her brow with her arm and started again. She looked up at the TV out of the corner of her eye. BBC news showed the house she was at last night. A timely reminder where she should be going considering what she had to do this morning. Ashley punched the bag one last time and started to unwrap her MMA gloves.

**

@GMP, fancy moving your vans from my road, some of us have work this morning! #Hatemondays

Big police thing going down near Didsbury this morning! #Anothermurder?

Great to see @GMP cleaning up our streets with another murder happening? #Whenwillitend?

Urgh, why is the traffic round Didsbury extra shit this morning! #notinthemood

Ashley pulled into the carpark of the City Tower with the radio still on, going on about selling tickets to a festival.

Ashley opened the door into the office to see that it was deserted. Ashley turned the TVs to BBC news, that were talking to one of the couples on Strictly. No doubt her mum and sister would be glued to the TV for such a thing. Ashley leaned over and picked up a banana from the side and ate while watching. The local news came on and showed the report, which was on earlier, highlighting the murder she went to last night.

"Police are appealing for information on the murder of a local man who was found in his home last night."

Thankfully they hadn't put two and two together; an investigation like this always became more difficult when the media got involved. They tended to get carried away with these sorts of things.

Ashley walked to her desk, turned her computer on and looked at the post-its that had been left on her desk.

Ashley checked her e-mail, once she waded through the department spam about nights out, charity collections and building changes she was left with a small list.

The first one was from the Home Office saying that they had been able to contact Joyce Kettings on her cruise and that she had been informed of what had happened at her house. They said that she was going to be on an early morning flight back to Manchester and was due back today at some point. Ashley emailed back her thanks and forwarded the email to McArthur.

The next one was from the Coroner's Office confirming that the autopsy had been carried out and that the report was ready but that they would like someone from the department to come and formally ID the body. Ashley sent it to print to put on McArthur's desk, then e-mailed back to confirm that someone would be over later in the day while also saying that Stan's mother was going to be in to formally ID her son.

The one after that was from North Wales Police saying that they finally caught up with Gordon Ferrets ex-wife. She and her boyfriend were in Zante for the last two weeks, which ruled out Armstrong's theory of a vengeful ex-Wife. The email also said that she was willing to speak to them if they needed her to. Ashley emailed back thanking them for taking the time and that they would send someone to speak to her in due course, while forwarding it to McArthur.

Another one was SOCO sending over the file from the scene along with photos as well. Ashley sent those to the printer as well, to put on the board. Ashley walked to the board and updated it, adding Stan Kettings with his details. Ashley added photos from the crime scene and pointed out the similarities of the two bodies.

She went over to Gordon Ferrets and rubbed the link about his ex-wife off the board thinking of the horror on Armstrong's face when he saw it. Ashley heard her computer *ping*, telling her that there was another e-mail. Ashley finished updating the board and went back to her computer. The statements from the neighbours had been e-mailed over.

Ashley opened them up and sighed at their length. She looked over at the clock. Hopefully, she would be able to sort through them all before people started to come in. It was the most boring part of the job, sorting through statements like this, but it was how most suspects were nabbed, making the small connections.

People were starting to come in dribs and drabs but most of them went to their desks, not paying her any attention. Ashley was busy going over what they knew about their new victim. Shy, not sociable, hardly seen. Stan Kettings seemed like a recluse, practically house bound… maybe agoraphobic.

"You burn the candle at both ends." Ashley looked up and saw McArthur looking at the new board.

"I wasn't busy," Ashley said, getting up from her seat. "Besides, everyone else does shit boards." McArthur laughed lightly.

"I like it," he said, tapping the board. "What have we got?" Ashley picked her notepad up.

Ashley told him about the Home Office getting back to her but also that SOCO and the neighbours' statements had come back to them.

"I haven't had a chance to go through it yet. The coroner came back, the autopsy has been done and they're waiting for someone to ID the body and for you to go over. I've forwarded everything over to you."

"Very good Fenway," McArthur said, walking down to his office. "Tell everyone when they get in, I'll brief them at nine."

"Yes Sir." McArthur went to his office at the back of their segment and closed the door; she went back to the statements.

As she was doing this, members of her team came through in drips. Parland was first, followed by Murphy who went to get a cuppa each.

A little later Armstrong came strolling in; he looked to see who was in and saw Ashley.

"Morning Fenway, you wouldn't mind making us a cuppa, would you?" He laughed at his own joke, while Ashley just gave him the finger without looking at him.

McArthur's door opened, and he came through.

"All right everyone, gather round we have a busy day ahead of us." McArthur walked to the board and turned.

"For those of you not there last night we have a potential second victim." He tapped the board on Stan Kettings photo.

"Stan Kettings, age unconfirmed but we're guessing it's close to our first victim. For those wondering why he was referred to us, please look at the photo here." He brandished a photo of Stan Kettings on his bed with his throat cut.

"He was found tied up like our last victim with his throat slashed. Coroner hasn't confirmed that he was cut in the same way as our first vic, but I can safely say that they are related. He was found in his mother's house; autopsy puts his time of death between ten and midnight on Saturday, so he was in bed all day."

McArthur banged the board.

"We need to know everything this guy was into. IT are doing their thing to his computers, but we need to know what else he gets up to. Any friends? Girlfriends?"

There was a smattering of laughs.

"Stop that, but you get the idea, previous jobs, things like that. I want to print a pretty picture of this guy like we did with Ferrets."

McArthur watched his team take down notes and nodded his approval.

"Right, me and Armstrong are going to the coroner and getting the low down on how he died and hopefully onto his mother, find out what else we missed." He turned to Parland and Murphy.

"You two, I want you to go talk to our friend downstairs and shake him down. He's been stewing for about eight hours so he should want to sing like a bird, find out who his contact is. Then go back to the neighbours and have a once over on what they were doing last night and what sort of person he was. Let's try and find a former place of work, something like that."

"Yes boss."

"Fenway." Ashley looked up from her desk. "I want you to stay here and pour over everything from our first victim, hopefully try and find a link between the two of them and get this Kettings' financials and phone records." Ashley had hoped for something a little more exciting, but she was a DC, and this was her job.

"Yes Sir," Ashley said, forcing a smile.

Everyone started to file out of the office leaving Ashley on her own to finish sorting through the reports from the neighbours.

Ashley went to go through the statements that were brought in last night. They pretty much all said the same thing about what had happened. No one had come or gone from the house since Joyce had gone on holiday that they've seen; Stan Kettings was a loner who no one hardly saw. The more she looked at them the more they all started to look the same. Ashley was writing up a summary when the phones rang around the office. She waited till hers rang and answered it.

"Fenway," she said, pinching her brow, the lack of sleep catching up with her.

"Hi, it's Bill from IT. We've finished the deep forensic exam on Stan Kettings' computer."

"Brilliant, what was on it?" Ashley asked, prepping her note pad.

"You might want to come down here, there's a lot to take in," Bill replied. On the one hand it usually meant something complicated, but she was desperate to get some sort of lead.

"I'll be down now." Ashley ended the call and walked away from the desk.

The City Tower not only housed the Major Crimes Unit, but it also housed the new IT support suite. Ashley got the lift down to their floor and walked in. Unlike her office which seemed to be perpetually light, this place was darker. The curtains were drawn across the windows with odd beams of light coming in. Sat at their desks were people who seemed to be stick thin or overweight, hunched over the many screens.

Ashley walked to the reception; the girl behind the desk just as engrossed on her work as the other lab technicians.

"Hi, I'm looking for Bill's team?" Ashley asked. The secretary didn't even look up from her screen.

"Section D4, back of the room."

"Thanks." Ashley looked up and saw the office had been spread into sections. She walked to the back of the room and found section D4. She leaned over the top of the office divider. There was a group of five of them all typing away. She recognised one of them; Aaron.

Aaron started around the same time Ashley did and their paths crossed a couple of times on cases and on nights out. Her old unit used to tease her that Aaron had a crush on her. She always denied it and said that they were just friends, besides, Ashley would eat the poor boy alive. He fell under the thin category of people who worked here with curly, brown hair and fashionable glasses. He looked up and saw her but quickly went back to his work.

"Hi, I'm looking for Bill."

"And that's me." A large jolly-looking fellow turned to Ashley and held a fleshy hand for her to shake. "You must be DC Fenway."

"Yes, I am."

"Well please, take a seat." Ashley pulled up a chair next to Bill and looked over at Aaron who was looking firmly at his work.

"So, what was on his computer?" Ashley asked. Bill cleared his throat.

"Well, it's a very sophisticated system," Bill said, with a touch of admiration. "Eighteen triple-encrypted firewalls, up to three quantum processors. Without a doubt the hardest computer we've had to break down."

"Sounds complicated," Ashley said, trying to make small talk. "Now, what was it you found?"

"This." After clicking a couple of buttons a few files came up on screen. Ashley frowned and looked up at the numbers and ledgers.

"Is that... Bitcoin?" Ashley asked.

"Very good detective," Bill said, like she had just learned a new trick. "Yes, it appears that Mr Kettings was indeed involved in Bitcoin."

"In what capacity?" Ashley asked. "Are we talking investor or...?"

"He was a miner, that's when someone keeps the ledgers and payment on Bitcoin running smoothly and are rewarded with more Bitcoin."

"So, was he proficient at it?" Ashley asked.

"Very much so," Bill said, pulling up his ledger. "Judging from this it looks like your victim was a millionaire." It took a moment to process the information.

"A millionaire?" She asked, looking over at Bill. "You must be joking."

"Aaron checked this morning; Stan Kettings was worth almost ten million pounds when he died." That was motive.

"So, did he make his money just from this mining?" Ashley asked. Bill shook his head and pushed his chair in closer to the screen.

"The makers of Bitcoin are shrouded in secrecy. I think that maybe your man was one of the founders or knew someone very close if he had access like this." Well, that explained why he spent so much time in his room.

"What was he spending his Bitcoin on?" Ashley asked. "It wasn't on indie movies, was it?"

"Indie movies, no, but it was movies." He was being evasive. Ashley shuffled in her seat and looked at him as to say carry on.

"It was child pornography."

"What?" Ashley sat up in her chair, suddenly more alert at a potential link between the two victims.

"Well, that's what he spent the bulk of it on," Bill said. Ashley was looking at the screen hoping that some of it could please make sense to her.

"How big was his collection?" Ashley asked.

"The biggest found in this country. We finished going through all his hard drives and it's well over seven terabytes, all ranging from grade 1 to 5."

"Is any of it homemade?" Ashley asked. Bill shook his head.

"It's all come from other sources. He probably had contact with people who do make this material." Ashley had a thought.

"Does any of it link up to victim one?" Ashley asked. Bill muttered something under his breath and pulled up a computer programme.

"We ran a comparison and over seventy five percent was found within victim two's collection."

"Were they in contact?"

"We haven't found anything to suggest that they were in contact," Bill said. "But they might have been through different means." Ashley wrote down to search for a link.

"You said he spent the bulk of his Bitcoin on this, what did he spend the rest of it on?" Ashley asked. "Are there any patterns?"

"We noticed that there are a series of outgoing transactions that sync up," Bill said. "I think that it's converting Bitcoin into cash and then he's picking it up at an exchange." Tim mentioned that Ferrets went to an exchange; maybe there was a direct connection.

Ashley wrote down to go over the financials of Stan Kettings to find out where the exchange was.

"What about the transactions he made to people, can we track them down?" Ashley asked. Bill shook his head.

"People like bitcoin because it offers complete anonymity," he explained. "Once transactions are made, they can be wiped straight away." Ashley swore under her breath, there went her lead on connecting the two of them directly.

"Can you e-mail this to me?" Ashley said getting up, "I'll forward it on to DCI McArthur. Can you please work on seeing if Kettings and Ferrets had any contact on the computer?"

"We'll do our best, but we won't make any promises," Bill said, preparing to send the file over to her.

"Can you also go back over Ferrets' laptop and see if he was involved in Bitcoin in anyway?"

"That we can do," Bill said, looking up at her. "I'll call you when it's finished."

"Great, I should be at my desk, if not Aaron's got my number."

"Oh, does he," one of them said, the whole team turned to Aaron who had blushed.

"We're just friends," Ashley said, walking out. She walked out into the stairwell, Ashley got her phone out and phoned DCI McArthur.

"McArthur."

"Sir, it's Fenway, IT have finished their analysis on Kettings' computer."

"Excellent, you're on loudspeaker. Go."

"IT have found out how Kettings made his living. He was a Bitcoin miner."

"Argh, not one of those tossers," Armstrong piped up. "Constantly going on about their 'investment'."

"He was a miner, not an investor, there's a difference," Ashley said. "He used to solve the problems that awarded Bitcoin." Ashley walked to a banister on the landing. Before her the late morning sun shining down on a busier Manchester.

"So, did he have a few bob then?" McArthur replied.

"He was worth nearly ten million pounds before he died," Ashley said.

"Fuck off, like bollocks he was," Armstrong said, disbelievingly. Ashley rolled her eyes but smiled at a couple of people making their way down the stairs. She half-sat on the metal railing.

"Well there's motive," McArthur said. "Was our other vic involved in bitcoin?"

"Tim Williams said about Ferrets going to exchanges so I've asked IT to look into it," Ashley said. "But there is a link."

"Go on." Ashley looked round and walked into an alcove on the staircase.

"He's also got the largest known child pornography collection in the country," Ashley said. There was a long silence from the other end. "All of the images Ferrets had were in Kettings' collection."

"So Kettings was dealing with Ferrets then," Armstrong said. "He must have been right, with Ferrets paying him in Bitcoin."

"IT haven't confirmed that but they're looking into it," Ashley said. "They said that he might have converted Bitcoin into pounds at some sort of exchange; they don't know where though."

"There can't be that many who won't recognise him. Fenway, I want you to put together a list of possible exchanges he could have used around the area."

"Yes Sir." Ashley bit her lip. She had a thought. "Sir, maybe this is a revenge attack."

"Revenge attack?"

"Maybe this is a vigilante killing. Ferrets had accusations of paedophilia laid at him in his life, Kettings looks like he's involved too."

"Two killings don't usually make a pattern, Fenway," McArthur replied. "I can see your point though, maybe it's an angle to look at. Go back over Ferrets' case and see if he and Kettings intersect in anyway, especially with these child fantasies they both seem to have."

"Maybe Kettings wasn't into that stuff, maybe he was just a seller," Armstrong offered.

"Another good theory, we have plenty to work from, let's get back on it."

"We're going to phone Murphy and Parland to compare notes, and then question Joyce Kettings. She's staying at her friend's place; we'll meet you at the station later for a debrief."

"I'll call you if I find anything."

"You do that. Good work Fenway, speak soon." McArthur ended the call.

Ashley walked back up the stairs to the office thinking over what could connect the two of them. She pushed the door open to the office and sat down. The deep forensic report had been sent up to her.

Ashley opened it up to have a look at it for herself. She was mostly interested in the Bitcoin account that he had.

His computer must have had some sort of quantum processor to solve the complex equations needed to mine Bitcoin. Ashley looked at the transactions that he was making. Although most them were incoming (probably to buy the pornography), there were some outgoing transactions. Ashley used her computer to highlight them on the screen.

She leaned back in her seat and looked at the highlighted lines. Most of them were scattered across the month with some hefty amounts going out. Probably to buy new material, thought Ashley. She thought back to when she was in uni, her mum forever complained about getting rent from her sister at the end of the month when she got paid. If he didn't have a regular job and this was his only income, he would have needed it to be converted.

Ashley looked across the dates to see if something linked, a certain day or week and a certain amount. She pulled up Gordon Ferrets' financial history too, maybe there was a link between the two of them in their transactions.

This would be so much easier if she had a list of Bitcoin prices. Ashley then remembered the exchanges. She closed down the files and opened Google.

'Bitcoin exchanges'

Ashley searched and Google came up with a list of mainly pawn shops in the area. Ashley got the statement that Tim Williams gave. He said the exchange he followed Ferrets to was the Skipp Pawn Shop in the city centre.

Ashley brought up the financial records for Ferrets and the ledger of Kettings. She was looking for a day that Ferrets withdrew money and Kettings got an order. After eliminating bills and other groceries from the list Ashley looked at expenditures, but again saw nothing. Maybe Ferrets had another account, or an off-the-books method to avoid leaving a paper trail to him.

"Smart," Ashley mouthed to herself, more than anyone.

She might have to pay his house a visit when she went to visit the exchanges she thought, while jotting it down. Just as she finished a new e-mail came through. Ashley opened it up. It was Stan Kettings' bank with his bank account information.

Ashley instantly sent it to the printer and forwarded it to McArthur. Ashley got the printout and laid it down on the desk. Going through it she could see that Kettings didn't have much physical money savings. Almost all the money going in was interest accrued on the small amount in his account. So, he was getting the converted Bitcoin cash in hand.

Ashley went back further and finally saw a pattern. It was from 1974. Regular payments into the account from the Royal Mail.

"He must have been a postie," Ashley said to herself. She got a highlighter from her desk and highlighted it. If this was in 1974 then Kettings must have been in his twenties at least and this was the last payment. Ashley frowned. He must have done something else between then and when Bitcoin came about.

Ashley opened the SOCO report on her computer and searched the inventory for the bedroom he was found in. The only bank card found on there was his Barclays account.

Her trail of thought was snapped when her desk phone went off.

"Fenway."

"Hi, it's Bill from earlier."

"Yes, Bill. What do you have for me?"

"I looked back over Gordon Ferrets' computer like you asked, and I found some mild Bitcoin software on his hard drive."

"Good," Ashley said. "I don't suppose there is anything on there about an exchange?" Bill hummed. Ashley heard him typing away.

"There are a few searches on Bitcoin exchanges," he said. "And directions to an exchange in the city centre." Ashley felt her spirit lift.

"Can you send me all the information on it please?"

"I will certainly do that," he said. "Is there anything else?"

"Yes, there is actually," Ashley said, looking at Stan Kettings' financial reports.

"Can you see if Stan Kettings has any other accounts apart from the Barclays account he used on his computer?"

"I will have a look."

"Thanks, bye." Ashley placed the phone down and waited for Bill's e-mail.

When it came through Ashley had a look. Thankfully Ferrets wasn't as careful as Kettings. Ashley picked up a photo of Ferrets and logged off her computer.

Chapter 26

Ashley pulled up outside the pawn shop that Tim had described to her and the one that Gordon Ferrets had frequented. It was a tacky pawn shop with lots of old and new trinkets in the dusty windows and bright neon lights which said 'Skipp Pawn Shop'. Ashley looked at some of the tacky jewellery in the windows and in the corner of the shop window was a small Bitcoin sign.

Ashley walked into the shop which set off an electronic bell. The walls were covered in glass cabinets with two island cabinets in the middle and a hatch at the far end. Ashley walked over to the hatch and pressed a bell to attract attention. She heard a chair wheel over. Sat in it was an overweight man with a balding head, yellow teeth, grey and ginger stubble and wearing a wife beater vest.

"Hello love." His voice was gravelly and smoke damaged. "I bet you saw some of our rings in the shop window, didn't you? Well, I can do a good deal for a pretty little thing like you." Ashley raised an eyebrow.

"Even if I was the jewellery type." Ashley shook her head and pulled out the picture of Ferrets and held it up against the hatch glass.

"Have you seen this guy come around here?" She asked. The man narrowed his eyes.

"Who wants to know? Boyfriend pawn off a ring of yours?" He asked. Ashley sighed and pulled out her ID and placed that on the glass too.

"I run a legit business. I haven't done anything wrong."

"Now why would you assume I was questioning the legitimacy of your business?" Ashley asked, putting her ID away.

"You'd be surprised how many of you lot we get in here trying to get things back."

"Well I don't care about that," Ashley said. "Now, this guy." She pointed at Gordon Ferrets.

"Has he been in here? Do you know him?" The man looked up shiftily at the photo.

"No," he said. Ashley rolled her eyes; why did they always make it more difficult?

"Are you sure?" Ashley asked, in a slightly patronizing tone.

"Yeah, never seen him."

"Strange," Ashley said, putting the photo down. "Because I have a witness seeing him frequenting this place and have him searching for directions to this shop." The man behind the hatch breathed heavily through his nostrils.

"If you knew already, why did you ask?"

"Test of character," Ashley said with a smile. "To see how trustworthy you are." He didn't look impressed.

"So…" She held up the photo again. "Do you know this man?"

"Yes," he said, in a patronizing tone.

"Great. What did he do here?" Ashley asked.

"Oh, you know, pawn a few things off." He was lying.

"Really? Like what?" Ashley asked. Calling his bluff.

"Jewellery, a bit of football memorabilia," he said.

"No crypto currency?" Ashley asked flatly.

"We don't deal with that sort of stuff, officer," he said flashing, his yellow teeth at her. Ashley laughed slightly.

"So, what's the Bitcoin sign in the window for?" She asked. His jaw locked.

"A gimmick," he said, flashing a smile. "But it is something we've thought about expanding into."

"So, if I were to come back with a warrant, we wouldn't find anything?" Ashley asked.

"Whoa, wait a minute." Ashley held her impassive look. "There's no need for that."

"I know there isn't," Ashley said. "I'm sorry if you don't like my honesty, in fairness I don't like your lies." He couldn't hide his displeasure.

"It's not against the law," he said. Ashley smirked.

"No, it isn't. It's the wild west," Ashley said. "You didn't need to get so defensive about it."

"You're a little obnoxious, has anyone told you that?"

"All the time; now." She pointed at the picture of Ferrets. "Did he come in here?"

"Yes, he did, didn't have a clue at first, but he soon got into it," he said. "He wanted to convert it and have it sent to an online ledger he owned." This was music to Ashley's ears.

"Right, I need the information of the ledger." He laughed. With his gravelly voice it seemed a little unnerving.

"I can't do that," he said, chuckling. "Customer confidentiality." Ashley quirked an eyebrow.

"You're not a lawyer and this is not a doctor's surgery," Ashley retorted. "Confidentiality rules don't stretch that far. It's a ledger that a warrant can easily give me."

"If that's the case, why are you asking me?"

"Because if you don't, I will bring blues and twos down here with all the media to show off what an untrustworthy place this is, that gives away client's information."

"What about him," he said, pointing at Ferrets. "What would he have to say about it?"

"He can't, he's dead," Ashley said, flatly. "And we think it was something to do with his Bitcoin transactions." The colour drained from his face.

"That wouldn't make a good newspaper headline now would it, and who knows what else we might find with a warrant?" Ashley said looking around at the shop. He breathed out and thought for a moment.

"OK," he said. "If I give this information to you… what are you…?"

"It's not going to be like the movies you watch," Ashley explained. "You're going to hand over the computer and the ledger and let me work in peace." He looked down, weighing over the offer.

"It's in the back," he said, with a gruff sigh. He got up and waddled over to a door. Ashley heard it open; he pushed it open and beckoned her in. Ashley walked in and he showed her to the computer which was a modern looking machine similar to the Stan Kettings computer.

"Nifty piece of kit," Ashley said, sitting down at the seat. "Buy it yourself?"

"Uhm… it was pawned off," he said. "Owner's never been back for it so…"

"OK." As if on cue the bell to the shop went off. The man looked at Ashley.

"Go on." The man sighed heavily and went to the front of the shop to deal with the new customer, while Ashley started the computer. When it loaded Ashley opened the Bitcoin software, she recognised it from Kettings computer. Ashley opened it and it came up with a sign in page.

Ashley clicked on the sign in and it came up with multiple log ins. Ashley studied them, they all looked like burner e-mails, made solely for this; Gmail accounts that didn't make sense. Ashley looked at the list of addresses that Ferrets would have used, trying to see if there was anything of a similar name.

Ashley's eyes darted between them and saw one.

FSA1965@gmail.com — FerSprAca@gmail.com

FSA.

"Ferrets Sports Academy," Ashley whispered. Ashley clicked on it and thankfully the password came up with it. Not very smart.

Ashley logged on and it came up as an account for Ferrets. Ashley was amazed to find out that he didn't even own one Bitcoin. His account read it as 0.00005. Didn't seem like much. Ashley opened the account page and looked at payments in. They were all conversions from this exchange. She looked at expenditure; it showed the money going out but nothing on who to.

Ashley looked up and saw the shop owner looking back at her. Ashley looked back at the screen. Maybe with a list of transactions they could see if Ferrets was buying from Kettings. That meant though impounding this computer.

Ashley copied the e-mail address. She changed the password on the account so she could access it at the station. She emailed the information to her work address and logged out.

"Are you done?" He asked. He didn't look impressed as Ashley walked out with the computer.

"Hey, where do you think you're going with that?" He asked.

"Sensitive material, being impounded as evidence now," Ashley said, shutting the door behind her.

Chapter 27

Ashley dropped the exchange computer at IT and asked them to get all the information on the transactions that they could from it.

When she arrived back at her desk Stan Kettings' phone records had been sent to her. Ashley opened them up, she got herself a cup of tea, sat down and started to go through both the home phone number as well as Stan's mobile.

And there wasn't a lot to write home about. Ashley also had a list of people that Joyce Kettings phoned frequently so there was a list of numbers for them.

Ashley got her highlighters out and started to go through the list. Unsurprisingly there wasn't any odd numbers that couldn't be explained, that Stan Kettings would phone. Ashley moved onto his mobile phone which was a little more interesting.

There were a few calls to what looked like businesses. Ashley searched the numbers and sure enough they were phone calls to small businesses. All of them in different fields and doing different things; butchers, bakers, bike shops and clothes shops all within the Manchester area.

This looked like a small business. Maybe out-sourced IT or something like that. Ashley brought up google and searched "Stan Kettings IT".

A few things came up but more specifically was a LinkedIn page which Ashley clicked on. It was a local page giving out IT advice and out-sourcing for small businesses. Maybe someone called him who might have been abused by him Ashley thought.

Ashley went back through the list and wrote down the names of the businesses so she could visit them; but one came up which Ashley didn't expect. She called a number.

"Hello Mr Oatley's office." Ashley frowned and span back to her desk. "Hello, Mr Oatley's office," the voice repeated. Ashley ended the phone call.

Oatley, as in Oatley Developments? Surely not... Ashley got up from her chair, paced a little and went back to the computer. Oatley Developments was one of the biggest employers and builders in Manchester. This was a big company; Kettings wouldn't provide IT services for that.

Then why was he calling the direct line of the CEO? The lady on the other end said Mr Oatley's office.

Ashley looked up how many times this number came up. If it was a one-off then it could be explained, but it wasn't. In fact, this number had called out and received calls from Stan Kettings for a while. These records only went back a year, but they were what Ashley would call frequent. (About the same amount of times she called her mum.)

Ashley wondered even more now what they were talking about. Plus, how long had this gone on for? Could this have been going on for years?

"You OK Fenway?" Ashley looked up at Murphy who had walked in. Ashley shuffled in her chair and folded her arms, her mind going a mile a minute.

"Yeah, I found something interesting though," Ashley said.

"Well don't keep up the suspense," Murphy said, coming to her desk.

"Phone records show that Kettings was doing some small IT work for various small businesses — no problem; except this," Ashley pointed. Murphy leaned down and looked at it.

"It's a popular one according to your highlighters. What's special about this number?" Murphy asked.

"It belongs to Oatley Developments." Ashley went to speak again but was cut off by Murphy.

"Ashley, there are lots of numbers relating to Oatley's," Murphy said. "He's probably the biggest employer in Manchester after the NHS."

"Yeah, I thought that too," Ashley said, a little annoyed. "If you let me finish, I could tell you that it was for Will Oatley's office." Murphy let out a low whistle and frowned.

"You're sure about that?" He asked.

"Hundred percent, heard it myself." Murphy was thoughtful.

"Was it a one off?"

"No, they've been talking frequently over the last year or so, maybe longer." Murphy ran a hand over his face and thought for a moment.

"We better tell McArthur about this," he said, straightening himself up.

"Why?" Ashley asked, sensing there was something else to it.

"Of course, you're not Manchester born, are you?" Murphy said. Ashley shook her head.

"But neither is McArthur," Ashley pointed out.

"He's been here long enough, come on, let's go see him." The two of them went to his office.

"Come in." Ashley and Murphy went in.

"Please tell me you have something," McArthur said, putting the phone down.

"Ashley's found something good," Murphy said.

"Regale me." Ashley went to answer but Murphy cut in front of her.

"She's found a link between Stan Kettings and Will Oatley." Ashley watched McArthur's reaction, which looked a little suspect.

"Not surprising," he said. Ashley could have killed Murphy. "He's a big employer."

"To Oatley's private line," Murphy clarified. "They've been calling each other for a while." Now McArthur became more alert.

"You're sure?" He said looking at Ashley who nodded.

"Sir, what's the significance of this?" Ashley asked. McArthur pressed his fingertips together.

"Close the door Fenway and take a seat," he said, nodding at the seat in front of him. Ashley did so along with Murphy. "You do realise that what we are about to discuss stays between us."

"Of course, Sir," Ashley said, not really knowing what was going on. McArthur sighed heavily then began.

"A few years ago, myself and Murphy were part of the team that dealt with elements of the Rochdale scandal." Ashley knew of that, a highly organised child exploitation ring that preyed on vulnerable young girls. Gangs of men would give the girls drink and drugs and then abuse them at various locations around the Rochdale area.

Ashley would have called it sophisticated if it wasn't for police ineptitude, that made sure that they went unchallenged for years.

"We had to take statements and quite a few girls said that Will Oatley was involved with the abuse," McArthur continued.

Ashley was stunned, she didn't see that coming. Will Oatley was famous in Manchester for his charitable donations and causes. In fact, he'd paid for the pitch at Ashley's hockey club to be upgraded from astro-turf to the new water-based pitch a couple of years ago.

"We tried to subtly build a case, but one by one things started to break down," Murphy continued.

"There's no evidence of it, but we think Oatley scared some of the girls into silence or bribed them," McArthur said. "Him now being linked to someone like Kettings, well, it raises a few eyebrows."

"You could say that again," Ashley agreed.

"It wasn't just then," Murphy said. "There's been rumours about him for years; to be honest I thought that all this *me-too* thing would get him."

"Why was nothing ever followed up?" Murphy and McArthur looked at one another.

"Unfortunately, Fenway, this is one of those things. Oatley has friends in high places. Higher than we have."

"What about now?" Ashley asked.

"If the evidence points that way we will," McArthur said. "So far we only have two murders to solve." Ashley nodded.

"I'll catch up with the businesses and see what Kettings did for them," Ashley said, getting to her feet. "Do you want me to go to Oatley Developments too?" She asked.

"If you can, yes," McArthur said, picking the phone up. "I wouldn't hold out hope though." Ashley took this as her cue to leave along with Murphy.

When he left, Ashley looked up Will Oatley; see what he looked like. His face had been on billboards around the city since she moved here. He had slick, grey hair and a distinctive grin.

Ashley grabbed her coat and bag as well as the list of businesses she had to now go to.

***

It went much how she suspected. Stan Kettings provided IT services to small businesses that couldn't afford it. He also repaired computers that they had on site. All of them were sad at his passing and had to arrange other computer services.

"It's a shame." Ashley was at a baker's shop that Kettings went to, it was the last one on her list. The baker handed Kettings photo back to Ashley. "He was a decent guy."

"He didn't complain or anything, problems at home, things like that?" The baker shook his head.

"Not to me he didn't. He came in and did his thing, had a doughnut for the road."

"He didn't have any enemies that you knew of?" The Baker shook his head.

"Sorry I can't be more help."

"No, it's fine," Ashley said, her eyes now scanning the assortment of cakes and pastries on display. She noticed one that made her bite her lip.

"Is that an almond tart?"

Ashley didn't tell them about who he really was or how he died, but they all said that he was quiet, respectful and had cheap rates. Well, he was a millionaire Ashley thought, but there usually was a causation between philanthropy and guilt.

Ashley got back into her car and finished her almond tart, which was delicious.

She crossed another name off and licked the glaze from her fingertips. The last business now being Oatley Developments. Ashley thought to herself; he did have the biggest causation of wealth and philanthropy in Manchester. Maybe he did have a lot of guilt. Ashley checked the time and how far away she was from Oatley Developments on Google maps. She was half an hour away and nearly at teatime.

She fired the car up.

Chapter 28

Ashley could see Oatley Developments from the entrance to the business park. A large, glass building which showed everything from corridors to canteens. Ashley pulled up in the staff carpark and walked to the front of the building where a few people were having a smoke break.

Ashley walked through the automatic doors to the reception area which had a large white wall with Oatley Developments in silver letters on it and an assortment of plants round the edge of a large white desk.

To the left of the desk were a set of terminals with plastic barriers. One guy walked up to it and flicked a badge over a reader to be let through. Ashley needed one to get beyond the reception.

A pretty, blonde woman in a business suit was at the desk typing away at a computer that Ashley couldn't quite see.

"Can I help you?" She asked, before Ashley had reached the desk. Probably had a CCTV monitor behind the back of the desk.

"Yeah, I want to speak to Will Oatley if that's all right," Ashley said. The receptionist let out a light laugh.

"Mr Oatley is a very busy man," she said, going back to her typing, not affording Ashley a second look. "You'll have to call and make an appointment with his own personal secretary."

"You see, the thing about that is that I don't have time to call for an appointment," Ashley said, getting her ID out. The receptionist looked up, probably going to ask, 'Who do you think you are?' and saw her ID.

"Oh," she said. "Then I'm sorry but you'll have to formally speak to him before I can allow police in."

Ashley was getting tired of this. She didn't want to be here any more than the receptionist wanted her to be, but she was doing her job.

"Look, can you just call his secretary? I won't take too much of his time."

"I'm sorry, but it's out of my hands," the receptionist said, with a fake smile that screamed 'take that bitch'. "Maybe you should have phoned ahead." Ashley was going to let it slide but after that comment she wanted to smack the conceited look off her face.

Ashley got her phone out, dialled the number to Oatley's phone and let it ring. His secretary answered the phone.

"Hello, Mr Oatley's office."

"Yes, I want to make an appointment to speak to Mr Oatley," Ashley said. The receptionist at the front desk smirked to herself. Ashley might not get an actual appointment, but she could be creative.

"I'm sorry, who is this?" His secretary asked.

"Detective Constable Ashley Fenway, Manchester Major Crimes," Ashley said. "I just want to ask Mr Oatley some questions about an investigation."

"Well, Mr Oatley is much too busy today to answer questions Ms Fenway. I have a gap in his schedule for tomorrow around noon if that's OK?" Not long enough.

"That should be fine," Ashley said. Time for GCSE Drama to help her out.

"He'll see you then, goodbye Ms Fenway." The call ended. Ashley kept her phone to her ear.

"And how will I get up to the office?" Ashley asked into the phone. "What, the girl at the desk will give me a badge?"

The receptionist looked up at Ashley who was aware of it, but she was looking at the lettering on the back wall.

"Good, I'll be up in five minutes," Ashley said, now putting her phone in her pocket.

"Excuse me," Ashley waved to the receptionist. "I have an appointment with Will Oatley. His Secretary said you could give me a badge to get through." Mission accomplished. The smirk was wiped from her face as she gave Ashley a badge.

"You'll need to sign it out," she said, through gritted teeth.

"Thanks," Ashley said, signing the form and taking the badge from her. Ashley walked to the left of the desk where the terminals were and scanned the badge. It bleeped and the barrier opened, letting Ashley through.

Ashley went to the lift. The only problem with this plan was that she had no idea where Oatley's office was. She gathered her thoughts. Will Oatley was the big CEO of the company; his office was going to be on the top floor. Ashley got into the lift and pressed for the sixth floor.

A few people got into the lift along the way but got out on other floors. A couple of guys did double-takes when they saw her in the lift, but were too shy to act on it, even if they tried to afford glances at her in the mirrors of the lift.

When it got to the top floor Ashley walked out and looked around. There was a small bull pen of people but there were lots of frosted office doors. Which one was Oatley's, Ashley wondered?

"Hi there." Ashley turned; a guy, five foot ten or eleven, smart appearance in shirt and trousers, worked out a little but not enough to be in an office job. Relatively handsome, dark, brown hair, blue eyes; not what Ashley was looking for right now.

"Hi."

"Are you lost?" He asked taking a step closer. Ashley sensed an opportunity.

"Yes, I am, it's my first day," Ashley said. "I'm meant to deliver a message to Mr Oatley's secretary from the finance director's secretary and I have no idea which office is his." He laughed and pointed to the back of the room.

"That's his office there, his sec will be right in front of it." Ashley looked where he was pointing; it was the only one which didn't have a secretary outside it. Perfect, she could ambush him in his office.

"Thank you so much," Ashley said, going to walk away.

"Well, if you're free later maybe we could get a coffee, you know, show you around."

"Oh, I couldn't possibly," Ashley said, now wanting to get away quickly.

"No, really, I insist," he said.

"Maybe some other time," Ashley said, with hopefully enough firmness that he would take the hint. "It's my first day and I can't be later than I already am." He seemed to take the hint.

"OK, see you around," he said, sulking back to his desk. Ashley made her way over to the secretary's cubicle, which was opposite another desk which looked equally lived in. Did he have two secretaries?

Ashley looked around the desk she was pointed to. It had been kept clean and organised, but there was no coat hanging up and a handbag under the desk. Probably out having a smoking break. Ashley walked up to the frosted door. She could make out rough furniture in the room but couldn't see if Oatley was in the office itself.

Ashley was wary of the time she was spending there, in case people started to become suspicious of her. Aware of this, Ashley put her hand on the door and went to let herself in.

"What do you think you're doing?" Ashley turned and saw an older woman, mid-forties come towards her, smartly dressed and looking annoyed.

"I'm here to see Mr Oatley," Ashley said. "DC Fenway, we spoke on the phone."

"I said you could talk to Mr Oatley tomorrow," she said, her voice harsh but quiet, probably so as not to cause a scene.

"Not soon enough I'm afraid."

"Mr Oatley left strict instructions not to be disturbed."

"That I did." Ashley turned to see Will Oatley now at the door. He was dressed in a grey suit and like in his picture, there was an uneasy presence about him.

"Sorry Mr Oatley, DC Fenway, Manchester Major Crimes, I just need to ask you a couple of questions about an ongoing case."

"I pencilled her in for tomorrow Mr Oatley." His secretary tried to explain.

"No, no, it's fine," Mr Oatley said to his secretary, his eyes rested on Ashley. "Anything for Manchester's finest, they have a difficult enough job without people like me delaying them." Ashley wasn't sure if he was checking her out or getting the measure of her.

"Although you could tell me how you were able to get up here." Suppose he deserved to know that much Ashley thought.

"I tricked the receptionist downstairs to give me a badge, I guessed your office was on the top floor and someone in here was nice enough to point out your office. Didn't get his name." Oatley smiled. Ashley found it unnerving with his brilliant white teeth.

"Clever," Oatley said. "I can see why you're in this job. Come on in, would you like a tea, coffee?"

"Tea please, milk no sugar."

"I'll have coffee, Julie." The secretary walked off in a huff as Oatley invited Ashley into his office. It was large and spacious with a lounge area as they walked in, with two white sofas and a coffee table in the middle. To the right was a raised level with a large, wooden desk, a couple of chairs and a large, wooden cabinet behind the desk that went from roof to ceiling.

Oatley sat down on a sofa which faced the door and Ashley sat down opposite him facing the window which spread across one side of the office.

"So, DC Fenway," Oatley said, clapping his hands together. "What can I do for you?" Ashley got her note book out and opened to a new page. "I won't need a lawyer for this, will I?"

"It's just a couple of questions," Ashley said. "We just need to ask about a couple of things that have come up in our enquiries."

"Oh, like what?"

"I wanted to talk to you about Stan Kettings," Ashley said. Oatley didn't look surprised by the name; if he did, he had a good poker face.

"What about him?" Oatley asked.

"How do the two of you know each other?" Ashley asked.

"We met in the Army Cadets," Oatley said. "Both our dads were enthusiasts. We developed a friendship. We kept in touch."

"How often did you keep in touch?" Ashley asked.

"Every so often," Oatley replied. "Stan isn't a social character." His face became more concerned.

"Is he all right?"

"You haven't heard?" Ashley asked a little surprised. Oatley shook his head.

"Stan Kettings died a couple of days ago," Ashley said. Oatley's face dropped a little. He took a moment to compose himself.

"I… I don't know what to say." Oatley took a deep breath. "How?"

"We think he was murdered," Ashley replied.

"You don't think I'm a suspect, do you?" Oatley asked. Before Ashley could answer, Julie came in with their drinks on a tray.

"Thank you," Ashley said, taking her tea.

"Yes, thank you Julie," Oatley said, distantly. "Oh, Julie, please send some flowers and a condolence card to Mrs Kettings as well, with our sympathies."

"Yes, Mr Oatley." Oatley took a sip of his coffee and placed it down on his knee.

"How's the tea?"

"Perfect, thank you," Ashley said, placing hers down. "In answer to your question, no, we don't think you're a suspect."

"Then why are you talking to me?" He asked. He really did want to know the whole picture.

"From Mr Kettings' phone records we saw that he made a phone call to your direct phone line a couple of days before his death," Ashley said. "We just want to know why he called you?" Oatley nodded intently.

"Stan did some IT work for me. He was good with computers and sometimes I don't trust the people here to fix things."

"Why don't you trust them?" Ashley asked.

"My competitors will do anything to get dirt on me, Miss Fenway," Oatley said, seriously. "People can be bought."

"And Stan couldn't?" Ashley asked; maybe Oatley knew about his Bitcoin business.

"Stan's a friend. Was a friend," Oatley said. "I knew I could trust him. Trust is something money cannot buy."

"Did he call you about an IT issue?" Ashley asked.

"Yes, about a server at home," Oatley said. "I've had a new security system installed which was playing havoc with the WiFi. He just called to say that he had fixed it and we chatted, said I had to get into the Bitcoin business, but I don't go in for all that." Ashley nodded and looked down at her notepad.

"I'm just curious, if you trusted Mr Kettings so much with your computer network, why didn't you offer him a job?"

"I did," Oatley replied. "Lots of times. But he refused, he preferred being freelance and I respected that." Ashley nodded. Did she reveal the

209

information that Kettings was a paedophile? It might get to reveal some more information, but at the same time it could have a negative effect.

"Do you know of anyone who would want to kill Mr Kettings?" Ashley asked. Oatley shook his head.

"I have no idea," he said. "Stan was shy and a little reclusive but ultimately a nice person. I can't think of anyone who someone would want to kill less." Someone had a reason to, Ashley thought.

"OK, do you know a Gordon Ferrets?" Ashley looked at his face and the poker face fell a little, he obviously knew the name but hadn't expected Ashley to say it. She could see the cogs in his mind formulating a response.

"No, is he connected with Stan's murder?" Oatley asked.

"Yes, he's been murdered as well, in the same way," Ashley said. "Are you sure that you've never heard of this name before? He was quite prominent on the local charity scene." Oatley paused.

"We might have bumped into one another then, but he obviously didn't leave a lasting impression," Oatley said.

Ashley didn't believe him; Ferrets' Sports Academy had links to charitable causes that Oatley was surely linked to. She would have to do some digging into their connections.

"Well, Mr Oatley," Ashley said, getting to her feet. "Thank you for your time."

"No, it's quite all right," Oatley said, getting to his feet and seeing Ashley to the door. "And if there is anything I can do, please let me know."

"We will Mr Oatley, thank you." He saw Ashley out and closed the door behind her. Julie didn't look too impressed with her as she walked past, but she was too busy thinking about that look in Oatley's eyes when she mentioned Gordon Ferrets. Maybe Oatley knew a little more than he was letting on.

Ashley made her way down to the reception area and handed her badge back to the moody receptionist, who may have just had a scolding from upstairs as she didn't look at Ashley in the eye or converse with her. Ashley smiled to herself when her back was turned and went to walk out of the building.

"Hey, wait." Ashley turned to see the guy who pointed out Oatley's office jogging towards her. Great, just what she needed.

"Did you find his office OK?" He asked.

"Yes, thanks, you were very helpful," Ashley replied.

"Are you going on a smoke break?"

"No, I have to get back to work," Ashley said. His brow furrowed in confusion.

"But you said it was your first day?" Ashley got her ID out and showed him.

"Oh."

"Convincing, wasn't I?" He laughed.

"Yes, you were," he said, with a touch of admiration. "Listen, that drink offer still stands if you want to?" Ashley smiled sadly. "You're spoken for aren't you?" Ashley nodded.

"Yeah, but thanks, I needed a confidence boost today. Have a nice day."

"You too…"

Ashley walked across the reception area and outside into the cold air. She had a feeling that there was something about Will Oatley that was a little strange. She didn't believe everything she was being told about him either. She started to the car. She wanted to talk to the neighbours.

***

Will Oatley watched Ashley walk to her car from his office. He sank his coffee, pulled a burner phone out of his pocket and dialled a number.

"Harold? It's Will." He narrowed his eyes at Ashley getting into her car.

"Something's come up. We need to talk."

Chapter 29

Fawkes Avenue looked very different in the light, if anything it looked better. The dark, bare trees giving the road a homely feel, with neatly kept houses either side. But with swarms of police officers and SOCO still on the scene it didn't look like a nice place to live.

Ashley opened the file with the witness statements and started to read through them to see who she wanted to talk to again. Ashley read through them, cursing other officers for their piss poor notes.

Stan Kettings was reclusive, didn't socialise with anyone.

Quiet boy, no other friends to speak of.

Fixed my printer once.

The trick with neighbourhoods like this Ashley knew, was that there was one local busy body, one person that knew more about other peoples' lives than they did. How do you know who it is?

Ashley picked out the thickest file and began to scan through it. Perfect. She checked the name. Mrs Anders, 27 Fawkes Avenue. Perfect, right across the road from the Kettings' house. Ashley got out of her car and walked across to number twenty-seven. A moment later the door opened to a small, old woman who Ashley could instantly tell was the busy body.

"Hello?"

"Hello Mrs Anders, my name is DC Ashley Fenway, I'm with the Manchester Major Crimes Unit." Ashley showed the woman her ID.

"I was hoping I could ask you some follow-up questions from your statement last night." Ashley trailed off when she noticed Mrs Anders looking at her up and down.

"How tall are you?" She asked.

"Sorry?" Ashley replied, thinking she hadn't heard the woman right.

"How tall are you?" She asked again. Ashley frowned in confusion.

"Five, nine," Ashley said in confusion.

"You're very tall for a woman." Great, secondary school all over again.

"Not enough for the WNBA," Ashley quipped. "Can I come in?"

"Of course, yes, yes." Mrs Anders stepped back and let Ashley in. The floor was carpeted in a green, floral pattern which lead into a living room which had the same carpet but a ghastly yellow and green floral wallpaper.

Ashley looked at the floral-patterned chairs, two armchairs and a sofa which all faced a modern TV. Sitting in one of the chairs was what Ashley could only assume was her husband, his face hidden behind a broadsheet copy of the Daily Telegraph.

"See Bert, there's a policewoman here." Mr Anders growled from behind his paper. "Please, take a seat." Ashley sat down on the sofa and got her note pad out.

"Would you like a tea, coffee?"

"Tea please, milk no sugar." Mrs Anders walked out of the room and Mr Anders folded his paper to look at her. His mean expression grunted and then flipped the paper up to avoid seeing her. Ashley was wondering if she should have skipped on the tea. Usually she spent this time looking round peoples' houses, but now she had to sit still.

A couple of minutes later Mrs Anders came back with a tray of tea and placed it down on the coffee table. She handed a cup and saucer (floral pattern of course) to Ashley, who took a courtesy sip.

"Mrs Anders." Ashley placed the cup and saucer down. "I just wanted to talk to you about the Kettings family." Mrs Anders hummed and nodded. "What can you tell me about them?"

"Well, they moved across the way in the summer of '65." She said. "Little Stan was nearly seven or eight at the time." Ashley wrote that down.

"What were they like?" Ashley asked.

"They were very nice and helpful," Mrs Anders said. "Isn't that right Bert?" Mr Anders just grunted and rustled his paper.

"What about Stan?" Mrs Anders thought for a moment.

"He was a quiet boy," she said. "We asked our own boys to try and make friends with him, but he always enjoyed reading and electronics rather than going outside." Mr Anders grumbled something from behind his paper which made both women look round.

"Anyway," she continued. "After his father died, he was still a bit reclusive; he worked as a postie for a bit before starting that computer business of his. Helped us out a few times hasn't he Bert?" There was nothing this time.

"So, you wouldn't know of anyone who would want to harm him?" Ashley asked.

"Oh no," Mrs Anders said, shaking her head. "No. He was such a nice man. I can't think of anyone who would want to."

"Did he have a girlfriend at all, anything like that?" Ashley asked. Mrs Anders posture suddenly became serious.

"No, he didn't have a girlfriend." Being so old-fashioned Ashley thought to herself that they might have suspected that he was gay.

"But he did have 'ladies of the night' come and see him."

"Prostitutes?" Ashley clarified, taking a sip of tea. Mrs Anders nodded. Well, that was something Ashley didn't know. Mrs Anders nodded stiffly.

"How do you know this, if you don't mind me asking?" Ashley asked.

"Well…" Mrs Anders looked either side uncomfortably. "It was late one night. Joyce had gone on one of her cruises with her friend. I was about to go to bed when I head a car door slam and what sounded like shouting."

"Like an argument?" Mrs Anders nodded. "What were they arguing about?" Ashley asked.

"I won't repeat the colourful language, but it was something about money," she said, as Ashley wrote it all down.

"Did you get a look at this woman?" She asked hopefully.

"Yes, she was slight, blonde hair and wearing a fur coat." Ashley wrote the description down.

"How can you be sure that she was a prostitute?" Ashley asked.

"The way she dressed, the way she talked," Mrs Anders clarified. "That and she came out of that house three hours later."

"Was this a regular occurrence when his mother went away?" Ashley asked. Mrs Anders nodded.

"Oh yes, I wanted to tell him that he shouldn't, but how should one broach the subject?" She said. "I mean he was making good enough money according to Joyce so why he needed them was beyond me."

Maybe because his tastes ran a little more peculiar, Ashley thought to herself. She wrote down about the frequency of the visits.

"Was it always the same girl or was it different?" Ashley asked.

"It looked like the same girl, with blonde hair," Mrs Anders replied. "But sometimes there were different guys."

"You haven't seen any strange vehicles or people outside, things like that?" Ashley asked. Mrs Anders shook her head.

"No, I haven't. I just can't believe that someone would do something like that in our neighbourhood. Can you Bert?" Mr Anders just grunted. Ashley half wondered as she drank her tea why she even bothered to ask him anything.

"Did you see or hear anything last night?" Ashley asked. Mrs Anders shook her head.

"I didn't hear anything until the sirens last night."

"What about the days beforehand?" Ashley asked. Mrs Anders thought for a moment.

"Yes, now you mention it, I thought I saw one of his 'women' walking round here the other day," she said. Ashley leaned forward in her seat.

"You did?"

"I'm sure of it." Ashley wrote it down.

"When exactly?"

"Must have been Friday."

"What time?" Mrs Anders thought.

"Must have been about teatime because I saw her as I brought Bert his tea, isn't that right Bert?" It was met by a grunt.

"Did she have any defining features, tattoos, things like that?"

"Oh, I know all the kids go in for things like that, but I didn't see one," Mrs Anders said. "She just looked normal. Blonde hair, for once conservatively dressed." Ashley jotted down the details.

"Could you remember her if you saw her face?" Ashley asked. She shook her head.

"Sorry love. I just thought that it was odd, maybe she wanted to see if he had a wife or something like that." With all the pictures of Joyce Kettings in the house Ashley doubted that very much, but it gave her enough to go on.

"Was she on her own?" Ashley asked, remembering that they were technically looking for a man. "No companion at all?" Mrs Anders shook her head.

"No, I just saw a woman."

"What about your husband, has he seen anything?" Ashley asked. Mrs Anders leaned over.

"Bert, Bert, the nice police lady is asking you a question."

"I haven't seen anything or nothing," he said from behind his paper. "I just keep my pecker out of other peoples' business." If Ashley didn't know any better, she'd say that that was a sly dig at his wife. Ashley finished her tea.

"Well thank you for your time, and the tea," Ashley said, getting to her feet. "You've been very helpful."

Ashley made her way out and looked at the notes she had made. The discovery that he was using prostitutes and that there was a woman outside the house not long before Kettings died gave Ashley some leads to go on.

First thing she did was go back round the neighbours and ask them if they had seen any women that didn't belong in the neighbourhood around or go into the house. A couple of people did and thought nothing of them as potential clients for his business.

She asked about the woman who was seen around the house in the afternoon. Most people were at work and couldn't help her; not even something to collaborate Mrs Anders' account with. That might have been a dead end, but the prostitute thing certainly had some merit to it. She'd go see her contact later to ask her to look into it. Ashley walked over to the SOCO van, where they were loading camera equipment into it.

"You OK detective?" One of them asked. Ashley nodded and looked at what looked like a tripod.

"Was that in the house?" Ashley asked.

"Uhm, yeah, in the upstairs bedroom." Ashley looked down at it.

"Can you show me please?"

The SOCO led Ashley back into Stan Kettings' bedroom, which was bare, now everything had been turned over.

"It was in here," the SOCO said, pointing to the wardrobe. Ashley opened the door and noticed that the mirror in the wardrobe door was two-way glass.

"How up to date is it?" Ashley asked.

"Pretty good quality," he said. "You don't think it was running, do you?" Ashley thought it over. He must have filmed his romps with the prostitute, maybe Armstrong's theory wasn't so bad after all. What if he was going to be using one the night he died?

"Dust it for fingerprints and have the contents sent to IT," Ashley said. "We might have caught the murder on tape."

Chapter 30

"That's a good lead," McArthur said. Ashley was on her way home and told him what she had learned.

"So why do you think he had the camera equipment?"

"I think he filmed them," Ashley said. "Maybe some of it isn't child porn but maybe girls who are young-looking."

"How do we track them down though?" McArthur asked.

"I have that covered," Ashley said, taking a left. "SOCO are dusting for prints and then they'll send what's in there to IT so they can extract what they can. But it still doesn't explain this woman walking past the house on Friday."

"Fenway, if I was you, I'd leave that," McArthur said. "Cramer thinks we're looking for a man."

"It could be an accomplice?" Ashley said. "Women statistically are more likely to be more approachable and trustworthy. It would explain why there was no forced entry on both victims."

"Unless you find something to back that up with, I would leave it," McArthur said. "We have a bit more to go on in this case. Any luck with the CCTV from the Cambrian?" Shit, that had slipped her mind, she did need to get back to the Tower and do some grunt work.

"No, but I'm on my way back now," Ashley said.

"I'll tell Parland and Armstrong to pick the pieces up on the camera lead," McArthur said. "OK, speak to you later." McArthur ended the call and Ashley sped on.

***

Ashley sat down in her chair and logged back into her computer. She got the CCTV from the Cambrian and loaded it up on to her dual screens. One screen showed the previous week and the other the current week. She was looking for anyone who came in around the same time and looked around.

She made herself a cup of tea, sat back down at her desk and loaded up the Sunday CDs.

Ashley was looking at the footage from the previous week, now keeping an eye out for a blonde woman; easier said than done when she saw lots of them. She was looking for someone who was looking around at exits, alternate routes and cameras.

Ashley could see why the killer had chosen this hotel, it was quiet and out of the way with not that many people coming through. The flip side of that was that if you acted strangely, you stood out. Ashley's mind then wondered, who would have chosen this rendezvous point? Ferrets or the killer?

After a couple of hours, viewing Sunday didn't provide anything so she went to Saturday and played that. She saw the couple from the next room along checking in again. Ashley made a note of it but thought they were telling the truth. To her at least.

Ashley put in Friday's tape and began to watch it. It would be the last one before she went home for the night; her tired eyes staring at the screens and everything still looked the same. Ashley yawned, stretched her body and looked at the time.

Half six.

Definitely time to go home now.

Ashley got her stuff and made her way down to the car park where her car was waiting for her. She had MMA tonight, but she needed to make one stop first.

***

Ashley pulled her coat more firmly round her against the night breeze. The Autumn nights were settling in nicely with fallen leaves scattered along the pathways of the local park. Ashley walked across the road to a line of shops which were mostly takeaways and hairdressers.

Ashley turned left into a small alleyway to a loading bay where a group of women were having a smoke and gossiping. As soon as one saw Ashley she scowled at her.

"Wha der yu want?" She asked, causing the others to turn around.

"It's OK, she's cool," one of the older ones said.

Kerry Thomas, or Cindy to her clients, had been on the game in Manchester for years. Ashley found her one night on her night patrol, beaten after a client turned bad. Although reluctant, Ashley had persuaded her to call the police and charge the guy, a jumped-up private school boy. The experience had forged a good, beneficial relationship.

Kerry provided Ashley with gossip on certain individuals while Ashley, when she was a beat officer turned a blind eye to her street walking. She was slim, with her hair in a pixie style with a pink fringe which complemented her black skin.

"Can we trust her?" The girl asked again. "She's a cop." Was it that obvious now? Ashley wondered.

"She's a good one," Kerry said, stubbing her cigarette out. "The only one." She walked over to Ashley with a smile.

"Here she is, miss big shot detective," Kerry said, hugging Ashley.

"Hardly," Ashley replied, not even bothering to find out how she knew, she just did. "Missing me?"

"All the time gurl," Kerry replied. "I take it this isn't a social call?" Ashley shook her head and pulled out the photo of Stan Kettings.

"Guy we're investigating," Ashley said. "Neighbours have said about girls going into this guy's house. I was hoping you would know of him, seems like a bit of a loner." Ashley handed the photo of Kettings over to Kerry who looked at it with a frown.

"I don't know him personally," she said. "Looks a little weird. How did he die?"

"Murdered," Ashley said, putting her hands back in her pockets. "Someone slit his throat." Kerry pulled a face.

"Nasty way to go," she said. "I'll have an ask around for your boy. Can't promise anything though."

"I know," Ashley said. "I have a hunch though, and I hope I'm wrong." Kerry gave her one last hug and went back to her group, while Ashley went the other way.

Chapter 31

Harold Donaldson parked up in the layby in his Range Rover and turned the lights off. He got out of the car and closed the door. It's loud echo around the deserted country lane signalling how alone he was. He pulled his coat collar up against the cold and walked down the country road. He came up to the large building he was walking to.

It was a large manor house that even in the gloom of night was a shade darker, with its tall spires standing out in the night. Donaldson pushed the gate open which creaked loudly into a driveway which was littered with moss and over laying branches from the unkept gardens.

Donaldson looked around. He remembered this place in its prime. It had been a beautiful house which he enjoyed going to.

His steps echoed on the stone steps up to a set of oak doors which was open slightly. Donaldson pushed it open to a large creaking sound. The inside of the house was just as dark as the outside, with only the moonlight lighting up certain parts of the house with white beams.

"Good, you're here." Out of one of the corridors Will Oatley came out.

"What's this all about?" Donaldson asked. "And why are we meeting here?" Oatley paced.

"Stan's dead." Donaldson turned his nose up.

"So?"

"Ferrets too," Oatley said, standing still. Donaldson stared at him.

"Since when?"

"Not sure, the police came round and asked me questions."

"What did you tell them?" Donaldson asked urgently walking towards him.

"Nothing."

"Will." Donaldson held on to his arm. "What did you tell them?"

"I told you, nothing!"

"Why didn't you call me?"

"Because then it looks like I have something to hide," Will said. "This way it was voluntary."

"Why did they contact you?"

"Because Stan, the fucking idiot, called me on his mobile and not a burner phone like I've always told him to," Oatley said. He walked over to the window which looked out on the front garden.

"The police searched his records and bam. That's why." Donaldson started to pace now, thinking it over.

"How much do they know?" He asked.

"Nothing," Will replied, looking back at him. "I told them that Stan did some IT work for me, which he does." Donaldson shrugged his shoulders in acceptance.

"OK, what else?"

"How we met, you know, normal police questions." Will got a cigarette out of his pocket and lit it.

"They didn't ask you about Gordon?"

"Yeah, they did."

"And?"

"I said I didn't know him, might have bumped into him but no, nothing."

"Fuck…" Donaldson walked up and down.

"I can find out if they've linked it with Thompson, I doubt it, but still."

"I need you to shut this down," Oatley said. Donaldson walked briskly towards him.

"Are you out of your mind? This is being done by the new Major Crimes Unit," Donaldson said. "We need that Unit to succeed."

"Even if it means taking you down to?" Oatley asked. "Because we both know what's going on."

"Taking me down?" Donaldson said, picking up on the not so veiled threat. "I think you've forgotten who's kept you out of prison all these years. Who kept all of you out of prison?" He pointed at Oatley. "This isn't just my sword to fall on Will, you push me and I will pull you down too."

Oatley didn't say anything.

"What we need is a plan," Donaldson said. "We need to lay low."

"No, we need this case gone as well. You did it with Rochdale."

"Will, that is beyond me," Donaldson said; he walked around. "This isn't some alcoholic thirteen-year-old we're talking about. We're talking about a full murder investigation."

"You did with Thompson." Donaldson shook his head.

"Things are different now," he said. "The police knew what sort of person he was. It wasn't long after they closed this place down," he shook his head. "I can't make this go away." Will paced again, he was thinking.

"What about Ian?"

"Who gives a fuck about him!" Donaldson snapped.

"If Stan and Gordon are gone..."

"What about Thomas, Dean, and all the others?" Donaldson said. "The police are going to make a link between the two of them eventually and we need to get ourselves out of the firing line."

"They don't know about this place though." Donaldson didn't look convinced.

"The only time I met Ferrets was here. The police don't know about it and the kids will be too young to put our faces to it. We're clean."

"Why did Stan phone you?"

"This again? I told you already."

"No, you didn't, why did Stan call you?" Will breathed heavily.

"We were organising a transaction." Donaldson swore under his breath and held the bridge of his nose.

"Please tell me it was for one of your new apartments on Newton Street."

"No."

"Jesus fuck."

"Will you shut up?"

"Will, this isn't the eighties anymore, you can't just buy and sell children like that; it's not that easy anymore."

"What makes you think we were doing that?"

"It's what you always do?" He said. "Has it occurred to you that the police have Stan's computer, his hard drives, his backups, his whole collection? And then the phone as well, what if they find the burner phone?"

"They can't trace it back to me."

"Why, because you two use Bitcoin? How high tech." Donaldson ran a hand over his face. "Money leaves a trail, no matter what, all it takes is someone with patience. All his transactions…" Donaldson stopped and walked away, anger getting the better of him.

"Right, if the police do find out, tell them you had no idea what he was sending over, you never opened the file. If they say you did, say you did it once to see what was inside. Got it?"

"The police won't come back to me," Will said, now having an idea.

"Why?"

"We give them something else to chase," Will said.

"Who?"

"Boyd. He still likes giving out beatings."

"How do you know that? And what does Boyd have to do with it?"

"Girls," Oatley said, not elaborating further. "He still likes beating them within an inch of their lives. We need a girl to kill him, same way as Ferrets and Stan, that way the blame goes on them. You can find that out, can't you?"

"Yes."

"We pay her to do it and then let her take the fall. Police investigation shifts." Donaldson thought it over.

"It doesn't solve who killed them though," he said.

"We don't need to. We give them a get out of jail free card, they won't risk killing anyone else," Oatley laughed.

"It's a root problem," he said, with a crooked smile. Donaldson didn't look impressed.

"OK. Who are we thinking?"

"Stan told me about a girl he fucks, Dora Sanchez, a prossie with a kid who's desperate for cash. Apparently stupid as fuck as well," Oatley sighed. "Stan called me because he wanted her out of the way."

"Didn't you ask why?" Oatley shook his head.

"Considering all the favours he's done for me this sounded relatively simple," Oatley said. "He wanted a prossie whacked, no biggie, no one was going to look for her anyway."

"So, what do we do with her now?"

"We pay her to kill Boyd, no one will miss him. We pay her to keep her mouth shut, you lean on the CPS to throw the book at her when she goes to trial. She comes out after however long, with money and her son, everyone is happy." Donaldson paced again, thinking over this plan.

"This all hinges on the fact that whoever's killing won't anymore after this," he said.

"If it's people from here it's a long list," Oatley said. "Whoever it is took out the two stupidest first. Whikley will be next, he wasn't that smart." Donaldson sighed.

"It might work."

"Of course it will. You find out how they both died, and I'll tell this Dora Sanchez what's happening. Remember that name."

"Yes, I will," Donaldson said.

"And I'll tell my contact to arrange the meet between Boyd and Sanchez." Donaldson sighed and looked around the hollow and empty room, where the walls were in various stages of full, stripped and large holes in them.

"Why did we meet here?" He asked.

"Nostalgia," Oatley said stubbing his cigarette out on the wall. "Don't act like you didn't enjoy it." Donaldson looked around the room he was in, with his back to Oatley.

"It's been a while," Donaldson said.

"I thought as much," Oatley said. "You should try and get back into it." Donaldson turned his head slightly back towards him.

"I'm in too high a position of power to do that." To Oatley it was unconvincing.

"Just means it's easier to get away with it."

"You've haven't changed one bit."

"I don't intend to start now," Oatley said, checking his watch. "Remember, I want to know how they died."

"Yeah, yeah, I will," Donaldson said, walking to the door. "How did you get in?"

"I own the place, remember?" Oatley tutted. "Idiot."

Chapter 32

Beep.

  Beep.

  Beep.

Ashley reached over and turned her alarm off; a cold chill swept her body that made her pull the duvet tighter around her. After a second, she was out of bed and getting her things together for the day, along with a cup of cold water. Gym stuff on and work stuff in her gym bag; she grabbed her keys and left.

***

Light Cardio.

  Arms.

  Core.

  Bag.

  Squats.

Ashley found the strength to push the bar up, letting out an audible grunt, and sighing in relief as it clicked into place. Ashley took a couple of deep breaths and walked to the bench while drinking from her bottle.

She sat on the bench, acutely aware of a couple of guys watching her. They had done since she started. More focused on her workout than their own. The problem with that was what that meant for her. Were they just admiring her technique, or were they thinking of something else?

Ashley checked her phone, that was all she had time for anyway. She finished her drink and made her way to the showers, thankfully none of them followed her out.

Ashley had a shower, changed into her work gear and went to walk to her car. When she got in, she checked her phone.

Kerry: *We know your boy. Meet at the usual time and place.*

"Bingo." Ashley started the car and drove away.

Chapter 33

The café they frequented was a greasy spoon in the dock area where most of the night workers came for a meal before clocking off home. Ashley was sat by the window, stirring her tea idly while looking out on the street outside. She looked across and saw Kerry and another girl who was wearing an overcoat at least three sizes too big for her, which concealed what looked like a tiny frame across the road.

Ashley looked up from her tea when Kerry and this girl walked in. She looked like a girl, maybe fourteen, maybe younger.

"Hey gurl," Kerry said, sitting down. "I want you to meet Nikita." The girl looked at Ashley like she didn't trust her. Ashley wasn't sure what much more she could do to be friendlier.

"Why don't you sit down?" She said pointing at the plastic chair. "Tea? Coffee?"

"Coffee, please," Nikita replied in a strong Russian accent and sat down next to Kerry and pulled the coat round herself more tightly.

"What about something to eat, have you two just finished?" Ashley asked. Nikita looked at Kerry to see if it was all right.

"It's all right, she won't hurt you," Kerry said. "Coffee, and have you ordered for me?" Ashley nodded. Kerry looked at Nikita who was still treating Ashley a little warily.

"Come on. She's paying, you can have what you want."

Ashley handed over a tenner and Nikita went to order at the front. After she ordered Nikita made her way back; they settled down to business. Kerry took the photo out and slid it to Ashley.

"We know your boy. He does use us," she said. "What's his name, you know, proper name?"

"Stan Kettings," Ashley said. "Is he one of yours?" Kerry shook her head and nodded to Nikita who was looking around the café.

"Toilet?" She asked.

"Down there and to the right," Ashley said, pointing behind her to a flimsy, white door. Nikita got up and went to the toilet.

"There's something you're not telling me about this," Kerry said, as soon as Nikita was out of earshot. "I know you," Kerry said pointing at her. "I'm a big girl, I can handle it." Ashley nodded, but hoped that Kerry trusted her enough to ask the questions. Besides, she was paying for breakfast, she should have some leeway.

"What about you?" Ashley asked with a raised eyebrow. "She barely looks old enough to be in secondary school, let alone on the game."

"She's legal if that's what you're asking," Kerry said. She took her coffee from the waitress and stirred. "But, some like 'em young, as you probably know." Ashley nodded and had a sip of her own tea.

"Just follow my lead," Ashley said, calmly. "I need to paint a picture, not a confession." Kerry nodded, Nikita sat back down and drank from her mug.

"Nikita." She turned around, she had bleached blonde hair and Slavic features touched up with cheap make-up. "My name is Ashley Fenway. I just want to ask you a couple of questions, nothing formal, I just want to know about this guy," she pointed to Stan Kettings. Nikita turned her nose up at the photo. She looked to Kerry.

"I know Ashley, she's cool." Nikita looked at Ashley.

"You won't turn me in?" She asked.

"You have my word," Ashley said. "Kerry trusts me, I hope you can trust me too." Nikita looked again at Kerry and back at Ashley and nodded.

"He's strange," Nikita said. "He always requests me, or girls like… me," she said, quietly.

"He likes you young," Ashley said. Nikita nodded.

"How long has he been using you for?" Ashley said, clicking the top of her pen.

"I've only been to him for couple of years," Nikita said. "Other girls longer." Kerry and Ashley shared a knowing look. Nikita was the only one willing to talk to her.

"Did he ever ask you to do strange things?" Ashley asked. "Wear anything you didn't want to?" Nikita got her phone out. She swiped a couple of times and showed Ashley what looked like a gown. It was grey with a white trim that seemed to go down to someone's feet.

"He made you wear this?" Nikita nodded.

"To start," she said, shrugging. "Not the weirdest though, he always made us take it off." Ashley jabbed her pen on her notebook. As she did so, Nikita and Kerry's food arrived. So, he was using prostitutes but only to stop himself from abusing again, Ashley mused.

"Does he do it to the other girls?" Ashley asked.

Nikita nodded. "He was harmless really," she said. "He had kinks like all other guys and girls."

"Was there anything else?"

"He liked us to cry," Nikita said. "He paid more, but that's what he wanted us to do." Ashley wrote that down, that was strange.

"But he wasn't violent?" Ashley asked.

"Rough," Nikita said, through a mouthful of food. "But not violent."

"Did he video you at all?" Ashley asked. Nikita fervently shook her head and swallowed her food.

"I don't like film," she said. "Other girls charge more but I don't." Ashley had a feeling that Nikita had been videoed without her consent.

"Did he ever pretend that you were someone else?" Ashley asked. "Some people ask for it?" Ashley was hoping that Nikita would give her a name, if he had a fascination with one of them then it could be a lead.

"Now you mention it," Nikita said, through another mouthful. "He did call me Lisa a couple of times."

"Lisa?" Ashley asked, not knowing where that name was coming from. Nikita nodded. Ashley wrote that down; who was Lisa and what connection did she have to Stan Kettings?

"Did he say that to any of the other girls?" Ashley asked. Nikita shrugged.

"He might do; we don't discuss client's personals unless they're really strange or violent," Nikita explained.

"Could you ask around if he did?" Ashley asked. "I want to find out who this Lisa is." Nikita looked at Kerry who nodded.

"I only talk with Cindy," she said.

"Fair enough," Ashley said. "Just tell her and she knows how to contact me." Ashley paid for breakfast and sent them on their way. Ashley got her phone out of her pocket and looked down at what she needed to do.

Chapter 34

Ashley walked back into the office. On the board for Kettings she took the pen and wrote about the blonde woman seen outside the house and circled if it was linked to his use of prossies. She sat back down in her chair, her stare piercing the board.

Did this mean that there were two killers working together or was it just the one? Based on the post-mortems they were most likely looking for a man, based on the force of the wounds to the back of the head and the neck. Plus, statistically speaking almost all mass murderers were men.

Ashley sat at her computer and logged into HOLMES, the police database which catalogued evidence for large cases like this. She used it to look at the inventory for Stan Kettings' house from SOCO. Ashley searched through it for any mention of a grey gown, but it wasn't on there... had the killer taken it?

Or was Nikita lying to her?

"Fenway."

Ashley turned her head and saw McArthur walking towards her.

"There you are, where were you this morning for the meeting?"

"Chasing down a lead, Sir," Ashley said.

"Which one?"

"The prostitute one, Sir."

"Well how did it go?"

"They confirmed that Stan Kettings did use them, Sir," Ashley said. "My source says that he had a particular liking to young-looking girls and has been using them for a number of years."

"All with the same preference?"

"Yes, Sir. I've asked them to look into it a little more but I'm not holding out much hope. Although one person said that he liked to call her Lisa."

"Lisa?" Ashley shrugged. "Have you come across a Lisa?"

"No. Ferrets never referred to a Lisa in his notes." Ashley said. "Maybe a girl he used to abuse?" McArthur nodded.

"She also mentioned that he used to make them wear this gown." She showed McArthur the gown. "But there's no mention of it in SOCO's report on HOLMES." McArthur frowned.

"Always take evidence like this with a pinch of salt," he said. "She could have been mistaken or maybe he got rid of it."

"Or the killer took it."

"Possible, but unlikely, why would they?" McArthur replied. Ashley didn't have an answer. "If SOCO didn't find it then he probably got rid of it. Also, we followed that Ewan around and we may have found his source."

"Who?"

"Some low life connected to the Tunnicliffe family," McArthur said. "We've referred him to the robbery section." When did they start getting into robbing people in that sort of area, Ashley wondered?

"Anyway, I have a job for you today," he said. Ashley pushed herself up in the chair. "That list of yours from the civil suit came really good but there's still one name on it that we can't track down."

"Kate Marsh?" McArthur nodded.

"I can have a look. She might have changed her name for all I know."

"Even so, I want you to take a look for me," he said. "Plus, there does seem to be a link between Ferrets and Kettings on the Bitcoin front; IT were able to pull the transactions from the computer you liberated."

"That's good, right?"

"Yes and no. Thanks to the ledgers Kettings kept we were able to line up payments which was a link, but we can't find anything on Ferrets' end." Ashley leaned back in her chair, what if Tracy Ferrets knew of one.

"You have an idea?"

"Maybe," Ashley said. "Maybe Tracy Ferrets knows of an account he might have used. Are you sure they went back through his compensation account?"

"Maybe you could double check for me."

"I'll get IT to send me over the ledgers, and I'll look into Kate Marsh as well."

"Thanks Fenway." McArthur walked off and Ashley fell back into her chair, wondering how she had been able to create more work for herself.

"Here they are, Manchester's finest." Ashley looked up and saw Harold Donaldson coming through with an entourage of people. Ashley looked over at Murphy who shared the same look of confusion.

"Working hard everybody?" He asked. McArthur came out of his office.

"Mr Donaldson," he said, shaking the Deputy Mayor's hand. "DCI McArthur, this is a nice surprise. I didn't realise you were coming."

"I was just making sure that the department had everything that it needed," Donaldson said. He looked around at the room and then at the boards.

"New case DCI McArthur?"

"Yes, Sir," McArthur said, looking at the board.

"Nasty way to go," Donaldson said, looking at the photos of Ferrets and Kettings.

"Would you like a tour, Sir?" McArthur asked.

"That would be great, thank you." As they all marched away Ashley looked over at Murphy.

"Bit bold isn't it. I didn't realise that he could waltz in like this," Murphy said.

"More to the point, we've been open for a while, why come in now?"

"Must be election season," Murphy said, getting up.

She set about gathering the information she needed. She ventured out into the new pool and got the records on Kettings' ledgers; once that was done, she phoned her friend Aaron, in IT.

"IT Aaron speaking."

"Hey stranger," Ashley said, flicking through the ledgers. "Can you do me a favour?"

"I'll add to the list."

"Can you send me over the analysis you guys did on the computer I brought in?" Ashley said. "DCI McArthur wants me to have a look over it."

"I can tell you now, it's shit."

"I grew up on a farm, I'm used to the smell," Ashley said. "How are things with you?"

"Fine, I guess," he said. "Been really busy, it's not just you guys who think we're at your beck and call." Ashley wasn't in the mood for people bitching about her doing her job.

"Well, we're all busy," she said, looking at her computer she saw the icon from Aaron come up on the screen.

"Thanks."

"Are you OK?"

"Fine," Ashley said, rubbing her eyes with the heel of her palm. "I'm just tired. I'll text you later." Ashley placed the phone down and sighed deeply, running a hand through her hair.

Ashley made herself a brew and started to go through the paperwork. She should have thought with someone with such a meticulous nature as Kettings would have his finances in order. The ledger had very specific denominations in which Bitcoin was transacted; the amount his processors brought, as well as all the costs that had been off-set.

Ashley highlighted what she needed to, checked the payments coming in and how Kettings recorded it all. From the looks of the names they were codes or nicknames.

Ashley checked all of Ferrets' financials to see if any payments synced up. Despite her best efforts Ashley couldn't see the link; Ferrets might have been using an account no one knew about.

"You look stressed, Fenway," Parland said. He had been milling around for an hour or so.

"Frustrated," Ashley said. "Why can't people have their financial affairs in order?"

"How are yours?"

"Not the point," Ashley said. "I think Ferrets has an account he used for his Bitcoin transactions. I just don't know what. With all the conversion rates it's stupid to track.

"Maybe his daughter knows," Parland offered.

"I thought that too," Ashley said.

"Fancy a drive?" Ashley needed air; she got up and grabbed her coat.

Chapter 35

Ashley pulled up outside Tracy Ferrets' house on the estate. There was a police officer standing outside the door with a now boarded-up window. Ashley and Parland got out the car and walked up to the door.

Ashley looked around the estate and saw people looking through curtains to get a peep at them. Others were more brazen and stood in their doorways.

Ashley looked up at the window at the front which was now boarded-up. On the woodchip someone had sprayed graffiti on it.

PEDO!

"Classy," Parland said, with a grimace.

"They don't know any better," Ashley said, nodding at the officer guarding the door. She remembered those long shifts standing outside, rain and shine. "Do you want a cuppa?"

"Could murder one," Ashley smiled to herself when he suddenly realised what he said. "Sorry, I…"

"It's fine," Ashley said, walking through. "How do you take it? The tea — before you get the wrong idea."

"Milk, no sugar," he said, rubbing his hands together. Ashley knocked on the door and one of their specialist officers opened it. It was Sharon from before.

"Good, you're here," she said, letting them in. Ashley went in first into the dark, cramped corridor which didn't feel much warmer. Ashley walked into the kitchen and began to make a cup of tea for the officer outside.

"So how bad has it been?" Parland asked.

"They had a brick through their window on Tuesday, Wednesday they had petrol shoved through the door; it wouldn't light, and then this morning," she pointed to the front door.

"I guess you saw what's on there."

"Yeah, we did," Parland said, sitting at the table. "Milk, one sugar Fenway." Ashley pulled a face and got another cup from the cupboard.

"People round here are really close. Lots of single mothers and young families on low income. Even if Tracy isn't involved it's guilty by association," Sharon said sitting down, her own mug on the table. "The thing is, she's just as much a victim."

"How are they coping?" Ashley asked. She went to hand Parland the mug.

"Cheers Fenway," he said, taking it.

"Oh, that's not yours," Ashley said. "I'm sure the officer at the door will be grateful when you take it out to him." Parland couldn't believe she had just done that. With a grumble he got to his feet. As he left, Ashley sat down in his space with her own glass of water.

"How is Tracy coping?" Ashley asked, as Parland walked out.

"It's been difficult for her," Sharon said. "She's been agitated about everything that's happened."

"Understandably so," Ashley agreed. "How did the locals find out?"

"Gordon was a well-known scout for one of the Manchester clubs. He helped scout a couple of boys from the estate." Ashley nodded and Parland came back in.

"Where's my tea?"

"Everything you need is on the side," Ashley said turning around, smiling sweetly at him. "Kettle just boiled too." Parland grunted irritably.

"Where is Tracy?" Ashley asked.

"She's outside, taken the kids to the park at the back."

"Is that really safe?" Parland asked.

"She has a couple of officers with her," Sharon wheezed. "She wanted to get the kids out."

"I'm going to talk to her," Ashley said, getting up.

"Detective!" Before Sharon could finish, Ashley was pulling the backdoor open and walking into the garden.

"She does that," Parland said, sitting down with his tea.

Ashley was in the back garden, which was full of overgrown grass, weeds, and broken, rusted toys that had been abandoned to the elements. Ashley zipped up her jacket fully and opened the gate into the park area.

The park was at the back of the estate with all the houses backing onto it. It was an oval field with a small park in the corner. Ashley could see them as she walked over. Tracy was on the outskirts of the rusted, metal gate of the park watching her two children playing. What Ashley could also see was four police officers, on each corner of the park. Tracy was waving to her daughter as she went down the slide.

"Finally showed up did ya?" Tracy asked not looking back. "Funny what you people will do." She still had her hair in a high, taught ponytail but there were visibly more lines and bags under her eyes.

"I didn't realise it was this bad," Ashley said, now standing beside her.

"Well, you try and keep two kids calm when the whole estate wants to kill ya," Tracy said, bitterly. "I didn't even do anything wrong." Tracy pulled a packet of cigarettes from her jacket pocket, she slipped one out and lit it quickly, puffing smoke into the cold air.

"Have you found him yet?" She asked abruptly. She gripped the metal railing, flakes of paint falling slowly to the ground.

"Sorry?"

"My dad's killer. Have you found him yet?" She dragged on her cigarette.

"We're still looking," Ashley said. "We have a couple of leads." Tracy laughed humourlessly to herself.

"I know how this works with people like him," she said. "Never going to look into the death of a nonce are ya?"

"Well, we are," Ashley said. "He was a person too." Tracy took a long drag.

"He was a good dad and grandad," she said, quietly. She dropped the cigarette which fell slowly in the wind onto the tarmac.

"He was a monster though." Tracy stamped on the butt.

"You know, I thought grief would be the worst of it," Tracy said. "But having to ask your own kids if grandad touched them at all, or took pictures." She shuddered at the thought. She slipped out another cigarette.

"But I still want justice," she said. "Maybe he had been a monster but he was still a good dad and grandad." Tracy looked down. "No one deserves to die that way." She puffed on her cigarette

"No one round here cares that he died. No one else cares if I die. Mum certainly doesn't care. It kinda feels like I have to."

"Do you know who attacked your house?" Ashley asked, trying to stay on point. Tracy pointed all around her with her hand.

"Everyone," she said. "Everyone's in on it." Ashley got her notepad out.

"Names?" Tracy scoffed.

"No bloody chance."

"How do you expect us to do something if you don't give us names?" Tracy flicked her cigarette away.

"Do you know why they didn't light the petrol in our letter box?" Ashley shook her head. "It was a warning," Tracy explained. "I want a safehouse. I can't keep the kids here any longer. That fucking mouth-breather Sharon is no bloody help." Ashley looked out on the park.

"Well, we don't give out something for nothing," Ashley said. "There are still a couple of things missing from your dad's personal affects."

"I told you all I know."

"Let me ask you the question," Ashley said. "It looks like your dad was involved with Bitcoin." She looked up at Tracy's blank expression. "It's a cryptocurrency."

"I know, I watch the news," she said, defensively. Ashley didn't believe her.

"Anyway. He wasn't using an account that we found on him or his flat. Was he using one that you knew about?" Tracy looked at the floor.

"Tracy."

"No…"

"Tracy, play the odds," Ashley said, shaking her head. "Can you really afford to not turn down our help now?" Tracy said nothing. Ashley pulled out the big gun. "Can you really afford to keep your kids safe from this place?" Ashley pointed around her.

"You tell me what I want to know, and I can have you and the kids in a safe house in an hour," Ashley said. "But you have to play ball with me. If not, what was the point of you calling us down here if you're not going to give us anything?" Tracy looked out on her kids.

"It can't be any worse than what you've had to go through already," Ashley reasoned. Tracy took a deep breath.

"My grandma died two years ago," Tracy said, looking down. "She was still getting money in from benefits, since dad couldn't work because of what happened," she laughed, humourlessly. "He was living off her benefits."

"What was her name?"

"Jenny Ferrets," Tracy said. "Look... I've been using it as well for a bit of... extra income." Ashley stopped taking notes momentarily. It seemed sad to her that this was what people were reduced to. She looked up at Tracy who was starting to cry.

"Look, it'll be OK," Ashley said. "Let me put the call in and get yourselves back to the house. OK?" Tracy nodded. Ashley walked back to the house and pulled her phone out, dialling McArthur.

"McArthur."

"Sir, it's Fenway. I've got a lead on the account Ferrets might have been using."

"Good work. What is it?"

"Ferrets' mum was on benefits. He was still raking the money in after her death." McArthur let out a low grunt.

"Right. Will you look into that?"

"Yeah, I will," Ashley said. "Tracy's also coming under some severe abuse from the estate she lives on; I think we should move her to a safe house, albeit temporarily."

"Do you think we should?"

"I think we should 'til it all dies down. Just a change of scenery could help her," Ashley said.

"OK, I'll have a word with a friend of mine," McArthur said. "You and Parland get back here and look for that account."

"Yes, Sir." Ashley opened the gate back into Tracy's garden.

"Parland, we have a lead on the account Gordon Ferrets was using," Ashley said. "Boss wants us back."

"What about Tracy?" Parland asked.

"McArthur's organising a safe house. Sharon you're going to have to help them pack," Ashley told her. "We've been called back."

Chapter 36

Ashley found the account Tracy told her about. Jenny Ferrets died in 2015 and had her benefits transferred into a Barclays account. Ashley was able to have it sent over to her and started to go through it herself.

It was hard work, but she was finally able to line up the payments, using the exchange converter Kettings used, and Ferrets' financials. Ashley was busy in one of the conference rooms with her highlighters and the calculator app on her phone, putting it all together.

"Jesus." Parland had come into the room.

"What have you found?" Ashley looked up at him. She blew a few strands of hair from her face and consulted the notepad that she had written her calculations on.

"I think my GCSE maths is right," Ashley said, frowning at her notepad. "In which case, I might have been able to link our two guys."

Parland looked at her calculations briefly and handed them back to her.

"I was shit at maths."

"Go figure," Ashley said. "You might want someone from the university look this over, but I think I'm right."

"I trust you," Parland said.

Ashley nodded, filed it away with the rest of the paperwork and went back to her other task; tracking down Kate Marsh.

While Ashley had Google open, she searched for Kate Marsh. The name came up, but she wasn't sure what sort of person she was looking at. She scrolled through the Facebook profiles and Twitter pages. She wasn't surprised they hadn't found this woman yet. They didn't even know what she looked like.

Ashley grabbed her coat and took the address Marsh had given the Evening News.

***

Ashley was in her car looking at Kate Marsh's last known address. It was a block of flats in a cul-de-sac, number seventeen on the first floor. Ashley was drinking a Lucozade Sport and looking at the house. The curtains were drawn, and no one had come or gone in the last two hours.

One suspicious thing she did notice was the same Audi A4 constantly driving up and down the road. It gave Ashley something else to think about.

The area was notorious for its recreational substances, so she guessed it was the drug squad for the local area.

But that was also likely to mean someone was spaced out in the flat. Probably not the same person, but then again, the police loved coincidences. She was now busy on her phone trying to find out who owned this place. Her only lead so far was that there was a renting company, Garrets, advertising all four of the flats up for rent; maybe they acted as an agent.

Ashley found the number and phoned up. The A4 was now parked across the street from her.

"Hello, Garrets' renting agency, Jemma speaking."

"Hi, this is DC Fenway with Manchester Major Crimes Unit. I was hoping you could assist me in an enquiry." Ashley's gaze was still on the A4.

"OK DC Fenway, how can I help?"

"We're looking for a Kate Marsh, we understand she was renting one of your flats in the Sound Edge area, seventeen Sutton Heights." The woman started to type.

"Yes, she rented that flat for a while," Jemma said. "She moved on about four years ago."

"I suppose she didn't leave a forwarding address?"

"She did but it's company policy to get rid of it after two years." Ashley wanted to swear.

"Can you tell me who lives in it now?" More typing.

"Jacob Musonda," Jemma said.

"Has he been in there since Ms Marsh left?" Ashley asked. A few more types on the keyboard.

"Yes, he has been, always pays his rent on time, not had any trouble from him." Ashley looked back up at the house and narrowed her eyes. She looked at the undercover squad in front of her.

"Thank you, Jemma, you've been very helpful." One of them got out of the car and walked towards her.

"Glad to help detective, have a nice day."

"You too." There was a rasping knock on her window. Ashley lowered it.

"Hi, is there a problem?" She asked. The man was youngish, short and stubby with a precise haircut, probably ex-army Ashley thought.

"DS Lewington, Drugs," he said, showing her his ID. Ashley smiled.

"I don't have any," Ashley quipped. Lewington's face frowned disapprovingly.

"DC Fenway. Major Crimes," she said, showing him her ID. "So, problem?"

"What are you doing here?" Lewington asked.

"Chasing a lead. You?"

"Not doing that much chasing if you're sat in the car for two hours," he said.

"Don't tell me you thought I was a suspect in something did you?" Lewington swallowed hard.

"The Tunnicliffe Family is known to use pretty girls as mules." Ashley quirked an eyebrow.

"Oh, I see how it is, one look at the beamer and that's it, drug dealers' car," she said.

"No, that's not what I meant."

"Who are you looking for, Private?" Ashley asked. Lewington narrowed his eyes at her.

"Jacob Musonda," he said.

"Small world," Ashley said, putting the window up and getting out. "So am I." Ashley shut her door.

"And it's Lance Corporal."

"Suppose that sounds better than seaman Lewington," Ashley said.

242

"We have him under surveillance on a long cover op," Lewington said, trying to sound impressive.

"So, why don't you toddle off home and ask my superiors for what info you need on him?" Ashley shrugged.

"I don't want him for drugs. I want an address from him," she said. "And don't talk to me like you're the dog's bollocks; if you were really important you would be in the car." Lewington went to speak but couldn't find the words.

Ashley walked past him to the house.

"Hey, you can't go up there!" He shouted after.

"Wow, really covert, private," Ashley said, pulling the hood of her jacket up. She turned around and walked backwards to the gate.

"How about you wait there and let the real officer do her work?" Ashley nodded at him and walked up the stairs, while it sounded like he was arguing with his colleagues over the radio. Ashley got to the first floor, walked across to number seventeen and banged on the door.

Nothing, just as she suspected.

She knocked again. Thankfully Lewington hadn't followed her up. She finally heard movement.

"One sec ma mon." The chain on the door came off and Jacob opened the door.

He was big, well-built, black with long, grey dreadlocks down to his shoulders. He was in sweatpants and shirtless as well.

"Who are you little bird?" He asked rubbing his eyes.

"You're not Kate," Ashley said.

"Do I look like a Kate to you?" He asked.

"She's a friend of mine, I just got out," Ashley lied. "She said I could come visit." Jacob shook his head.

"No, she gone little bird, way gone," he said, in his thick Rastafari accent.

"Did she leave her new address?" Ashley asked hopefully.

"Yeah, little bird." He went into his entrance hall where a small chest of drawers was. He had a route through and pulled out a card. He wrote an address down on a note pad by the phone, tore the paper off and handed it to Ashley.

"She lives there now little bird," he said. "Now unless you want some gear, can you let me sleep?"

"No, thank you," Ashley said, now walking back with the paper in hand. She walked back down the brick steps where Lewington was waiting for her.

"Well?" Ashley waved the paper as she walked past him.

"Did he say anything else?" He pressed.

"Offered me some gear, whatever that is," Ashley said. Lewington swore.

"Can you give a statement?"

"I'll type one up and send it over private," Ashley said, as she got to her car. "Sorry, love to stay but I'm chasing a lead." She pulled on the paper to make it taught. She could overhear on his radio.

"Mate, you should ask for your balls back from her before she goes."

"See ya round." Ashley started her car and drove off, leaving DS Lewington looking deflated.

Chapter 37

Ashley pulled up outside a nice suburban home; this was the last name on her list. Kate Marsh. Ashley could see her; brunette hair and a slim figure who was sat in the living room. Ashley got out of the car and walked to the front door. Before she got there though the door opened, and a man walked out with various camera equipment.

"Hi, are you a friend of Kate's?" He asked. At least she was on the right track.

"Not exactly," Ashley said. "DC Ashley Fenway." She flashed her ID

"Ian Whikley, I'm a photographer, just taken Kate's photo for her passport."

"That's nice, I just need to ask her a few questions," Ashley said, walking past him.

Kate Marsh was at the mouth the open door, there was something… familiar about her.

"Kate Marsh?"

"If you're a reporter I don't want anything to do with you," Kate said, going to shut the door.

"I'm not a reporter," Ashley said, showing Kate her ID. "My name is Ashley Fenway, I'm with the Manchester Major Crimes Unit." Kate narrowed her eyes at the piece of paper. She looked around to make sure none of her neighbours were watching.

"Come in," she said, walking back into the house and seeing Ashley through, before shutting it roughly. She walked down the hall and turned right into a tidy living room.

"Would you like a tea, coffee?" She asked.

"Tea please, milk no sugar." Kate nodded curtly and walked onward into a kitchen which gave Ashley the time to have a quick snoop around. The house was well furnished, newish sofa and large, flat-screen TV along with some art of fields on the walls. Ashley walked over to the bookcases.

You can tell a lot about a person by their bookcase, or lack of it. Most of them were romance novels; Sophie Kinsella being a favourite with some books on agriculture. Ashley heard the stirring of a spoon in a cup and sat down on the sofa. Marsh came in and handed her a mug.

"Thanks," Ashley said, taking her notepad out and clicking her pen.

"*You* are a very difficult woman to find," Ashley said. Kate half smiled and laughed.

"I knew that this might come out one day," she said, looking round her living room. "That's why I came here. That is why you're here isn't it?" Her gaze suddenly fell on Ashley, her eyes slightly constricting, as if to gauge her reaction.

"I'm here to talk to you about Gordon Ferrets," Ashley said. Kate half laughed again and shook her head.

"Ferrets is history to me," she said. "I've moved on, it's something you'll have to do one day. You'll have to leave all the hurt and the misery where it belongs. In the past."

"You were vocal about it at the time," Ashley said. "Why stop?"

"Because people didn't want to look deeper," Kate said. "I take it you spoke to all the others, that's why you're here." Ashley nodded.

"So, why now?" Kate asked.

"He's dead," Ashley explained. "We're looking into the people who were part of the civil suit."

"Oh yeah, that," Marsh said with disdain. "I'm sure everyone has told you that they'd rather just forget about it.

"That seems to be the case," Ashley said. "Was it really badly run?"

"No, we thought we had a good case," Kate explained. "Ferrets though was always cosy with the council."

She wondered what this woman's connection to Ferrets was. Ferrets was almost exclusively interested in young boys. Now she thought about it, Kate Marsh was one of the few names on the civil suit that was female.

"How did you get involved in the civil suit?" Ashley asked.

"Ferrets raped me when I was a teenager, after a night out," Kate explained.

"A friend mentioned the name Gordon Ferrets and about how he was…" She paused.

"It's OK, take your time," Ashley said. "I know it must be difficult." Kate looked up with a dark look on her face, probably not aimed at Ashley but still a little unsettling.

"Thanks," she said, now looking away from Ashley, as if her gaze was a bright light.

"She told me about how he was abusing kids. I wanted to show that he was an all-round sex predator, that way it would have more credence." Ashley nodded.

"Is there anyone who can back that up?"

"There are only a few other people who could confirm it. Connor Goldson and Emma Curtis are two I know of." Ashley nodded.

"Have you heard of a man called Stan Kettings?" Ashley asked. She shook her head.

"No, I haven't," Kate said. "Wait, wasn't he on the news?" She asked, handing Ashley the photo back.

"Yes, he died," Ashley said, slipping it back into her jacket pocket.

"What's he got to do with Gordon Ferrets?" Kate asked. I wish I knew too, Ashley thought.

"Just something we're asking people involved," Ashley said. Kate nodded in acceptance.

"Where were you on Sunday last week between three and six p.m.?" Ashley asked.

"In my allotment," Kate said, pointing out back.

"Can anyone collaborate that?" Ashley asked.

"My neighbour, Sally," she said. "I also help her with her allotment."

"Is she in?" Ashley asked.

"Yeah, I'm about to look in on her anyway," Kate said, getting to her feet. Ashley got up and saw a photo of Kate and what looked like her daughter; both had blonde hair. Something snapped in Ashley's head; the blonde woman Mrs Anders told her about.

"Are you naturally blonde?" She asked. Kate looked back with a quirked expression. Ashley pointed to the photo.

"No, I decided on a change a couple of years ago and changed back," Kate said. "I prefer it brown." Ashley smiled, annoyed that her idea was out the window. "Come on. Sally's waiting for us." Ashley watched as Kate grabbed a couple of things from the kitchen and went outside.

Ashley followed her to the next house where Kate pulled out a key and entered a dark house.

"Sally, Sally are you in here?"

"In the living room Kate." An elderly voice rang out. Ashley followed Kate through a dark house which looked like it hadn't been decorated since the '90s. They took a left into a living room where an old woman sat on a sofa. She was dressed but Ashley saw her milky white eyes.

She was blind.

"Hello, Sally, how are you?" Kate asked.

"I'm very well Kate," Sally said.

"I've brought you some dinner," Kate said. "It's chicken. I'll put it in the oven for you, just ask your carers to take it out when they come next.

"You have a friend with you," Sally said.

"Yes, I'm DC Ashley Fenway."

"Oh, are you in trouble Kate?"

"Me, no," Kate shouted from the kitchen.

"Is that true?" Sally asked.

"I just need you to confirm that Kate was here last Sunday afternoon," Ashley said. "She says she was helping you in the allotment?"

"Yes, she was," Sally said. Ashley couldn't hide her disappointment. "Kate's so helpful, she helps me keep my garden looking great." Ashley wanted to point out it was futile but instead nodded, which again was futile. But something was eating away at her, it seemed too plausible an excuse.

"How often does Kate come over?" Ashley asked. "You two seem to have a routine going."

"Kate comes and helps me most days," Sally said. "I keep telling her that she shouldn't, but she refuses. I used to babysit her daughter see."

"Right, if I can ask a personal question. How long ago did you lose your sight?"

"About five years ago dear," Sally said. "I have carers come in four times a day and they help me."

"So, what does Kate do?" Ashley asked, curious about what Kate did that carers couldn't.

"She just pops in to chat," Sally said, nodding. "She also cooks a meal for me for my carers to serve me and does some odd jobs about the house, and her daughter comes around to do some jobs too." Ashley nodded.

"And to do some work in the garden too," Ashley pointed out.

"That's more during the summer," Sally said. "But Kate keeps an eye on both our allotments." As she was explaining this, Ashley looked over at the door where Kate was putting a dish into the oven. Was Kate really a good Samaritan? Or had the police turned Ashley so cynical to the point where she questioned everyone's acts of kindness, as a dubious plot to undermine them.

"She's a nice person," Ashley said, finally.

"She is," Sally said. "I have a daughter who wants nothing to do with me. Kate is more of a child to me than anything." Sally's hand wandered around, Ashley looked round and saw a cup and saucer. Ashley reached over and placed it in her hands.

"Thank you," Sally said, taking a sip. "Kate said she isn't close to her parents." Can't imagine why Ashley thought.

"It's a strange type of family, but family isn't always blood, it's what we make it." Ashley nodded and Kate walked back in.

"Dinners on, Sally," she said. "And your washing is out on the line."

"Thank you," Sally croaked.

"I've taken up too much of your time," Ashley said, closing her notebook. "Thanks for talking to me Sally, take care."

"You too dear," Sally said, as they walked out.

"You do a good thing for her."

"I try my best," Kate replied. "She used to look after Tammy, my daughter when I was working, it's the least I can do for her." Ashley made her way to the front of Kate's house and she saw her out. While she walked down the path something came across Ashley's mind.

"Ms Marsh," Ashley said, turning back. "Did you know anyone called Lisa who was part of the case?" Kate paused, her lips pursing slightly.

"No. Can't say that I do."

"It's only because we're looking for a woman called Lisa too," Ashley explained.

"Must have been after my time," Kate said. Ashley nodded and went to walk away.

"Ms Fenway." Ashley looked back at Kate. Kate looked down at her feet and then back at Ashley. "If you need to talk to me again, you can always do so."

"Thanks," Ashley said, walking back to her car.

What an odd thing to say Ashley thought. The whole thing seemed too well thought out for her liking. She got into her car and afforded one last look at the window where Kate was looking at her. Ashley started the car and drove off.

"Phone DCI McArthur." The Bluetooth started making the call.

"Fenway, what have you got?"

"I've just finished speaking to Kate Marsh," Ashley said.

"Great, and?" Ashley took a deep breath.

"She seems to check out," Ashley said.

"You don't sound sure," McArthur said, sensing her doubt.

"Ever had that feeling that something falls into place too easily."

"All too often," McArthur replied. "What is her alibi?"

"A blind neighbour who she helps look after," Ashley said, "But it's not just that. Her whole demeanour is off."

"What do you mean?" Ashley breathed out, mulling over what was the best way to describe it.

"Remember how most of Ferrets abuse victims where bitter and twisted about what happened to them."

"Yes."

"She seems to have made peace with everything; she's moved on with her life."

"Maybe we should be happy for her then."

"I know what I mean," Ashley said. "I'm going to ask for a copy of the civil suit against Ferrets, I think there might be something in there. I'll talk to you tomorrow, I'm fried."

"OK, see you later." Ashley stopped the call and drove back towards the city, the odd interaction still playing through her mind. During her time with the police she had spoken to survivors of child abuse. Almost all of them were bitter and wallowed in self-pity, while Kate was seemingly over it. Maybe she was the exception to the rule.

Chapter 38

Beep.

    Beep.

    Beep.

Ashley turned around under her duvet, bleary eyed and turned her alarm off, her body still tired from hockey training the previous night. She instantly pulled her covers back and started to get her gym gear on and do her morning routine. She was in the kitchen making her lunch and listening to the radio, which was talking about Robert Mugabe being removed from government. But still no more news on their murders. They must be doing a good job of keeping it out of the public eye.

Cardio.

Arms.

Core.

Squats.

Bag.

It was going to be another long day — she could feel it. Hopefully the civil suit against Ferrets would be on her desk when she got in. She punched the bag one last time and took her gloves off.

***

Walking down Manchester high street, don't think I heard a word of English, what happened to integration? #ourcountryourlanguage

    Someone told me today I was beautiful in polish and I am over the moon! #canthisdaygetanybetter #damnright #boysgottaste

Ashley saw it on her desk from the door. A thick-looking box which could only mean one thing. Ashley walked over. On top of it was a note.

"Happy Hunting."

Ashley threw the note away, started her computer up and went to make her porridge and tea. She sat back down at her desk and started to look at the boards to see where they were with the investigation.

Tim Williams had been going back to his day job so surveillance on him had stopped. Ashley looked up and saw that her lead on the woman outside Ferrets' place hadn't been picked up by anyone.

Gradually everyone came in, while Ashley tied up a couple of loose things. McArthur came out of his office at nine for the morning briefing.

"OK everyone." McArthur stood in front of the board. "Let's have a quick brainstorm to see what's going on. Fenway, let's start with you." Ashley got her notes out.

"I found Kate Marsh," she said. "Saw her yesterday, and she has solid alibis for Ferrets and Kettings and didn't even seem to know victim two, so we can cross her off the list." McArthur put a cross through Kate Marsh's name.

"I've also got a copy of Ferrets' civil suit." Ashley patted the box of Ferrets case. "I'm gonna have a look through this and see if I can find anything else, but I'm not sure what else there is after that."

"Armstrong. How is CCTV around Fawkes Drive?"

"There's hardly anything Guv," he said.

"Manc Cams don't go out that far; none of the neighbours have CCTV and Kettings didn't even have one of this own."

"OK; Parland."

"Tim Williams is in the clear, I've been tailing him, and he's just been going about his normal life."

"So, what you're all saying is that we are no closer to finding out who killed these two men," McArthur said.

"We're ticking things off all the time Skip," Parland said. "We'll try and find some more links today."

"Yeah, do that. Fenway, has your source come back on the girls Kettings used?"

"No Sir."

"Let me know if anything else comes of it.

"I know a few people on the game, should I ask them?" Armstrong asked.

"Me too."

"Yes, ask around, it might be a murderous pimp going around," McArthur said. "Ashley put this up on the board as well, about a woman loitering outside the Kettings' house. Murphy, Parland, I want you two to go back to our vic's neighbours and ask them if they saw a woman loitering outside either of their houses." Both nodded.

Everyone dispersed. Ashley sat down and placed the paperwork for Ferrets' Civil Suit on her desk. She wanted to see why this suit came about. It was from a group of parents who were told by their sons that they had been abused by Ferrets on the way to training and at his house with the promise of stardom.

Ashley skipped through all the testimonies because they sounded pretty much all the same but stopped at Kate Marsh's.

Her testimony said she had been raped by Ferrets as she walked home from the pub, after a night out of underage drinking. She never reported it at the time but could identify him as he was known around her area. The report said that this happened in 1984, which would have made Marsh fifteen at the time of the attack.

But Ashley's previous hunch about Marsh being the only woman was correct, so her name stuck out like a sore thumb. Ashley looked at the lawyers reasoning for taking this to trial.

The defendant has a history of singular abuse cases which have been routinely covered up by local authority and charities. The defendant was also named in a separate case against the 'New Agers'; a religious sect embroiled in the abuse of young boys and girls brought by Didsbury Abused Women New Shelter.

Ashley reread the paragraph. Ferrets had been named in this? Ashley tried to find anything referring to this case, but it wasn't mentioned in the paperwork again.

Ashley got onto Google and tried searching for this case but was hit by a wall of 'no results found'. Ashley tried searching for Didsbury Abused Women New Shelter. A few sparse results came up but that was to be expected as they kept under the radar, but one did reveal an address.

Ashley got her coat.

***

The shelter was an old, red brick building which looked innocuous from the outside; it could have been a house that you walked past every day. Suppose that was the point, Ashley thought to herself as she walked to the door which had CCTV in the door and above it, with a keypad to the side.

Ashley walked to the door, not sure if she should knock or ring a bell. Her question was answered when a voice rang out on an intercom.

"Hello, how can we help?"

"Hi, I'm DC Fenway with Manchester Major Crimes Unit." Ashley held up her ID for the camera.

"I'm sorry DC Fenway but as you know there has to be prior warning before you can interview an attendee."

"I'm not here for that," Ashley said. "I need to talk to whoever's in charge, relating to a court case." There was silence but the door unlocked. Ashley walked into a bright and welcoming hallway, which had a reception to the side where an older woman was at a computer.

"The site lead, Ms Robinson will see you shortly. Do you want to take a seat?"

Ashley thanked her and sat on a chair. Opposite the reception area were a couple of women's magazines laid down on an old coffee table. Ashley though had her notebook open and was writing down the questions she wanted to ask.

"DC Fenway." A woman in her thirties was walking towards her, long, blonde hair and dressed smartly.

"Janine Robinson, site lead," she said, shaking Ashley's hand. Ashley didn't feel too good about this. The woman was far too young to have worked here when the case came about. Ms Robinson led Ashley upstairs to an office. Along the way she could see some of the women roaming the halls, along with a couple of children; most of them sporting scars and bruises.

"I must say I wasn't expecting a police visit," Robinson said, sitting down at the desk. The office was bright like the rest of the building, with the same colourful art on the walls.

"It's only come up today," Ashley said, "I wanted to talk to you about a civil suit the shelter put forward against an organisation called the New Agers. It would have been around 1990." Robinson shrugged.

"A bit before my time," she said. Well no shit, Ashley thought to herself.

"Are there any records of this happening?" Ashley asked. Robinson shook her head.

"Sorry, all records are destroyed every three years as per Government guidelines." Big waste of time. They could have told me over the intercom, Ashley thought. But she did have an idea.

"Who is your lawyer?" Ashley asked.

"Excuse me?"

"The lawyer for this place?" Ashley asked.

"Uhm, Kaye and Russel," she said, her voice wondering what the point of this was.

"And how long have they been the lawyers for this place for?" Ashley asked.

"Since I've been here." Again, no shit Shirley.

"Well thank you," Ashley said, getting up. "Hopefully I haven't taken up too much of your time."

***

Kaye and Russel had been much more helpful, they had been associated with the shelter for pro bono cases for years. They had all the information Ashley needed on the case she was looking for. Unfortunately, it was all in paper which came in a large box, though they were helpful enough to make her a copy to take away.

Ashley was now back in the office with a cup of tea and her box of paper and she started to go through it. She picked out the document relating to why the case was brought forward.

Plaintiff — Didsbury Abused Women New Shelter on behalf of Lisa Strachan. Represented by Mary D'Owda QC of Kaye, Russel and Minton LLP

Defendant — The organisation calling themselves the 'New Agers' Represented by Harold Donaldson QC of Gordon & Spencer LLP.

Ashley frowned. That name again, Lisa. Nakita talked about Kettings calling her Lisa during their liaisons. But the case was specifically for the New Agers, so how did Ferrets fit into all this?

Ashley resigned herself to a long day of sorting through the paperwork. The first thing she did was read Lisa Strachan's testimony on what had happened. She was skimming over it mostly, trying to see where Ferrets came up in this.

After a couple of hours searching through testimony after testimony it came up. The document stated that Ferrets provided sports training to the kids at this New Agers headquarters, so it could fulfil its legal obligations to become a school.

Ashley read about how he would systematically abuse boys under the sect's care; that he was one of many paedophiles that came to the house to abuse children and that it went on for over twenty years. Ferrets was one of a couple of people named in the case along with Frank Thomas and a Graham Boyd. Ashley made a note of their names so she could get the extended team to go through them.

Ashley searched Ferrets' name along with this New Agers cult. Not much came up in Google, but this would have been in the seventies or eighties. Ashley leaned back in her chair and thought it over. Ferrets had a connection but there was no mention of Kettings.

Maybe his mother knew. Ashley went to the computer and found her number.

Chapter 39

Ashley pulled up outside Joyce Kettings' house, the last time she was here it was at the dead of night with police swarming over it. Now it was a quiet, suburban street which had nice flowerbeds, but the lawn was still showing wear of the police going over it. The other things Ashley noticed was that the front door and the windows were different and there was a new 'For Sale' sign in the grass.

Ashley turned the engine off and got out. She pulled her collar up against the wind and walked up to the house to ring the bell. Joyce Kettings opened the door. A frail-looking woman with silver hair and tired, dark, circles under her eyes. Stan must have taken on more of his dad's features because he looked nothing like his mum.

"Hello Mrs Kettings, my name is DC Fenway, we spoke on the phone."

"Oh, yes…" She trailed off. "Please, come in." Ashley followed her into the house which in the dull overcast day was a dull grey. The pictures that adorned the walls were now placed away. Ashley followed her into the kitchen at the end of the hallway. It too, like most of the house was being packed away.

"Would you like a cup of tea?" She asked.

"Yes, thank you, milk, no sugar," Ashley said, sitting down at the small, wooden table in the middle of the room. Ashley looked around and saw boxes strewn all over the place, that were either full or partially full.

"So where are you staying at the moment?" Ashley asked.

"My friend, Sybil's," Joyce said. "It's just too…" She looked around the cupboards. "Morbid." She went back to making tea.

"I've only just placed it on the market," she explained. "The estate agents say I should wait a while before selling it, but I just want rid now." Ashley thought it was sad. She walked over with the tea, placed it down on the table and eased herself into the chair. Both women took a sip from their mugs.

"So, DC Fenway, what can I do for you?" Joyce asked.

"I just wanted to see how you were holding up," Ashley said. "A few of your neighbours said you haven't been back, and then you started packing away." Joyce nodded.

"They're very nice," She said. "But... there are too many memories in this house now."

"Good ones too." Joyce nodded.

"He wasn't perfect my Stan," she said. "But... I can't help but think about that room, knowing that's where he was last alive." Ashley nodded and sipped from her cup.

"Why was he so reclusive?" Ashley asked. Joyce looked up at her. "It's only because you seem more outgoing?"

"You can blame his father for that," she said. "Stan was a quiet boy, loved books and learning and the quiet, while Howard loved the outdoors and sports. Chalk and cheese the two of them. And Stan could never be the son Howard wanted but he couldn't love him for who he was."

"With you caught in the middle." Joyce nodded.

"Sometimes I wonder if I could have done better with him. Maybe encouraged him to go out and find a hobby. But he loved that computing thing, so..." Ashley nodded her understanding.

"My mum didn't like me playing hockey," Ashley said, trying to build a rapport. "She tried to get me into ballet; less contact." Joyce nodded.

"Howard wanted Stan to play rugby," Joyce said, with a slight chuckle. "I knew that was never going to happen. He did force him to join the Army Cadets. I agreed with him; it got him outdoors and some exercise, he also made some friends."

"Will Oatley." Ashley said.

"Oh yes, he was a very nice young man," Joyce said. "He helped Stan a lot, even after they left. He tried setting up an IT business which I supported but computers were still so new. Howard and I agreed on him getting a job in the interim period."

"The postman job?" Joyce nodded.

"A friend of Will got him the job. He argued with us, but we said that unless he got a job then that was it. He resisted at first, but it seemed like he made some friends while he was there."

"Did they do stuff together?" Ashley asked.

"Yes, they used to go camping. I thought though, Stan loved his computers too much to go camping," Joyce said. Probably out abusing children, Ashley thought. She shouldn't tarnish the memory of her son.

"Did you meet any of them?" Ashley asked hopefully.

"Oh no, Stanley was very particular about who he bought home. I only ever met a couple of them, including Will. He did have friends on those online games he played but I never spoke to them. But there was that nice young man who helped Stan when he was sacked from the post office."

"Why was he sacked as a postie?" Ashley asked, having a drink from the mug. "If you don't mind me asking."

"No, not at all," Joyce said. "He was sacked for supposedly taking mail that didn't belong on his route." She shook her head. "They never found anything, but I think they picked on him because he was so shy. But his friend was a young lawyer and it went to a tribunal." Ashley nodded. "They tried but they let him go." Ashley frowned to herself.

"I actually found the letter if you want to look at it?" Joyce asked.

"Yeah, could I?" Joyce got up and walked out of the kitchen, leaving Ashley alone. Ashley quietly got to her feet and had a look around the kitchen, more specifically the back door. She placed her hand on the slider and shook it lightly; again, no sign of forced entry.

"Here it is." Joyce's voice floated from the stairs. Ashley quickly sat back down as Joyce walked into the kitchen and handed it to Ashley.

The letter was a confirmation from his lawyer that he had his employment terminated for various reasons, how they had tried their best and he would help in any way he could. It wasn't really what she was looking for.

"Did he keep in contact with his friends after he left?" Ashley asked. Joyce nodded.

"He ended up doing some computing work for them, I'm not sure what. I didn't really understand, but they still went out a few times." Joyce's face fell a little.

"His IT business was really taking off. I thought he could set up a little office, maybe even get his own place." She laughed to herself softly.

"If only…" She composed herself. "If he only just told me he might be in trouble, I could have done something for him."

"You can't blame yourself," Ashley said. "We didn't know any of them were in trouble." Joyce nodded.

"Have any of his old friends been in touch?" Ashley asked, trying to change the subject. "Pay their condolences?"

"A couple of cards, which I binned." Great Ashley thought. "Will Oatley sent a nice bunch of flowers." Ashley was reading down the letter.

"You can keep that if you want," Joyce said.

"Is that OK?" Joyce nodded.

"I'd only bin it anyway."

"Are you doing that with all his things?" Ashley asked. Joyce nodded.

"I don't want it anymore. I can't even be in the street without people haranguing me about Stan," she said. "I'm too old for that."

"Do you have anything else planned?" Ashley asked.

"I have some money to buy a small seaside place," Joyce said. "I'm giving all of Stan's blood money to abused women and children centres. They need it more than I do."

"Mrs Kettings, have you ever heard of a group called the New Agers?" Joyce shook her head.

"I can't say I have," she said. "Was Stan involved with them?"

"I'm not sure," Ashley said. "Another person like Stan, was murdered and had a link to this religious sect," Ashley explained. "I wanted to know if he had a link." Joyce shook her head.

"I'm sorry."

Ashley's phone went off. She got it out and answered.

"Fenway."

"Any luck so far?" McArthur asked.

"No," Ashley said. "Ferrets was named in a suit against a religious cult called the New Agers."

"Never heard of them."

"Neither have I."

"Where are you now?"

"At Joyce Kettings place." Ashley looked at the letter she had been given. "I'm trying to see if Kettings was connected to this cult somehow."

"Forget that for now," McArthur told her. "One of Armstrong's sources came through on the prossie link."

"You're kidding," Ashley said, walking into the hallway.

"No, one of the girls who Kettings used has been recently arrested for killing a man in a fit of anger. Slashed his neck." Ashley paced the hallway.

"Let me ask my source about it," she said. "What's her name?"

"Dora Sanchez," McArthur said. "She's currently in holding at Styal Prison; me and Armstrong are on our way there now to question her."

"OK, I'll get back to you. Also, ask her about Lisa."

"Lisa?"

"Apparently Kettings liked to call his girls that."

"We'll ask. Speak to you later." McArthur hung up and left Ashley to contemplate. She needed to phone Kerry and get more info. She walked back into the kitchen where Joyce was.

"Sorry, something's come up, I have to go," she said.

"No worries dear," Joyce said, smiling kindly. "You have a busy job."

"I'll call you soon with news," Ashley said. She walked out of the house to her car and got in.

"Phone Kerry." The phone rang and she picked up on the fifth ring, by which time Ashley was already moving.

"Hello."

"Afternoon Kerry," Ashley said. "Fancy a late lunch?"

"What? Ash, it's barely lunch time."

"Maybe for you," Ashley said. "I need to talk about Dora Sanchez." There was a long pause from the other end of the line.

"I fancy a Maccies," Kerry said. "Meet you at the one in the town centre in an hour."

"OK, see you then." Ashley shifted down and drove back towards town.

Chapter 40

Ashley couldn't remember the last time she came to McDonalds sober; must have been when she was at uni. When she walked in Ashley checked her phone.

Got my food, get a drink and meet me upstairs.

Ashley got herself a milkshake and went up the stairs where Kerry was sitting on her own in the corner eating. Ashley put the straw in and sat down opposite her.

"What up gurl," Kerry said, taking a bite of a burger.

"Dora Sanchez."

"Amigo."

"What?"

"That's her nickname, Amigo," Kerry explained. "Spanish I think," she said, through a mouthful of food.

"Does she have a temper?"

"She killed one of the regulars who was known to beat girls," Kerry explained, as if it was no big deal.

"Who was her pimp?"

"A nasty piece of work called DeShawn, supposedly a pimp with the Tunnicliffes," Kerry explained. "Only girls who are really desperate go to him."

"Because of the company he keeps I assume?" Ashley said. Kerry nodded. "Why do girls go to him?"

"He pays more, means they get a bigger slice of the pie," Kerry said.

"Was Dora desperate?"

"She'd just given birth and some of her regulars didn't want her, she got into bed with DeShawn to make some money quickly."

"Including sleeping with a guy who beats you?"

"She was prepared to take one. Just not one like that." Maybe this was the person they were looking for. Did Kettings and Ferrets have other perversions that got them killed? Ashley had some of her drink.

"Is she the violent sort?" Ashley asked. Kerry put her burger down and looked out of the window onto the street.

"I know the guy she killed," Kerry said. "He's an old boy, old school. Would pay for the sex but mostly just wanted to inflict as much pain as he could on the girls. When I was really young, I did a stint there."

"You didn't?" Kerry nodded.

"Desperate times gurl," she said. "I was one of the lucky ones." Ashley looked down at the table.

"Sometimes we're pushed to our brink. I took a guy's eye out when he didn't play by the rules." Ashley couldn't hide her surprise. Kerry had another bite of her burger. What was someone capable of when pushed to the brink?

"Do you think she would be capable of killing others?" Kerry shook her head.

"No," Kerry said seriously, her eyes narrowed. "Do you guys see her for the other two?" Ashley nodded.

"The girl has a kid who she adores. She wouldn't waste her life in prison to kill three people."

"But she did kill one." Kerry shook her head.

"Yeah, she did," Kerry conceded. "But she didn't kill the other ones."

"Was she one of the ones who went to Kettings?" Kerry's silence was all Ashley needed to hear.

"It doesn't look good," Ashley said. "Did she ever mention a guy named Ferrets at all?"

"I don't know, but I can ask around," Kerry said.

"What colour hair does Dora have?"

"She's a blonde, why?" Not what Ashley wanted to hear.

"There's been sightings of a blonde woman outside one of our murder sights."

"Fuck."

"I'll look into it, I promise. It doesn't fit with the post-mortem of our victims."

"It doesn't?" Ashley thought about the two-person theory.

"They think we're looking for a man," Ashley said. "Does Dora have like a boyfriend, partner, anything like that?" Kerry shook her head. "What about her baby, who's the father?"

"I don't know," Kerry said. "But you are the detective, you figure it out."

"Thanks," Ashley said, picking her drink up and walking away. Kerry looked back at her and went back to her burger.

Ashley got into her car and breathed out deeply. She needed a plan. She got her notepad out and wrote down what she needed.

Dora Sanchez's baby's dad.

Was Dora mentioned in Ferrets' notes?

Was Dora mentioned in Kettings' notes?

Ashley looked at her notes; she needed to get back to the station. She left a message with McArthur to tell him what she'd learned and drove off.

***

Ashley strode into the office. Murphy was sitting at his desk.

"Are you busy?" Ashley asked.

"You got something?"

"Maybe," Ashley said, getting onto her computer and turning it on. "Are you looking into Dora Sanchez?"

"Finding out about background."

"Me too," Ashley replied.

"And?"

"I know who her pimp was. A guy called DeShawn who sells girls to abusive clients," Ashley said. "Also, she had connections to Kettings before she had a baby, and she's blonde."

"Matches up with the blonde being seen outside Kettings' house." Ashley nodded. "So, what do we need to know?"

"Who's her baby's dad," Ashley said. "I've already asked McArthur to ask her."

"OK, what else?"

"Back through everything to find out if Dora Sanchez was related to Kettings or Ferrets."

"I'll take Ferrets," Murphy said, getting to his feet.

Ashley got a board and wrote 'Dora Sanchez'. She got her arrest file and started to add the information that they already knew. She printed her mugshot and placed it on the board. Latina looking with dark skin, a petite frame and dyed blonde hair.

Ashley sat down in her chair and started to go back through the Kettings' file looking for a sign of Sanchez.

"I can't find anything," Murphy said.

"The only link we have with Kettings is that he used to use her," Ashley said. "He must have used a burner phone to arrange girls which we didn't find."

"Until she gives us alibis, we have nothing to go on," Murphy said.

Armstrong and McArthur came in. Both their expression unreadable.

"How did it go with Sanchez?" Ashley asked.

"We might have a killer," McArthur said. "There's still a few things we need to work out."

"OK, like?"

"Let's start from the beginning, what do we know about Dora Sanchez?" McArthur asked. "Fenway, what did your source say about her?"

"She's been on the game in Manchester for years," Ashley said. "Recently gave birth and tried to get back into it. Was working under a pimp known as DeShawn to get back into the game. He was notorious in supplying girls to clients with shall we say, particular tastes."

"Like the guy who beat her half to death?" Armstrong asked. Ashley nodded.

"My source also says that she did go to Kettings as well," Ashley said. "If that was arranged through DeShawn or someone else, I don't know."

"Any link with Ferrets?"

"None yet," Murphy said.

"Did she say who her baby's father was?" Ashley asked.

"No. She said she didn't know," McArthur replied. "Social Services have taken a swab from the kid and we're going to run it in the system to see if a match comes up there."

"What were her alibis?" Murphy asked.

"She said she was on the game the night Kettings was murdered," Armstrong said, looking through his notes. "Apparently with a regular."

"OK, and Ferrets?"

"At home with the baby."

"Did she say who the regular was?"

"A man named Jason," Armstrong said. "Couldn't give a last name."

"Maybe not even his real name," Ashley said. "Did she at least give a location?"

"Yeah, and you're gonna love this." Ashley didn't even have to ask.

"The Cambrian," she finished for him.

"In one Fenway," Armstrong said, impressed. "You might make a half-decent DS."

"I'm better than you so I'm already a half-decent DS."

"Kids. Focus," McArthur said, sternly.

"We need to focus on her alibis. Murphy, I want you to talk to her neighbours and see if she was at home with her kid. Ashley, since you're so familiar with the Cambrian CCTV see if we can locate this 'Jason' character." Great, more CCTV work.

"OK," she said, almost forced.

"Right, let's see if we can wrap this up in a couple of days," McArthur said. "Metro are dealing with Dora Sanchez's killing so they have all info on her if you need it." Perfect, Ashley said to herself. First thing Ashley did was phone Dave.

"DS Hughes, Metro CID." It felt good to hear his voice.

"DC Fenway, Major Crimes," Ashley said, with a small smile.

"I bet it felt good to say that."

"Yes, it did," Ashley admitted. "I hear we are in business."

"If you can call it that. We get a killer and you lot want to pin your murders on her," he sighed. "Is there a link?"

"We have reasonable cause," Ashley said. "She was a regular of one of our victims."

"Great, what about the other one?"

"Looking into it."

"So why are you phoning?"

"Catch up," Ashley said.

"We're going out for drinks later in the week if you fancy it?"

"Love to," Ashley said. "I don't suppose you guys have been looking into Dora's regulars, have you?"

"We have to see if there is a pattern of violence, why?"

"Have you come across one called Jason?"

"We have." There was a long pause.

"Can I have it please?" Ashley asked. "It would save me loads of time."

"Is there something the great department can do for us with all your connections?" Dave asked.

"Maybe, depends on the nature of it."

"We've got Dora's phone which we think might pave the way for incriminating someone in helping her try and cover up the murder, but IT are sitting on it."

"I can try and get it bumped up," Ashley said, thinking Aaron could help with it. "When can I get what I want?"

"Emailing over to you now. Thanks, Ash."

"Don't mention it and thank you." The icon came up which showed Jason. Ashley hung up and opened it, sending all of it to the paper so they had a hard copy. She next sent an e-mail to Aaron to ask him nicely to bump Dora Sanchez's phone to the top of the queue for unlocking, as it was related to their case.

She got an e-mail back saying that he would try his best. Ashley thanked him and asked if Metro CID could get a copy of the analysis when it was done.

Ashley went and gathered the paperwork from the printer and started to assemble it in the right order.

From the paperwork, this Jason was a businessman who came to Manchester to work occasionally but lived somewhere else in the country. Ashley frowned, he looked familiar; he looked very familiar. Ashley leaned back and tried to remember where she had seen him before.

"Pennington," Ashley said, leaning forward. She searched her desk and found CCTV for the day Ferrets died and put it into the dual player. She found the day after Ferrets died and loaded that. Ashley looked at the hotel reception area and pressed play. She was looking for either one of them to come to the desk. Low and behold, at ten in the morning she saw 'Jason' coming into the lobby and buying a room.

About twenty minutes later Dora came in with a friend. Dora was carrying a car seat with a baby in it. She gave her friend the car seat and they left. Dora checked her phone and went to the lift. Ashley played the tape for the day after he died. After the lockdown both Dora and Jason left around midday, he handed her an envelope which she looked reluctant to take but did anyway and they went their separate ways.

"Murphy," she said, looking over at him. "Her alibi is false."

"How do you know that?" He asked.

"She was at the Cambrian the day Ferrets died," Ashley said. "I have it on screen."

Murphy came over and Ashley showed him what she had learned, explaining to him about Jason and Dora.

"And here's our guy and girl."

Murphy let out a low whistle.

"So, she was at The Cambrian at the same time as our vic?" Ashley nodded. "So, this Jason could be the person that we're looking for?"

"We have to track him down first. What about the night Kettings died?"

"It could be with that Jason."

"We need to talk to her again." Ashley was looking at the screen with her arms folded.

"What's the matter?"

"I talked to them," Ashley said. "Her and this Jason were next to the vic." Ashley swore and looked at the screen.

"It's not your fault," Murphy said, placing a hand on her shoulder. "We couldn't have known." Ashley sighed. It was a part of the job she hated.

"Were they at the Cambrian the night Kettings died?"

"I haven't even got that far yet," Ashley said. "But maybe we don't need to. We can take this to her and scare a location out of her."

"No, boss wants everything watertight," Murphy said. "Let's get the alibi for Kettings before doing anything else."

"Well since I did all this, why don't you go and get the Cambrian videos for the eighteenth and I'll tell the boss," Ashley said.

"Sounds fair. Well done Ash, that was a good hunch you got there," Murphy said, getting his coat and going. Ashley went into McArthur's office and told him about the alibi situation.

"That's great, is there any way we can track this Jason guy down?"

"We might be able to get him on Manc Cams," Ashley said, thinking out loud. "According to Metro he might not be from Manchester, so he might be going to a train station or bus station. We could track him from there."

"Can you track him?"

"From the hotel? Yes. But you'll need to talk to her again to get a straight answer."

"Me and Armstrong are going again tomorrow. Where are we with the other alibi?"

"Murphy's gone to the Cambrian now for the CCTV tapes for us to look over."

"I want you to track this Jason and see where he went. Good work you two." Ashley wanted to say it was mostly her but she decided against it.

"I'll tell Murphy when he gets back." Ashley sat down at her desk and looked at the map of central Manchester she had printed out for Tim Williams.

She took that all down and started again. Logging the time that Jason left the Cambrian and caught him on an outside Manc Cam, Ashley placed a tack on the board and followed him into the city centre, where he stopped at Byron Burger with what looked like a work colleague. Ashley wrote down the times and a note to stop there for CCTV.

He went back along the main road to a pub with his mate; again, making a note of times and to get CCTV. Ashley noticed him coming out, him and his friend parted ways and he walked to Manchester Pic for around half three.

Ashley looked down at her notes. More CCTV and tracking down. Time though was of the essence. She got her coat and went out.

Chapter 41

"So, you went to a burger joint, a pub, and a train station?"

"Yep," Ashley said, taking a sip of tea; looking at the images of 'Jason' and his friend having a burger. Nothing seemed to carry the attention of anyone around them. Possibly two guys meeting for food.

"You could have got me something."

"Not my remit," Ashley said. "And maybe a nice cold one to wash it down with."

"Read my mind." Ashley rolled her eyes. Both men got up and walked out to the pub. Ashley changed over to the pub and watched them order and chat some more.

"I can't see them," Murphy said.

"Maybe you're not looking hard enough," Ashley countered.

"No, I'm sure," Murphy said. "I've looked over this at least three times, neither are on here."

"Look at it again in a slower rate," Ashley said. "He goes in first, then her, try looking for one with a baby carrier." Murphy grumbled something but went back to it. A couple of hours later 'Jason' left the pub and started to walk towards the train station.

Ashley took the pub one out and replaced it with the train station CCTV. Ashley was now looking at a crowd of people in the main part. She synced up the times and pressed play in slow motion. Ashley watched 'Jason' walk in at 15:32:15 on the Manc Cam. Ashley watched him walk in and followed him with her finger.

He walked over to a ticket machine and waited in the small queue. Three minutes later he collected his tickets and stood in front of the large station board. He waited there for about twenty minutes before going to Platform Five. Ashley watched him get onto the train.

She went back to the board and saw him looking up. She toggled the camera to see the board and watched, her eyes scanning over the board at the different destinations, which ranged from Glasgow to Euston. The board allocated the platform number five for Leeds.

"Are we on speaking terms with Leeds?" Ashley asked.

"Are you a footie fan?"

"God no," Ashley said, pulling a face.

"Then you should be fine," Murphy said. Ashley first had to phone the train company, Trans Pennine, and get them to send over CCTV. After navigating a very unhelpful train company they said they would send a copy over to her in the morning. She next moved onto Leeds train station who said the same thing.

"Not much more I can do now," Ashley said, putting the phone down and rubbing her eyes. She started to write down on the board about Dora Sanchez and her links to both Ferrets and Kettings.

"Well we're making progress," Murphy said, with a concerned look. "I don't think though she was here."

"Haven't you seen her or Jason?" Murphy shook his head.

"She's lying about where she was that night." It didn't look good for Dora it had to be said, and probably this Jason as well, wherever he was. Ashley wrote down on the board that her second alibi was a fake one as well.

McArthur came out of his office.

"Where are we with this Jason?" McArthur asked.

"He's in Leeds," Ashley said. "Station Cams have him going to Leeds, I've got the train company to send CCTV for the train he was on."

"Well whatever station he gets off at I want you and Murphy to go there tomorrow and find out where he went," McArthur said. "What about her alibi for Kettings' murder?"

"I've looked through the CCTV for the Cambrian, neither she nor this Jason are there," Murphy said. McArthur nodded.

"Good work. We can at least find out where she was. Hopefully somewhere in Kettings' neighbourhood. You two go home, you've done well today."

"Thanks Sir," Murphy said, getting to his feet and his coat.

"Are you coming Ash?"

"I'm gonna work on the board a bit more," Ashley said. "I want to make sure we have everything." Plus, she had an hour and a bit to kill before MMA.

"Suit yourself. See you in the morning."

"Yeah, see you in the morning," Ashley said, writing out in detail what they knew on Dora Sanchez, adding photos and looking at this Jason character. When she was satisfied with the board, she got her coat and went home.

Chapter 42

Beep

   Beep

   Beep

Ashley reluctantly moved her arm across and tapped her phone to shut it off, her body still stiff from MMA. She sat on the edge of her bed, yawning and stretching. She got her phone and checked her messages; a couple of friend requests from Facebook from some guys she didn't even know. She checked how far it would be to travel to Leeds.

"I need diesel," Ashley said, getting up.

***

Cardio.

   Squats.

   Legs.

Ashley hated leg day but it had to be done, and since she was going to be spending most of the day in the car anyway, she didn't see a problem with it. She did her last set of weights on the legs press and gratefully let it down. She took her towel and drink and gingerly walked out of the gym. Again, she could see the same guys that had been watching her work out.

After a shower and slightly awkward walk to the car, Ashley filled up with diesel and went into the office.

She sat down at her desk with her tea and porridge and went through her e-mails. There was a thank you from Dave for getting the phone through quickly and one from the train company, who had sent the CCTV over.

Ashley loaded that up as well as the train station CCTV and watched. She saw Jason walk onto the platform and get on the train on the third carriage. Ashley located the third carriage and watched Jason get on and sit down. He made a phone call, spoke for ten minutes and the train departed. Ashley sped up the cam a little.

"Morning Ash," Murphy said, as he came in.

"Morning Herschel," Ashley said, smiling. "Train company CCTV came back."

"And?" He asked sitting down. "Where do we get to go today?"

"Not sure, I'll tell you in a sec," Ashley said. Murphy went to make himself a tea. Ashley sped it up again a little more. He was on the train reading a book while people got on and off. Nothing conspicuous about him at all. A face you would easily forget.

The train stopped and he got up. Ashley paused it and saw the station. Morley. Ashley checked on Google maps; it would take over an hour to get there, that was if the traffic was kind which it never was in Manchester. They would set off after the briefing.

"Where to?" Murphy asked.

"Sunny Morley," Ashley replied.

"Never heard of it."

"Hopefully it has somewhere for lunch."

**

"I take it we're using my car," Ashley said, as her and Murphy walked down to the car park.

"I don't think my car could make it that far," Murphy replied. They got in and set off, getting stuck in the traffic going out. They then got onto the picturesque roads into Yorkshire. They had a good chat in the car; he was easy to get on with Ashley found.

He still mocked her for her taste in radio station but what else was new? Everyone did.

"So, are we going to the station first?" Murphy asked.

"Yeah, can you call ahead and make sure they have what we need ready for when we get there?" Murphy made the call.

"You can?" Murphy said hopefully.

"That is amazing, thank you very much."

"Don't forget to ask if they have CCTV outside?" Ashley asked.

"Sorry? No, not you, my partner."

"Do you have CCTV outside?" Ashley asked loudly.

"Yeah, what she said," Murphy said. There was a pause.

"Yeah, they got that too," he said. "We'll need that as well. Is there somewhere on site we can watch it? We're coming from Manchester."

"Perfect, thank you very much, see you later, bye." Murphy ended the call. "Guy says he'll have a room available for us, tea and biscuits as well if we want it."

"Perfect. We also need to phone Morley police station to see if we can have an interview room if we find this Jason."

"Good point," Murphy said, now looking through his phone.

"You know, I was happy with my old phone. These bloody new ones are too complicated."

"You sound like my dad," Ashley said.

"Here it is," he said, now calling.

Ashley laughed to herself, but Murphy secured an interview room for them if they did find this Jason. They reached Morley, very northern and industrial and a small town with very Yorkshire routes. Ashley should probably keep her Lancashire roots to herself. They drove round, looking for a left that Ashley didn't think would come.

"Who's Dan?" Murphy asked. Ashley checked her phone which was showing Google maps but also a message from Dan, which began with 'Hello gorgeous.'

"No one," Ashley said, feeling herself go slightly red. She pressed on her phone to highlight the map. She found the turning which went down to a single lane.

"Didn't look like no one," Murphy said, with a slight smirk. Ashley glared at him. Thankfully they were quite close to the station. She parked up quite briskly in the small carpark.

"We're here," Ashley said, noting how hot she felt and getting out.

"We sure are," Murphy said getting out too. Ashley took the police laptop they were issued and looked around. It was a small station with a small outbuilding which went on to the platforms. Ashley looked up at a couple of the streetlights that were around and saw a CCTV camera attached onto one.

"This wasn't really what I had in mind," Ashley said, now looking at the dark, grey clouds over head.

"I know it's not the best," Murphy said

"Let's just hope the CCTV's good." They walked into the station house which only had one ticket booth which was being manned by an old man. Murphy went up and knocked on the window.

"Well hello you two," he said, cheerfully. "And where are you off to today?" Ashley couldn't help but smile at his cheerful demeanour.

"I'm DS Murphy, I think we spoke on the phone," Murphy said, showing him his ID. "It was about using the CCTV you have here."

"Oh yes, yes," he said, walking back to the back of the booth and letting himself out.

"We don't get many police visitors," he said, beckoning them to a side door. "So, this is a really rare occurrence."

"We're very grateful," Ashley said, as he led them into a small room which had a single computer and monitor.

"Rusty is the guy who files it all away. I'm not sure what order he keeps it in."

"It's fine. Thank you," Murphy told him.

"Can I get you guys a couple of teas?"

"Thanks, milk no sugar for me."

"Milk, and two for me."

"Do you need a hand at all?" Ashley asked.

"No, no, you guys get on with catching the bad guys," he said, round a laugh. "I'll be a second."

"He was nice," Ashley said, setting up her laptop.

"Well let's find what we're after," Murphy said, looking at the monitor. "What date are we looking for again?"

"The thirteenth of November," Ashley said. She checked the CCTV. "We're looking for the 16:43 coming into the station from Manchester Pic." Murphy looked through the files which were helpfully in date order and split up in hour slots. Murphy isolated the date and looked at the cameras which were marked A, B and C. A and B looked on the platforms and C the car park. Camera A showed the train coming in.

"He's on the third carriage," Ashley said, looking at the timestamp on the computer. "He should be coming off at 16:43:30."

Ashley came around and looked at the monitor. When the doors opened Jason stepped out of the third carriage and checked his phone again. He walked down the platform to the station house and out to the carpark where he got into his car.

"So, he's local," Murphy observed.

"DVLA will be able to give us name and address," Ashley said.

"What car does that look like to you?" Ashley looked at the monitor; it looked like a Vauxhall Insignia.

"Insignia," Ashley said. "But they're quite popular." Ashley looked at the camera.

Before they could talk more the guy from the front came in with a tray of tea and biscuits.

"Oh, thank you," Ashley said, taking it from him. "You didn't have to give us biscuits," Ashley said, noting the bourbons.

"I'd only been eating them. And I need to watch my shape." Ashley laughed.

"How long have you worked here for?" Ashley asked, taking her mug.

"Since '65."

"Really. Don't you think about retirement or anything like that?" He laughed.

"No. it would be very boring, and my wife would go mad with me home all the time." Ashley laughed again.

"Thank you very much," she said. "I hope I'm half as active as you when I get to your age."

"Age is just a number," he said, walking back out.

"Right, we have a name," Ashley said, looking at the laptop. "Glenn Young, he's local to Morley, lives just down the road as well."

"Good," Murphy replied. "I'll make a copy of these and we are good to go." They packed their things and made their way to Glenn Youngs home, which was a nice detached house with a big drive. Ashley though still parked up next to it.

Her and Murphy walked up to the door; Ashley knocked. The door was answered by a woman who looked a little stressed when she opened it. Ashley could hear a couple of kids in the background.

"Hello," she said, almost abruptly.

"Hello, I'm DS Murphy and this is DC Fenway, we're looking for a Glenn Young," Murphy said, showing her his ID.

"He's at work," she said slowly, her interest peaked. She folded her arms across her chest. "Why?"

"We need to ask him a couple of questions regarding an investigation," Ashley said. "Are you his wife?"

"Yes…" she said, her eyes darting between the two of them. "Is Glenn in trouble?" She asked.

"We just want to ask him some questions, nothing to worry about," Murphy said. "Where does your husband work?"

"He's a finance director." Murphy and Ashley looked at one another.

"Is it OK if we come in and ask you a couple of questions?" Murphy asked.

"Why?"

"You see, we're from the Manchester Major Crimes Unit," Murphy explained. "We need some information on your husband's movements." Mrs Young nodded and led them inside to the living room.

"Let me just get the kids upstairs," she said, moving into the house.

"Fiver says she's calling him right now," Murphy said.

"He won't go in the wind, he'll panic and come home," Ashley said, looking around the living room which was slightly messy with kids' toys around the floor; not where Ashley would have thought a double murderer would live. Mrs Young came into the living room. Ashley noticed her slim jeans now had a noticeable phone-sized bulge in the pocket.

"Mrs Young, does your husband work away a lot?" Ashley asked.

"Yes, he has to go to Manchester sometimes for work," She said in a worried tone.

"And how often does he go?" Mrs Young shrugged.

"Every couple of weeks or so. He has friends in Manchester as well, so he goes and sees them too." She looked to Ashley and Murphy.

"He's… not in trouble, is he?"

"When was his last trip to Manchester?" Ashley asked, ignoring her question. It might seem callous, but you need to keep the questions on point.

"Last week, he had work there and spent the weekend with a friend." Murphy frowned.

"Mrs Young, do you know where your husband was the night of the twelfth of November?"

"I… he was away with work, a last-minute thing," she said, fiddling with her shirt collar. Ashley felt sorry for her, she had no idea what her husband was up to, or maybe even capable of.

"So just to clarify on the twelfth and eighteenth of November your husband was in Manchester?" Ashley asked. Mrs Young nodded.

"Mrs Young, where is your husband now?" Mrs Young shook her head.

"He's at work," she said. "I… I called him."

"Is he on his way here now?" Murphy asked. Mrs Young nodded mutely. "We'll wait for him then."

"Is he in trouble? Like, big trouble?"

"That remains to be seen," Ashley said. "Would you like a cup of tea?"

"I think I need something stronger," Mrs Young said, now sitting on the sofa arm.

"Come on, let's go to the kitchen." Ashley helped Mrs Young to the kitchen and started to make her a tea. Ashley didn't like making other people drinks in their own kitchens because she didn't know where anything was.

"It's bad isn't it?" Mrs Young said, out of the blue. Ashley didn't answer.

"If it was minor then you would tell me," she said, her gaze focused blankly on the floor. "I witnessed a mugging a few years ago and the police came around to take a statement. You just got what you needed and left. Glenn didn't know but you told him…"

"It's the nature of the investigation," Ashley said, handing her the tea. She muttered her thanks and took a sip while Ashley sat next to her.

"I… I didn't mean to call him," Mrs Young said softly. "I just…"

"It's OK." Ashley reassured her.

"Will you question him here?"

"No, we have a room at the local station to do so." There was a knock on the door. Strange, Ashley thought, wouldn't he walk into the house?

"Excuse me." Ashley walked back into the living room where Murphy was talking to a lawyer, the suit gave it away. He was tall with a mop of greying hair and a relaxed demeanour.

"Who's this?" Ashley asked.

"James Asworth, Mr Young's solicitor," he said seeing, Ashley and shaking her hand. "Mr Young phoned me to come ahead."

"So, he's on his way?" Murphy asked.

"Yes, he as anxious to get this misunderstanding cleared up as anyone," Asworth said with a smug smile.

"Well that's good to hear," Murphy said. Ashley went back to the kitchen where Mrs Young was still sitting.

"Is that James?" She asked.

"Yes," Ashley said, sitting back down. "Do you know him?"

"I hate him," she said. "He's one of Glenn's friends." Ashley got her notebook out.

"Is it all right if I take a statement from you confirming your husband's movements?" Ashley said. Mrs Young nodded.

"Yeah, if that bastard thinks he can sneak around he has another thing coming." Ashley took her statement and she could confirm them with phone calls made to him.

"Ash," Murphy came in. "He's here, we should go." Ashley nodded.

"Thank you," Ashley turned to Mrs Young. "We shouldn't be too long."

"Take your time with him," Mrs Young said with venom. Ashley walked out of the kitchen into the living room where Glenn Young stood. He looked very different from the bathrobe Ashley saw him in when they first met. When his eyes saw Ashley, they dropped.

"Remember me, don't you?" Ashley said.

"Need I remind you two that this is a voluntary questioning by myself and my client," Asworth said.

"Yes, we know," Murphy acknowledged. "If you two would be very kind as to follow us."

Chapter 43

Morley Police station reminded Ashley a lot of the police station in her village back home; a blink and you'll miss the building. A brown brick building on a roundabout next to an equally dilapidated fire station. They parked round the back and led Glenn Young into the station which was a small maze of cramped hallways and rooms.

The Chief Inspector, a portly man by the name of Sides who was happy to have something interesting going on, showed them to the interview room. Young was taken down to holding to meet his lawyer.

Sides led Ashley and Murphy into his office.

"Nasty business this," he said, sitting down. "We haven't had a murder in Morley for decades."

"We don't think he did any here," Murphy said. "We're grateful for you allowing us to conduct the interview here."

"It's not a problem," he said, with a hearty laugh. "If you don't mind, a couple of my officers want to look in on the interview, something like this doesn't happen very often round here you understand."

"So long as they're behind the screen then that's fine," Ashley said. "We were hoping if we could use some of your facilities," Ashley said, wanting all the evidence to be there and waiting for them.

"That should be fine, PC Gallow can show you where everything is." Sides got up from his desk and went to the door.

"Gallow!" He shouted. An older PC came to the door.

"Can you assist DC Fenway with her evidence gathering?"

"Sure thing, Sir," he said. He showed Ashley and Murphy to one of the computers, showed them where the printer was and left them to it. About an hour later he came back with some sandwiches for them which he left on the side.

When they were done Ashley took her sandwich and sat down with Murphy who was tucking into his.

"I was hoping for a pub lunch," he said.

"It's better than nothing," Ashley said, opening her tuna and sweetcorn and taking a bite. Passable as sandwiches went.

"So, come on," Murphy said turning to Ashley. "Who's Dan?"

"I told you, no one," Ashley said, not looking at him and taking another bite.

"So, everyone messages you saying, 'Hey Gorgeous' then?"

"Why not?" Ashley countered. Murphy smiled knowingly at her.

"Come on, who is he?"

"Nobody," Ashley said, looking down at her sandwich. "No one concrete."

"Do you want him to be?" Ashley didn't say anything.

"I don't know. It's complicated."

"What is he, married?"

"No."

"Seeing someone else?" Ashley sighed.

"Then I don't see what's so complicated."

"Why the sudden interest in my life?" Murphy shrugged.

"Why are you so defensive about it?" Ashley couldn't answer. Murphy laughed and shook his head. "Life's too short for you to care about what other people think."

"I don't," Ashley said, finishing her sandwich and going on to the next one. "Everyone else cares." The door to the small room opened and Sides poked his head around.

"Detectives, they're ready for you."

"Saved by the bell," Murphy said, getting his file. Ashley smirked and followed him out, down the small maze of corridors. Ashley got a quick look at the viewing room and there was about ten people crammed in. This must have been the biggest thing to happen to them in a while.

They walked into the room, unlike the Tower which was bright, this one was dark with a solitary bulb handing above the metal table in the room. Opposite was Asworth and Glenn Young with their file.

Ashley and Murphy sat down.

"Are you OK Mr Young, is there anything else you need or require before we begin?" Ashley asked.

"No, I'm good," he said. By the sound of his voice he couldn't believe how this had happened. Murphy loaded the tape which blared out that unbearable noise.

"This is Detective Sergeant Herschel Murphy, seeing this interview at Morley Police Station of Glenn Young on 23rd November 2017 at 14:44pm with..."

"Detective Constable Ashley Fenway."

"And James Asworth."

Ashley opened her file and looked up at Glenn Young.

"Mr Young." Murphy opened his file too. "Before we begin, I have to caution you. Although you are not under arrest at this time, you do not have to say anything, but it may harm your defence if you do not mention when questioned, something which you later rely on in court. Anything you do say may be given in evidence. Do you understand?"

"Yes."

"Do you travel to Manchester a lot Mr Young?" Murphy asked.

"Yes, I travel with work, I'm a finance director at an advertising firm," He said, in a calm voice, well as calm as he could.

"Do you travel solely for work?" Young closed his eyes and took a deep breath.

"No, I have friends in Manchester, I meet up with them from time to time," he said.

"Do you get up to anything else while you're away?" Murphy asked.

"Are you leading my client?" Asworth asked.

"No, it's a simple question to try and establish the sort of clientele your client likes to keep," Murphy replied, coolly.

"No, I don't know what you mean." Murphy looked at Ashley.

"Does the name Dora Sanchez mean anything to you?" Ashley asked. Young turned and looked at her, his breathing becoming more rapid at the mere mention of the name.

"I..." He took a deep breath. "No comment."

"Well, I know you know Dora Sanchez," Ashley said. "If your lawyer doesn't already know, Dora Sanchez is a prostitute in Manchester who Mr Young frequents." Ashley pulled the photo of Dora out.

"I'm now handing Mr Young document ND1." Ashley pushed the photo of Dora's scared mugshot across the table.

"I am also handing Mr Young document ND2, a transcript of my own notes from the thirteenth of November where I interviewed a Mr and Mrs Pennington at The Cambrian Hotel with regards to the murder of one Gordon Ferrets." Ashley slid the other document over. Asworth instantly took it and scanned it.

"For the tape this Mr and Mrs Pennington were staying in the room next door to the deceased person."

"How can you be sure that my client is the one in the room?" Asworth said, still reading.

"If you are unaware Mr Young, Dora Sanchez has been charged by Manchester Metropolitan CID with the murder of Graham Boyd," Murphy said. Young looked up in surprise. He went to say something but stopped. Murphy continued.

"She killed him with a single slash wound to his neck. While investigating this, our friends in Metro CID gave us intelligence on a man they wanted to question in relation to this, who called himself Jason." He gulped. Ashley hoped they got that on film. Ashley took out another document.

"DC Fenway is handing over Document ND3." Dora Sanchez testimony of 'Jason'.

"DC Fenway recognised this person as you, based on the information given by Dora Sanchez who said that she would meet this 'Jason' at the Cambrian hotel for regular sex." Young breathed deeply. "We then followed you on the Manchester Street Cameras to a number of different places."

Ashley handed over the map of his movements.

"We have handed over Document A5," Murphy said.

"On the thirteenth of November you left the Cambrian hotel and as shown on Document A5 picture NDA you went to Byron Burger." Asworth laid out all the pictures.

"Picture NDB shows you leaving Byron Burger with an acquaintance and going to the Mildred Arms, as shown in Picture NDC. Picture NDD shows you are leaving. Picture NDE shows you at Manchester Piccadilly Station. Picture NDF from the station shows you boarding a train to Leeds Station. Picture NDG through NDK shows you coming off at Morley station and getting into your Vauxhall Insignia, which is registered to you. Is that correct?" Young sighed.

"Yes, it is," he said.

"So, were you with Dora Sanchez on the morning of the thirteenth of November?"

"Yes, I was," he said.

"Mr Young, were you with Dora on the night of the eighteenth of November?" Ashley asked.

"No," he said. "I was working." Why lie? Ashley thought.

"We are showing Mr Young document MA1; MA1 is a statement from Dora Sanchez that says she was with you the night of the eighteenth," Ashley explained, getting out another document and pushed it over.

"For the tape we have given Mr Young a copy of Document A6," Ashley said. Young rubbed his head.

"Do we have to go through the rigmarole of you denying it and then we prove it, or can you give us a straight answer?" Young nodded.

"I was with Dora," he admitted. "We were supposed to go to the Cambrian but after the murder there it was so risky."

"For you to be exposed." Mr Young looked up darkly at Ashley.

"Yes," he said, drawing the one word out.

"So, where did you go?" Ashley asked.

"We went to the Premier Inn in west Didsbury," he said. Ashley looked at her phone and typed it in, it wasn't that far away from her Hockey Club and only ten minutes away from Kettings' house. Ashley got it on Google maps and gently tipped it to Murphy for him to see.

"What time did you check in?"

"About six."

"To confirm, you were with Dora Sanchez on the night of the eighteenth of November and into the nineteenth?"

"Yes," Young said.

"Was she with you all night?"

"Yes, she stays till the morning and then goes," Young said. Ashley had a feeling that his and Dora's relationship was deeper than they thought.

"Mr Young, did Dora leave the hotel room at all?" Murphy asked.

"Not while I was awake."

"What time did the two of you go to sleep?" Ashley asked.

"About eleven." Matched up with time of death as well.

"And she didn't get up in the night at all?" Young shrugged.

"I don't know."

"What about the day you were in the Cambrian?" Ashley asked. "Did she leave the room at all? You said in your statement to me that you and your 'wife' were asleep between two and four, which cuts right across the murder time of our first victim." Young started to laugh nervously.

"You don't think I had anything..."

"You were at the first crime scene at the time of murder, as well as ten minutes away from our second victim on the night he died." Young looked down at the table.

"If that's not a coincidence I don't know what is," Murphy said. Asworth tapped the table.

"Do you have any DNA evidence which puts my client in the same rooms as your murder victims?" Asworth asked.

"Not yet, but we're running his fingerprints now," Murphy said.

"Then to me, my client is only a victim of circumstances," Asworth said.

"Right." Ashley got out another picture and handed it across.

"I'm handing Mr Young document ND8 which shows a sequence of photos, MA1 to MA9 of a transaction between Mr Young and Dora at the Cambrian on the morning of the thirteenth of November. As previously stated, the payment for their liaisons took place in hotel rooms, so what was this payment for?"

Young said nothing, he just looked at the picture.

"Because what I see there is hush money," Murphy said. He nodded at Ashley to show him the CCTV footage from The Cambrian.

"We are showing Video MA1 which is from The Cambrian CCTV on the thirteenth of November. It shows Mr Young and Dora Sanchez when Mr Young hands her an envelope. She shakes her head and tries to hand it back. After much insistence though she takes it and you leave." Ashley stopped the video.

"So, I reckon that during your 'nap' Dora woke up, saw you had gone, heard what was happening next door. Saw what happened and you bribed her for her silence."

"That is an unfounded claim, detective," Asworth said, in a harsh voice. "Unless you have proof of this, which you don't, I would respectfully remind you that it is just speculation."

"What was the money for Glenn?" Ashley asked. "Was it for the baby?" Glenn looked up, he blinked at Ashley and nodded.

"Are you the father?"

"No," Glenn said. "We carried out a paternity test but..." He was starting to break down. The choice was simple, admit the affair or be looked at for murder. He admitted.

"The money was for the baby," Young said, wiping tears from his eyes. "I felt sorry for her, she got pregnant from one of her regulars who wanted nothing to do with her after."

"Did you still go to her?"

"I was the only one, her only source of regular income," he said.

"How did you find out she was pregnant?" Ashley asked.

"She told me," he said. "She was honest with me, she thought that like other people, I would find someone else."

"Why didn't you?" Murphy asked. Young took a deep breath and looked up at the dark ceiling.

"I enjoyed Dora, I liked her," Young said. Ashley though could see through it.

"You like pregnant women, don't you?" Young nodded. "So, you have a fetish for them."

"In fewer words. Yes," Young said. "I missed my wife being pregnant, I paid more and it was worth it. We bonded, we grew closer, what was once a month suddenly became once a week."

"Did it ever occur to you that she was using you?" Murphy asked. Young shook his head.

"Dora wasn't like that," he said. "I never lead her on, she knew exactly where she stood."

"So, what was the money for?" Ashley asked.

"Dora said she was struggling, even with our new arrangement." He took a deep breath. She even did porn while pregnant but that had dried up. It was a passing comment, but I felt that I could help her."

"Was that why she was hesitant?" Ashley asked, pointing at the photo.

"She didn't want it, but I insisted," Glenn said. "We've become friends." There was a thick pause, Ashley decided on another plan of attack.

"Is she capable of killing three men?"

"I don't know..." he said. "All I know is that I didn't kill them. I know it doesn't look good but..."

"Have you ever heard of Gordon Ferrets or Stan Kettings?" Ashley asked. Young shook his head.

"No." Ashley looked at Murphy, who had folded his arms and was staring at Young.

"Is there anyone else who can vouch for your movements on the dates we've asked?" Murphy asked.

"Only Dora." Ashley leaned over to Murphy.

"We need to speak to McArthur and Armstrong, see what they've learned," She whispered in his ear. Murphy nodded.

"Well Mr Young, you've been helpful, but we need to speak to our colleagues," Murphy said, reaching over to the recorder; Ashley was busy setting up a conference. "Interview paused."

Chapter 44

Ashley and McArthur went to the Chief Inspector's office so they could set up Skype. As it turned out McArthur and Armstrong wanted to speak to them again. Not long after Ashley sent the message, they Skyped. Ashley accepted. The screen showed McArthur and Armstrong sitting in a very bland room, no doubt somewhere in the prison. Once the pleasantries were out of the way they got down to business.

"Did he tell you where he and Dora were on the eighteenth?" McArthur asked.

"They were at the Premier Inn in west Didsbury," Ashley said. "Apparently they were there all night and left in the morning."

"We can ask Parland to get CCTV," McArthur said. "Well Miss Sanchez has been most unhelpful. Her legal team are telling her to say no comment for pretty much everything."

"Well she and Glenn have a close relationship, if you can call it that," Ashley said. "The money he gave her was allegedly for her baby and not hush money."

"According to him."

"Yes, according to him," Ashley said, as though it didn't need explaining. "His lawyer did make a good point though. We have no DNA or eyewitnesses that put either in the room when either victim died."

"Well we're still waiting on that," Armstrong replied.

"Ashley has a point though," McArthur said. "Most of what we have is circumstantial, and Kettings' case is increasingly looking remote. How far is the hotel from the crime scene?"

"Ten minutes on a good day," Murphy said. McArthur shook his head.

"I don't think this Glenn Young is connected to them," he said.

"He can explain some of the money coming through in her financials though," Ashley said, thinking about her old team in Metro. "He also said that she did porn while she was pregnant to support herself."

"Did she confess to Boyd?" Murphy asked.

"Sang like a bird. Well they did catch her with the blade in her hand and covered in his blood," Armstrong said. "She's refusing to take the can on our two though, having her close to the second killing though could push her over the edge."

"That's probably why she's saying no comment," Ashley said. "CPS wont charge on this."

"Then we need to work harder. Hopefully the CCTV at that hotel they were staying at shows them wandering out at some point."

"Maybe we should drop her in it," Armstrong said.

"No," Murphy said, shaking his head. "Any confession she would give would be inadmissible if anyone found out we talked about setting her up too. She might even confess to protect him. And if we find out she's not our killer after… It's not worth it."

"I agree," McArthur said. "Personally, I think that Young is in the clear, that Sanchez used him as a cover story to deflect," he said. "Although we could use the nature of their relationship to get something out of her," he said to Armstrong.

"Can you ask her if Young was with her during the whole night, that he didn't get up at all?" Ashley said. "That's the only thing that's holding him back."

"Yeah, we'll ask her," Armstrong said, writing it down.

"Is there anything you want us to ask him?"

"Try and get a general picture of her moods," McArthur said. "See if this is a onetime thing or if she was prone to mood swings."

"Did she say anything else?"

"Yeah, she keeps on saying that she was set up," Armstrong said, dismissively.

"Set up? By who?" Ashley asked.

"She says by Will Oatley," McArthur answered.

"What does Will Oatley have to gain by setting her up?"

"Nothing, that's the point."

Ashley's phone started to go. It was the SOCO lab.

"Sorry, I have to take this," Ashley said, going out into the hall and answering.

"DC Fenway."

"Hi, this is Gloria from the SOCO lab."

"Yes, hello Gloria. What can I do for you?"

"Well it's something we've come across that we think you'd be interested in. We got your DNA profile from the Stan Kettings' case and we have a match on the system."

"He doesn't have any priors though," Ashley said confused, she checked herself, that's why they took the sample.

"Not on your system, on ours. We thought it was odd."

"Why?"

"It's a match for an Emilia Sanchez." Ashley could have dropped the phone.

"So, is Stan Kettings the father?" Ashley asked.

"99.9% chance of it according to the stats."

"Gloria, I need you to e-mail this to me right now," Ashley said.

"OK, I take it it's good news."

"Maybe, thanks, call if it won't send." Ashley rushed back into the room.

"Who was that?" Armstrong asked.

"Lab," Ashley said, sitting back down. "They got a hit on Emilia Sanchez's DNA profile."

"Good, with who?"

"Stan Kettings," Ashley said, now checking to see if the e-mail had come through yet. Ashley looked up and saw the other three staring at her.

"You're fucking with us," Armstrong said.

"No," Ashley replied. "Young said that he did a parent test with Dora that said he wasn't the father. What if she did it to others without knowing?"

"I suppose she's able to get the DNA easy enough."

"Armstrong, gross," Ashley said. She saw the e-mail come back through and sent it off to McArthur. "I've sent the e-mail confirming it now."

"Maybe she knew Kettings was the dad and that's why she killed him," Murphy said. "Deadbeat dad who wouldn't pay for the child he bore."

"Kettings stopped seeing her when she was pregnant though," Ashley said. "How would she get DNA from him?"

"Maybe she didn't show until late," McArthur chipped in. Plausible, Ashley thought.

"Motive?" McArthur said looking at the e-mail on his phone. "We can use that to see if she did know."

"We can use it to see if Young talks," Murphy concluded.

"Right, call us on the way back."

***

Ashley walked past the packed observation room and into the interviewing room where Young and Asworth were waiting for her.

"Are you OK? Do you two need anything?" Ashley asked before sitting down.

"No, thank you," Glenn said, as Murphy walked in.

"Mr Asworth?"

"No, thank you," he said, sitting down too. Murphy clicked on the recorder.

"Recommencing interview of Glenn Young at Morley Police Station. Still present is DS Herschel Murphy."

"DC Ashley Fenway."

"James Asworth."

"As per previous recording the caution still remains in place Mr Young, do you understand?"

"Yes, I do."

"Mr Young, would you consider Dora to be a violent individual?" Murphy asked. Young shook his head.

"No, she wasn't. If anything, I thought she was a little timid," Young said. "She's petite as well. I don't think she has the strength to hurt anyone." That was true, Ashley thought.

"Did you ever see her have any violent outbursts?" Young shook his head.

"No."

"What about towards her baby's father?" Ashley asked. Again, he shook his head.

"No."

"Was there any particular reason that she asked to go to Premier Inn in west Didsbury on the eighteenth?" Ashley asked.

"She said it was convenient for her," Young answered.

"Did she ever tell you who the father was?" Asworth interjected

"Detectives, the questions are a bit scattered."

"OK, did she ever tell you who the father of her baby was."

"She just said it was one of her regulars," Young continued. "She never said who it was."

"Did she want to find out?" Ashley asked.

"If she did, she never told me," Young said. "I took a test voluntarily."

"Was she angry towards the father?"

"I would be lying if she wasn't a little resentful," Young mused. "I suppose it was her livelihood more than anything."

"She complained about it?" Murphy clarified. Young nodded.

"Don't think bad of her," he said. "She just wanted her child to be looked after." Ashley could sympathise with that.

"Did she ever mention a man called Stan at all?" Murphy asked.

"If she did, I can't remember," he said. "I'm sorry. I don't know how much more help I can be."

"Are you sure she didn't mention the name Stan?" Ashley pressed.

"I've told you no I —" His eyes narrowed. "Was he the father?"

"Yes," Ashley replied, while nodding. "We're investigating his murder. Of which due to Dora's location and motive makes her the prime suspect."

***

"We can't charge him on anything," Murphy said to Ashley once they were outside the room. "This is wrong place, wrong time, wrong person."

"I agree," Ashley said. "I'm going to call Metro and tell them that we have someone in custody that they might want to have a look at."

"OK, I'll talk to McArthur and Armstrong and tell them."

***

A couple of hours later she and Murphy were on their way home, stopping at a pub for a bit of dinner. Murphy had a steak and Ashley had fish and chips. The atmosphere in the pub was lively but their table a little more sombre.

Murphy was busy tucking into his food while Ashley played around with hers. Her mind going over what this could possibly mean for their investigation.

"What's the matter with you?" Ashley moved some food on her plate.

"I'm thinking."

"About?" Ashley sighed and placed her fork down.

"Where do we go from here?" Ashley asked. "Is Dora Sanchez really our killer? It doesn't match up with anything we have."

"CPS might think we have enough circumstantial evidence to place her at the scene of the crime," Murphy said, taking a sip of his beer. Ashley had stuck to J2o since she was driving.

"And carry out two?" Ashley shook her head. She was trying to picture how someone as small as Dora Sanchez could generate the force to stab someone in the neck. Before that she would've had to have hit Ferrets and Kettings on the back of their heads, tie them up on a bed and dealt the killing blow.

Would she be able to do it? The original blow didn't have enough force to kill the victims, only to knock them out. Carry them up the stairs and tie them to the bed before they woke up. Even with her active lifestyle she wouldn't have been able to do it in time.

"We have to go where the evidence goes Ash," Murphy said, breaking the silence. "First it was Tim Williams, now it's Dora Sanchez. You're still relatively young to the detective game, investigations like this take twists and turns."

Ashley had to concede that this was true, she had only been a detective for nine months or so and this really was her first big case.

295

"It's not always like on the TV shows where you have one suspect in a big case like this. There are loads of threads."

"Maybe you're right," Ashley said. "Does this mean another comb over the records?" Murphy nodded. Ashley wished she had something to drink now.

"I was impressed with your questioning though," he said. "I think you'll stick it out." Ashley half smiled.

"I hope so too," Ashley said, having another drink.

Chapter 45

Will Oatley closed his laptop and got up spritely from the chair. He laughed in his head at how easy it had been to organise this; usually it required much more planning and a lot more luck. This time all he needed to do was send his wife on holiday, for a free house.

Maybe he should have listened to Stan more often, the internet was a pool of untouched potential that he hadn't thought to use; he had always been so successful in his own way that he didn't see the need to branch out.

Even if the oaf phoned him, the police wouldn't suspect him in his murder, a simple IT phone call, nothing more. Even his death wasn't that big of a loss, Kettings was careless in some ways. His infrastructure was second to none but when it came to the dirty stuff, he didn't know the care and precision that came with executing the vision.

Will made his way to the bedroom to make sure that everything he needed was there. Fresh sheets on the bed, candlelight, but there were a few other things lying around if things became really naughty.

A couple of ties that could act as restraints and a bottle of lube in the top drawer.

He walked down the stairs of his house. A modern, brilliant white, floating staircase against a white wall with pieces of contemporary art on the walls, with the lights down low to create the atmosphere.

The doorbell went. Will pulled his phone out of his pocket and saw the agent at the door; they had already messaged ahead to say that they would be wearing a hoodie. They were careful, he liked that. But what they discussed wasn't. He got another phone out of his pocket and called the burner number they agreed on.

Will watched through the camera as the agent picked up the phone.

"It's rude to keep a guest waiting." A voice scrambler, another smart move, he liked this guy more and more.

"You seem to be a guest short," Will replied.

"I have to make sure this place is safe," the agent replied. "Make sure that no one can see us, nothing that can compromise me." Will laughed.

"I assure you."

"I didn't become who I am by taking other people's 'assurances'," the agent said. "Either we do it my way, or not at all. I can find another willing person to buy what I'm selling."

Will smiled and nodded to himself. This was the problem with the new ways, he had to give up the control he craved. But he appreciated the care this guy put into his work and could understand it. No one became this good by being careless.

"Very well." He cut the call and security feed and walked to the front door. He unlocked the door and opened it, before it was open Will was struck across the head.

***

Will wasn't sure how long he was out for. It could have been hours or seconds but what he could feel was being dragged up the stairs with his head hitting each step on the way up. He looked up and could see his attacker who had removed their hood to reveal what looked like blonde hair.

He tried to focus but the pain in his head was too much.

He tried to move his hands, but they were bound along with his feet. He felt his head against the carpet of the upstairs landing before blacking out again.

Will woke up again, more alert this time. He was on his bed.

"You do know who I am don't you?" He called out to his attacker, who he suspected was still in the room with him.

"I'll have you hung drawn and quartered for this!"

"I know," his attacker said, a little out of breath. "That's why I decided to beat you to it." Oatley tried to move his arms again and felt that he couldn't. He was on his bed with his hands and feet tied to each of the four corners. Will tried to break free but they were tight.

"I wouldn't try that if I were you." Will still couldn't see his attacker but they had removed the voice scrambler.

"Look, I have money, maybe we can come to some sort of arrangement," Will said, straining against his bonds.

"I don't want your money," the attackers said, now coming into view. "If I wanted it, I would have taken it years ago."

Oatley let out a fearful breath, he knew that face.

"You recognise me," there was a smile in the voice. "Good. The others didn't until it was too late."

"Others?" Will could see them nod.

"Look, I'm sorry," Will said. "For everything."

"You know, if someone who didn't know you heard that they might just believe you," his attacker said. "But you always abused us with a smile on your face because, how sorry were you really? I bet you were jacking yourself off to your collection before I even got here."

Will now felt really stupid. He should never have gone on the internet, he got sloppy, complacent, all the things that get other people caught; not him.

"But don't worry, everyone will know what sort of person you are, I've already seen to that. All your charitable blood money will be poisonous, your company ruined and your name resigned to nothing more than a slur!" His attacker got in his face.

"No one will remember any good that you ever did." Will closed his eyes, he could feel the straps loosening, he must have disturbed them while waking up.

He saw them walk across him and behind, so they were behind the bed. He saw the knife come up.

"WAIT!" Before he knew what was happening the knife came down hard into his neck and a searing pain spread through his body. The thrashing of his body made his bonds snap.

Help, was what Will thought; he needed help. Will tried to get to his feet but he could tell that he was losing blood too quickly. He felt a searing pain in his stomach. He looked down at the knife slide slowly out of him.

He looked at his attacker who just watched him. They knew that it was over. Will tried to reach out and hit them, scratch them, anything; he wasn't sure if he did on not.

Will though tried to get to safety, he stumbled out of the door with his hand over the wound, to the stairs. He slumped to his knees and looked up at the landing light.

This was it. This was how it all ended. He fell forward onto the cream carpet with a bang and the life left his eyes.

Chapter 46

Beep.

    Beep.

    Beep.

Ashley was already awake when her alarm went off. She'd spent the last five minutes debating going back to bed or getting up. She turned over, her body a little stiff from hockey training the night before.

She reached over, turned her alarm off and got out of bed.

She got her phone and saw she had a few messages from guys on Facebook. Ashley opened them up and started to go through them, all starting with some variation on the word, 'Hey'.

"Fuck! No, no, no!" Ashley threw her phone on the bed and went to get changed. An unsolicited dick pic. Just what she wanted in the morning.

Cardio.

Arms.

Squats.

Bag.

Ashley hugged the bag for a second and looked up at the TVs which were talking about the latest celeb going to rehab. Ashley pushed herself off the bag and went to have a shower.

***

This government does more u-turns than @Clarkson on the @Grandtour #Loudnoisesandnosolutions

    Anyone still want to talk about the famine in Yemen? No, didn't think so. #Openyoureyespeople

My cat just bopped me on the nose and stole my crisps in my vulnerable state. #Victimofcrime #crimewave #catburglar

Someone mentioned a collapse at work and instantly thought about @England Cricket #roughsummer #hitforsix

Crime still on the rise in @Manchester. @GMP what's being done about it. #hollowpromises

"Are our kids at risk of online predators on their games? A BBC investigation has shown that almost a quarter of children playing on popular games such as Fortnite and Overwatch have been asked by someone they don't know, to engage in chats."

"Surely the parents should take responsibility," Ashley said, as she drove to the office.

"Some kids as young as six are playing on these games, what if they don't know any better?"

"It's the responsibility of the gaming developers making sure that these platforms are safe for children to use." Ashley shook her head. Anything for people not to take on responsibility. She turned into the car park.

Ashley got into the office, she finished her banana and threw the skin into the bin. Breakfast and tea sorted, she got out the post-mortems of their two victims. She sat at her desk and looked at the details of how they died.

She examined the force that the blade was brought down at. It was the reasoning by the pathologist that they were looking for a man. Ashley looked at the full body shot of Dora Sanchez. She was quite petite with not a lot of arm muscle. But even then, a height advantage could compensate for it, but Dora was five two.

Ashley checked how high the bed was off the floor. Again, not enough to generate the force to make the cut. Ashley's phone went off. She reached into her pocket and pulled it out. It was McArthur.

"Sir." Ashley put the phone to her ear, still comparing the reports.

"Are you in the office?" McArthur asked.

"Yes," Ashley answered. "Why, do you need something?"

"You're gonna hear about it in the next five minutes, the press is down here already." Ashley looked out of the window at the other people in the office. Nothing looked out of the ordinary.

"Sir, what is it?"

"Will Oatley is dead."

"What!" Ashley said getting up.

"Get down here, everyone else is still getting their tights on." Ashley got her coat.

"How ironic. Where?"

"His estate, on the outskirts."

Ashley checked on Google maps.

"I'll be twenty minutes."

"See you there." Ashley got her coat on and walked out to see the few people in the office looking at their phones.

Chapter 47

Ashley could see the flashes of blue light from further down the road. She pulled up near the cordoned off area which had a few neighbours milling around. She found herself in an affluent area, but if this was the Oatley family it was a given.

The Oatley's owned much of the land in central Manchester and along the suburbs, it was prime real estate that they had made money off.

As Ashley got out of the car, she realised that they weren't neighbours. Reporters. As soon as she strode forward one of them recognised her and shouted her.

"Detective!"

"No questions, bugger off," Ashley said showing her ID, allowing her through, the press still asking questions as she walked to the open gate of Oatley Mansion.

The new house was modern with white walls, oak exterior and glass walls which had been dimmed. In the drive was an Aston Martin V12 Vantage along with an Over Finch Range Rover, which SOCO were combing over. Outside she could see McArthur on the phone; he wasn't speaking but had a stern look on his face which told Ashley that he was being shouted at.

His eyes flicked up and saw her. He snapped his fingers to get her attention. Although she hated it Ashley went over, being summoned. She didn't take it personally. He probably didn't want to interrupt the person he was talking or being talked at to."

"Yes Sir, it's my highest priority," McArthur said, in a measured voice. "Yes, I appreciate it." He rolled his eyes. "Well Sir, I'm here so I'm going to have a look now. Thanks, bye." He closed his phone and looked at Ashley.

"Assistant Chief Constable," McArthur said. "As if I don't know what we're dealing with." He walked towards the house and Ashley followed.

"How bad is it?" She asked.

"Will Oatley, *was* one of the most prominent men in Manchester," McArthur said, putting emphasis on the 'was'. The scene logger at the front door took their names and ranks.

"Wife phoned early this morning in a right state," McArthur said, pulling on overalls. "Unable to speak, just screaming."

"Where is she?" Ashley asked.

"Hospital, being treated for hysteria," McArthur said, looking around at the SOCOs. "Responding officer said that it was a bloody mess." They walked up the stairs, Ashley looked around, it was the sort of house that was never lived in. Everything was in order as if you were ordering from a catalogue.

When Ashley got to the top of the stairs, she saw it. A naked male face down on a cream carpet with a pool of blood staining it in a near perfect circle. What drew Ashley's attention was the victims outstretched arm.

Ashley looked at McArthur and could see that he was thinking the same as her. Cramer was busy fussing over the body while his assistant took photos. McArthur ran a hand through his hair and looked down at it.

"Is it him?" He asked. Cramer nodded. McArthur sighed heavily, as though the world added more loads onto his shoulders.

"How long ago are we talking?" McArthur asked.

"Based on body temperature I'd say he died last night, probably between midnight and two," Cramer said. "Died in the same vein as the others, and like victim two has the same sort of wound at the back of the head. I am surprised though he made it this far; but this should interest you." He turned Oatley's outstretched hand out and showed them his fingers.

"Blood," Ashley said, noticing the red tips on the nails. She looked down the arm and saw that it wasn't a sustained wound. "From the killer?"

"I hope so," Cramer said. "With any luck there should be some skin there as well." Ashley got up off her haunches and looked at the trail of blood coming from the living room. She looked down at the floor and saw another pool of blood by the victim's abdomen.

"Another wound?" Ashley asked.

"Yes, it's consistent with the knife wound on his neck, I would wager that they didn't hit the carotid arteries on the throat, but blood loss more than likely the cause of death." Ashley moved away from the body, following the trail of blood on the cream carpet to a bedroom.

The bedroom was much like the house, barely lived in; the only thing that gave it away was the crumpled-up sheets with blood on them. Ashley looked around the room and noticed a dressing table. She walked over to it, opened the drawers and saw a jewellery box which was unopened.

Wasn't a robbery gone wrong. Another personal vendetta. Ashley walked over to the bed and inspected the knots. The rope was frayed and not of good quality. Ashley poked the knot and it slightly came away. Very poorly done. The others were tied properly, so why this?

Ashley followed the blood trail back to where McArthur was standing.

"What do we think? Same people?" Ashley nodded.

"I think we're looking for a pair," she said. "The knots used are different and poorly done." She looked down at the body. His bloodshot eye looking up at Ashley.

"That's why he got away," Ashley concluded.

"Well, we don't have the luxury of press autonomy anymore," McArthur said. "Everything we do now is going to be under the microscope."

"Joy," Ashley deadpanned, just thinking about the amount of paperwork she would have to shift through to find links between Oatley and their other victims. Hopefully his computer would shed some light on that; but that brought something else up. Ashley walked down the stairs and McArthur followed.

"He couldn't really be a... you know?" Ashley asked with a frown.

"There's a distinct possibility," McArthur said, as they got to the hall.

"I've already sent Murphy and Armstrong to his office to confiscate his computer and files," McArthur said. "I want you to go back and search for a link between Oatley, Ferrets and Kettings." Ashley nodded.

"What about his friends, enemies?" Ashley asked.

"Parland can handle that," McArthur said. "It should be a few hours before we get DNA from here." They walked round the house which was lit by a greyish hue from the large skylights.

"What do we do now about Dora Sanchez?"

"Fuck, yeah. I almost forgot about her," McArthur said. "Well at least we know she isn't our killer, or this Glenn Young."

"We put a lot of work into that," Ashley said.

"Well both were in custody forty miles away. We can't change circumstances."

"Can I make our evidence available to Metro?" Ashley asked. McArthur replied, with a questioning sound. "They're doing the Dora Sanchez case."

"Yeah, yeah, we need friends," McArthur concluded. They walked into an office where someone from IT was looking at a fancy MAC computer.

"Been able to get in?" McArthur asked. The technician shook his head.

"We'll have to get this back into the lab to break it down," he said.

"Make sure you get any laptops and iPads, even his wife's," McArthur ordered. "We just got bumped up to priority on everything." He continued talking to the technician, Ashley though walked over to a small box on the side of the door. Archimedes Security Systems.

Ashley got her phone out and searched it on Google. The company website was the first result and Ashley had a look. They were a locally based, private security company which provided bespoke security solutions to a range of clients, footballers and 'celebs'; the main clientele. Ashley read the main 'about us' section on the website.

We at Archimedes Security Solutions take your safety seriously. Our engineers and security team provide detailed plans and networks unique to your homes and businesses, with everything from motion detectors, infra-red cameras and panic rooms all linked to a central CCTV hub which can only be viewed by our team of twenty-four-hour support staff.

"Sir." McArthur came over, Ashley pointed to the box, most likely a motion detector.

"What is it?" Ashley handed him her phone so he could read it, from the look on his face he had the same idea as her.

"Come on Fenway." He handed her, her phone back.

"What about you?" Ashley asked.

"More like us," McArthur said. "We're going to speak to this company. You can drive." Ashley raised an eyebrow. She'd never been asked to help interview a suspect with a leading detective.

"Fenway, are you coming?" He asked.

"Yes Sir," Ashley said, with a small smile as they walked.

Chapter 48

Shocked about Will@OatleyDPLC dying @GMP, what's going on?

@OatleyDPLC was one of the kindest and generous people I've ever met, really cared about his community. #oneofakind #RIP

Will@OatleyDPLC helped keep my local community shelter open when it was about to go under. Wondering today what might have been if he hadn't helped. #oneofakind #RIP

Manchester has lost one of its greatest characters today. So senseless, I hope they find who did this and put them under. #Oneofakind #RIP

See you in hell @OatleyDPLC When I see your grave, I'm gonna piss on it, you fucker!!

@OatleyDPLC you changed this city for the better and it will be worse off without you. #RIP #oneofakind

Anyone else shocked that @OatleyDPLC was murdered? No, me neither. #thetruthwillcomeout #everythigcatchesupwithyou

Archimedes Security Solutions were based on the same industrial estate as the bus company, so Ashley knew the way.

It was the same sort of unit with a shiny metallic front, which unlike the bus company was cleaned regularly, probably for the sake of keeping up appearances, as most of the units were badly worn. There were a fleet of cars stationed outside with the name and insignia on the vans. Ashley parked up and they walked over to the front door.

Inside was a sleek and modern interior which wasn't anything like the outside. There was a young guy on the front desk typing away.

"Hello, welcome to Archimedes Security."

"Hello, DCI McArthur and DC Fenway, Manchester Major Crimes Unit." Both McArthur and Fenway showed him their IDs.

"How can we help you detectives?" He asked.

"We need to speak to your manager about a client of yours," McArthur said. "Will Oatley."

"I'm sorry, we can't discuss client's personal matters with police unless in exceptional circumstances."

"He's dead," Ashley said. The man at the desk turned to her. "Exceptional enough?" Dumbstruck the man uttered his apologies and rang a number.

"Our owner is coming to meet you now," He said quietly.

"Thanks," McArthur said with a slight smile. A minute later a well-dressed man with sleeked-back, black hair came from the door behind the desk. Ashley instantly got the impression that he was a bit of a show-off.

"Hello officers," He said, shaking both hers and McArthur's hand. "Chris Smallwood, why don't we go talk in my office?"

McArthur and Ashley followed him into his office which had a piece of modern art on the wall and the same sleek interior as the reception area, all out done by a large mahogany desk which he sat behind.

"Please, take a seat." Ashley and McArthur sat down on two comfy chairs in front of the desk. "I'm not sure if my mate out front misheard you, but he said that Mr Oatley is dead."

"We can confirm it," McArthur said. Chris let out a long breath.

"I can't believe it," he said. "He was one of my first customers, said he believed in giving small, local businesses a fighting chance."

"Were the two of you close?" Ashley asked.

"Very much so," Chris replied. "He was an investor in the early days, helped us get on our feet, and get new clients with his contacts." He ran a hand back through his hair.

"Sorry, would you like a tea or a coffee?" He asked, picking his phone up.

"No, we're good," McArthur said. "I know this must be a trying time, but we need to ask some questions."

"Of course, anything."

"Well Mr Smallwood, Mr Oatley died at home," McArthur explained. "Looking at your website it says there is a continuous feed that relays back here."

"That's correct," Chris said, now typing away on his computer. "Mr Oatley had one of our most secure packages, including electronic keys as well as exterior CCTV cameras. So, no one would have been able to have got in without his express consent."

"Is there any way Mr Oatley himself could have seen the feed?" Ashley asked. Chris nodded.

"His system included an app where he could look at any of the cameras," Chris explained. "From that app he could contact us, the police, or lock his house down if he felt threatened." It matched up with the others of letting the killer in.

"Were there any internal cameras?" Ashley asked. Chris shook his head.

"Mr Oatley only had them outside. He didn't want his house to become in his words 'a prison.'" Ashley could sympathise with that. She wouldn't want everything she did in her house looked at. Her mother certainly wouldn't want it to be.

"What about the motion detectors?" Ashley asked again. "There were quite a few of them around the house."

"It's a smart system we've been trialling," Chris explained. "The house picks up where people are using the motion detectors so it knows how many people should be in there. Then after a certain time if more movements are picked up when say, the person's in bed it notifies the person."

"Do you collect the information?" Ashley asked.

"It's stored on our servers."

"Can we take a copy of the CCTV and have a look at them?" McArthur asked.

"Of course, but for confidentiality purposes you'll have to view it here in the interim period while we go through our process of release," Chris said. McArthur and Ashley looked at each other; most of the time security companies were shitty about CCTV so to see it on site was a bonus.

Chris led them to a room which had a couple of monitors and a computer where a technician was waiting for them. Chris made the introductions but excused himself to make a call.

"If you need anything else, please call me." He got a card out. McArthur went to take it, but he handed it to Ashley who gingerly took it.

"Thanks," she said. Chris smiled at her and walked away. McArthur and Ashley exchanged awkward glances.

"So," the Technician said. "What is it you are looking for?"

"We need to look at the front and back door CCTV cameras for Will Oatley last night," McArthur said. The technician got the feeds up.

"Between nine and six," Ashley said, consulting her notes. The technician pressed play and they watched.

"I take it there's no audio," McArthur said. The technician shook his head. Ashley and McArthur looked at the screen as nothing came up on the front or the back doors.

"There!" Ashley pointed to the front monitor when someone in a black hood came down and pressed the bell. The technician paused it. From the angle the camera was at Ashley couldn't see the person's face.

"That's him," McArthur said. "What happens next?" The technician pressed play, a couple of seconds later they answered a phone and spoke. A few seconds after that they were let in, but they made an aggressive step forward and quickly closed the door.

"That explains the head wounds," Ashley said. "They must have been expected and then attacked as they go through." McArthur nodded in agreement.

"What time does he leave?" They fast forwarded it and just after midnight the footage stopped.

"Where's the feed?" McArthur asked.

"I'm not sure," the technician said, typing something into the keyboard.

"Can someone disable the security using the app?" Ashley asked.

"Only with fingerprints," the technician replied. Ashley and McArthur looked at one another.

"Disable the security for a clean getaway."

"Seems that way," McArthur said. "Can we get a printout of our hoodie guy?" He asked.

"I'll just have to ask Mr Smallwood if that's OK."

"Well you go and do that," McArthur said, and the technician walked out the room. McArthur got his phone out.

"I want you to find out which hospital they took Mrs Oatley to," McArthur said. "I'm going to find all the CCTV in the area and find out who this bastard is."

Chapter 49

Ashley could see McArthur looking round at her car with the same confusion that Murphy had when he got in.

"Nice car," he mused. The hospital Nicola Oatley was in was ten minutes away.

"Thanks," Ashley said. "Murphy liked it too."

"I didn't have a car like this at your age." McArthur said.

"Did they have cars this powerful when you were my age?" Ashley asked. McArthur smiled and chuckled.

"It suits," he said. "You a big fan of cars?" Ashley shook her head.

"No, they're to get to A and B," she said. "But when I got this car, I realised just how much I love driving it." They came off the ring road towards the hospital.

"Before this I drove a Corsa." Ashley allowed herself to reminisce about the old battered car, which was now her brothers.

"But some guys get very defensive if a girl has a better car than them," Ashley said.

They pulled up outside a plush private hospital on the outskirts of the city centre with sprawling grounds and large oak trees where the leaves were falling onto the road. The road with a circular end, led up to a large manor house.

Ashley parked in a visitor space at the side of the building and they walked to the big oak doors and let themselves into a large spacious waiting area. McArthur and Ashley walked to a blonde-haired receptionist who was busy typing away.

"Hello," McArthur said, in a welcoming tone. The receptionist looked up at him with a beaming smile.

"Hi, how can I help?" She asked, with youthful exuberance.

"We're here to talk to Cynthia Oatley," McArthur said, showing her his ID. "She was admitted a couple of hours ago."

"Oh, I see." She frowned and consulted her computer, she looked up at them before going back to the screen.

"Ms Oatley was admitted and is on the Lubia wing. I'll phone ahead for you." Before either of them could reply, she had already picked the phone up and was phoning. She had a brief conversation with someone on the other end.

"If you follow the signs to Lubia, Dr Stevens will see you," she said, with a smile.

"Thank you very much," McArthur said, leading the way.

"I'd rather she didn't phone ahead," McArthur said, when they reached the corridor.

"Element of surprise."

"Bingo," McArthur said. Ashley could see the logic; phoning ahead gave people a chance to formulate a lie in their head. Not that she was a suspect in this, but most murders were domestics gone wrong. They reached the Lubia wing which was a corridor of private rooms with polished walnut doors and frames.

Outside one of the rooms was a doctor in a long white coat. He was tall, with a sharp jaw line, with soft stubble and short, curly, blonde hair. He looked up and almost did a double take at Ashley who rolled her eyes.

"Dr Stevens?" McArthur asked.

"Yes," he said, after a pause and shook McArthur's hand.

"I'm DCI McArthur, this is DC Fenway." He smiled broadly at Ashley when he shook her hand, which made Ashley a little uneasy.

"We're here to see Mrs Oatley," McArthur said, putting his hands back into his coat pocket. Dr Stevens looked at Ashley again.

"Yes, well she's here, I have to warn you that we've had to give her a slight sedative to calm her down so she might be a little... slow."

"We'll call if we need anything," Ashley said, following McArthur into a large room which had a bed on the left, and a media centre on the right. Ashley noticed a smart suit that was pressed and folded on a chair in the room, no doubt by an orderly.

Mrs Oatley was sitting in a large, high backed chair which was looking out onto the gardens. McArthur walked towards her. She had a blank expression on her face and her skin was pale.

"Mrs Oatley, my name is DCI McArthur and this is DC Fenway. We're very sorry for your loss." Mrs Oatley nodded mutely.

"Thank you," she whispered. McArthur nodded to Ashley who took the other seat next to her.

"Mrs Oatley, can you tell us where you've been?" Ashley asked.

"I was away with the girls for a spa week. Will paid for it," she replied. Ashley and McArthur looked at each other with knowing looks.

"Where was this?"

"The Kasbah Tamadot in Marrakech." Ashley nodded, sympathetically. Her phone buzzed in her pocket.

"And you got back this morning?" She nodded.

"How was Mr Oatley before you left?" McArthur asked. Ashley checked her phone.

Unknown: *DC Fenway, care to comment on the speculation that Will Oatley has bit the dust? S Lingard.*

Ashley placed her phone back in her pocket.

"He was excited, he said he potentially had a big contract for a new hotel in the city centre. He said it would be better if I was out of the way." Ashley and McArthur again showing knowing looks.

"Did he spend long days in the office?" Ashley asked. Cynthia nodded.

"He was very busy," she replied. "The expansion of the city centre was a big project that needed his input."

"Mrs Oatley. Is there anyone who would have records of your husband's itinerary?" McArthur asked. "So, we can retrace his last movements."

"His personal assistant, Ella," she said. "She doubles up as my PA as well."

"Do you know where she is now?"

"She should be at work," Cynthia said. McArthur nodded and looked at Ashley that this was their cue to leave. Ashley got to her feet and bid her goodbye, telling her that they might be back.

"How is she? You didn't upset her at all?" The doctor asked.

"No, she was helpful," Ashley said, as they walked away.

"How do you deal with guys checking you out all the time?" McArthur asked, as they walked back to her car.

"I just ignore them," Ashley said, opening the door to the carpark. "Besides, if I'm interested in someone, they know about it."

"You don't strike me as the clingy type." Ashley smiled to herself.

"Good job you have good instincts," Ashley said, sitting down and doing her belt up. "Where do we go now?"

"We have a PA to talk to."

Chapter 50

With one of the city's wealthiest sons murdered, it was amazing how much manpower was suddenly available. The Oatley building had a much more subdued feeling than when she pulled up here the other day.

Uniformed officers were there talking to employee's and taking boxes of papers out of the building.

"What the fuck? Pull up here." Ashley pulled up and McArthur got out of the car before she stopped. Ashley swore under her breath and followed him to a Senior Officer. More specifically Assistant Chief Constable Delany.

"Oh shit," Ashley muttered.

"Ah, Donald, nice of you to come," he said. "I was busy making sure you have what you need."

"There was no need. I already had my team down here."

"Well not soon enough for the Chief Constable's liking. I don't have to remind you."

"That Oatley is one of Manchester's revered sons," McArthur said. "I don't suppose you'll have to say that once they know he's a paedophile." Delany's face instantly hardened, from the smug look he was wearing when they got there.

"I've heard rumours about the case you've been doing," Delany said, in a low voice. "You better make sure he's not part of it."

"We'll go where the evidence takes us," McArthur said, as they walked past him. Ashley kept her head down as she walked past but could feel Delany watching her. Ashley had hoped after the press conference the she wouldn't have to see him for a while.

"He's only looking for a chance to show off Sir," Ashley said, as they walked into the large reception area.

"By tomorrow the Chief Constable will be down here too. Oatley was a big donor, not to mention the Police and Crime Commissioner too," he sighed.

"I really could have done without it," he said in a tired voice.

"Come on, we have a secretary to question." Ashley led them upstairs to the large office area. Oatley's office was at the back which was being manned by a smart looking woman who was sat at her desk.

Her blonde hair was tied back in a tight bun, with sharp eastern European features and sharp blue eyes.

"Ella?" Ashley asked. Ella nodded tearfully, her expression blank as Ashley and McArthur sat down. "Hello Ella, I'm DC Ashley Fenway and this is DCI McArthur. We just want to ask you a couple of questions."

"I'm here legally," she said abruptly, in a soft Polish accent.

"We're not looking into your legality," McArthur said, reassuringly. "We want to talk to you about your boss, Mr Oatley, you were his PA were you not?" Ella nodded.

"Sorry, how silly of me," she said.

"It's OK," Ashley reassured her, getting out her notebook.

"How long have you worked for Mr Oatley for?" McArthur asked.

"I joined seven years ago as, a cleaner," she said. Ashley noted the forcing of the A. McArthur nodded his head.

"And how long have you been Mr Oatley's Personal Assistant for?" McArthur asked.

"Three years," Ella said. "I replace Mrs Hawthorne." She closed her eyes, mentally scolding herself. "I replaced Mrs Hawthorne. His previous PA."

"Well that's quite the rise," McArthur said. "Did it go straight to that or was there a middle-step?" Ella nodded.

"I joined the pool first," she said, putting emphasis on joined. "It's a small group which helps the associates. He was impressed with me." Again, the cynic in Ashley said it was only for her looks but looking at Ella's desk everything was filed in logical places with lots of separate trays for various things. She even had two calendars, a Labrador one for what Ashley could only assume was for herself and a generic landscape one with Oatley's schedule.

"How was your relationship with Mr Oatley, was it good?"

"Oh, very good," Ella said. "He was like father to me." Again, she grimaced. "He was like a father to me."

"He gave me a chance when no one else would, I wanted to repay him so much," she said, wiping her eyes.

"Ella, had Mr Oatley been acting strangely or out of character in the last week or so?" McArthur asked. Ella thought for a moment.

"He was busy with a new hotel that needed signing off," Ella said. "But he seemed, happy, more than he had in a while."

"Before that?"

"Irritable," she said. "Not to me personally but to other people." As she talked to McArthur about it, Ashley noticed a photo on the desk of Ella and what looked like her daughter. The girl had the same bright blonde hair and looked like she was about thirteen. Ashley frowned slightly.

"But he was always so nice and always asked about my daughter."

"Is this her?" Ashley asked, interrupting and pointing to the photo. Ella looked at the photo and nodded. Ashley and McArthur sharing knowing looks.

"Does she come into the office?" Ashley asked.

"A couple of times. Why?" She asked.

"Curiosity," McArthur said, easily.

"Do you have Mr Oatley's schedule for the last two weeks?" Ashley asked.

"Of course," Ella opened her computer; Ashley noted again that it was organised. She printed out a few sheets of paper for them.

"Before we go Ella, is there anyone you know who might want to harm Mr Oatley?" McArthur asked. Ella bit her lip.

"Ella, it's important that you're truthful with us," Ashley said.

"There were phone calls," Ella said, quietly.

"What type of phone calls?" McArthur asked.

"You have to understand. We sometimes have to deal with angry people on the phone. Mainly from people whose houses are in the way of developments."

What a shock, Ashley thought.

"But these were different," she said.

"Different how?" McArthur asked.

320

"Threatening," Ella said. "They would talk about how they show the world what sort of person he was. Nothing about work."

"What did they talk about?" Ashley asked. Ella shrugged.

"They just, shouted, things that didn't make sense."

"Was it a man or woman?" Ashley asked.

"It was masked.".

"How often did these calls come through?" Ella shrugged.

"Not that often."

"Did you record any of them?" Ashley asked. "Or call the police over it?"

"I ask Mr Oatley about it," Ella explained. She again closed her eyes and cursed herself for not saying 'asked'. "But he said to ignore it. Some jealous friend he said."

"OK Ella, thank you for your time and the schedule," McArthur said, getting up. "We're just going to have a look in his office." He nodded to Ashley and they walked through a ceiling-high, glass door into Oatley's office.

"Phone calls? Sounds weird," McArthur said, putting his hands in his pockets.

"Maybe he knew he was untouchable," Ashley said, looking at the wall. They were adorned with Oatley, at his various charitable foundations, and framed newspaper articles. McArthur came over.

"Could be like Jimmy Saville?" McArthur asked. He looked at the desk where the desktop used to lie, which was hopefully being combed over by the lab technicians.

"What if we get the phone records for the line and see where they came from?" Ashley suggested. "They might have been dumb enough to do it from the same spot."

"Good shout," McArthur said. His phone went off again. "McArthur... right, I'll be there now." He ended the call. "Right, contact the rest of the team, we need to have a brief in an hour."

"Yes Sir."

321

Chapter 51

"Great, if you can send those over as quickly as possible, I'll be really grateful," Ashley said, putting the phone down. Phone companies were really pissy when it came to data, but they had signed up to a twenty-four-hour turnaround for phone records. She had also chased up the social media guys to confirm that the picture of their suspect had been circulated. Her phone went off and she checked the message.

Dave: *Thanks for the evidence Ash, owe you one.*

"Phone records are en route, so are credit and debit cards," Ashley said out loud. She walked to the board, slipping her phone back into her pocket and ticked off the list.

"How's the press situation?" Parland asked. Ashley walked to the window. The small pool had swelled three times the size with more TV crews as well.

"I think they got wind," Ashley said, walking back to her desk.

"Probably one of the hired helps," Parland said. "Autopsy's been pushed up, but it won't be done 'til the end of the day at least."

"Where's McArthur?" Armstrong asked.

"Briefing the overlords," Ashley said. "With what piss poor evidence we have so far."

Parland walked to the boards. A jumbled picture which so far didn't fit, all three of their victims led different lives yet were killed by the same person in the same way. What was their link?

The only link Ashley could see so far was the one between Kettings and Oatley as friends. There must be something more there, something that would have got them both killed. Maybe they ran in the same paedophile circles as Gordon Ferrets.

"Maybe there's something in his company's accounts and archives," Parland said, he looked over at Ashley's desk. "How big is it?"

"Annual reports go back to the fifties," Ashley said. "Not to mention paperwork from the company, we're talking close to 20 000 pages of documents which are unsearchable electronically."

"But we don't know what we're looking for," Parland said.

"Well let's look at what we do know," Murphy said, picking up his report. "He was killed with a slash to the neck and tied to a bed like the others. But he broke free."

"Knots were sub-par," Ashley said. "Anyone could have broken out of it."

"What about the houses?" Armstrong asked. "All of them were locked, the killer was invited in. The CCTV from the security firm proves it. So, it's someone who they all knew."

"I suppose with two contrasting social circles like Ferrets and Oatley should narrow it down." Ashley said. "But there's days' worth of material here. Days is something they won't let us have." Ashley pointed with her finger at the pool of reporters.

"What do you suggest?" Armstrong asked.

"We need a link, a lead, something to work from," Ashley said. "I bet my future pension that he's a paedophile too."

"Fair statement, but where does it give us a lead?" Parland asked. Ashley smiled. She was hoping they would ask.

"I went to his office. The walls were covered in photos of his charitable deeds," Ashley said. "Tell me how a powerful and rich paedophile gets his kicks, more to the point, how does he keep his victims quiet?"

"Money?" Armstrong suggested.

"Guilt," Ashley said. "The big picture is who stands to lose more. One person, or hundreds?" The team looked at each other.

"The lead is in one of his charities," Ashley said. "Someone who was abused by him. We find that, cross reference it with people in our two victims' social circles."

"Bingo killer," Murphy said.

"Good, let's track down the ones he was most involved with; we'll need to pull files from the charities commission," Parland said, getting to his desk. "Bring up a new board and let's go through them."

"I think we should keep an eye on the social media feeds as well," Ashley suggested. "See if there are people glad of his death."

"Good idea Fenway. Phone IT and assign someone to monitor it." Ashley phoned up IT and Aaron answered.

"IT forensics, Aaron speaking."

"I hope your day's as good as mine."

"Maybe worse if possible," Aaron said. "This Oatley thing has sent us into a shit stream."

"Tell me about it. Anything on his computers?" Ashley asked hopefully.

"Barely started," Aaron said. "Something tells me though you want to add to my workload."

"You know me so well," Ashley said. "We need a monitor on the social media feeds."

"What are you looking for?"

"Anything negative on Oatley's death," Ashley said.

"Should be easy," Aaron told her. "Loads of people are mourning. You would have thought that Manchester would be going to the dogs if it wasn't for him."

"Can you keep a forty-eight-hour watch on it?"

"Writing the algorithm. Fancy a drink over it later?"

"Read my mind," Ashley said, she looked up and saw McArthur coming in. "Thanks for this, I'll text you later." She put the phone down.

"Right, where're we going?"

"We're looking at the possibility that Oatley might have abused kids at his charities; we're putting a list together and going to search through them."

"Good, what else?"

"IT are setting up a watch on social media on anyone saying anything negative on Oatley, and they're just starting on the breakdown on his computers." McArthur nodded.

"I suppose I don't need to tell you that the powers upon high want this brought to a swift conclusion," McArthur said. "Evidence isn't offering up much in the way of suspects, but I know there's something there."

"We were saying social circles have been made smaller," Parland said. "There cannot be that many people who run in the same circles as these guys." He finished pointing at Kettings and Ferrets.

McArthur sighed and looked at the board up and down.

"Sometimes I hate Fridays," he said. "Good work everyone. Let's get that list so we can hit some of the charities tomorrow, let's not forget the work we have to put in with Ferrets and Kettings as well. Let's see if there's a link between all of them before you all go." He swept into his office and they set to work.

Ashley was looking back over the evidence they had so far, to see if there was anything that linked them and Oatley. After going over the same papers and evidence nothing was showing Oatley or any of his businesses.

She had been at this for hours without a break and her mind was frazzled. Ashley leaned back in her chair, gulped down the last of her tea and looked at her teammates. The same frustrated and tired looks reflected her own mood. She looked at the time. It was nearly time to clock off anyway.

She rearranged the files and put them back in order, some of the evidence for Oatley would be back tomorrow and they could start afresh.

"Clocking off?" Murphy asked.

"I need a break. Everything is starting to blur together," Ashley said, pulling her coat on. "How about you?"

"Just a couple more charities and we can hit them all tomorrow," Murphy said. "Today's been hard."

"Well tomorrow is going to be much worse," Ashley said. "Tomorrow they want a suspect and we don't have one."

"We'll find one," Murphy said with a smile. "Good night."

"Night."

Chapter 52

Ashley got her Bud from the bar and sat down in a nice, comfy chair. It had been a shit day and was about to become even shitter, so she could enjoy a beer or two. The décor of the bar she was in was dark and purple with lots of business and young people having an end of week drink.

Ashley looked up at one of the TVs dotted around which was showing a football match. No doubt Matty was watching it. Ashley scanned the door and Aaron walked in. He clocked her and walked to the bar and got himself a drink (a lager) and sat in the seat next her.

"Fuck this day," he said, checking the score.

"Amen to that," Ashley replied. "Metro CID was so much easier."

"Amen to that," Aaron agreed, and they clinked drinks.

"So, is he?" Ashley asked.

"Looks like he is," Aaron said. "His personal home computer has a cluster of encrypted files which are taking a long time to break down, but it should be done by the morning."

"How can you be sure?" Ashley asked.

"Because we can find confidential documents in his normal servers," Aaron said. "Why encrypt something like that?"

"Point taken."

"Plus, his computer has access to the dark web."

"He could be hiring hitmen," Ashley deadpanned.

"Damn those people who want to keep their houses, right?" Aaron said. Ashley shrugged, looked up at the TV again and finished her bottle. She got the attention of one of the bar staff and asked for another.

"Bitcoin," Ashley said.

"Hmm?"

"Was he into Bitcoin?" Ashley asked. "At least it would provide a link between the three victims."

"I'll look into it," he said, nervously. He looked at Ashley who was staring into nothing.

"Still no luck?"

"No, and the lines are getting more and more blurred," Ashley said. "There must be a reason, I just don't know what so far. Bitcoin seems like the best bet to find it"

"And their porn tastes."

"Yeah, and their porn tastes," Ashley said, shaking her head. She wondered if there really was a link between them or if they were just random.

"What about that social media watch. Anything come up from that?" Ashley asked. Aaron reached into his bag and pulled out a couple of sheets of paper. As he was doing that the waitress came over and gave her a beer which Ashley paid for with contactless.

"A few people," Aaron said, handing them over.

Ashley looked at them. They were printouts of tweets and Facebook posts. All of them glad about the fact that he was dead; but you don't get to where he was without making a few enemies.

"Was this just from when I asked?" Ashley asked, looking at Aaron who nodded. Ashley was hoping that it was still running, but this was more than enough to get her started. There was nearly five pages of solid social media to go through.

Ashley checked her phone. It was nearly half nine and she could go back over some of this. At least try and rule a few people out.

"So…" Aaron was never the best at small talk. "How are you finding it?"

"Finding what?" Ashley asked.

"The Major Crimes thing?"

"It's fine," Ashley said. "Same sort of shit, different sort of day. How are you finding it?" Aaron shrugged.

"It pays more and there is something different every day," he said. Ashley laughed, sometimes she wished her job was as simple as his.

"What's funny?" He asked.

"Nothing."

***

Ashley closed the door to her apartment, threw her gym gear in the washing machine and switched it on. She flipped the radio on, got her dinner out of the fridge and put it in the microwave. She fished into her bag and pulled out the social media posts.

"Deputy Mayor Harold Donaldson had this to say." Ashley turned to the radio and turned it up.

"I speak on behalf of the Mayor's office when I express our profound sadness at the death of Will Oatley in such tragic and horrific circumstances. As we all know, Will worked tirelessly for our local communities with his philanthropy and his commitment to make home ownership a dream that everyone could wake up to.

"Of course, we hope like everyone else that those responsible are caught and tried to the full extent of the law and we encourage anyone with any information to come forward and contact the police. Thank you very much."

It was going to be a long night.

She sat down with her dinner on the sofa and her laptop and set about working. Ashley systematically went through every post on the list and the people who were posting them.

Many of them were victims of Oatley's developments, a few basic searches showed posts that related to their removal from properties.

Kerrie Smith.

Mid-thirties, was removed along with her entire street to make way for a new housing development. The people were promised new houses but where shafted and their 'affordable houses' were sold for higher profit, leaving her and the rest of her neighbours homeless.

Her post rambled on about how great it was that Oatley was dead and that he finally got what was coming to him.

Joe Gamble.

Mid-seventies and an ex-employee of one of Oatley subsidiaries, who along with over a hundred other people were screwed by Oatley when the company was sold to a rival developer, who stole the pension pot and left him penniless.

328

The guy was still working two jobs just to make ends meet. At least that's what his daughter says.

Again though, not the sort of guy with the means and knowhow to kill Oatley.

Kevin Thompson.

Ex-security guard at the same place of work as Gamble and lived on the same estate as Smith. A double-axe to grind, and judging by one of his earlier posts he was very graphic in the slitting of Oatley's throat. He would be someone they should have a look at in the morning.

Kyle Burch.

Similar story; screwed over by Oatley on another housing development; shit, how did this guy not get killed sooner? Ashley thought. He was obviously good at keeping his nose clean. Ashley rubbed her temple; there must have been a reason why Oatley kept on getting away with shit like this.

Ashley made a note of some of the more aggressive posts before she came across someone who hadn't been evicted from one of his properties.

His post was giving it all about how much he hated Oatley and how he was better off dead, but all his posts were like this.

"Demari Wright," Ashley said, delving deeper. He shared a lot of posts about Oatley's developments with rants about how he destroyed everything he touched.

Ashley searched for Demari Wright. Nothing of interest on Google but his Facebook and Twitter profiles made for interesting reading. In a way it reminded Ashley of Tim Williams. He saw himself as a gangster wannabe, also saw himself as a musician.

Ashley listened to some of his music which wasn't to her taste, but the underlying tones of resentment in the lyrics were a little on the nose. It was like he wanted people to know he was touched up as a kid.

Ashley finished her dinner and tried to look back deeper into Wright; he was the main man so far. His Twitter profile also bragged about an arrest so he must be in the system somewhere, but she still didn't see him for murder but...

Ashley leaned back on the sofa, looked up at the ceiling and breathed out. Her eyes flashed to the clock and saw that it was nearly eleven.

Ashley shook her head. She could find him in the morning. After a hot shower she crawled into bed, turned the lights off and closed her eyes.

Chapter 53

Still lost after the death of @OatleyDPLC, hopefully there is some sort of donation page set up for him #Oneofakind

We at the Labour Party express our mourning over the death of Will @OatleyDPLC, our thoughts and condolences to his family and friends at this sad time. #Oneofakind

@OatleyDPLC well thank fuck you've bit the dust.

I still hope @OatleyDPLC will continue its charity work, it's been the lifeline of some communities #Oneofakind

Ashley allowed herself a break from the gym, she had a small lay-in and drove straight to work. She was surprised to see that she wasn't the first person, in. When she got in, she saw McArthur's office light on.

Ashley walked to her desk and saw three other people inside with him, along with Parland and assistant Chief Constable Delany. Maybe they were expanding the team to deal with Oatley.

Ashley started up her computer, got her morning tea and breakfast and sat at her desk. She brought up the NPC and searched for Demari Wright. As she expected he had a record and he had an address which she wrote down. Ashley sent an e-mail to Aaron, asking him to send up what else the programme had picked up.

When she had finished, the door to McArthur's office opened. The two other people in suits came out along with Delany. Two of the other guys clocked Ashley and shared a joke between themselves and Delany. Ashley ignored them, Parland came out, saw her and came over.

"What was that about?" Ashley asked.

"They want to expand the team into these murders," Parland said, taking a seat next to Ashley. "Three DCIs, an army of DSs and DCs with Delany having oversight of it all.

"It's still McArthur's team though, right?" Ashley asked.

"Yeah, he's SIO on it still," Parland said. "We're looking after the Oatley case while the others look over Kettings and Ferrets."

"So, who were the other guys?"

"DI Taylor and DI Deacon," Parland said. "Not sure what order they're running this on but there's going to be a big conference at ten so we can all compare notes on what we're dealing with." Ashley nodded.

"So, McArthur wants us all here, so no excursions," he said, nodding at Ashley's screen.

"Promising lead on what we had yesterday," Ashley said. "I want to talk to him. He has a lot to say about Will Oatley."

"Everyone does."

"Not the good kind," Ashley said, giving Parland a knowing look. Parland just grunted.

"Well, boss doesn't want anyone going anywhere just yet so sit tight." Parland went and sat at his desk.

"Fenway, a word please." McArthur went back into the office. Ashley got up, followed him inside and closed the door.

"I'm sure Parland's already told you that we're expanding the investigation team."

"Yes Sir," Ashley replied. "How big is it going to be?"

"Around fifty," McArthur said.

"Is that good news?" Ashley asked.

"Now onto the bad news," he continued. "I know you love your boards, but we've been allocated an office manager. DS Sarandon, but everyone calls him Sue."

"Ah, OK," Ashley said, quite an unfortunate surname; could never be said that the force didn't have a sense of humour.

"You'll need to talk to him as well, he's a nice chap, he'll look after your board."

"Thanks, Sir," Ashley said. "I'll see you later."

***

Underneath their floor there was a free office which they were using for this huge briefing. Ashley went down with Murphy who was surprised by it all.

"There must be at least fifty people," he said as they walked in.

"Maybe they've palmed off lots of other things on local CID," Ashley said. They stood near the front. At ten sharp McArthur came down.

"Right everyone, thank you for coming," he said "As you should all know by now you have been absconded into Operation Overline. Our main objective is finding the person or persons involved in the murders of these three people." McArthur banged the board.

"Gordon Ferrets, Stan Kettings and now Will Oatley. DI Taylor and his team will look after the Ferrets investigation, DI Deacon the Kettings one and DI Parland the Oatley one, and I will have oversight on all of them. We'll all be working on the eighth floor. Sue will be the floor manager and look after the boards and the evidence logging. I'll be having meetings with your DIs on a regular basis so don't be shy in telling them what you learnt, as well as meetings at nine every morning with everyone. All of you will also have access to the HOLMES database on our victims so far; be sure to add to this, so others can look at what we have all found out.

"Go back with your DIs, go over the evidence and get a plan of attack; I don't need to remind you that the press is looking and wanting us to fail. Don't do anything to reinforce that. I'll let you all go back and familiarise yourselves with your case."

***

Ashley sat down, unlocked her computer and wrote down the address of Demari Wright.

"Great, press love a serial killer," Armstrong said. "What do you reckon they'll call him?"

"Armstrong, now's not the time," Parland said. "We have to start looking into the autopsy as well."

"I've got a potential lead from his charities," Ashley said, checking her inbox. "I also had IT do a scan on social media profiles regarding people who didn't like him. I thought maybe we could hit them if they have an axe to grind."

"The Oatleys have enemies everywhere. It's not going to be a short list." Ashley shrugged.

"We have to start somewhere."

"I agree with Ashley," Murphy said. "We can cross off some people." Parland nodded.

"OK, me and Armstrong are going to see the body with McArthur. Murphy is going to chase up the lead we have on the use of the burner phone in the general area outside his house and Fenway has a lead too. We should have uniform as well to go around. Maybe see if a blonde woman was seen around there."

Ashley knew who she wanted to see first.

Chapter 54

Ashley pulled up to a row of terraced homes which had seemed a staple of Manchester since she arrived. The sky was a murky, grey which told Ashley that she was right to pick her hooded coat.

Ashley walked up to number fifty-six and knocked on the door. She looked up at the house and then at the windows which had the curtains open, but from her knock she couldn't hear any signs of life. She banged on the door again, it was nearly ten o'clock and Wright didn't have a job that she knew off.

She banged a third time and heard a muffled sound.

"OK, OK, I'm comin'." Ashley heard the door unlock and pull back. She saw the frizzy, black hair of Demari Wright. He looked at Ashley up and down with suspicion.

"Who are you?" He asked.

"DC Ashley Fenway, Manchester Major Crimes." she said, showing him her ID. "Are you Demari Wright?"

"Who wants to know?"

"I want to talk to you about Will Oatley."

"Fuck off," he spat, venomously. He looked around before his gaze went back to Ashley. "I had nothing to do with him dying, you feel me?"

"I just want answers." Ashley pulled her phone out and showed him his tweet. "Not something you say about one of Manchester most revered sons is it?"

"Shit, even now he's dead you lot are still in his pocket," Demari said. "You wanna bang me up for a fucking tweet?"

"No, I want answers," Ashley said. "Something stinks with Oatley and you seem to be the only one willing to speak about it, better I come and talk to you than someone who wants you to stop." Demari looked down and at her.

"How can I trust you?" Ashley shrugged.

"You only have my word," Ashley said. Demari closed the door, opened it and appraised Ashley. Ashley could see that he had been out drinking and she had probably woken him up. Ashley walked into the hallway.

"Is he really dead?" Demari asked. Ashley turned her head towards him.

"Sorry?"

"Like, dead."

"I've seen the body," Ashley said. Demari walked past Ashley into a messy living room which was littered with cans of larger and bottles of spirits. Demari sat down on the sofa and rubbed his sinuses. Ashley sat down on the sofa and got her notepad out.

"Why the tweet?" She asked. Demari shrugged. Clearly, like Tim Williams he was a man who couldn't formulate his feelings into actions. Well, the right ones.

"So, you thought you'd do it for what, a laugh?" Ashley asked. Demari exhaled loudly and looked away from Ashley.

"When did it start?" Ashley asked.

"Did what start?" Demari asked, almost accusingly.

"You know," Ashley prompted. "From this case we can assume that the people dying have some dark pasts." Demari squirmed on the sofa.

"Pasts that involve children," Ashley said. "We think someone is hunting them down, people with personal grudges." Demari didn't say anything.

"Demari, my superiors have already had it in for someone who was abused by one of our victims who holds a grudge, please, tell me what we're dealing with." He was quiet for a moment. He was looking down at the floor.

"A monster," he said.

"When did it start?" Ashley asked again, knowing where this was now going.

"I must have been twelve," he said, "Do you know the Civic?"

Ashley nodded. The Civic's full name was Johnson Memorial Civic Centre. It used to have a bad reputation as a hangout for gangs, but it had been through an upheaval in recent times.

"I was there before he threw his money at it," Demari explained. "But they... he said he wanted to make it better, and he did." Demari wiped his mouth.

"They would do these fundraisers," he said. "Money back in the community and things like that, anyway... it happened at one of those." Ashley went to ask him a follow up question, but he cut her off.

"I don't want to talk about it," he said. "All I know is that people were too busy counting the money he was throwing at the centre to care about some black kid saying he was touching them up." Ashley nodded.

"Did you try?" He nodded, he got to his feet and pulled up his jumper. His black skin was littered with lots of marks that looked like whip marks.

"Jesus..."

"That's what you get for speaking out against Will Oatley," he said, pulling it down.

"Was he actively abusing children at the centre?" Demari nodded.

"There are loads, he bought most of them off. Houses, cars, drugs. Everyone has their poisons."

"What was yours?" Ashley asked. Demari looked at her with a quirked expression. "Well, you haven't spoken out about him until now. What did he promise you?"

"My life," Demari said, matter of factly. Now it made sense, the scars, the silence.

"That's how they kept me quiet," he said. "Any time I thought about it, there would be a reminder."

"Was it still going on?" Ashley asked.

"I heard through the grapevine that Oatley was still doing it," Demari said. "Shouldn't be surprised really. He always knew he wouldn't get caught, if you throw enough money in the right places you can never be caught."

"Tell me about this centre."

336

"He has others like it," Demari explained. "It's the same gig that Jimmy Saville used. Make a place too dependent on you, then you get away with murder." Ashley nodded.

"I need to ask you this, but where were you on the night Will Oatley died?" Ashley asked.

"I was out last night with my sister. Celebrating," he said. "I was down The Crown; they have video, you can check it out."

"Thanks," Ashley said, getting up and walking to the door.

"Listen." She turned and faced Demari. "Now he's dead… you can speak out." He laughed.

"You want help?"

"We could do with it," Ashley said. "Make a statement." Demari shook his head. Ashley smiled sadly. She pulled her card out and placed it on the table by the door.

"If you change your mind," she said, patting it.

Ashley walked out and felt the breeze of the door closing behind her. Though what Demari said about Oatley was interesting; he was supplying youth projects with cash and abusing youngsters at them. People turned a blind eye because of the money.

No, it was because of the good that he did, the good the money did. She could imagine Oatley smugly telling people who caught him to think of the good his money did and how it could all go away if they spoke. Ashley got into her car and searched for the centre, thankfully it was only around the corner. Ashley started the car.

Chapter 55

Ashley pulled up outside the community centre, a modern building which had recently been erected in one of Manchester's poorest neighbourhoods. The outside was neat, but she saw one of the low-lying walls had a large crater in it.

Ashley walked up to the wooden door and pushed it open into a warm, open area where a group of old people were playing bingo while teenagers handed them cups of tea. Society in motion. It would be a shame if this did come all crumbling down.

"Excuse me, can I help you?" Ashley turned to see a young woman, almost dressed like a librarian with smart glasses a long, tartan skirt and a simple, white blouse.

"DC Ashley Fenway with Manchester Major Crimes," Ashley said, flashing her ID. "I wanted to talk to you about Will Oatley."

"Oh, I heard about him," she said with a frown. "It was so sad. He's a huge patron of the centre."

"I'm sorry, you are?"

"Sarah, I help run the centre," she said brightly, extending her hand which Ashley shook. "Are you investigating his death?"

"Yes, we're going to all the charities Mr Oatley was a patron of," Ashley explained. "We're looking into his dealings."

"Right, of course," Sarah said. "Shall we speak in my office?"

"Lead the way." Sarah smiled and Ashley followed her to a door by the reception. "How long have you been part of the centre?"

"I've been here for years," Sarah said, getting a key out and opening the door. "I was here before Mr Oatley took over. When he did, he asked me to stay on to look after it. Please, take a seat."

Ashley sat down and her eyes scanned around the office wall which was adorned with paintings from kids and pictures of various events that the centre had held, with Sarah mostly in the middle of them. It was a diverse age of young and old but one thing that stood out to Ashley was that Oatley wasn't in any of them.

Strange, Ashley thought.

"Would you like a tea, coffee?"

"I'm good," Ashley said, getting her notebook out, which made Sarah look nervously at it; another thing Ashley noted.

"So, forgive me but what is it that the centre does?" Ashley asked. "I read up on it, but it only really scratches the surface." Sarah smiled nervously and let out a small laugh.

"Well, we try and cater for all walks of life," she said. "We help the elderly with bingo days and classic film nights." Ashley opened her notebook and started to write, noting that Sarah bit her lip, now nervously.

"And for the youngsters we do game nights and video game tournaments, but we have started a book club which has really taken off." She laughed nervously but soon stopped at Ashley's passive expression.

"We, err, also rent out to some support groups as well: Alcoholic Anonymous, a depression forum."

"Very good," Ashley said. "I'm more interested though in the things that Mr Oatley was interested in."

"Oh, yes, of course," Sarah said, with another nervous smile. "Well, Mr Oatley was very active in our youth wing. He wanted to make sure that kids were off the street and, you know, valuing the community they lived in rather than trash it."

Admirable, Ashley thought.

"Were there problems around this area?" Sarah nodded.

"Yes, anti-social behaviour, drugs, violence. The centre gave kids a place to go, but like everything else they just abused it. We were on the brink of shutting down before Mr Oatley intervened." Sarah glanced again on the notebook as Ashley made notes.

"Seems very different now," Ashley observed.

"Discipline and boundaries," Sarah said. "Mr Oatley said that leadership should be more like business heads. Have a set of house rules to control the small things and then the big things fall into place."

"It looks like he's done a lot for this place," Ashley said. "Brand new building and interior, state of the art equipment."

"Mr Oatley said that he wanted to give something back to the community that had given his family so much. His father was a generous man as well." Ashley nodded. "He wanted the centre to be a beacon of what community could achieve. It was his idea to include the old people in the centre as well."

"So, did he just write the cheques or did he come down himself?" Ashley asked. Sarah took a deep breath.

"He comes down occasionally. He shows his face at some of the functions for the publicity, it helps us raise money and get new backers."

"Does he do this for all the charities he's a patron of or just for yourselves?" Ashley asked.

"Mr Oatley introduced us all to his other charities, that's how we set up some of the other programmes," Sarah explained.

"He's very charitable," Ashley said. "You said that this place was going before he helped." Sarah nodded. Ashley stopped writing and looked up at Sarah.

"Was everyone happy about it?" Ashley asked. She wanted to gauge Sarah's reaction, which was the one she expected.

"Of course, they were," she said, a little flustered. "Mr Oatley is a known benefactor for the area."

"So why is there a smashed wall outside?" Ashley asked.

"Some people don't like the rules that are in place," Sarah replied quickly.

"What about the lawsuit by Demari Wright?"

"A misunderstanding," Sarah said, round a breathless laugh.

"What about the fact that Mr Oatley isn't in any of these pictures?" Ashley said. Sarah abruptly got to her feet, the scraping of metal on the floor stopping Ashley from asking her follow up question.

"I think, detective," Sarah said with an odd finality. "That you should leave."

"Whatever it is he had on you, it's over," Ashley said. "I just want the truth." Sarah looked away.

"I think you should leave." Ashley nodded.

"I will be back," she said, walking so she was by Sarah's side.

"And whatever it is you're hiding for him will be public knowledge," Ashley said. "Is money really worth that much to you?"

"Just... go," Sarah said. Ashley walked past, she opened the door and slammed it shut which sent a shiver through Sarah.

Ashley walked to the car and got inside; there was something wrong about this place. She looked down her list of other charities.

It was interesting what Sarah said about the charities being all connected by association. Ashley heard an e-mail come through her work phone. She checked it; some of the classified financials from Oatley's accountant had come through.

Ashley started the car. She had got a good lead and now she had a reference to start from.

Chapter 56

The group of reporters had swelled even more since the morning; hopefully the others had done a little better than her. She slowly edged her way through the group and parked up.

She made her way to the office and went back to her computer where Demari Wright's details were still up. Ashley walked to the board and put on it that he was, in fact, a victim of Oatley.

Ashley looked quickly at the board on Oatley. According to the autopsy he died between eleven and one onwards.

She typed up her report on Wright and looked at the boxes stacked by her desk which contained Oatley's private and confidential business financials.

The contents were almost seven hundred documents. Ashley swore; this paper tree was deliberately confusing to stop people looking into it. She put the first one on her desk and at the side. Thankfully whoever did box them up had the decency to sort them by business and personal. One thing she did know was that her desk wasn't going to be big enough.

Ashley walked to one of the conference rooms which was free. Ashley moved the boxes with personal financials into the conference room. Ashley opened the boxes and started to look at what was inside them. They were tax returns and investment forms along with directorships for the numerous subsidiaries of Oatley Developments.

The forms for directorships didn't show anything useful for Ashley so she discounted them. She started to look through the personal bank accounts.

She got her highlighters out and began to look at the patterns that came up. From what she could see Mrs Oatley had a huge cosmetics and clothing budget while the food bill was exceptionally high. The house was ancestral so there was no mortgage to worry about, one-off payments for insurance but a couple of large payments were explained by receipts for cars and luxury holidays.

Ashley was organised, but every large payment from his accounts was accounted for and the patterns were constant throughout. It certainly wasn't about money, but they knew that already from the other two victims.

Ashley downed her tea and looked at the reams of paper in front of her. Not what she wanted. A knock on the door caught her attention and Murphy poked his head round the door.

"Boss wants an update," he said.

Ashley walked back to the bull pen with Murphy where McArthur was waiting for them.

"Fenway, nice of you to join us," McArthur said. "So, IT have come back on his computers and have confirmed he is a paedophile as well." There were a few murmurs around the team. "That's not even the worst of it. Based off some of his e-mails it looks like Oatley was still abusing, which makes it harder. Does anyone have a lead on potential victims?"

"His charities," Ashley said. "I spoke to one who was abused at the Civic Centre. He knew it was still going on."

"How did you find them?" McArthur asked.

"I was looking at people who were slagging him off on social media. Most of them were for his developments but his ran deeper."

"Good, let's bring him in to answer some questions," McArthur said. "Are IT still running that scan?"

"I assume so," Ashley said.

"OK, good, anyone got anything else?"

"The PM came back, he died of blood loss rather than asphyxiation," Parland said. "But he was able to break free before the killer could cut the windpipe and the arteries in the throat."

"But he still had enough time to get himself free before collapsing from the blood loss," Murphy said.

"Maybe the killer panicked," Ashley suggested. "Tried to flee?"

"Neighbours didn't see anyone come out of the house."

"Maybe Oatley keeled over when the killer fled. He was old, he wouldn't have been able to last too long with blood coming out of his throat."

"Sneak out at night like the rest of them," Murphy said. "So, no one saw them."

"Is this one even like the rest of them?" McArthur asked.

"Cramer said the knife and initial wound were the same and the knots were consistent with the others," Parland said.

"What about the blood and skin under his fingernails?" McArthur asked.

"We're still waiting on that," Murphy replied.

"The way he died seems to be the biggest shock," Armstrong said. "He has a reputation for being a ruthless bastard. Many of the people we spoke to were surprised it didn't happen sooner."

"He has a bad rep," McArthur said. "We're going to have to search through all of the people who had a thing against him."

"That could go into the hundreds," Parland said, dropping a file onto the floor.

"Then we get the list together and give it to uniform since we got them," McArthur ordered. "In the meantime, we need to go over every complaint ever made against him and find some of the kids he abused. I need to inform the powers that be of this because we need to get a message out."

"Wife's not going to like that," Armstrong said.

"No, she won't," McArthur agreed. "Hopefully DNA and SOCO report should be in tomorrow so we can look over that. I also have a press thing later today to talk about the photo of the person at Oatley's house. Just continue to pore over this, there's a lead in there somewhere. Fenway, a word."

McArthur went to the lift and Ashley followed him.

"I want you to come to Oatley's wife's house," he said. "She knows you."

"Are you worried she might be —"

"Hysterical, yes," McArthur said, pushing the button on the lift. "How do you expect anyone to react after they find out their husband was a paedophile?"

"Maybe she knew," Ashley offered. There had certainly been stranger things that women had tolerated over the years. But as the saying goes, money talks. From the looks of it, Oatley had plenty.

"Well, I want you there," McArthur said, as the lift door open. "I think a woman's touch might be needed." Ashley shrugged.

"When do we go?"

"Give me an hour and I'll meet you downstairs, in the press room," he said, as the doors closed.

Ashley walked back to the conference room and started to look through the company accounts, which was more of a minefield. Thankfully Benison and Co kept detailed accounts and again everything she could see so far was accounted for. Heck, even the lawyers had receipts.

Ashley looked at her phone, her hour had nearly passed. She got her coat and went downstairs to the press room.

Chapter 57

"I hate these things," McArthur said, both his and Ashley's steps echoing round the small corridor.

"I hated mine too," Ashley said.

"PR is different to press," McArthur said. "It's an animal that likes feeding but will maul you if you hold back its food."

"Is this a mauling?" Ashley asked.

"If they find out there's two other murders then yes," McArthur said.

"It should be a quick one; confirm death, get the suspects face out there, preach the number, all that. If I can get away with questions, then great. I'll see you after."

He went to get his microphone put on and Ashley went to the back of the room. The press room was medium-sized with a large screen at the back in front of a table. So far, the back was adorned with the Greater Manchester Police insignia.

Ashley stood at the back of the room where the press was assembled. Normally there would only be a few people from the local news when deaths happened, but Will Oatley was a big deal. The room was filled with television cameras from the national stations and all the national newspapers.

When McArthur walked out onto the stage with the big players in Greater Manchester Police, the cameras went wild with flashing and clicking. They sat down and McArthur spoke.

"Thank you all for coming," McArthur said. "As you are aware and we can confirm, that Will Oatley has died, and his death is being treated as unexplained at this time. We cannot go into the specifics of his death until a full post-mortem is done. We would like to offer our condolences to Mr Oatley's family and ask that you please respect their privacy at this difficult time." McArthur shuffled in his chair.

"We would however like to speak to this individual in relation to our case." The screen behind them turned into a picture taken from the CCTV.

"We want to speak to this individual in relation to the incident. This picture was taken on the night of Thursday the twenty-third outside Mr Oatley's mansion. So, if anyone recognises this person or knows someone who might, please contact us on the below number. Also, if anyone saw this person in the local area please contact us on the number below. We believe that he was in the Didsbury area between twelve and three o'clock." Assistant Chief Constable Delany then took over.

"I want the public to know that we are doing everything we can and that every available resource has been made available to DCI McArthur and his team." Ashley thought that this would be it and went to walk back.

"Now, DCI McArthur will take a couple of questions," Delany said. Ashley looked back. On the press table McArthur glanced sideways at Delany. Ashley felt her stomach knot uncomfortably and took her place at the back of the room. In this time the assembled reporters had gone crazy with shouting questions.

McArthur regained his composure and shuffled his shoulders and physically tightened his jaw. He nodded to one at the front.

"Emily Hash, North West Tonight. Do you think this man killed Will Oatley?"

"We only want to talk to this individual," McArthur said. "He was spotted outside our crime scene and we believe him to be either a valuable witness, or a potential suspect."

"One more," McArthur pointed at someone.

"Haley Baldwin, Manchester Evening News. We have on good authority that the Major Crimes Unit is looking into two similar murders in the same vein as Mr Oatley, can you confirm this?" For all the noise earlier, the room went very quiet.

McArthur's anecdote about feeding the press was coming true, and now, he was in the lion's den with the beast baring its teeth at him.

"We don't comment on speculation." Safe answer, or a backwards step from the beast. The reporter though poked it forward.

"Gordon Ferrets and Stan Kettings, two confirmed paedophiles who have been found murdered." Ashley swore; McArthur looked back at her.

"Are we looking at vigilante killings?"

Fuck.

"I'm not sure where you're getting your information from but —"

"You're evading, DCI McArthur," she said. "Do we have a paedophile hunter in our midst?" Just as McArthur was about to answer Delany cut across him.

"Thank you, that'll be all, no more questions!" At that the room erupted into a spate of noise and shouting. Ashley scarpered out the back. Just as McArthur thought he was getting out the pit alive someone closed the door on him.

Ashley made her way to the back of the stage. From some of the headlines that the reporters Ashley walked past were coming up with, it was going to be a rough couple of days ahead. When she got there, she could hear McArthur who was arguing with Delany.

"Of course, I don't fucking know how it got out!" She could hear McArthur's thick, Glaswegian accent from down the hall.

"Well the press thinks they're all linked now!" Delany shouted back at him.

"Yeah, and how do you think they got that? From you cutting off the questioning, you muppet!"

"I am still in charge of your department, McArthur, you can't talk to me like that!"

"Well thanks, to your monumental fuck up I now have the full force of the press on me as well as public scrutiny!"

"I didn't say anything!"

"That's the problem, you didn't let me say it." The door banged open and McArthur came out with a face like thunder.

"Fenway, when he comes out, I want you to give him the filthiest look you've got then follow me. Got it?"

"Absolutely, Sir." Delany came out to have the last word. He saw Ashley who gave him her dirtiest look and followed McArthur, leaving him in a stunned silence.

"Well done Fenway, come on, we have work to do." They went down to the car park.

"Good meeting?" Ashley asked. McArthur shook his head.

"When you make DCI, Fenway, you'll see the politics that comes with the job," he said, opening the door.

"Are we going to get in trouble for this?" Ashley asked, starting the car.

"Maybe, if we beat the Chief Constable there. He's insisting on being there for his 'Lifelong Friend' of about a month." Ashley smirked and started the car.

"Would be a shame if we got there before them then," Ashley said. The BMW roared and shot out of the parking space.

Chapter 58

Mrs Oatley was staying with a friend in Salford. Like her own neighbourhood it was secluded, with every house having its own protective gate which had two policemen and a small pool of reporters outside of it.

As they pulled up the reporters began to surround the car and shout questions at them. Thankfully they opened the gate quickly and Ashley swung in. Thankfully, the drive was circular and she could drive round to the front door.

"Detectives, what's the latest on the Will Oatley Murders!"

"Is Mrs Oatley involved at all!"

"Do you have any suspects?"

As they walked to the door it was opened by a liaison officer. They walked in with the sounds of the press still ringing in their ears.

"When did they turn up?" McArthur asked, taking his coat off.

"A few hours ago," the liaison officer said. "They must have got a tip off from the hospital."

"Make sure no one gives a statement without passing it by me first," McArthur said, hanging his coat up.

The house they were in had a more traditional feel to it than the Oatleys', which was more modern. Ashley and McArthur walked down a corridor into a spacious living room, where Mrs Oatley was sitting with her friend with a game of scrabble between them. They were sitting on an old sofa and armchair respectively, with a fire burning in front of them.

"Mrs Oatley," McArthur said. She looked up from the game.

"Oh, DCI McArthur, is there news?"

"Yes," McArthur said, "But we also need to ask you a few questions if that's OK?"

"Do I need my lawyer?" She asked.

"You're not a suspect Mrs Oatley," McArthur said. "You have a watertight alibi. But a couple of things have come up about your husband that we need to ask you." She thought about it for a moment before nodding.

"Do you want me to join you?" Her friend asked.

"No, no it's OK," Mrs Oatley said. "Can we use the kitchen?" Her friend nodded and they walked into the kitchen which again was traditional. They sat at an island bank, she shrugged as if to indicate that they could start.

"Mrs Oatley, is there anyone who you think would want to harm your husband?" McArthur asked. Mrs Oatley chuckled to herself and looked down at her tea.

"How long have you got?" She said looking up at them. "Will had enemies left, right and centre. Not just his own but also his fathers too." She shook her head. "We had death threats every other week from people." She nervously played with her fingers.

"Some of them were justified," she said. "Will was ruthless, and sometimes I struggled to sleep at night knowing that others who had a roof over their heads one day, didn't because of us." She ran a hand through her hair. Ashley was surprised by her frankness.

"What did you do to offset it?" Ashley asked.

"I'm a patron for Shelter," she said. "I also donate to the Low Families Income Fund as well. Will never knew about that. The money came from an old trust fund of mine."

"Is there anyone you know who would really want to kill your husband?" McArthur asked. Mrs Oatley thought hard for a moment.

"Kyle Burch," She said. "He threatens us every opportunity he gets. We have a restraining order against him, but it doesn't stop him." Ashley made a note to talk to him. He was one of the people Ashley had been researching from the social media posts.

"Mrs Oatley, this might be a bit much for you take but…" McArthur looked at Ashley and back to Mrs Oatley.

"But?"

"But we found pornography on your husband's computer," McArthur said. Mrs Oatley shook her head.

"Well, he's a bloke, you'd expect that right." Their faces must have shown it all.

"Right?"

"It was child pornography." Her jaw slacked.

"What?"

"I'm sorry but we found a lot of hardcore child pornography on his personal computer," McArthur explained.

"No, no you must be mistaken," Mrs Oatley said. "It must have been... planted. Yes, planted!"

"I'm sorry Mrs Oatley but that wasn't the case," McArthur said. "Not only that but we think that he was killed because of it." Mrs Oatley let out a small whimper and then burst into tears.

"I know this must be difficult to hear," Ashley said. "But... has there been any —" Before she could finish the question Mrs Oatley started ranting.

"I can't believe it," she said, now looking up. Her eyes stained with tears. "He never let on, why didn't... why didn't anyone tell me?" Ashley thought it best not to bring up the bribery and the emotional blackmail of his victims.

"I mean it's not hard, it's..." She got up and started to pace the kitchen. "You know people warned me he was a bit of a player, but kids!" She stood by a set of French doors that went outside.

"He told me not to worry about that bloody reporter!" She seethed. McArthur and Ashley looked at one another with confusion.

"What reporter?" Ashley asked. Mrs Oatley turned around. Her eyes full of rage.

"About six months ago this reporter from the Evening News ambushed us at a restaurant," she said. "Said she had a source from some old home that could implicate Will in something; and he told me not to worry about it!"

"Do you remember what it was about?" McArthur asked. "Any little detail would help."

"Will told me not to worry about it," she said. "Said it was a smear. It happened all the time, but he always sorted it." She shook her head.

"Oh god," she said, all the pieces falling into place. She stopped. "Was he abusing?" She asked. With the silence she looked around.

"He was, wasn't he, you know."

"We've had individuals come forward," McArthur said. "We're exploring all lines of enquiry." She nodded tearfully.

"I'm going to sell that house the first chance I get," she said. "What a sick bastard." She went back to the window.

"I'm glad he suffered now," Mrs Oatley said. "I did think how bad it was that he died that way but... maybe he deserved it." Ashley looked at McArthur who was remaining passive. Ashley was a little unnerved at the sudden change of tone from Mrs Oatley; but what Mrs Oatley said about her husband taking care of it was what interested her more.

"Have there been other instances of your husband taking care of problems?" Ashley asked. Mrs Oatley thought for a moment.

"There have been a couple of times, but Will never let me really know them," she said. "I trusted him, why wouldn't I?" Ashley made a note to look through his financials and phone records again. See if there was a link after these incidents came up.

"I don't suppose you knew who the reporter was?" Ashley asked.

"They were with Manchester Evening News, that's all I know," Mrs Oatley said, she chuckled to herself. "Maybe I should be thanking them."

"Do you remember what they looked like?" Ashley asked hopefully. Mrs Oatley shook her head.

"No, I can barely remember her," Mrs Oatley replied.

"Mrs Oatley, is there anything else you know that could help us?" McArthur asked. Mrs Oatley shook her head.

***

Ashley and McArthur were able to negotiate their way out of the press with what they had learned still fresh. McArthur made a phone call to Parland and told him everything that Mrs Oatley had told them.

"Yeah, we need to call the Evening News, see who came up with the story on Oatley."

"We do that and they're going know something's up," Parland said. "For all the shit we give them they're smart, they'll put two and two together."

"We need that lead though," McArthur pressed. "It could open up a clue for the other two as well."

"It's your call skip." Parland thought for a moment. Ashley would have gone to the Evening News. It was the lesser of two evils. They needed a lead, higher management needed a lead, but at the same time they didn't want the press to get a whiff.

"Try and find someone, anyone with a contact there and try and extract it. If we have to play politics say we'll give them an exclusive only if we have forty-eight-hour wiggle room."

"OK, anything else?"

"While you're at it try and track down a Kyle Burch. Apparently, the Oatley's had a restraining order against him. He might still hold a grudge. I want to know where he was on the night of the murder."

"Yes Sir," Parland said, putting the phone down.

"Burch came up in the social media search," Ashley said. "I didn't know the Oatley's had a restraining order against him."

"You found a good lead doing that, so don't beat yourself up," McArthur said. "I want you to do some digging into Oatley 'taking care' of these problems."

"I looked through both his personal and business accounts," Ashley said. "Every large purchase was accounted for."

As they pulled up to the station there was another large crowd gathered outside the gates, say for the usual reporters. Both Ashley and McArthur leaned forward.

"Who the hell are they?" He asked. The group looked like an ordinary group except they had placards which they were waving around.

We want justice!

The police were in on it!

Oatley was a monster! How many more are there!

"Looks like the cavalry's out," McArthur mused. "This is just the start of it."

"Start of what?" Ashley asked.

"People coming out of the woodwork," McArthur explained. The man on the gate allowed Ashley through to the carpark.

"So, what do we do about Oatley?"

"People like Oatley are clever," McArthur said, as they pulled into the station. "They're not your garden variety criminal." Ashley parked up and McArthur got out.

"With them, the devil is in the detail," he said, leaning on her open door. "In my experience no one ever paid over the odds for a new toilet seat." He smiled, closed the door and walked away, leaving Ashley to think about what he had said.

Ashley went back up to the office.

"Heard shit went down with Oatley's wife," Murphy said.

"She just found out her dead husband was a paedophile," Ashley said. "Amazing how someone gets over grief when they find something out like that."

"Well Parland and Armstrong are out getting Burch," Murphy told her. "I'm trying to find anyone on the force who has a contact in the Evening News." Ashley frowned.

"Why, what are you doing?"

"I'm looking back over Oatley's financials," Ashley said. "I think there's something I missed. Can you keep an eye out and see if Oatley's phone records come through?"

"Will do." Ashley made herself another cup of tea and went back to the conference room with all the paperwork from earlier on. She went back over it, thinking about what McArthur said.

"No one paid over the odds for a toilet seat." Maybe he had a point, maybe the money was being funnelled somewhere else; maybe through a different company. This was for Oatley Developments plc. He wouldn't funnel money through this. It was too obvious.

Maybe one of its subsidiaries though. Ashley picked up the annual report for Oatley Developments and looked at the subsidiary list. Thankfully it gave a brief description of what each subsidiary did. Ashley had the deflating feeling that she was now in over her head. There were quite a few subsidiaries, bordering a hundred and fifty.

Ashley looked down the list; there were quite a few holding companies. Ashley knew companies used holding company structures but over half of the subsidiaries were. What were they for?

Ashley went back to her computer with the list and went onto Companies House. She chose a random one: Oatley Charity Holdings Limited. Been incorporated since 1971 and was a holding company which held the shares of various charities which had a standard revenue stream.

But unless she had receipts for what all a hundred and fifty people were buying and selling it would be tough.

"You OK?" Murphy asked.

"This is the face of someone who has just made more work for themselves," Ashley said. "McArthur seems to think that Oatley was paying people off through his companies, but I can't see the link."

"What makes him think that?" Murphy asked.

"His wife said that someone from the Evening News turned up one day and threatened to expose him for something. According to her no story was ever published."

"Maybe we need to look at people who left the Evening News then," Murphy said.

"Don't suppose you know someone on the payroll, do you?" Ashley asked hopefully.

"No, but it wouldn't be too hard to find, would it?" Ashley looked down at the reporter pool.

"We can have an ask around, but I would be discrete," Murphy said.

Ashley walked back into the conference room with the printouts of Oatley Maintenance Limited and Oatley Services Limited. Ashley sat down at the table with a fresh cuppa and opened the box for Oatley Services Limited, incorporated in 1984.

Ashley took the paperwork out and started to read through it. The turnover or money in wasn't remarkable, and the company was buying new equipment like floor cleaners, cleaning chemicals and office equipment.

Ashley started to look at receipts which again accounted for expenditure on these things. Ashley turned her attention to the next company.

Oatley Maintenance Limited, incorporated in 1996.

Ashley looked at the expenditure, which was close to three million, with money coming in at nearly five million. What sort of maintenance was this company doing?

Ashley started to look through their financials; the bulk of the money was coming through on small things like stationery and lightbulbs. Ashley didn't buy it, who were they buying these lightbulbs from?

Mrs Oatley said this confrontation was nearly six months ago. So, did this company happen to make an order of lightbulbs? Ashley checked back six months and sure enough the company had bought nearly a hundred thousand lightbulbs at a cost of £100 000. Ashley got the receipt. It was from Lifeways Electrical Limited.

Ashley had never heard of it. Had they bought from this company before? Ashley searched back through the paper trail in the box. Again, payments made to this company of very specific amounts.

Ashley took the few sheets of paper she needed, went back to her desk and made her computer come back on.

"Found something?"

"Maybe."

"They got Burch in interviewing," Murphy said.

"That's nice," Ashley said idly, opening up Google. "Murphy, have you ever heard of a company called Lifeways Electrical?"

"No, can't say I have," He said. "Why?"

"No reason," Ashley said, looking at the results. The more she researched it the more it looked suspicious. Google showed a link to the Cayman Islands' registry. Ashley clicked on it.

The registry showed that Lifeways Electrical was a Cayman Islands registered company since 1996. Any offshore tax heaven was bad news; one, because it almost always meant tax avoidance, but two, they also gave a certain degree of anonymity as you couldn't access their yearly filings like with Companies House.

Ashley went down the search page but again found very little for it. She clicked on a few random links which were copies of the registry. She clicked on a link for a Hong Kong Government website. Ashley searched the document and Lifeways came up. It was a joint venture between a

Green Energy company incorporated in Bermuda and a company called ODHF LLC, which was in Delaware.

"Trail gets murkier and murkier," Ashley said. She searched for ODHF LLC in Google and it came up with a link to the Delaware registry which showed that this company had been made up six months ago.

"Yeah, that's not suspicious," Ashley said. She went back to the Government website, she looked to see who the shareholders were in this Green Energy company. She found a list of the top twenty shareholders. Right at the top.

Oatley Overseas Investment Holdings Limited, who owned 49% of this company. Well at least there was a link. Ashley printed off what she had found and went back to this Delaware LLC. But for the life of her she couldn't find any documents for it. If she had to guess, this reporter had to of been given a bribe through here.

Ashley picked the phone up and called Aaron.

"IT Forensics, Aaron speaking."

"You need to work on your phone voice," Ashley told him.

"To be fair not many people call me directly."

"Well, I am in need of your skill set."

"What do you need?"

"I'm sending you an e-mail with a company name. I need any documents you can find for it," Ashley explained as she sent it off.

"How legal is this?"

"I'd rather not answer," Ashley said. "All I need to know is if it received a payment of £100 000."

"Oddly specific."

"It might have been used for a payoff," Ashley explained.

"Well, looks like you are in luck," Aaron said. "Don't ask how but that company did receive a payment from a Green Energy Company, of which half of it was transferred to a private bank account."

"Which bank?" Ashley asked.

"HSBC."

"A name?"

"A. Franks." Ashley wrote it down.

"Thanks, can you send it over to me please?"

"Already done." Ashley looked at her e-mail and saw it.

"Thanks, owe you one.

"I stopped keeping count."

"Probably for the best. Speak to you soon." Ashley put the phone down and looked at the report. He was right, £50 000 given to a public account with account number and everything.

Ashley opened a tab for Google and searched Manchester Evening News, A. Franks. A few articles came up but nothing recently. Ashley found her on Facebook as well. She was pretty with brown eyes and red hair.

But there was no flaunting of wealth, not even a lie of coming into money. Not a post in six months.

"Got her," Ashley said.

"What?"

"The reporter. Got her," Ashley elaborated. "Her name is Amelia Franks, hasn't posted anything in six months."

"So, she might be a suspect?"

"She tried to bribe him once, maybe she went back and got greedy," Ashley suggested.

"And the other two?" Ashley shrugged.

"If not, Franks can tell us what she was going to expose Oatley for." Ashley said. "If he's a known paedophile it might be someone with an axe to grind." Murphy smiled.

"Got an address?"

Chapter 59

Ashley was wondering if she had the right address. Amelia Franks' house looked as though it was condemned. The house was derelict, with moss on the outside walls, overgrown grass and with mouldy, drawn curtains.

"Do you have the right place?" Parland asked.

"This is her last known address," Ashley explained.

Ashley got out of the car, walked up to the front gate and walked up to the door with the uneasy feeling that she was being watched.

"Maybe she wants to get off the beaten track," Ashley offered. "I saw what Oatley did to Demari, maybe she wanted to avoid that."

She got to the door and knocked hard on it, half expecting it to fall off its hinges. From inside there sounded like scratching. Ashley knocked on the door again, placed her ear to the door and could hear that same scratching and shuffling.

"Hello?" Ashley called. "Hello, I'm DC Fenway with Manchester Major Crimes."

"Go away!"

"Is that Amelia Franks?"

"Piss off!" That's a yes. Ashley looked at Murphy who shrugged.

"Amelia, I just want to talk to you," Ashley said. "I wanted to talk to you about Will Oatley." There was a stiff silence.

"Go around the back," Ashley mouthed, and Murphy did so.

"Amelia."

"If you're here to kill me..."

"No, no, I don't want to... kill you," Ashley said, with a small grimace. "Will Oatley is dead." Another stiff silence.

"What?"

"Will Oatley died a couple of days ago," Ashley repeated. Ashley heard scrambling from inside the house and the door creeped open. It was Amelia Franks all right, that distinctive auburn hair from her Facebook profile hidden partially under a hat. She looked thin and very dishevelled.

"Are you alone?" She said, looking round.

"No, I sent my colleague round the back because I thought you were going to bolt," Ashley said.

"Right, best you come in," Amelia said, walking back in. The house was just as grubby on the inside, with mould on the wallpaper and bare floorboards.

"Murphy, she's opened the door." Ashley walked in and followed Amelia into a living room which, like the entrance hall had poorly maintained wallpaper and exposed floorboards, with a disused fireplace and very little light coming in from the curtains. There was a sleeping bag on the floor along with a paraffin gas hob, with a few wrappers of discarded food.

"How did he die?" Amelia asked. Ashley heard the door close and Murphy came through. Ashley pulled her notebook out.

"He was murdered." Amelia let out a half laugh.

"Figures," she said. "Any suspects?"

"One we can't give out," Murphy said. Amelia nodded.

"You threatened Oatley with something," Ashley said. "I want to know what it is." Amelia smiled coyly.

"I threatened to expose him," she told Ashley. "Not threaten him personally, there's a difference."

"What were you threatening to expose?" Ashley asked. Something though told her she knew the answer.

"It's the worst kept secret in Manchester that Will Oatley liked little boys and girls," Amelia said. "His old man was good at keeping it out of the news, but he perfected it."

"How?" Murphy asked.

Amelia explained. "Fear and intimidation under a façade of goodwill. Make yourself so indispensable to the community that they turn a blind eye." Ashley nodded. The exact same thing happened to Demari.

361

"But surely people knew about this?" Murphy said.

"Oh, they do," Amelia said, nodding her head. "Everyone did. But I tried to convince people that there was safety in numbers. This is in a time of the Me Too movement where victims are listened to instead of victimised."

"How far did you get?" Ashley asked.

"I went back," Amelia explained. "There are hundreds of victims, ranging from his secondary school to where he works. Everywhere held documents of internal investigations, police reports and witness statements and I found them."

"So, what happened?" Ashley asked.

"There was one place," Amelia said. "It would not only bring down Oatley but lots of influential people, not only in Government but nationwide."

"What place?" Murphy asked.

"Limehouse," Amelia said. "A house leased by a religious sect called the New Agers." She knew that name.

"He didn't strike me as the god type," Murphy muttered.

"Oatley owned the house," Amelia explained. "He rented it out to this cult who exploited children. Once Oatley knew, he wanted in. Then he informed paedophiles from across the country who would join him at these rape parties. MPs, judges, celebrities, businesspeople, people with real influence."

Ashley couldn't believe it. Maybe the police might be involved, maybe in covering it up.

"Why had nobody come forward before?" Murphy asked.

"Who are you going to believe?" Ashley said. "A vulnerable teen from a cult or a person in power?" Amelia nodded.

"But lots of them went on to become stable people, some didn't," Amelia explained. "We built up enough credible witnesses to be taken seriously and my editor was going to run it. This was going to be bigger than Watergate." Something in Ashley's head told her that this was what she was looking for.

"What happened then?" Murphy asked. Amelia sighed.

"Someone in the paper loyal to Oatley saw what we were going to do and tipped him off," Amelia said. "Her son would have lost his kids' club if Oatley was exposed. She told him and he found me," she shuddered.

"He came to my house with his suave personality, tried to reason that these were nothing more than malicious smears from competitors. But I knew the truth."

"Then…"

"Then he showed why he was called Ruthless Will," Amelia said. "He'd already deposited £100 000 in my bank account from the two different offshore accounts. He said that if the story went to print, he could prove not only this payoff but that my sources as well were nothing more than smears. Of course, all this time he was busy roughing-up people daring to speak against him; fear or money, pick your poison."

"That's why they dropped out," Ashley said. Amelia nodded.

"Nearly six months of hard work down the drain. Not that I could blame them."

"So why have you retreated to here?" Ashley asked.

"Because Oatley said that if I so much as wrote on a napkin, he would ruin me as a fame loving whore who would sell out vulnerable people for a quick by-line. And I was scared, I knew he wasn't bluffing." Amelia walked to the window.

"Sometimes you have to know when you are beat, and Oatley played the game perfectly. He left that money in my account as a reminder that he had won, knowing I wouldn't spend a penny of his blood money."

"So, you quit the paper." Amelia nodded.

"It was the only thing I could do," Amelia said. "I came to the furthest place I thought he would never find me."

"But what about the story?"

"Without people willing to step forward it becomes nothing," Amelia said. "If I know Will Oatley like I think I do, then those people won't want to talk anymore."

"Where were you between eleven and one on the twenty-third of November?" Murphy asked.

"Right here. I think the neighbours will be able to back me up, they complain about the smell enough."

Ashley though had a feeling that they might have stumbled onto their link.

"Limehouse."

"Seems a bit too far-fetched for me," Murphy said. "A nationwide network of abusers that's somehow gone under the radar for decades; you've heard of those fantasists, right?"

"Yeah, but Amelia said that there was a paper trail for other assaults from Oatley's past," Ashley said. "Why not for this Limehouse too?"

"If it was me and I owned it then I would burn it all," Murphy said. "Make sure no one gets it. And if he did own this Limehouse then that's exactly what I would do." Ashley rasped her fingers on the steering wheel while they waited at a set of traffic lights.

"He must have seen it as a threat though if he got involved," Ashley said.

"Sometimes the hint of scandal is enough," Murphy countered. "I know they say there's no such thing as bad publicity but something like that could be damaging. We are in a world where it's guilty until proven innocent now, in the court of public opinion."

As much as Ashley wanted to disagree, she knew Murphy was right. Even the police nipped scandals in the bud before they could get out. Ashley's phone started going. It was McArthur, Ashley answered.

"Fenway."

"Where are you?"

"Following up on a lead," Ashley said. "I found one through all that shit you made me wade through, but I think I may have something."

"Well, Burch can't account for his movements for our three victims," McArthur said. "Quite a violent chap too. So, we need to get some backstory on him. Financials and phone records have been requested and should be here tomorrow."

"I'll look through them," Ashley said. "Besides, Oatley's phone records should have come through now anyway."

"Well we might have to pull some late nights because the press is baying for info. Plus, we have people coming out of the woodwork with allegations on him."

"They're going to be true."

"Well we need to wrap this up quickly. Come back to base for a meeting. We need to plan our next move."

"Yes Sir."

Chapter 60

Ashley and Murphy walked into the office where McArthur was sitting at Parland's desk. The rest of the team were in deep discussion when they walked in.

"Right, now we're all here," McArthur said. "Mr Burch doesn't have an alibi for the nights that either of our victims died, he says that he was at home alone, but a neighbour saw him leave, which casts doubt."

"So, where did he go?" Murphy asked.

"Fenway, I want you to follow up his alibis."

"There's more than one?" Ashley asked.

"We have to be thorough," McArthur said. "At the moment, Burch is our number one suspect; I want his confession all wrapped up in a little bow for the press and the DCS." McArthur walked away but Ashley grabbed her evidence and went after him.

"Sir."

"Make it quick Fenway, I'm busy."

"Sir, I've found a promising link that might link our three suspects."

"Does it involve Burch?"

"Well, no."

"Then I'm not interested in it right now, Fenway," McArthur said, calling the lift. "Burch is prime suspect number one, and I want a link to him."

"But Sir." Ashley quickened her pace, so she was in front of him. "I did that digging through the financials of Oatley like you said and I found a payment made to a reporter from the Evening News. The story she was going to print would expose Oatley and a host of other people."

"Does this exposé include Burch?"

"No, but —"

"Fenway, maybe I didn't make myself clear. I want Burch, not this, if you can link the two of them then by all means." The lift came and he walked forward, Ashley had to side-step out of the way.

"You want to impress me, go get me that evidence." The door closed. Ashley looked down at her work.

"Screw you too," Ashley said, walking to her desk and throwing the paperwork into a drawer. She huffed and looked at the drawer. She could have a look into it herself, there was nothing stopping her.

Ashley went to the Charities Commission and typed in 'Limehouse'. Not to her great shock nothing turned up. She leaned back in her chair and stroked her chin. She looked over at the file on Limehouse and saw the New Agers. Ashley's eyes flickered between the two. She leaned forward and typed in the 'New Agers'.

The list came back with something more to her liking with only one result. Ashley opened it up, which gave Limehouse's address along with trustees and directors. They only had one, Dennis Thompson. It also showed that its charity status dissolved in 1989.

There was also the possibility of buying documents for it as well. Ashley got on the phone to the Charities Commission and requested every report and document they ever placed in. Ashley even paid for the next day delivery, she didn't want to wait for the four-day delivery in case another body showed up.

Ashley watched back through Burch's interrogation, making notes on were he said he was going and what he was doing; in the end it ended up being three different stories she had to check out. She sighed and wrote down where she needed to go on three different pages.

Ashley got her coat and bag and went down to her car.

***

Alibi one:

"Where were you between Saturday the eighteenth between eleven and one?" McArthur asked. Burch looked down at the table.

"I was at home, pizza guy delivered around half nine and I rented a film."

"Which film?" Armstrong asked.

"Top Gun."

"Good choice, love that film," Armstrong said. "And, the pizza place would be able to back this up?"

"Absolutely."

Ashley parked up outside Joey's Pizza. As dirty pizza places went Ashley knew this was a good haunt, a couple of nights out had ended up here. It was nearly seven, but it was starting to get busy, but there were a group of delivery drivers outside who stopped talking as she went past.

Ashley walked in and skipped the queue which caused a bit of ire.

"Don't worry, official police business," Ashley said, showing them her ID. The girl at the front sighed.

"Just because you're police, doesn't mean you can cut the queue."

"I'm not drunk enough to have one," Ashley said, getting her phone out.

"I need a receipt for an order placed on the eighteenth, for a Kyle Burch," Ashley said, showing her the date and time Burch ordered. The girl sighed.

"It might be in the log," she said, reaching underneath the till and getting out a large, black, leather-bound book. She flipped a couple of pages back and pulled out a receipt and handed it to her.

"Thanks." Ashley turned back and looked at it. The order was under Burch and it was to be delivered by CJ. Ashley placed the receipt into a plastic bag and sealed it.

"Is CJ around?" Ashley asked, handing the book back. The girl nodded outside.

"He should be outside." Ashley walked out into the bitter wind to the group of three guys on scooters, who were having a smoke.

"CJ?" Ashley asked. The black one of the group nodded his head.

"And what can I do for you?" He asked with what Ashley thought was supposed to be a smoulder, but he just looked ridiculous.

Ashley got her ID out again and the smirk was wiped off his face.

"I need to confirm that you made a delivery on the eighteenth of November," Ashley said, handing him over the bag with the receipt.

"Yeah, Burchy."

"Is he a regular?" CJ nodded.

"What time did you deliver?" Ashley asked.

"About nine," he said nodding. Odd, Burch said his pizza was delivered at half nine.

"Are you sure?" Ashley asked.

"Yeah, second half of the football was about to start. I asked him the score." CJ said, now frowning. "He's not in trouble, is he?"

"No, just asking for an alibi," Ashley said. "Thank you very much." Ashley walked away back to her car and wrote down that Burch was lying about what time his pizza was delivered.

Alibi Two:

"All right, where were you the on the twelfth of November between three and seven?" McArthur asked. "Think carefully."

"I was at the pub," Burch said, his face visibly strained. "I always go on a Sunday. The landlord can vouch for me."

Ashley pulled up next at The Thorny Crown, which was a much as an old man pub as there could be. There were a few mutters of disapproval as Ashley walked in. Inside was stuffy and full of laughter but very old fashioned, the sort of place Burch would visit.

Ashley stood at the bar, the barman looked at her and came over.

"That was quick," Ashley thought.

"Sorry miss, no girls allowed," he said. Ashley quirked an eyebrow, got her ID out and showed it.

"Fuck."

"Yeah, fuck," Ashley said. "Good job I'm not investigating inclusion today." She got the photo of Burch on her phone and showed him to the barman.

"What's that bird doing in here?" Someone shouted.

"Derek, leave it!" The barman shouted back. "She's not going to be here long."

"That depends on you," Ashley tapped the screen of her phone.

"The twelfth of November. Was he in here?" The barman nodded.

"Burchy comes in most Mondays after work but he wasn't in here last one," he said. "I'm not sure where he was."

"Does he talk about Will Oatley at all?" Ashley asked.

"Never fucking shuts up about him," the barman said.

"Did he mention if he went after him at all?" The barman looked around.

"He always talks big about giving Oatley what he deserved." Ashley wrote that down.

"Thanks, can I take a name?" Ashley asked.

"Gerry Donnell."

"Thanks. You've been very helpful."

Alibi Three:

"Have you even been to the Cambrian Hotel, Kyle?" Armstrong asked. Burch shook his head.

"Can't say that I have," he said.

"Lovely and quaint place outside of the Arndale," Armstrong said, sitting down trying to gauge if he was inept or soulless.

"Where were you last Thursday between eleven and one?"

"At work," he said. "My boss will be able to back that up."

Ashley was outside the Amazon warehouse by Manchester Airport. She walked up to the reception area of the building which was unmanned. It was nearly eight anyway, so they probably sent the receptionist home. Ashley rang the bell for attention. About five minutes later a manager came through and she explained why she was there.

"Yeah, Kyle was here," the manager said. "He's a good worker, a bit moody but —" He shrugged.

"Are you sure?" Ashley asked, sensing another dead end.

"Yeah, he comes in, does his twelve hours and goes home."

"Does he have a timecard or something in writing that can prove it? Not that your word isn't enough."

"Yeah, he has a timecard, I'll get it for you now." A couple of minutes later he returned with the timecard which oddly enough proved his story.

"Can I get a copy of this?"

Chapter 61

Ashley opened the door into her apartment and dropped her gym stuff down. She finished her drink off and flicked the radio on. She just wanted to forget the day and forget work. She had a long, hot shower, made her way into her kitchen and made herself a salad, making a mental note to get some more stuff later in the week.

She walked into the living room and picked a book up from her bookshelf before sitting down.

She sat down on the sofa and started to read and eat, she got a few chapters in before her mind started to wonder about work. She wasn't confident that they could pin the Ferrets and Kettings murders on Burch. He might have a reason to kill Oatley but the other two didn't make sense. What would be a reason to kill all three…?

Ashley's mind wandered back to what Amelia said about that place that could bring down lots of people.

Limehouse.

It sounded familiar.

She could see how Oatley would be involved but what about the other two? Ferrets was a football scout not a star. Although with all the allegations surrounding that it might not be that far of a stretch, but where did Kettings, a postman, fit into all this as well?

Ashley shut her book. The pieces were there, she could see them. The gown in Kettings wardrobe the focus in her mind, along with Ferrets' slashed neck and Oatley's cocky grin.

"No, Ashley, you need sleep," she said tiredly, rubbing the side of her head. Ashley got to her feet, washed her bowl out and put it away, turned the lights and radio off, went into her room and got into bed. She closed her eyes and tried to shut her mind down, but she was still formulating a theory in her head.

If all their victims were linked to this place, along with countless other celebs and people of power, the victims could run into the hundreds…

It didn't bear thinking about.

Ashley moved onto her side and closed her eyes; if there was a link, she'd find one. Where though? There might not be that many documents on the internet. But if those three are connected there might be more.

"Dammit." Ashley got out of bed, went back into the living room and turned her laptop on, went to the kitchen to make herself a decaf tea, she sat back down in front of the screen and started to research Limehouse in more detail.

It was an old manor house that was owned by an affluent family until the second world war. It got its name as the original owner was the local lime quarry owner who built the house. When the quarry went bust however, it was sold.

"Sold to who?" Ashley wondered. Ashley used her police log in for Land Registry; Limehouse was sold in 1960 to Oatley Development plc.

"There's a link," Ashley said.

When it was sold to Oatley's father, the family fell into arrears. It was leased out as a house for famous singers, actors and actresses when they were on tour or working in the north west. But then it was leased out to a reclusive Christian group called the 'New Agers'. Ashley frowned, that was the name of the sect in the civil suit brought against Ferrets.

Ashley was looking at a photo of the New Agers; they were wearing gowns in the middle of a field. The same gown that Nikita showed her; the one Stan Kettings made her wear. They mostly looked like children and teenagers. There was something in their eyes that Ashley couldn't quite put her finger on.

The picture was from an old Christian magazine piece which praised the New Agers for their commitment to god, by giving up material possessions and living a simple life of honest labour. The programme was run by Dennis Thompson, a former banker and missionary who had become disillusioned.

Ashley tried searching his name in Google but nothing came up for him. Ashley tried searching for the ''New Agers in Google and got some more promising results. The results were about the good charity work that the Agers did.

She saw the three of them softly linked to this Christian cult. The gown from Kettings wasn't found at his house; she only had Nikita's word for it. Maybe there was something more solid linking them? Ashley tried searching their names with the New Agers, but nothing came up.

Ashley sighed, ran a hand through her hair and looked over at the board she had in her room, which had Ferrets' name on it with the name Lisa Strachan and a question mark. Lisa Strachan was part of a cult.

It said so on her board.

Ashley walked over to the board and wrote 'Limehouse?' This had to be the place Lisa Strachan was at. The more Ashley thought about it the more it all fitted. Lisa Strachan first accused Ferrets while at this… Limehouse. If she was at Limehouse Oatley would have access, if he had access then Kettings would have too. Ashley got her notebook and wrote down to check Ferrets' civil case, confirm where the cult Lisa Strachan was in were based.

Ashley sat back down on the sofa and ran her hands down her face. This was a promising lead; if she wasn't chasing up these duds, she could devote more time to this.

But there was such scarce information on it. Maybe there was a link in old newspapers. It was a long shot, but Ashley checked the local newspaper websites, but none of them did old issues.

Ashley was looking at the Manchester Herald which had the death of Oatley on its front page. Ashley though searched the website for archives.

Nothing.

Ashley thought for a moment. She nodded and Googled 'newspaper archives in Manchester'; a few results came up, but the one she was interested in was Manchester Public Library's website which had a large archive, which had recently been digitised. That would help in searches. Ashley made a note of the address, shut her laptop down and looked at the time. It was going to be a long day tomorrow.

Chapter 62

Beep.

Beep.

Beep.

Ashley's arm rose out of the puddle of her duvet, felt around for her phone and turned off the alarm. She pulled the duvet back and sat on the edge of, the bed, cursing herself for her lack of sleep. Not what she needed on a game day.

Ashley made herself breakfast and sat in front of the TV watching the Monnargan Moment which was now talking about kids who were spending too much time on games. Ashley though was too busy thinking about Limehouse.

She turned the TV off and got all the links she had made last night and put them into a spare folder she had lying around. All the links and connections she made last night were still there; she would try and get to the library after the game which was in Alderley edge, and she was designated driver today. Ashley put her file away and got her hockey stuff ready.

***

"Led Zep? Queen? Blondie?"

"Yeah, take your pick," Ashley said.

"Sorry girl but my dad listens to this," Di said, dangling Queens Greatest Hits in front of her.

"It's what I like," Ashley said, moving Di's hand out of the way.

"Nothing wrong with the classics," Eliza said, from the back. Di turned her head to her.

"Your ideas recently haven't been the best," Di said. "Dean?"

"Fuck you."

"You may as well have tried to fuck Ash."

"Enough, my car, stick Queen on."

"Queen?"

"As in her majesty," Ashley said, in a mock, posh accent. Di huffed and placed the CD in.

"Does this one have Radio Gaga on it?"

"That's greatest hits two," Di shook her head.

"Is Bo Rap first?" Ashley shook her head.

"It goes Killer Queen then Bo Rap."

"Can't we put that on first?"

"No!" Eliza and Ashley chorused.

"Killer Queens a classic, let's keep that."

***

"Remember, let's try and keep the ball, keep it ticking over in the midfield. They like playing the counter so let's invite them onto us and find the space in behind. Ash!"

"Yep."

"You're in the centre, so keep that ball, protect it, move it, arrive late, got it."

"Crystal," Ashley said, pulling her under armour on.

"Eliza, Di, no hanging back, run in behind and catch them cold, Ash and Kim can find you with their passing."

"Got it," Eliza said.

"Tough game today girls, always is between us. Show no fear and don't pull out of challenges. Go out there and win."

Ashley walked out into the light drizzle in the air, jumping up high to get the blood going on this cold day. She stood in the middle of the pitch, bounced up and down on the spot, stretching her back then bending over and touching her toes, she raised her stick over her head and shook her hips.

Time to do this.

What Ashley liked about hockey was that as soon as she crossed those white lines, all her problems went away. For an hour, nothing else mattered. But they were always there when she got off.

She was walking off, a hard-fought victory, two assists and an OK performance in her book. Her trail of thought was interrupted by Eliza jumping on her.

"Have I told you how fucking good you are?" Ashley smiled.

"Often, when I set you up," Ashley said. "Although you'd have to be brain dead to miss those chances."

"Less of that," Eliza said. "You fancy going out?"

"Can't tonight. I have work to do."

"Girl, all you do is work," Eliza said. "We need another girls' night as well, your turn to host."

"Yes, yes. Sorry, new job's been hectic recently. They weren't happy I was coming here today."

"Feel better after that?"

"Loads," Ashley said, with a smile.

***

"See you on Tuesday!" Eliza walked back into her apartment building. Ashley looked at the time. She got her phone out and checked when Manchester Library closed.

She had time, she went home, showered (properly) and was back out.

Ashley drove to the Manchester library. She walked up the large, stone steps to the Greek style front with its large pillars and sloping roof. Ashley put her hands in the pockets of her jacket and walked into the foyer, with her boots echoing her footsteps on the marble floor.

She walked into the main hall which was nearly empty; only a caretaker and a couple of students preparing to pull all-nighters. It reminded her of own uni days.

The old newspaper records were kept on computers in the corner of the room. Ashley sat down in front of it and opened the application which brought up a search bar. Ashley typed in the name of ''Gordon Ferrets and Limehouse.

The search icon turned into a rotating hourglass; it came up with a list of newspapers, which had, issue number, date and page number. Most of them were feel-good pieces about his academy, nothing that they didn't know already. But one did catch her eye, the headline was about education being provided to youths.

Ashley clicked on it and the article came up, a grainy black and white image of three men standing with a group of youngsters behind a large manor house.

"Limehouse," Ashley muttered to herself, tapping her temple with her finger.

The children were wearing the gowns and they all looked miserable, while the three men beamed. She looked at the line under the photo.

Leader Dennis Thompson, director of the Ferrets Sports Academy Mr Gordon Ferrets and Owner of Limehouse, Will Oatley. Picture by Ian Whikley.

Ashley leaned forward. This provided a link between all their victims so far. Ashley got her phone out, went back through her photos and found the one that Nikita had sent her of the gown Kettings wanted her to wear. Ashley looked up at the screen and felt a shiver go up her spine. She was onto something. She could feel it. Ashley saved the link and went back looking.

Limehouse.

A few more articles came up. Most of them were feel-good pieces but more recent ones were about abuse at the cult's hand. Ashley opened one of them up about a woman who claimed that she was abused at the cult.

Ashley read intently. It detailed the same abuse that Amelia told her about. Ashley went back to the top of the article to see the woman's name. Claire Wellbeck. Ashley opened Google and typed in the name. Not much came up for her, apart from an obituary.

She died a few years ago but the cause wasn't explained in the piece itself. Whoever wrote it did a good job and it was very moving, going on about the failed justice she had over the years with Limehouse.

Ashley frowned. Maybe this was what Amelia meant, warning her away from digging too much into Limehouse. Something was going on there. She needed to find out what.

She looked up the name of the person who wrote the obituary, Matilda Kaye. A quick search was on Google showed that she wasn't on the internet much. The electoral roll would have her name on there.

Ashley scrolled back to the photo of Oatley and Ferrets with this Dennis Thompson. What was his story now? Ashley went back to Google.

The name was a popular one with many people on Facebook and doing a wide range of professions. This guy could still be alive, or dead for all she knew, she had to see what had happened to him.

Ashley added that to her list as well.

"Lisa Strachan" The icon twisted round, Ashley rapping her fingers on the desk. What she feared came up.

Nothing.

She printed off the articles she needed and pulled her coat on, the autumn chill racking through the library.

***

Another great game by our Ladies 1st team who beat Alderley Edge 2–0. #GOTG Eliza Williams #Upthenorthern

@Nottingham Men's Uni team beating @Derbyuni 3–0. #MOTM Hat-trick Hero Matt Fenway. See his second on @grassrootgoals. It's a doozy. #R1+O #Whatahitson! #Topbins

That hollow feeling when you finish your newest @Netflix binge. #Feedme!

Day 45 without sex, my dad asked the dog who's a good girl and I said, 'Me Daddy.' Without thinking. He thought I was being innocent... #Nothingofthesort #Ineedtogetlaid

"Shouldn't you be on the piss?"

"I've got a paper due tomorrow." Ashley laughed.

"Lightweight. I usually did both."

"What did you get again?"

"Double-first," Ashley said. She was lying on her sofa with her dinner in her lap and the articles on Limehouse and the New Agers around her.

"How's the paedophile hunter going?"

"Words reached there has it?" Ashley asked. She was reading a piece on Dennis Thompson and his cult. Self-serving was all Ashley could think about.

"It's all people are talking about sis," her brother said. "We talked about it in my business class." Ashley sighed.

"Does anyone think we're doing a good job?" Ashley asked.

"Grow up, you're the police, no one thinks you do a good job." Ashley lowered the article.

"Thanks for that, just what I needed," Ashley deadpanned.

"You know I think you do the best."

"I try," Ashley replied, going back to reading.

"Do you guys ever, you know, think like that?"

"Like what, Matt?" Ashley asked running a hand through her hair. He paused.

"Like… should we let this guy get away with it." Ashley thought about it for a moment, lowering the article slowly. Was it tempting to? Sorely. But the there was a reason why they all did what they did.

"No," Ashley said.

"Even if there —"

"We just don't Matt," Ashley said, cutting him off. "I have a job to do; bring this person in. If we condone the acts of one person killing people, it just doesn't end. Soon they'll be justifying killing litterers to save the turtles."

"Suppose you're right."

"Yes, yes I am," Ashley said. "Listen, I have to go, I have to work early."

"Yeah, me too. Only two thousand words left to go."

"Redbull."

"Monster."

"That stuff is like battery acid."

"Keeps me going longer."

"Nice, speak to you next week, bro."

"Speak to you soon, sis." Ashley ended the call and looked at the photo of Thompson.

He was described as charismatic and charming, which was how he could get people to join his cult, but from reading some of the stories about this place it was like a house of horrors.

Regular beatings from Thompson himself and cult elders, slave labour, prolonged punishments and more disturbingly the use of children as sex slaves. How could a place like this go under the radar for so long, Ashley wondered?

Ashley got her laptop up and searched for Matilda Kaye on Google, Facebook, Twitter... nothing. The woman must have been quite old or had got married since the articles were published, or maybe she had died like Claire Welbeck.

She spent most of the evening reading notes and reworking her board to include Thompson and the New Agers. She yawned, stretching her body and flopped her arms down. The links that had made sense a second ago, now making no sense whatsoever.

She cleared her things away and got into bed; the last thought in her head thinking what she should do for girls' night.

Chapter 63

Ian Whikley sat on his sofa playing with his fingers. The news of Will's death had spread more quickly than he could have imagined. He had cancelled the liaison he had planned. It was too risky now, first Ferrets, Kettings, now Oatley.

The agent wasn't too happy with his change of heart, but he had refunded him in full; but now he was more paranoid than ever before. Someone was hunting down people who were part of the ring. The CCTV he ordered would be here tomorrow so he would be safe.

Tonight, was supposed to be the night that he had the girl, funny how things change. He could be dead, he erred on the side of caution; he should go to the police with this but it would expose him.

It made him think back to those days at Limehouse, the perfect institution where people like him could do what they pleased, but no one could link him to it, he was sure of it.

The pictures of all of it were on a hard drive that no one could find. He always found it useful to keep such information just in case.

The doorbell went. In his jittery state he jumped up. He looked at the door of the living room, daring it to ring again; a couple of seconds later it did. Whikley scrambled round for his diary. He flipped the pages to today's date which showed that he had someone coming to pick up some photos, it also showed that he had someone coming tomorrow morning as well.

Whikley got up slowly off his sofa and walked over to the door. His steps echoed and his breathing heavy. He checked the peephole.

It was his neighbour Kate. He breathed a huge sigh of relief and opened the door.

"Hi Kate."

"Are you OK?" She asked.

"Yeah, sorry," he said, around a nervous laugh. "I thought you were someone else for a second." Kate laughed.

"No, just me, I was wondering if you had mine and Tammy's passport photos? I'm going to the post office." Relief flowed through him.

"Of course. Yes, please, come on in." Kate smiled and followed him into the house."

"They came back this morning," he said, trying to make small talk. "In fact, they've turned out really —"

Before he could finish, he was struck across the back of the head and fell onto his knees and then the floor, with Kate looking down at him.

***

When Whikley came to he found himself on the bed. He groggily tried to get up but found his wrists and ankles were bound to the bed. He struggled against the bonds, but they weren't coming loose from the grips.

"Don't bother." Whikley looked down at the end of the bed and saw Kate looking through the albums and rolls of film. He could only see her outline, her face concealed by the darkness.

"Kate... what are you doing?" He asked.

"It would have been easier for you if you just went through with it," she said. "Accept the offer I gave you and then... well actually it would have ended up like this."

"I don't understand."

"I'm the agent," she said. "You were hard at the thought of fucking a girl, that you didn't think it through."

"But, the voice, the pictures."

"A ruse, Jesus, I thought paedos were supposed to be smart. Now. Where are they?"

"Where are what?"

"The pictures," Kate said, calmly. "The pictures of me."

"You?"

"Yes, the pictures of me."

"The passport ones?"

"No! Not the fucking passport ones!" She shouted.

"I don't know what you're talking about!" He shouted back.

"Really?" She said breathlessly, Kate got up and walked into the light of the room. "Take a long hard look." Whikley squinted his eyes at her, the realisation suddenly dawned on him who she was.

"You."

"I may have dyed my hair but, yes," Kate said. "Now, about those pictures."

"I don't know."

"Don't lie to me!" Kate spat.

"Look, I'm sorry, I really am," Whikley said, tears in his eyes. "But they're gone."

"I doubt that. You always had a thing for me, I can't believe you would just destroy them," Kate said, now at the side of the bed.

"I was a child," she said. "We all were, and you did nothing." The tears flowed freely down his cheeks.

"You really are pathetic," Kate said. "The world won't miss you. It'll celebrate that you're gone."

"Please, please, you know I wasn't like the others."

"No, you were worse," Kate agreed. "More manipulative. And so arrogant that I was under your nose the entire time, there must have been something in the back of your head that recognised me."

Whikley fell back on the bed and Kate got back to her feet.

"Last chance for some redemption," she said, evenly. "Where are the photos of me?"

"I don't know."

"You never did make things easy," Kate said pulling a knife out of her bag.

"I'm gonna turn this place upside down, now we can make it quick if you tell me, or long and painful if you don't play ball. So." She kneeled down beside him.

"What's it going to be?"

"You were a slut then, and you still are now!"

382

"So be it." Kate got to her feet and cut the back of his knees. Whikley screamed, cussing and screaming at her. Kate walked behind him and placed the knife to his neck and slowly cut across it.

"I'm not going to cut the jugular, not yet, the air across the wound will be bad enough." Whikley was squirming; Kate went back to searching through the film.

"The police will love this," she said. "And don't worry about little old me." Whikley tried to say something but was gasping on air.

"The police have no idea it's me, and they never will." She walked over to him.

"I thought the likes of Oatley were the worst but no. No, you're the worst, you do something much more depraved." She got onto her haunches.

"Hope, you gave me hope and then took it away. But don't worry, you're not the last name on my list." She could see his skin turning white. It was near the end. Kate walked behind the bed and readied the knife.

"Nice, big smile sweetheart." It's what he always used to tell her.

She finished the job. She watched the blood seep down his chest and his struggling movement turning to nothing.

"Right, where are those pictures?" She said going back to the albums.

Chapter 64

Ashley was staring at the ceiling, her alarm due to go off in about half an hour but her mind was on other things. The thought of Limehouse was swimming around in her head to keep her awake, trying to figure out what this all meant and how their victims were connected to this place.

Ashley got out of bed, her body stiff from yesterday. She winced and looked down at her vest. She pulled it up to see an ugly bruise on her side. Her mind wandering back to yesterday when she was fouled. One of the Alderley Edge players stepping across her after Ashley had taken the ball past her; making sure her thigh and stick caught Ashley.

Ashley pulled her vest down and went about getting her things ready for the day.

Cardio.

Weights.

Squats.

Core.

Sauna.

Ashley wiped her brow and looked at the swirling steam in front of her. Thinking about Claire Welbeck, Matilda Kaye and how they fitted into what she was looking into with Limehouse.

Could Claire Welbeck and Lisa Strachan possibly be related, could they have been there at the same time? Well, time to find out, Ashley told herself as she got up.

***

"The reports of abuse by Will Oatley have slowly gone through the roof after his death earlier this week, with witnesses detailing the scale of abuse he carried out."

"I think more worryingly is the sudden spate of people who refuse to condemn the actions of this individual. Even going as far as asking that the police not look into these crimes until it's done."

"Well why not? It's what the public wants."

"And what if someone is incorrectly labelled a child molester and they end up dead? People are already concerned that these vigilante gangs tracking paedophiles are going too far. Is this really the message we want to send out?"

"That if you abuse a child you end up dead. I think that's a deterrent enough."

Ashley made it to the office just before half seven, she was surprised to see the group of people asking for information on Oatley had swelled up. When Ashley got inside, she turned on the lights, computers and the TV which was still running with the death of Will Oatley. Ashley got her porridge from under her desk and watched another interview with another Oatley victim.

With porridge and tea in hand Ashley brought up the NCD. She consulted her notebook, first she looked up Matilda Kaye on the Electoral Roll. There were a few in the UK but thankfully only one in the Manchester Area, well, Warrington. Ashley wrote down the address, she would have to find time to go and talk to Kaye about her connections to Claire Wellbeck.

Next on her list, Dennis Thompson. She checked the Electoral Roll, there wasn't a Dennis Thompson in the Manchester or surrounding area. Ashley checked the NCD now it had warmed up. She did a nationwide search for Dennis Thompson.

Only one result.

That was odd, even for the NCD. Ashley clicked on it and up came the details on the case. An unsolved murder. The problem with the NCD was that it only gave a brief outline of the case, the hard files had to be requested from archives.

Victim was in his late forties in a poor and run-down area of Carrington. The victim was found in a state of undress on his bed with a single knife wound to his neck. Ashley had seen enough and placed a request. Knowing that it would take hours for the request to be processed Ashley picked up her phone. She had another bite of porridge and a slug of tea before it was answered.

"Archives, Constable Stiles." The voice was old and croaky, years of smoke abuse.

"Hi, I'm DC Fenway with Major Crimes."

"What can I do for you doll?" Doll?

"I placed a request for a file just now, I was hoping to skip through all the procedure and come down and get it now?"

"Listen love, I haven't even had my coffee yet let alone turned the computer on," he said.

"So, what, you just come in early for the bacon sandwich, it's gone half seven." He coughed from the other side of the phone; probably couldn't believe a woman had talked to him like that.

"Well, we're all busy DC Fenway."

"That we are," Ashley agreed. "So, I'll be down in about ten minutes, the case reference is ND-2356746JJ, if the computer doesn't warm up. I know what they're like."

"Hold your horses, I haven't even got a pen. Are you this pushy with your husband?"

"I don't have one."

"Boyfriend?"

"Nu uh."

"Probably explains it."

"ND-2356746JJ, see you in ten." Before he could get a word in, Ashley placed the phone down and finished her porridge.

Since the City Tower has lots of space, they'd allocated a basement floor for a section of archives.

She made her way down. When she got to the door, she saw that a few letters had been scrubbed away. She opened the door into a dark waiting area which separated the archives by a mesh window.

Ashley walked forward and rapped her knuckles on the mesh.

"You DC Fenway?" A gruff voice asked from behind the rows of files.

"Yes I am." A portly man came from behind the files with a file under his arm and eyed her up. Not in a sexual way, but to get the measure of her.

"Huh, you're not what I suspected," he said, walking to the mesh office front.

"What were you expecting?" Ashley asked.

"Someone older," he said, placing the file down. "So, do you know how this goes?" He asked.

"Don't I have something to sign?" Ashley asked.

"Clever girl," he said, getting out a folder with a sheet of paper which Ashley filled in.

"Thanks," she said, turning around.

"Do me a favour next time?" Stiles asked. "Put in a request after eight."

"I'll consider it," Ashley said, winking and closing the door.

When she got back to her desk, Ashley opened the file. The victim was indeed Dennis Thompson. Early forties and found murdered in his bed.

There were no leads in the case, this was done in a time before social media and the internet and no one could connect the dots. Neighbours said he moved in recently but didn't say from where; a couple of them saw prossies coming and going. She might go to Kerry and ask her.

He was found on his bed with a slashed throat but not tied up. There was booze and a little cocaine in his system, but no signs of poison.

The front door was unlocked, so the killer was trusted to be let in... but left in a hurry. Ashley frowned; just like their murders. Ashley turned the page and looked at the knife wound. The pathologist report said there was one initial wound of great force in the neck, before the neck was slashed fully. Ashley thought back to criminology one-o-one.

The initial wound was one of fear, the other of vengeance looking at the result. Ashley heard the door open but didn't look up. This was a crime of opportunity. Someone, probably from Limehouse, saw the chance and took it. But why would Thompson invite someone from there into his house?

Ashley turned the page and saw a picture that made her blood run cold. Ashley picked up a picture of a grey gown with a white trim. The same one that Nikita showed her and that was in that photo of Limehouse.

Ashley bit her lip and tapped her chin. Maybe this had to be someone who lived at Limehouse while the abuse was going on. Ashley looked up and saw one of the detectives from the other team making tea in the kitchen. Maybe the murders were related.

Every killer had to learn their craft, and the photo from the paper proved a link between two, potentially three victims. Ashley had to approach this carefully. McArthur was under stress already with the death of Will Oatley and wasn't in the mood for unnecessary links and leads right now.

The phones round the office rang. Ashley waited for hers while flicking through some of the photos and profiles of Dennis Thompson.

He was working as a salesman, go figure, obviously had the gift of the gab.

"Major Crimes, DC Fenway speaking," she said, placing the phone between her shoulder and ear.

"Hi, this is Dean Henderson with the coroner's office. I thought you guys would want a heads up." Ashley's attention was taken from the file, and the swooping sense of dread threatened to bring up her porridge. She leaned forwards and took hold of the phone.

"Heads up for what?" Ashley asked, as the red sunlight spread down outside.

"You have another one."

"You're joking."

"You know as well as I do, we're not in the joking trade," he replied.

"How can you be sure?" Ashley asked.

"Male, late fifties, tied to a bed with his throat slashed," Henderson said. "Your type of cases, correct?"

"Correct," Ashley said, her posture slacking so her head was being held up with her left hand. "Right, where is it and who called it in?" After he told her the details, Ashley placed the phone down and rang the rest of the team.

"Fuck," McArthur said, the strain evident in his voice. Ashley could hear him pacing.

"I know. I've sent everyone down there now," Ashley said.

"Right, I want you to stay there and make some headway on the Oatley case," he sighed heavily. "How bad is it?" McArthur asked.

"I really don't know Sir," Ashley said. "You can phone me with some info on the guy and I'll see if his name comes up with our other victims."

"OK, you might as well release Burch as well while you're at it too," McArthur said.

"I'll do it later. Something doesn't seem quite right with him."

"He's a lunatic, that's why," McArthur said. "Out of curiosity how many of Burch's alibis checked out?"

"One," Ashley said, opening a new case on the computer. "He's a very lucky boy."

"Wish we could charge him with wasting police time," McArthur said.

"I'll caution him. Then I'll get everyone to carry on looking into Oatley."

"Yeah, yeah, I will. Is there anything else?" Ashley paused, should she tell him about the link between Dennis Thompson and their murders, but with a new victim coming in she couldn't just swan off and do her own thing like she wanted to.

"Fenway, is there anything else?"

"No, Sir," Ashley said. "Speak to you later."

"Yeah, see you later." Ashley ended the call and laid back in the chair.

"Shit, shit, shit," she said, getting to her feet when someone let out a low whistle. She ignored it, she got a new board and wrote 'Victim Four'.

Chapter 65

The more people are talking about Will Oatley I think that he might have been a nonce. #justsayin

Can't wait for the @Netflix documentary on Will Oatley.

If this man was so evil why didn't people come forward earlier? #notbuyinit #peoplelie

Funny how people who support all survivors matter suddenly go quiet or 180 when someone they like is accused. #doublestandard #hypocrites

I knew Oatley was a slimy bugger, this just proves it.

To be fair this is just confirmation of what we all knew and he fucked everybody!!! #illseemyselfout

After Ashley had left instructions for the extended team, she walked down to the holding cells where Burch's lawyer, Gail Downey, was tapping her foot impatiently and looking at her phone. At the sound of Ashley's footsteps, she looked up.

"About time," she said, dropping her phone into her handbag. "I've been waiting all morning." Ashley walked straight past her and let herself into the holding cells. "Are you charging my client at all? Because his treatment by your officers has been nothing short of inhumane."

Downey followed Ashley down to the holding cells where the desk sergeant was waiting. Ashley handed over the paperwork to release Burch.

"Hello? Can you tell me what the fuck is going on?" Downey asked. The desk sergeant looked up with a wry smile on his face and handed the paperwork back to Ashley.

"Which cell is he in?"

"Cell one."

"Thanks. Can you open the door please?" The sergeant waved her onward.

"Are you releasing my client?" Downey asked, following Ashley to cell one.

"Kyle Burch, we are releasing you on bail pending further enquiries." She unlocked the door and looked down at Burch who was sitting on the concrete bench, his mean features looking up at her. He got to his feet. He was over six foot and towered over her.

"You are to report back to this police station at ten and four every day, pending said further enquiries, do you understand?" He grunted.

"Is that a yes?" Burch looked at his solicitor, who nodded.

"Good." Ashley stepped aside and he walked out.

"Before you go." Both stopped and turned around. "Mr Burch, I also have to caution you as well."

"Why?" Downey asked. "My client did everything he was asked to."

"Everything, apart from tell the truth," Ashley said. "We checked his 'alibis' that he gave us and only one of them checked out." Downey looked angrily at Burch who shrunk under her gaze.

"Lying to the police is an arrestable offence. But since we can clear you of our three murders this time, we are willing to let you go." Ashley handed him the caution notice.

"I remind you that if you lie to us again, it wouldn't be beneficial to you," Ashley said. "You can go."

Downey took Burch by the scruff of the neck and took him outside. Ashley shook her head and went back upstairs to her desk.

When she got there, there was a couple of large parcels on her desk. Ashley walked over and looked at the labels; they were from the Charities Commission. Ashley opened them up: two large boxes of printed documents.

"Great," Ashley said to herself, placing the lid back on the box.

She looked at her desk which was a mismatch of different documents. She rubbed her tired eyes and set about trying to get the paperwork into some sort of order. A thankless task and one that raised more questions than answers.

"You OK?" Ashley looked up and saw DS Sarandon come over.

"Yeah, I'm fine. You might want to add another board. We have another one."

"Christ. Do we have a name?"

"Not yet," Ashley replied. "I'll let you know when I know. I've given you a head start." She pointed to the board which had victim four on it.

"Thanks," he said, now looking at her notes on Limehouse and Dennis Thompson's murder file. "Does this need to be catalogued?" He said, pointing at her file.

"No," Ashley said quickly, she saw his confused face. "No, it's… something I'm working on."

"Hmmm, looks complicated," he said. "Are these for the —?" He pointed to a pile of documents.

"Yeah, they are," Ashley said. Sarandon took the documents.

She made herself a tea and sat down at her desk. She looked over at Sarandon organising the board and then at her file on Limehouse.

Ashley opened the drawer to get her highlighters. Her phone started ringing.

"Fenway."

"Ian Whikley." McArthur told her. Ashley got her notepad out and started to write the name.

"OK, what else?"

"Fifty-eight years old, found murdered in the same way, can you please get all the essentials. I'll text you over his account details."

"I'll put the phone calls in," Ashley said. "Is it as bad as the others?"

"Maybe worse," McArthur replied. "It's a bloody mess in here. Find out all you can on Ian Whikley; we should be back in a couple of hours. Can you also find his next of kin?"

"Will do, speak to you later."

"It looks like he's a photographer as well if that helps with your searches, quite a lot of lenses and stuff lying around." Weird, Ashley thought.

"OK, thanks." McArthur ended the call and she looked down at the file on her desk on Limehouse. Again, other things to do, but she would talk to McArthur about it when he got back.

She walked over to Sarandon.

"Ian Whikley, fifty-eight, found the same as our other victims."

"Perfect," he said, starting to write it down. "I take it McArthur has put this on you?" Ashley nodded.

"I'll reallocate the Oatley stuff in the interim."

"Thanks," Ashley said, going back to her desk

Ashley located a next of kin; a niece who lived in Liverpool. Ashley sent McArthur the address.

Ashley opened the NCD and typed his name in. She tapped her fingers on her cheek and the results came back in. He only had one previous conviction for harassment of a former colleague, but due to the nature of it the person's name was redacted. Ashley put in a request to get the file.

Ashley opened Google, Facebook and Twitter and searched for their guy. McArthur seemed to think that he was a photographer. Facebook came in first with a Whikley's Photography. It looked like a small-time business. The page was adorned with images of smiling babies, families and weddings. There was a photo of Ian himself. Slightly plump, wore a brilliant, white shirt and had long, grey hair in a tight ponytail.

His Twitter page again promoted his business with the same photos, it too had a company website which again was for the photography.

On the website there was an 'about me' section which Ashley checked out. According to this Whikley was an ex-freelance journalist / photographer for various newspapers in the north west. Ashley made a note to try and find some of his pieces. The article went on to talk about how he was now following his first love of 'capturing the one in a million moment for people'.

Ashley rolled her eyes and continued to read it, which was a bunch of self-serving spiel. Ashley closed it down. She found it on Companies House; she found the accountants and went about ordering all the essentials, phone records, financials and company records.

When all that was done, she went about looking for articles that Whikley wrote about. Unfortunately, again, it would have been old issues because not much came up. Ashley looked down at the information she had so far.

Maybe this guy was part of it too. A journalist would be good at covering up the scandal but…

Ashley looked back at her computer screen. He was a photographer as well. How was evidence collected against these people of power?

"With photos," Ashley said, writing down pictures on board four 'pictures, Limehouse.' They would be in his house or computer, just… somewhere. Maybe he was the lynchpin which stopped this all coming out.

What if the killer already found it?

"Good theory Ashley but all we need is a link," she said. Her phone buzzed in her pocket. Ashley pulled out her phone which had a message from McArthur asking for her progress. Ashley texted him the address of his studio, there might be someone there who could provide a lead.

Ashley though started to pore over the documents Oatley had because he had the most evidence, along with Amelia Franks' testimony.

The phone on Ashley's desk rang. It was an internal number from the PR department.

"Major Crimes, DC Fenway speaking."

"Hi, it's Pam from PR." Of course it is.

"Hi Pam, what can I do for you?"

"You're working Will Oatley's case, aren't you?"

"With those skills you could join me in here," Ashley said, sitting down.

"It's only because we have people phoning asking for comments."

"A statement will be given in due course, isn't that the usual BS?"

"Well, not when they say that Oatley was a paedophile to rival Jimmy Saville." Fuck, how did that get out, Ashley thought.

"They're asking for police comments."

"We don't comment on speculation," Ashley said.

"So, has this come up?"

"We don't want this getting out Pam," Ashley said. "Who's asking?" Ashley got her note pad out.

"Local newspapers and regional news stations," Pam said.

"Names would be helpful," Ashley said, sensing a lead.

"Evening and Herald, along with BBC news."

"Perfect," Ashley said. "I'll let you know if we need anything else from you." Ashley ended the call. "I almost take back every bad thing I said about PR."

Chapter 66

McArthur swept into the office, an air of frustration on his face. Probably just come back with a conversation with Delany about their new victim.

"Right, Ian Whikley, what do we know about him? Fenway."

"Fifty-eight, a photographer by trade and previously a reporter and photographer for various local papers across the north west. Now owns a small photography studio where he does the usual photography bollocks."

"What about his house, Parland?"

"House was a bloody mess," he said, checking his notes. "Vic was found the same way as our three, tied to the bed, blow to the back of the head and no sign of forced entry. The only difference is that the house was turned over top to bottom."

"They were looking for something," Ashley said.

"I guessed that too but we have no inventory from anyone," Parland said. "Did we find next of kin?"

"A niece in Liverpool," Ashley said. "But I doubt she's going to know every little thing in the house."

"The body didn't look any more beaten up than the rest of them," Murphy mused. "If they were looking for something why not just torture him until they got what they wanted?"

"Maybe they panicked?" Armstrong offered.

"They lost control," Ashley said. The room turned to her. "Maybe they meant to torture him, but they were so angry they killed him in a fit of rage."

"Maybe he was the worst of them," Murphy offered. "Or are they doing this in order?" Ashley looked over at the TV; they were outside Whikley's house. There was a young male reporter by the police cordon.

"Sir." Ashley pointed to the TV.

"Fuck." Armstrong unmuted it and they listened.

"The discovery of Ian Whikley is the fourth body found in a spate of grisly murders that have surrounded Greater Manchester in the last week.

Whikley, a local photographer we believe, died in the same vein as Gordon Ferrets, Stan Kettings and Will Oatley although the police will not confirm that. It also raises questions over the lifestyle of Mr Whikley, as the others have been confirmed as predatory paedophiles which has put Whikley into this bracket as well; which confirms our suspicions that there is a vigilante killer among the Manchester streets."

"Shall we brainstorm a catchy nick name?" Armstrong asked, dejectedly. "I feel like pissing the press off."

"No point, they'll find one," Parland said, he turned to McArthur. "We can't have them though saying there's a vigilante killer on the streets."

"Panic?"

"No, acceptance," Ashley said. "Have you not been listening to the radio?" By the vacant stares they didn't. "People are already on their side, why not kill paedophiles? Who wants them around anyway?"

"People on the radio are saying this?"

"Radio Two does come in useful."

"And Radio Four," McArthur said. "Even the wife has heard about it on the daytime talk shows. We want the media on-side."

"They'll want something."

"Yes, I know," McArthur snapped back. "First things first, let's go through all the usuals. Does IT have Whikley's computer and hard drives?"

"They should have them after SOCO have finished dusting them all for prints," Parland said. "To be honest everything in his house has been taken away so they can dust it."

"Neighbours?"

"No one saw anyone coming or going to the house," Parland said. "Or any weird vehicles over the last few days."

"Who found him?" Ashley asked.

"A bride who went to pick up her wedding album," Parland said. "Killer left the door open and went straight in."

"Was it a scheduled appointment?"

"Yeah, she was going away to see family and wanted to pick it up early."

"He was on the NCD," Ashley said. "A harassment claim was made against him by a former colleague, but the file is locked; I've already put a request in for it."

"OK, let me know when it comes back." McArthur's phone went off.

"McArthur." He frowned.

"Right, yes, yes Sir, they are related, I don't see how a press conference right now can..." He was cut off.

"It'll cause a problem and a panic. The TV stations are already saying there is a vigilante on the streets and..." He went into his office and closed the door.

Ashley was looking at the TV which was now on a generic morning programme.

"He's not going to do a press conference, is he?" Murphy said. "That'll be the worst thing to do right now."

"Armstrong, turn it up," Ashley said, nodding to the TV.

"The discovery of another body in the Greater Manchester area would normally send chills through the local community; or maybe not, as this might not be the case now. Gordon Ferrets, Stan Kettings and the now infamous Will Oatley, are hardened and predatory paedophiles who preyed on young boys ang girls for the best part of forty years. As a consequence, with more and more allegations coming out every single day, speaking to locals we have found that they're not as worried as you might think."

"The more of them in the ground, the better," one old woman said.

"I feel safer knowing that there are three less of those sickos on the streets," a young mother.

"Well whoever they are I have names of other ones they can take out if they want to," an old man.

"Aren't you afraid?"

"No, I haven't got anything to hide," a teenage woman. "The only people who are afraid are the ones that have something to hide."

"She has a point," Armstrong said.

"We don't deal in satire," Parland said, he swallowed thickly. "Even if they are right. Mute it and let's stay on point." Armstrong muted the TV and turned back round.

***

Ashley stood at the back of the room waiting for McArthur to come. Interesting to see Delany hadn't joined him. McArthur took his seat and got his notes out.

"Good Morning, Ladies and Gentlemen of the press. I can confirm that earlier on today we recovered the body of Ian Whikley. We believe that his murder is connected to our previous three victims, of Gordon Ferrets, Stan Kettings and Will Oatley. We reiterate that we are doing all we can to find those responsible and have a few promising leads already."

The cameras were still going off like crazy and some of the reporters were getting tetchy.

"Of course, it goes without saying that if anyone has information on these crimes they should —"

"Is one of those leads Kyle Burch?" One of them shouted. Ashley could see McArthur's jaw lock.

"Who are you?" He asked.

"Hugh Bell, The Sun."

"Of course," McArthur muttered under his breath. "We did question Kyle Burch in connection to Will Oatley's murder. He provided an alibi and was let go."

"Not what he says."

"As if you lot weren't already famous for kiss and tell. We have new lines of inquiry and my officers are constantly making strides."

"DCI McArthur, Melisa De Luna, the Guardian. Considering we now have four dead bodies of suspected paedophiles, is it safe to say that we have a vigilante killer in our mist?" McArthur sighed.

"I know you lot like running away with things like this," he said. "Ian Whikley hasn't been confirmed as anything other than dead."

"But you suspect that he is?" De Luna pressed.

"Unlike you, we don't suspect anything, we get the facts."

"So, this is the work of a serial killer rather than a vigilante killer?"

"No, it isn't, we —"

"Which is it? Do we have a serial killer on the loose or do we have a vigilante killer taking out paedophiles?"

As much as Ashley hated De Luna, she put McArthur into a corner superbly. This was what they wanted; fear sold news. People always wanted to know what could make them afraid. As soon as she said it more of her colleagues jumped on as well.

"We need to know!"

"Are there other people at risk!"

"Are normal people at risk!"

"Should people feel safe with this person walking the street!"

Ashley didn't know what she would do in the same situation. Probably what McArthur did.

"No more questions!" He said getting up and walking away to a flurry of questions and camera snapping.

Ashley snuck out and went to the pressroom where she could hear McArthur shouting. One of the PR team came out.

"I'd leave him for five minutes if I were you," she said.

"Shame, I have to speak to him," Ashley said, going inside.

"Delany is a bloody prick!" McArthur said, he was sat slumped in a chair. "You knew it was going to be a shit show when he said he couldn't make it." He banged his fist on the table, then took a deep breath.

"I'm sorry, I just made your jobs more difficult," he said.

"I'm sure I'll cry over it later in my life," Ashley deadpanned.

"This has lit a huge bonfire under us," McArthur said. "I can see the headline now." Ashley checked her phone and went on the BBC news app.

"Something like this?" The first page was a breaking news headline of vigilante serial killer on Manchester streets.

"Bollocks." McArthur leaned back to rest his head on the wall. "I'm gonna kill Delany when I see him."

"As much as I'd love to see that we need to get a suspect," Ashley told him.

"Yep, you're right," McArthur said, getting up. "Come on, we got work to do."

They made their way up to the office where the rest of the team were in animated discussion. From the looks of it Parland was the one trying to get his point across to the rest of them.

"I think it's a good idea," Murphy said.

"You would. Think about how much work we'll have to go through."

"We didn't get into this business to cut corners," Parland told him.

"What's the idea?" McArthur asked. Ashley sat back down in her chair while the others looked to Parland to explain himself. He took a deep breath.

"What if it's one of those paedophile hunters?" Parland suggested.

"Based on what exactly?" Ashley asked.

"Well that's the thing, we need to look into it, but maybe one of them was targeting all four of them. Things got out of hand…"

"It would make sense if the killer was suspected for something other than coming and slashing their necks," McArthur mused.

"Like a potential victim showing up," Murphy said. "They would answer the door quicker than they could get their trousers off."

"And it might explain how they were contacted," Parland said. "Someone gets a bit too far worked up, a bit pissed at these people not getting what they deserve."

"Whack them before anyone can let them get away with it," Armstrong said. "It's as good an idea as any."

"Where do we even start?" Murphy asked.

"Didn't you track one of them down, Fenway?" Armstrong asked.

"I figured out rather than tracked," Ashley said, running a hand through her hair. "Look, these people don't want to be found, we might have to ask them."

"Not really the show of force I was hoping for," Parland said. "If we round them all up and bring them in then it might actually look like we're doing something."

"And systematically piss off every member of the public because they're doing exactly what they want us to do," Ashley said. "What if we're wrong?"

"Well we try again," Parland said angrily, trying to shut down the conversation.

"With the press breathing down our neck and questioning our motives," Ashley shot back. "We stand more of a chance by asking them to come in and asking them to be co-operative. If we go in using force it will just be bad for everyone." Parland looked to McArthur.

"Sir?" McArthur was deep in thought.

"I like the idea," he said. "But we go with Fenway's approach. Let's ask them in to comply. If, however, they decide to be difficult then we should use force."

"Fine by me," Parland said, although judging by his face he didn't look too happy.

"OK, get it done," McArthur said, going to his office.

"The press wouldn't be such a shit show if he hadn't been such an idiot."

"Parland, enough," Murphy said. "We have enough people on our backs without resorting to infighting." Ashley agreed.

"Right, Fenway, get onto the phone to those people you talked to, the rest of us will track the rest of them."

Chapter 67

Terror in Manchester as killer roams the streets!

Four bodies pile up and the police with no leads.

Are people safe to walk the streets?

Are they just targeting perverts?

What's the pattern? The motive?

How can I make my children safe!

Their probably safer than they've ever been.

Can't say I'm really surprised with the ineptitude of the police trying to catch a pedo hunter #justsayin #Publicservice

I bet there some people having sleepless nights tonight. #Good #Youknowwhoyouare #hescomingforyou!

Does anyone actually want this person to be caught? #notme

"Why do you read that shit?" Kerry asked. Ashley was flicking through her phone.

"It's part of the job," Ashley said, now putting it in her pocket. "Gauging public perception."

"Well whoever they are they're a champ, how's that for perception."

"You agree with they're doing?"

"They're taking sickos of the street. I'd vote for them to be my MP."

"What about their families?"

"Probably in on it too. Some weird 'Hills Have Eyes' shit."

"Fun for the whole family?" Ashley asked sarcastically, with a raised eyebrow.

"You can tell you've never been on the game."

The two of them were sat in the café having a late lunch, or early dinner depending on how you saw four o'clock. Ashley was having a cheese and ham toastie and Kerry, pie and mash. After spending the morning going through paperwork and coming up with nothing, Ashley had decided on a new approach. She was going to shake all her contacts for anyone that fell into this pile of hating paedophiles and search them top to bottom.

The rest of the team were back at the station, Parland had an idea of getting known paedophile hunters in for questioning, people with an axe to grind; it made sense, rather than be drowned in alibi chasing. Ashley fancied something to eat.

"Girl, you should have like a bat signal for this guy," Kerry said. "As soon as you find one you tell him and boom! He's there to take care of them." The idea was appealing on a personal level, but she wasn't in the mood.

"And after they're all gone?"

"Rapists, murderers, people who try and short-change a gal like me." Kerry took a massive bite of her pie. "You can look at me like that all you like but it's what the people want."

"People want justice."

"No, they want fairness," Kerry said. "Think about it. My aunt was killed by a drunk driver, some hot-shot business guy. After his lawyer was done with it, he only got two years on licence. He didn't even go to jail, how is that fair?"

"It isn't," Ashley agreed.

"You remember that guy who beat me up?"

"Yes."

"How many years, sorry, months did he get?"

"Ten."

"He was out in five while I had over eight in rehab and physio," Kerry said, shaking her head. "Fairness."

"These guys didn't kill anyone though."

"They did something worse," Kerry said. "They ruined someone's life and then left them to deal with all the fucked up mental problems that come with it. Imagine living with all that confusing shit inside you as well." Ashley never really thought about it like that. It made all the bitterness towards them seem more relatable.

"Have you worked with people like that?" Kerry nodded.

"This one girl. Really not right in the head at all, could only get the big O with her uncle after he touched her up as a kid. Always ended up going back to him because that's the only way her body would respond."

"Jesus Christ."

"That ain't the worst of it," Kerry said, shaking her head. "You must have gone down the rabbit hole enough to see how messed up people are?" Her mind cast back to Kate Marsh and the life she had created for herself.

"Some people get over it."

"The majority don't," Kerry said. "And then who do they have to turn to when it's all over?"

"OK, that I agree with, but why does the public, people who have never had this done to them want this person dead?"

"So, it doesn't happen to them or people they love. Fucking hell, I thought you said you had a degree in this shit." That was low.

"I'm gauging public opinion," Ashley replied, her voice stiff from the low jibe. "My boss had the bright idea of tracking down every paedophile hunter in Manchester and has got them all in for questioning, thinking one of them will snap."

"Not a bad route to go down. Not often I give you lot credit."

"That's very true," Ashley agreed. "Still doesn't solve my case though. In fact, I don't think anyone wants us to solve it just yet."

"Like I said, it's fair," Kerry said. "That's why people are buying into it. They might not agree with killing every criminal but people like Oatley, Ferrets." Kerry shrugged to make her point.

"Deep down you agree with him too."

"How do you know it's a guy?" Ashley asked. Kerry put her knife and fork down.

"Do you know why there aren't that many women serial killers?" Ashley quirked an eyebrow.

"No, why?" Kerry smiled deviously.

"It's because we know how to clean blood off every surface." Ashley wanted to keep a straight face but failed miserably and spluttered out a laugh. It must have been the first time she laughed in days and it almost hurt.

"That's good," Ashley said. People in the café were looking over at them. "I never thought of it like that." Kerry smiled.

"Now come on, I know that you don't buy me a decent meal without wanting something in return."

"You know me too well," Ashley said. "Who would you know that would want to do something like this?" The conversation died a little.

"Girl, that is a long list," Kerry said, shaking her head.

"You said you knew girls who this had happened to?"

"Yeah, I did, what it didn't mean was an intrusion into their private life," Kerry said. "Besides, most of them decide that they just want to try and get on with whatever life they have. They don't want to bring that shit up. Sorry."

"No, I can see where you're coming from," Ashley said. "Have you ever heard of a place call Limehouse?"

"Limehouse? What is it?"

"An old house out in the sticks," Ashley said. "Home to a cult called the 'New Agers.' Apparently, there were quite a few rape parties that used to happen there in the seventies and eighties."

"Before my time."

"Thought so," Ashley said.

"Another lead?"

"Maybe," Ashley said, taking a bite of her toastie. "Have you heard of Dennis Thompson?" Kerry thought for a moment.

"It sounds familiar, don't know where from."

"He used prossies in the early nineties, he was found murdered in his house."

"Another Dora Sanchez case?" Ashley shook her head

"Unsolved, so you tell me." Kerry put her cutlery down.

"The name's familiar, but I don't know much more than that," Kerry sighed. "There are others who might know but… girl, not many people stay in the game for decades. Even then, whoever might have gone to your guys' house might not be around. She could be dead or something now."

That was what Ashley was afraid off.

***

405

Ashley drove back to the Tower, taking a more leisurely drive than normal. She found herself thinking about what Kerry said about people being more inclined to accept what was happening because they thought what had happened to the victims was fair.

Ashley found herself gazing at people walking down the streets, thinking what if they thought that their victims deserved to die.

Who else did they think deserved to die?

The questions were still plaguing her mind as she walked into the office, which was busy with people going over Parland's idea of the hunters being the ones carrying it out.

"Fenway." Parland was shouting her from his desk.

"Where have you been?"

"Talking to a contact," she said, sitting at her desk.

"Did they give you anything?"

"No," Ashley said, unlocking her computer.

"Well I've allocated you to carry out alibi checks as well on the CPG. You know them so I've been told." Ashley looked at her e-mails and their statements were in her e-mail box along with some other stuff.

"Can any of them say for certain that they were talking to our victims?" Ashley asked.

"They could be using aliases," Parland said in a strict tone, as if anyone had the cheek to poke holes in his brilliant idea.

"IT are going to be working on that as well as the break down on the computers and hard drives when they get them," he said. "They may not like it right now but that's their problem, not mine.

"Where are the others?"

"Doing the same as you," Parland said. "I'd get a move on."

"Prick," Ashley muttered under her breath.

Ashley spent the rest of the night confirming alibis for the paedophile hunters who weren't at their computers for the nights of their victims dying. Most of them going to support meetings or going down the pub. She wanted to confirm with IT the ones that were on their computers working, put they were so drowned in stuff that they weren't getting back to her.

Ashley looked at the clock and saw it was seven, she got her coat and bag and left.

***

Ashley walked into her apartment, opening the door awkwardly with a box of Limehouse paperwork balancing on her hip. She kicked the other one in, placing the other one on top. She turned the light on in the kitchen, went to the living room and turned the lights on.

She changed into shorts and a vest and made herself some dinner; smoked and peppered mackerel with salad. She moved the boxes to the living room and opened the tops. Ashley picked out the incorporation document for the New Agers and started to read it with her dinner.

The cult was set up in 1969 under the preface of carrying out simple living, for people who wanted to. It didn't get charity status until six years later in 1975. Ashley had a quick scan through the reports leading up to it with the New Agers gradually losing more and more money. The timing of the charity status was rather fortuitous with more and more money coming in under grants.

Ashley took a bite of food and checked the document setting up the charity status. It was carried out by Gordon & Spencer LLP. Ashley could only wonder why they did it. She next checked the lease, which as she knew already was leased by Oatley Developments plc.

In the years after their charity status they suddenly got a lot of donations and grants which saw them even turning a profit over the last decade; companies no doubt using it as an offset for their CSR. Little did they know that this was now the perfect tool to see who was going to these rape parties; maybe they used the grants and donations as some sort of membership fee.

Ashley took her plate to the kitchen, new information swirling in her head; trying to make a link between the donations and people who visited this place. If she was right, they might be able to know who was next on the killer's list from this.

Ashley got herself a beer and sat back down, making a list of the companies donating. A powerful pharmaceutical firm, a few law firms, the local council, government officials, an MP and a few celebrity donations.

"Damn…" Ashley said. This money trail was almost yearly. The odd person going in and out, but this was promising. Ashley took another swig of beer, wondering why something like this would be left so brazenly in the open; probably as an insurance so people didn't think about going to the police about it. Ashley felt a very cold shiver go down her spine when she saw that the police federation had donated to it in the past.

Ashley put together the reports, the lease and the charity status completion form in her Limehouse folder which was starting to get quite chunky.

Ashley sighed deeply, resting her head on her palms behind her head and looking up at her ceiling, wondering just how far this Limehouse thing went, and who on the police was going to Limehouse?

Her stomach growled. Ashley turned onto her back, looked up at the ceiling and back to the board.

"I'll get to you later," Ashley said, now getting to her feet. She showered, got herself some Carte d'Or ice cream from the freezer and put some in a bowl. Ashley sat down on the sofa feeling slightly more refreshed, but the board was still looking at her. Ashley tried turning the TV on to distract her. After watching part of a film, she was still finding herself looking at the board.

She got up and walked over to it, starting to go back over it to see if she could add to her theory. She got her notebook out. She added Ian Whikley to the board and wrote down what she knew about him.

She couldn't see how though he would fit into this web of people. Maybe being a journalist, he had some way to keep it out of the papers.

But the links were slowly coming together. she added the information on Thompson as well to the board as their potential first victim, adding the link with the gown found at the scene. His link to them all would be Limehouse which Ashley wrote on her board. Again, she put down the information she had on him and looked at the case history.

The police didn't look as though they were too bothered if they solved it or not. Maybe they knew what sort of person he was and decided not to pursue it. Maybe because there was a lack of evidence as well; no concrete suspects and no DNA or fingerprints were found at the scene and no eyewitnesses saw anything that night. Like Kettings he used prostitutes as well, but no one was willing to talk to them. They decided in the end to put it on ice as a cold case as the family didn't seem that bothered if it was solved or not.

Ashley tapped her pen against her chin. Looking at all the links she had amassed, the gown and the photo of Ferrets and Thompson with Oatley being the main ones. But so far, a suspect alluded her. If the stories of the abuse at Limehouse were true almost anyone there would want to murder them. The only people she knew that were there, was Lisa Strachan who had disappeared and Claire Wellbeck who was dead.

Ashley sighed and ran a hand through her hair, she could deal with this in the morning. She added more pieces of paper to her Limehouse file, she turned the living room and kitchen lights off and walked to her bedroom.

Chapter 68

Beep.

 Beep.

 Beep.

 Ashley's hand instantly turned her alarm off, and she got out of bed and did her morning routine. She walked through the living room and saw her board. She shook her head, picked up her gym bag and work bag and walked out.

 Cardio.

 Arms.

 Core.

 Bag.

 She really needed this today. She was practicing some of the new moves Clarence had taught her on the punch bag. After releasing a rather vicious combo she stopped, panting heavily and hugging the bag. She looked up and saw the TV, a morning news show which was still running with the serial killer story. Ashley read the subtitles, the anchor talking about if the police had any clue what was going on. It went on to say about how they were bringing in known hunters for questioning.

 Ashley had seen enough. She got her gloves off and walked towards the changing rooms.

***

"Manchester Major Crimes seems to have taken a serial killer approach to their serial killer problem and are picking random people off the streets to question."

 "What the fuck. No, we are not," Ashley said in disbelief. The drive to work was littered with things about work. The crowd outside the station had swelled with a new group of people with placards which were defending the paedophile hunters.

After making her way through Ashley got up to the office which was unusually busy for this time of the morning. Ashley turned her computer on, got tea and porridge and sat down at her desk. There were a few e-mails she had to answer and send but she also had a new pile of alibis to go through as well.

Ashley was putting them in order when McArthur called a meeting between them. Everyone having seemed to have got in an hour earlier. Ashley could see his complexion was visibly stressed and the lack of sleep was catching up with him.

"Right, where are we with the alibis for our dark justice wannabes?" McArthur asked.

"Still going through them," Parland said. "We should have them cleared either today or tomorrow at the latest."

"Make it today. Where are SOCO on the computer and hard drives; anything?"

"Still trying to pull any prints off it," Armstrong said. "I've been chasing them up and hurrying them along but nothing."

"Well as soon as they're done, I want IT to break them down." McArthur ran a hand through his hair.

"Is there anything else that we're missing?" He asked out loud. "Any luck with neighbours?"

"We sent another team over, but they said the same thing," Murphy said. "We talked to the woman who found him, and she didn't know anything."

"The other teams aren't having much luck but have a few leads as well. Does anyone else have any ideas or theories?" Ashley saw her chance.

"I have an idea," Ashley said. The team turned and looked at her. She was looking round to gauge the reaction of people. Some was shock, while others showed apprehension and amusement.

"OK, let's hear it," McArthur said rubbing his temple, as if it couldn't hurt. Ashley took a deep breath. She got up from her chair, taking her Limehouse file from her bag and walked over to the spare

411

board in the room. She picked the pen up and scrawled 'Limehouse' across it and popped the lid back on.

"What the hell is a Limehouse?" Armstrong asked.

"It's a place," Ashley said. "It was home to a religious sect in the seventies and eighties called the New Agers, which was owned by Will Oatley and that Gordon Ferrets provided sports training to," Ashley explained. "Now, according to Amelia Franks —"

"Wait, hold up." Armstrong cut in. Ashley took a deep, calming breath. "Who the hell is this Amelia Franks?"

"She's a journalist," Ashley said. "She was the one who uncovered the Limehouse scandal."

"Scandal?" McArthur said, sceptically.

"This house, Limehouse," Ashley said, banging the board lightly. "The sect was using it as cover for an undercover paedophile ring, that was what Franks found out. Oatley was in on it along with lots of famous celebrities and powerful individuals, MP's, judges, celebrities, that sort of thing."

"Why didn't any of the kids tell people about it?" Armstrong asked.

"Well they couldn't, the sect stopped them while they were there."

"What about after?" Parland asked.

"Who are you going to believe?" Ashley said, the silence that followed told her the answer. "Rochdale, the scouting scandal, we all didn't believe it until it was too late, just like this." She went back to the board.

"Some did try but they were pushed back and discredited, money and influence at work," Ashley continued. "I'm trying to find out just how many there are over the years, but people have changed their names or died."

"When was it shut down?" McArthur asked.

"The house was shut on the cusp of the nineties," Ashley explained. "People were talking too much. I think the powers that be decided it was attracting too much attention and so they dissolved it quietly."

"Move on to something else?" McArthur said.

"They say Rochdale started in the early nineties," Armstrong mused. "Maybe that's what filled the void left by this." McArthur nodded.

"OK, plausible," he said. "So, you think our killer has a link to this Limehouse then?" Ashley nodded.

"All we need to do is find out who links them."

"It's a who?" Murphy questioned.

"Yes, who." Ashley pointed with her pen at the board. "The answer isn't on a piece of paper it's with a person."

"And who is this person?" There was a long silence as Ashley thought it all over in her head.

"I think it's someone called Lisa Strachan."

"Lisa Strachan, who is she?" Armstrong asked.

"Didsbury abused women shelter filed a case on behalf of a Lisa Strachan against the New Agers who were at Limehouse." Ashley explained, placing the plaintiff sheet on the board.

"In her testimony she said that Gordon Ferrets was complicit in this abuse, with Oatley owning the building and Kettings had a gown that was used by the cult in his wardrobe which he made girls wear."

"OK, and how do we find this person?" McArthur asked.

"… I don't know. There's no other mention of her after this court case."

"And what links our fourth victim to this?" Ashley made a pained face that the others couldn't see.

"I don't know." McArthur sighed heavily. "But there are links between the rest —"

"It's a good theory Ashley," He said placing a hand on her shoulder. "But a lot of it is too circumstantial. The link between Ferrets and Oatley is coincidence based on the case itself. Plus, this doesn't even give us a lead to go on or tell us what we are looking for?"

"Hopefully it'll show up in Whikley's photos," Ashley said.

"You think he's a nonce too?" Armstrong asked.

"I bet my future house on it," Ashley said. "Some of the cases against Limehouse that I can find, the victims say that some of the abuse was recorded in photos and videos."

"So that would make Whikley what, the cameraman?" Armstrong said.

"Yes. I think his computer would show it."

"And Kettings?"

"The distributor," Ashley continued. "He was the one who got it all sent out. Make the money from selling what they did, that's how they kept it going." Hopefully she could find a trail to back that up.

"Fenway. I just don't see it," McArthur said. "Maybe this Limehouse thing should be for the cold case team, but for the here and now?"

"Cold cases have tried and failed," Ashley snapped.

"How do you know that?" Parland asked.

"Because Ferrets wasn't the first victim," Ashley said. "The leader of the sect, Dennis Thompson was." Ashley placed his photo on the board.

"He was killed in 2000. Single slash wound to the neck. His murder was never solved, all they found was his body and this in the bathroom." She placed the photo of the bloodstained gown on the board along with the photo from the paper about Limehouse and the photo of the gown Nikita sent her.

"Fenway…"

"No, listen to me," Ashley said. "I think we are looking for someone from Limehouse. Kettings had the same gown that was in this photo." Ashley pointed to it. "Who else would have access to the gown unless he had been there?" Ashley looked around at the doubtful faces in front of her. She felt her stomach twist uncomfortably.

"You don't believe me."

"It's a good story Fenway," Armstrong said. "But I'm with the Guv. There's a lot of leaps here."

"Maybe if we all work on this then maybe we can find something, right now we have the same thing, leaps." The room acknowledged that fact with silence, but to Ashley it looked like nothing was going to change.

"You would rather search top to bottom again than listen to me?" Ashley asked.

"It's not that it's coming from you Fenway," McArthur said. "We have to weigh up resources and time. The press is already hammering us for not getting anywhere and the public want this person for prime minister, so we need to finish this quick."

"So, what are you suggesting we do?" Murphy asked. McArthur thought for a moment and ran a hand through his hair.

"Right now, we can only wait for the fingerprints and computer content to come back from Whikley before we go jumping to conclusions," he said. "It might give us a promising lead, or, it could connect with Ashley's theory about this Limehouse place."

"So, we still shake down Oatley leads," Ashley said, in disbelief. McArthur nodded.

"Until we get something new, that's the plan, go over everything with a fine toothcomb," he said, walking back to his office and closing the door. The others went back to their desks, but Ashley grabbed her coat. She needed some air.

***

Ashley was sitting on the railings outside with her feet resting on the first rail with a cup of tea to warm her against the wind.

"That went well," she muttered to herself, taking a sip of her tea. She couldn't believe that her theory had been shot down. She had to get the evidence to make them see. She thought it over in her head; if the newspapers were already interviewing people then they had leads. Ashley took her phone out of her pockets and texted Sam Lingard at the Evening News.

Got any dirt on Will Oatley?

She took another sip and saw Aaron come out and get a cigarette out of his pocket.

"I thought you were quitting." Aaron jumped at the sound of her voice.

"Jesus fuck," Aaron breathed, turning around and looking at her. "How do you do that?"

"A lot of planning and forethought," she replied. "Not that it's helped me so far." Aaron slipped another one out and offered it to her.

"No thanks, never had one," Ashley said. "Though I feel like I could do with one."

"Maybe you could drink?"

"Not while I'm on duty," Ashley replied, looking at her tea. "I'm just sick of people killing one another and trying to get away with it." Aaron put his cigarette into his mouth and lit up.

"I'm sick of looking through nonce's computers," Aaron said. "Join the police and fight cybercrime they said." He puffed out. "It'll be fun." Ashley shrugged.

"So Whikley's a nonce too?"

"It'll only be a matter of time," Aaron said, taking another drag. "What leads have you got?"

"Nothing so far," Ashley said, looking back out onto the forecourt. "We've got nothing that links them other than they're paedophiles. They're vigilante killings."

"Maybe it's someone in the system then."

"None of them were ever charged."

"OK, maybe they all abused the same kid and they want revenge?"

"Like looking for a needle in a haystack," Ashley said, shaking her head. She looked up at the grey sky and had more tea.

"So, what are you doing now?" Ashley's phone went off. She looked down and saw she had a text from Lingard.

Maybe, why?

Ashley smirked.

"Why are you smiling?" Ashley texted back.

Fancy something to eat?

"I may have a lead," Ashley said, jumping off the railing with a smile. "See you later." She walked to her car and called Amelia Franks.

"Hi, I wasn't expecting to hear from you again."

"I was going to ask if you wanted an early dinner." Franks sighed.

"This isn't going to be for free, is it?"

"No," Ashley said, as she got into her car. "I need some names."

Chapter 69

Ashley and Amelia pulled up outside the greasy spoon near the dock. Both women got out of the car and walked towards the café where Sam Lingard was sat at a table.

"You didn't mention this," Amelia said, frostily.

"Swallow your pride," Ashley said, sitting opposite Lingard.

"I still think we should have gone to Jamie's Italian," he said.

"Too expensive for three people," Ashley said, shuffling a seat along.

"What do you mean?" He turned around and saw Amelia and his eyebrows shot up. "By that…"

"Hi, Sam" Amelia said, sitting down.

"You have some nerve you know that?" Lingard said, pointing at her.

"Kids, stop it," Ashley said, as the waitress came over. "Tea for three please."

"OK, I thought it was just the two of us," Lingard said.

"We have info we all need," Ashley said. "Amelia is here to dot some I's for me."

"You do know who she is?" Lingard said, pointing at her. "Said she had the biggest story of the year, was going to put us on the map and then poof. Fucked off quicker than you could say washing up. Tell me, how is Oatley's dirty money?"

"I had no choice, he put me into a corner!" Amelia whispered, viciously.

"We revel in choices!"

"Shut up, both of you," Ashley said, looking at the menu. "Jesus, anyone would have thought that we are after the same thing."

"And what is that exactly?" Lingard asked. Ashley pulled Oatley's picture out and slid it into the middle of the table.

"I know you've had people coming to you with stories about Oatley," Ashley said, looking at Lingard. "Along the same lines that Amelia did years before." Lingard's eyes darted to Amelia.

"We may or may not have."

"Cut the shit," Ashley said. "One of your reporters phoned us for a comment."

"Amateur," Amelia muttered. Lingard regained his composure.

"I take it it's cheaper to print it when they're dead," Ashley continued. "Or it could be libel."

"OK, what do you want?"

"Names," Ashley said, she was taking a risky gambit with the next part. "I want to know who they are. They could hold the key to solving four more murders."

"Wait, four?" Lingard reached into his pocket and pulled out his own pen and paper as their tea arrived. Ashley took her tea and took a drink, all the while looking at Lingard.

"That doesn't sound like a name," Ashley said.

"But you said four murders."

"Did I? Because what I was looking for was names," Ashley said. Lingard took a second, obviously weighing up in his mind if this was worth it.

"Who else knows?"

"No one else around this table," Ashley said. Lingard flipped a few pages back, looking up at Amelia every so often.

"How many people have there been?" Ashley asked.

"Quite a few," Lingard replied. "A lot of it is just noise. But this girl however, she's the real deal." Lingard got his phone out. After a couple of seconds, he showed Ashley the picture of a woman.

"Emma Curtis." Ashley paused.

"I know that name," Ashley mused.

"You do?" Ashley looked at the eyes, something very empty and vacant around them. But she remembered what Kate Marsh said.

'There're only a few other people who could confirm it. Connor Goldson and Emma Curtis are two I know of.'

And that was relating to Gordon Ferrets. What if she knew about Will Oatley and Stan Kettings as well?

"Do you have an address for her?"

"Is she genuine?" Lingard pressed.

"Wait, who is she?" Amelia asked. "I've never heard of an Emma Curtis."

"An address?" Ashley pressed.

"Not until I get a quote."

"A quote? No, I don't give out quotes, all I can tell you is that there are four other murders linked to Oatley's," Ashley said. Lingard wrote out something on the paper and tore it. He tapped his pen on the table and looked up at her.

"Give me one name."

"Thompson, the new ager," Ashley said, grabbing the paper from his hand. "Budge up," she said to Amelia, who stood up to let Ashley pass.

"So where are we going now?" Amelia asked.

"'We aren't going anywhere. I have a lead, you're staying here," Ashley said, walking to the exit.

"Hey, you're my ride!" Amelia shouted after her.

"I thought you two might want some time alone," Ashley said. "You know, you said you were looking for a new job, that file is your CV." Amelia looked at the file Ashley left at the table, but when she looked up Ashley was gone.

***

Ashley pulled up outside Emma Curtis's house which was a smart-looking house in Didsbury. She pulled her zip up against the cold, walked up the drive and knocked. The door partially opened and she could see Emma Curtis's brown hair.

"Yes?"

"Emma Curtis?" She nodded. "My name is DC Fenway, I'm with the Manchester Major Crimes Unit. I was hoping to ask you a couple of questions."

"Regarding what?" Emma asked, quietly. Ashley looked around.

419

"Maybe it's something we should talk about inside." Emma nodded.

"Just one second." The door closed, but instead of the unlocking of the door Ashley heard something else. Fast footsteps. Running.

"Fuck sake." Ashley ran around the side of the building just in time to see Curtis running out of the side door and down the path that ran down the side of her house.

"Emma, stop!" Ashley said, starting to catch up with her. Emma darted down another side path. Ashley slowed her speed so she didn't slip on the wet leaves. Ashley set off again, Emma was running alongside the canal, side stepping joggers and dogwalkers.

She wasn't that fit and finally keeled over with a stitch. Ashley walked over to her.

"Emma, please." Before she knew what happened, Emma swung her fist round and hit Ashley on the jaw. Ashley fell to her knee.

"Mother fuc —" By the time she got over it she could see Emma already running away.

"Right, out with this bitch." Ashley sprinted down the road and caught up with her; Ashley threw herself forward and tackled Emma to the ground, making sure that she landed on Emma to cushion her fall.

"Ow, please!"

"Trying to appeal to my better nature went out the window when you punched me," Ashley said, placing a knee in her back to stop her squirming.

"Ow!" Ashley pulled Emma to her feet.

"Let's go sunshine," she said, taking her back to the car.

Chapter 70

"Sometimes, we just hit the proverbial goldmine," McArthur said, looking at Emma Curtis talking to her lawyer through the two-way glass of an interrogation room. Ashley was sitting on the rim of a table, her fingers rubbing the small bruise on her face.

After booking her in and the rigmarole which came with a suspect, it was three hours into their questioning period. Ashley had gone upstairs to finish looking through Whikley's phone records, when McArthur had called her down to do the interview with her.

"Why were you looking for her again?"

"A hunch," Ashley said. "I think she's a link between three of our victims."

"Why?"

"She was going to talk to the papers about Ferrets a few years ago," Ashley said. "And now she's going to talk to them about Will Oatley."

"How did you find that out?"

"Good old-fashioned detective work," Ashley said, dryly.

"Why do you think she ran?" Ashley shrugged.

"Maybe she has something to hide."

"My thoughts exactly," McArthur agreed. "How's the jaw?"

"My pride hurts more," Ashley said, sourly.

"Do you want to talk to her?" McArthur asked. Ashley nodded, they walked around to the door into the interrogation room. Both Emma and her solicitor, Heather Potts were still talking as they went in.

"Is there anything we can get you before we start?" Ashley asked. "Tea, coffee?"

"No, thank you."

Ashley and McArthur sat down opposite Emma and her solicitor. Ashley reached over to the recorder and set the tape which let out its usual groan.

"This is Detective Constable Ashley Fenway conducting an interview with Emma Curtis at Manchester Major Crimes Unit HQ, City Tower police station on twenty-eighth of November 2018 at 6:30 p.m. Also present are…"

"DCI Donald McArthur."

"Ms Heather Potts, solicitor for Miss Curtis."

"Before we start," Ms Potts looked at Ashley and McArthur. "I would like to apologise on behalf of my client for her striking DC Fenway in her apprehension of Miss Curtis earlier today." Ashley subconsciously rubbed her jaw where she had been hit. A smart move on the solicitor's part; make sure that there would be no bias on the account of being socked.

"That has been acknowledged," Ashley said, determined not to give a millimetre so early on. "So, Ms Curtis, we'll start with a simple question. Why run?"

Emma looked down at her fingers and started playing with them. Ashley watched intently at Emma holding each of the fingers on her left hand with her right and squeezing them reassuringly.

"I don't know if I'm honest," she said, in the same quiet voice she had used on Ashley at the door. "I just… panicked."

"Do you have anything to hide Miss Curtis?" McArthur asked. Ashley watch Emma squeeze two of her fingers.

"No," she said. "As I said, I just panicked… it was a… what do you call it. Fight or flight."

"Well we know you're capable of both," Ashley said. "Are you sure there isn't a reason why you ran?" Emma shook her head.

"Miss Curtis has shaken her head to indicate the answer to DC Fenway's question as no. But for future reference she must answer all questions orally," McArthur pointed out.

"No, I really can't explain why." Time for the shock value. Ashley leaned back in her chair.

"Does it have anything to do with Will Oatley?" She asked. Emma stopped playing with her fingers for a second; that was all Ashley needed. The air was thick while Ashley and McArthur waited for a response.

"No…" That was a lie, Ashley concluded.

"OK, how about Gordon Ferrets?" Emma bit her lip and squeezed her fingers.

"Are you OK Emma?" Her solicitor asked.

"I'm fine," Emma replied through gritted teeth, but her stare was still on Ashley.

"I'll cut to the chase Emma. What do you know about the two individuals I've just mentioned?" Ashley asked. Again, Emma squeezed her fingers.

"Because both have ended up dead in the last week," Ashley continued. "Now, we have it on very good authority that you are going to be in an exposé on Will Oatley, isn't that right."

Ms Potts jumped in. "I don't think that's any of your business."

"I don't think a lawyer on the Manchester Evening News retainer can really talk right now, do you?" Ashley asked, turning to her. Ms Potts backed off.

"It's not a crime, we know what he's been up to," Ashley said, turning back to Emma. "In fact, you are not the only one to do so, quite a few are. No, what we're interested in is the fact that you were going to do the same to Gordon Ferrets as well." Emma said nothing.

"We know what he was like too," McArthur said. Emma looked away from them. "You're not in trouble, Miss Curtis," he reiterated. "Why specifically those two?" Emma didn't say anything, some of her hair had fallen into her face and obscured their view of her.

"Did they attack you?" Emma nodded.

"Miss Curtis nodded to DCI McArthur's question," Ashley said, now having some idea of why Emma had run from her.

"Are you OK, do you need a moment?" Ashley asked. Emma shook her head fervently.

"No, no I'm OK I just…" She took a relaxing breath out. "I've been running from this for too long." Ashley and McArthur nodded.

"Can we talk about Gordon Ferrets?" Ashley asked. Emma nodded.

"He scouted my brother for City," she said. "Because it was just us and my mum and she worked three jobs, he used to take him there for his trials and training sessions."

"Did he take you?" Ashley asked.

"No, I was home alone, I was a teenager," Emma said. "But I saw the change in my brother. He was more distant, angrier, more... everything. Soon, he stopped wanting to go to football, but my mum made him. She got stars in her eyes, he was going to be the next George Best and take us all away from there." Emma sighed.

"But... she didn't realise what it was doing to him." She looked up at Ashley with a hard stare. "What he was doing to my brother."

"How did you find out?" McArthur asked.

"You pick up on these sorts of things," Emma explained. "He was so distant. We all thought it was because he was focused on trying to get into the academy. But I knew him, he wouldn't have acted like this unless something was wrong." Emma squeezed her fingers again.

"He was ten, fucking ten years old and that bastard stole his dream from him for some sick thrill." She relaxed the grip on her fingers. Ashley spoke next.

"How long did it go on for?" Emma wiped her eyes.

"'Till he was fifteen. He was let go for poor attitude. It's difficult enough with boys at that age but he was so confused about everything that he couldn't concentrate, schoolwork, the football, it all went to shit." Emma squeezed her fingers again. "In the end we had to send him to a rehab clinic, he took so much meth."

"I was in my twenties when he confessed everything," Emma said, quietly. "My brother told me when I asked him why he did all those things. I was sick to my stomach because I thought... not him too." Ashley had a very good guess who Emma's abuser was.

"Where is your brother?" Ashley asked. Emma wiped her eyes more thoroughly

"He's dead. Threw himself in front of a train when he heard Ferrets had got off scot-free." Well, that was one theory down the drain.

"Was he part of the civil action suit against Ferrets?" Ashley asked.

"Yeah, we both were, one of your officers came to talk to me about it," Emma said. She smiled. "God, I was so happy when I found out he bit the dust. Got what he deserved if you ask me."

"A lot of people have said that," Ashley muttered.

"Did you ever confront Ferrets?" McArthur asked, keeping them on point. Emma nodded and her face changed again. Ashley noted that she squeezed her fingers harder than she had before.

"I did..." She said quietly. "I confronted him after my brother confessed." Ashley decided not to press too much on that front. "I knew then what he was doing, I always had but I never wanted to face up to it. I tried telling my mum, but she didn't believe me. She had been wrapped up in her fantasy of being a footballer's mum. I sometimes doubted myself so much that I thought I was wrong."

McArthur looked sideways at Ashley who looked down at the table.

"Did you report him?" Emma laughed.

"No, the police didn't want anything to do with him. They didn't believe me either. Gordon Ferrets is an upstanding citizen they said." Emma shook her head despairingly. "So, I went and confronted him," Emma said calmly, but Ashley saw her grip her fingers more tightly.

"What did he do?"

"He told me I was crazy, told me that I was jeopardising my brother's chances of becoming a pro with stuff like this." She took a deep breath. Whatever happened to Emma, flashing before her eyes.

"He hit me," she said, squeezing her fingers tightly.

Emma said matter of factly, "After, he threatened me, saying that if I said a word to anyone then he would ruin me. That no one would believe my story, my brother would be kicked out of the academy and that we would be bottom feeders for the rest of our lives."

Ashley was only just starting to realise just how ruthless and twisted these people were. Emma sighed and looked down.

"You said before, not him too," McArthur said. "I want to talk to you about Will Oatley."

"The main attraction," Emma said, with a small laugh. "The pervert in plain sight who could get away with murder."

"So, you knew him?" Emma nodded.

425

"Where we grew up was a victim of Thatcher, mining community, high unemployment and low spending from government which made a perfect storm of crime," Emma explained. "But the one thing we had was the local community hall which gave us all a place to go."

"Ran by Will Oatley," Ashley finished.

"Yes," Emma said. "Local Millionaire helping disadvantaged youths with his generosity. No one wanted to know the cost of it. But if they knew the cost…"

"Were there a lot of you?" Emma nodded.

"Yes, all different ages, boys and girls, it didn't matter, he loved the power element of it all. He loved that he could have who he wanted."

"Didn't any of the staff stop it?" Ashley asked.

"And risk not getting any funding? Unlikely," Emma said. "So long as the money kept rolling in then some of us would have to pay the price." She sighed. "Then you had that creepy guy taking photos of him all the time." Something clicked in Ashley's head.

"Pictures?" Ashley asked.

"Yeah," Emma said. "He always had a photographer that went around with him for the papers and shit like that."

"What did he look like?" Ashley asked, getting her phone out of her pocket. McArthur glanced at her out of the corner of his eye.

"I don't remember now," Emma said. "It was over twenty years ago, but if you found him, you would have a goldmine." Ashley and McArthur looked at one another. This was new.

"What do you mean?" McArthur asked.

"It didn't happen to me personally, but a few people said that he would take pictures of the abuse," Emma explained.

"What?" Ashley and McArthur said at the same time.

"That's why loads of us are going to the press about it. Hopefully something might come up. I thought that would be in your files about him?" McArthur and Ashley looked at one another.

"How sure are you about this?" Ashley asked. "I have to remind you that you are still under caution."

"On my brother's life," Emma said. "He followed Oatley round like some lovesick puppy, probably thought it was an easy gig, and feed his perversions too."

426

Ashley got the photo of Ian Whikley on her phone and showed it to her.

"I'm showing Ms Curtis a photo on my phone which will be documented as Image CA1."

Emma looked over at it.

"Is he the guy?" Ashley asked. A tight knot was forming in her stomach; if Emma confirmed this it would be a link between Whikley and the rest of their victims.

"He looks older but…" She paused and her brow furrowed. "What's his name?"

"Ian Whikley," McArthur said. Another pause.

"That's him."

"Are you sure?" Ashley asked. Her stomach fluttering with the feeling of success.

"I'm certain of it," Emma said, looking down at the phone.

Chapter 71

"Yeah, boss wants his house turned top to bottom, any hard drives or any albums since he's such a photography freak," Ashley said. The scene commander at Whikley's house muttered something but reluctantly agreed.

"Thanks," Ashley said, putting the phone down. Ashley sighed and held the bridge of her nose. Her head was starting to throb with all the information it had taken in over the last few hours.

So, her hunch had been right about him being some sort of photographer for the cult. Well, not that part but if he took pictures of people abusing kids it wouldn't be that far a stretch, especially someone with an ego like Oatley.

"What are you still doing here?" McArthur asked, coming in.

"I'm working," Ashley said, as if it was obvious.

"Not on my time you're not. Overtime doesn't stretch that far," McArthur said. Ashley looked over at the time. Nearly seven. A full twelve hours.

"I can still carry on," Ashley said. McArthur laughed.

"Fenway, do you know why the higher up the food chain you are the longer you work?"

"No, I don't."

"It's because of how much information you know in a case. As SIO, I know a little about a lot. As a DC you know a lot, about a lot."

Ashley went to argue. "True," she conceded.

"It also means you need more sleep than people like me," McArthur said. "Go home, rest. What have you got on tonight?" Ashley thought.

"Hockey," she said, absentmindedly

"Perfect, now go on or I'm not paying you."

"Thanks, Sir," Ashley said, getting to her feet, taking her bag and coat and leaving, while yawning loudly.

***

Ferrets was the sports guy. Ashley made a pass out wide and sprinted forward.

Kettings was the distributor. Ashley held her position.

Oatley made it all possible. The ball came towards her and it just passed her by.

And Whikley… Ashley's mind had been on autopilot. She watched the other team score and a blare on the whistle. She ran a hand through her hair. Fuck…

"OK girls, OK enough, get the cones in!" Ashley tried to catch her breath. Both Di and Eliza came over to her.

"You OK, you looked spaced out then?" Di asked.

"I'm fine," Ashley said, shaking her head.

"Ash." Ashley saw Karen in the middle of the pitch looking at her. "A word please."

"I'll meet you back at the changing rooms." Ashley walked over to Karen.

"Something the matter?" Ashley asked.

"You looked a million miles away," Karen said. "That last play was terrible."

"Yeah, it was," Ashley agreed.

"Something on your mind?"

"Work," Ashley said, no need to sugar coat it. "Work's been hectic, I was thinking about that."

"Are you sure you're gonna be all right for the weekend?"

"Yeah," Ashley replied. "Yeah, I will be."

"Is everything OK with work? I know your work is stressful; if you need a break or anything."

"No, no I'm fine," Ashley said, shaking her head. "Sorry, it was just a heavy day, I couldn't switch off."

"It happens," Karen said. "But make sure you're right for Thursday and Sunday or I will drop you."

"I know. See you on Thursday."

***

Ashley got in, put the radio on and had a shower, the warm water washing the day away. She changed into pyjamas and checked the fridge. Not much to make dinner with. Corned beef sandwich?

She checked the freezer and found a subway pizza. She put it in the oven and looked over at the living room where she saw her board with her theory on Limehouse. Ashley looked over at the sofa where she had thrown her bag down. The Limehouse folder showing its corner teasingly.

"Don't try and seduce me like that," she said, narrowing her eyes at it. She got herself a glass of squash and had a drink, but still found herself looking at her bag.

"Cover up, have you no shame?" Ashley muttered to herself, while looking away. She looked over at it again.

"Dammit." Ashley walked over to her bag, pulled out her files and spread them across her coffee table. Her phone went off.

Ashley checked and it was a WhatsApp message from Eliza.

Eliza: Earl's still asking about you…

Ashley opened the conversation.

I thought I told you to tell him to sling his hook.

He's persistent.

Do you want me to get a restraining order?

So, it's a no?

It's a no. If you want him, you have my blessing.

Eww, no, his friend was awful too.

I told you no.

Drunk me should listen more often. What are you doing tonight?

Ashley looked at her coffee table. She knew exactly what she wanted to do.

Depends on what you're offering?

Wine and a gossip?

Ashley was about to reply with 'yes' when Eliza beat her to it.

Sorry, I can't I have FWB coming over.

430

Well that decided it. Ashley said it was all right and that she would see her at training. She got her subway pizza out and sat down. She took a deep breath and went through Dennis Thompson's file.

She wrote on the board that he was the first victim based on the fact his death was so similar to the other four. Although he wasn't tied up, he was found in the bedroom with his throat slashed, and the gown in his bathroom. He was top of the tree at Limehouse.

Ashley stuck his picture at the top. Next was Gordon Ferrets, someone who kept a steady supply of children coming in to be abused, for the rape parties at Limehouse.

Will Oatley, who owned the place and with Amelia's evidence could be placed at Limehouse and carried out some of the attacks.

Then there was the new boy, Ian Whikley. Local journalist and photographer who could always steer the stories away and keep it out of the limelight. But it's what Emma Curtis told them about him constantly taking pictures of Oatley. She was sure a link would come up between him and their other victims when his computer analysis was done.

Ashley put the photo of Limehouse with Thompson, Oatley and Ferrets on the board. She looked at it and the picture description.

Leader Dennis Thompson, director of the Ferrets Sports Academy Mr Gordon Ferrets and Owner of Limehouse, Will Oatley. Picture by Ian Whikley.

"Son of a bitch," Ashley said, taking the photo off the wall and looking at it under the light to make sure.

"Got you," Ashley said, now able to make a link between four of them; again, they were leaps, not a solid link.

Ashley sat down on her sofa and tried to remember what they had about Kettings. He started in the Royal Mail in the seventies and through into the eighties. His mum said he was dismissed for something. Ashley looked back through the file and found a copy of his dismissal letter.

Fancy lawyer terms aside he was dismissed for hording mail and going places in his van that he shouldn't have. Ashley looked up at the board. In a time before the internet paedophiles had to distribute porn somehow.

What would look less conspicuous than a Royal Mail van? Ashley looked down through the letter to see who was responsible for the action.

Chris Cox.

Probably retired now, it would be interesting to know what route Kettings had with the Royal Mail, and where he was found with the van. The letter itself didn't go into too much detail about that. Ashley wrote her theory on the board and made a note to find out if she could get more details on Kettings' dismissal.

She frowned at the board. Something that was missing was now only coming to light.

"How did the killer contact them?" Ashley asked herself. Their victims weren't the most tech savvy, and the murders required a degree of planning. Ferrets was at a hotel, that needed to be organised, Joyce Kettings was away on holiday and Cynthia Oatley was away as well. There was a form of communication between them and the killer. Oatley's security proved it, although they never did find the phone Oatley used and none of the computer reports showed that they were using a messenger service on social media platforms.

Maybe they were using old school methods; she made a note to double check. Ashley sat down and looked at the board and thought about how someone would contact them. Texts, messages, the mail?

"Computers." Ashley circled it. There had to be something inside their computers.

Chapter 72

After the gym Ashley got into the office, she walked to her desk and saw another conference happening in McArthur's office.

She checked her e-mails and saw Whikley's financials and phone records had come through.

Ashley printed them off and went to the printer. She felt the hairs on the back of her neck stand up. She glanced up and saw one of the new DI's looking at her.

"It's DC Fenway, right?"

"Yes," Ashley said.

"DI Taylor."

"What can I help you with, DI Taylor?" Ashley asked.

"DCI McArthur speaks very highly of you," he said, now coming around so he was next to her.

"He's a good DCI," Ashley said, turning to face Taylor. He was smarmy, a cheeky smile and a guy who had a reputation among the PCs as a bit of a lady's man. Ashley did her homework.

"Listen, do you fancy going to get a drink sometime?" Ashley went back to the printer.

"I'm flattered, but no thanks." He laughed lightly, not quite believing it.

"That was very definitive," he said.

"Maybe McArthur should have told you that I'm quite definitive," Ashley replied, checking she had everything she needed.

"And I don't mix business with pleasure," she said, going to walk away. Taylor shook his head.

"I could show you a good time," he said. "If not drinks, dinner?"

"Try the PC pool," Ashley replied.

Ashley sat back down at her desk and looked up. She saw Taylor laughing to himself; oh great, Ashley thought. She knew she'd have to speak to him again, more to the point he would come and speak to her.

Ashley got her highlighters out and went through the financials. She was about halfway through when other people started to come in. Ashley went through her process of eliminating the obvious expenditure. Ashley looked at the big expenditures, most of which were explained with receipts: cameras lenses lighting and other shit photographers needed.

One though couldn't be explained, a payment from his company to the tune of £10,000. Ashley frowned and circled it in red. What was he spending this money on? She went further down. £5,000 had left the account to a Bitcoin exchange ledger. Ashley groaned, that really wasn't what she wanted to see.

Ashley sent an e-mail to Aaron. She needed to see if Kettings sold things to the Bitcoin account she had sent over to him.

Again, she didn't get the answer she wanted; Whikley and Kettings had no contact whatsoever. Ashley slouched in her chair, thinking, brooding, whatever she wanted to call it. Again, their new victim was not tech savvy. He would have needed help to find an exchange.

Ashley leaned forward. She asked Aaron to search for anything that eluded to Bitcoin exchanges on the computer. McArthur came out of his office.

"Right, where are we with Ian Whikley?" He asked.

"Just spoke to the scene commander and they found a few more albums in his house but none of them were of kids, at least in that capacity," Parland said.

"OK, what about his financials, have they come through, Fenway?"

"They came through this morning and I'm still looking through it but there are a couple of anomalies."

"Like?"

"He took £10,000 out of his business account and wired half of it into a Bitcoin exchange, but I don't know where, yet."

"Keep working on that, Armstrong. Murphy, what about his neighbours, anything there?"

"One neighbour, a Kate Marsh, said she went to pick some pictures up from him around six and then left. That seems like the last time anyone saw him."

"Kate Marsh?" Ashley asked.

"Yeah, know her?" Ashley nodded.

"She was part of Ferrets' civil case."

"Well she was pretty shaken up about it. No luck on what they were looking for either."

Ashley looked at the board, his house had been turned over, something that hadn't happened in the others.

"Anything taken?" Ashley asked.

"Not that we know of," Armstrong replied. "It could be anything, but all the valuables are still there."

"What about his associates?"

"Nice guy, good photos, no problems," Murphy said. "We're still asking around though and we have someone on CCTV around the area."

"I'm going to make a statement to the press later," McArthur said. "If anyone asks you for a statement, we're doing our best, yadder, yadder," McArthur sighed.

"It would be better if we had a suspect."

"Sorry, Sir," Parland said. "These are planned jobs. In and out without a trace. If we knew who they were going for next, it would be easier."

"Yes, well there's no recourse for that," McArthur said. "Keep me informed, I'm going to talk over with the other teams." He went out the room and Ashley could see morale dwindling. They needed something. Hopefully when IT broke down Whikley's hard drives they would find something to go on. She looked over at her bag with her file inside it and quickly looked away.

Ashley started to look at the phone records, they were primarily calls to clients, no real family or friends to speak of. Most of the calls were to unknowns but could be found on his client list, Kate Marsh included.

Ashley's desk phone went off, which she picked up.

"Fenway," she said, tiredly.

"And you said my phone voice needed changing."

"It does, what have you got for me?"

435

"Bitcoin exchanges."

"What about bitcoin exchanges?"

"Well that's why I'm phoning you, and my boss is phoning your boss," Aaron said. "He did, he searched for some in his local area."

"Did he have his own private ledger?" Ashley asked.

"Yep, has the software on there," Aaron said. "And before you ask, we don't know who he sent the money to."

"Any chance you can send me over the pages?" Ashley asked. "I can go around and ask if he's been in."

"Done and done," Aaron said, sending them over.

"You're the best, thanks. I'll speak to you soon."

"I try my best, see you later." Ashley hung up and opened her e-mail with the search pages. Ashley wrote down all the local ones and got her keys.

***

Ashley now found herself outside Skipp pawn shop. She sighed and went inside.

"Oh shit, not you again." The first one on her list was the shop Ferrets went to. The owner was happy to see her as always.

"Am I going to get my computer back?" He asked.

"Soon," Ashley said, getting Whikley's photo up on her phone.

"Does this guy ring a bell?" The owner let out a grunt and had a look.

"Yeah, came in round the same time as your other guy. I had to basically hold his hand in doing the conversion."

"Was it the once?"

"Yeah, just the once. Had his own private ledger so it was a simple transfer at the end of it."

"Hmmm, thanks for your help Mr Skipp," Ashley said, walking out of the shop. She walked back over to her car, wondering where to go next. She looked up and saw the Royal Mail sorting office. She could pop in and see if they kept files on Kettings. She was here, and it was not as if it had nothing to do with work.

At the sorting office they had been kind but sceptical that they had records that went back that far regarding employees.

"We keep paper copies for reference," the general manager said, leading Ashley across the sorting floor. "Management are very much sticklers for that, I'm not sure how far they go back though."

"Well I'm just grateful for that," Ashley said. "How long have you worked here for?"

"Since the '70s," he said, leading her up some stairs.

"At this office."

"No, I've been all over Manchester," he said, opening a door into a dim corridor. "I came here in '94."

"Don't suppose you heard of Stan Kettings?"

"Can't say I have."

"How long has it been since records were added here?"

"System came in, in 2003," he said, stopping outside a door. "And this building has been in use since the war."

"Guess I'll have a root around then," Ashley said, optimistically.

"By all means." He opened the door to a row of filing cabinets with no order on them. "Help yourself."

"Thanks," Ashley said walking in, her optimism replaced with a sense of dread. He shut the door behind her to a loud bang which made something fall. Ashley checked the first cabinet and pulled out the first file.

Rodney Atkinson 1941–1975.

"Dammit," Ashley said putting it down and starting to pick out the files, some of which crumbled in her hands they hadn't been looked at in so long. So, she should count her luck that they still had this here, but she cursed her luck that she had to go through it.

A couple of hours and a tea later, Ashley finally found it.

Stanley Kettings 1972–1983.

Ashley put the other filings in the cabinet away and placed Kettings' file on the table. She opened it up carefully. Thankfully the paper wasn't as brittle and the ink not that worn. He started working in the sorting office, had a good proficiency at it and was promoted to a postie.

Ashley looked at what she was here for, the discipline record. He was caught a few times going into districts that didn't belong on his route.

Most notably towards Kenworthy Woods. Ashley got her phone out and got Google maps open and put in Kenworthy woods.

Lots of open roads and greenery, the sort of place an old stately home might be. Ashley put the file into her bag and went.

***

The long and winding roads were great to drive down, but she was still looking out for hidden entrances; the hedgerows were quite tall and hid almost everything on the side of the road. She passed a couple of farmhouses, and she saw it.

Tall spires in the distance, black silhouettes in the grey sky which appeared and disappeared in the high tree line. Ashley slowed down and saw the entrance and drove into a large opening but also a large rusted gate.

Ashley parked up, got out of the car and looked up at the building. Ugly, grey brickwork which was now lined with green moss and dark, hollow windows. It reminded Ashley of skull eyes. It must have been quite grand back in the day. Now, it was like an open and rotting wound.

Ashley reached back into the car and from her file pulled out the photo of Ferrets, Oatley and Thompson. Ashley looked up, the same spires in the distance. This was the right place. Limehouse.

Ashley walked up to the gate and shook it slightly. The loose gate rattled but remained firm. This was in the same district that Kettings was found in, so it pretty much confirmed his place in this ring.

Her phone started to ring.

"Fenway."

"Where are you?" It was Murphy.

"Chasing up a lead," Ashley said.

"Boss wants you back, SOCO report should be coming in soon."

"I'll be half an hour," Ashley said, getting back into her car.

Chapter 73

Ashley got back into the office, sat at her desk and put her bag with her research on Kettings and Limehouse out of sight. Half an hour later everyone was downstairs for a large catch-up meeting, which McArthur was conducting.

Everyone gathered round the boards with their new victim and previous ones, which had been updated by Sarandon.

"So, PM came back on Mr Whikley. Cramer has confirmed he died like our other victims and is therefore possibly linked," McArthur said. "According to the autopsy he died between six and nine on twenty-sixth of November which is earlier than our other victims. That's not the only differences though; by the looks of it he was tortured first. To what end we're not sure."

"We're still operating under the assumption that it is a male carrying out the attacks given the degree of force used for the blunt force injury on the back of his head, as well as the cut and the strength necessary to move him round the house."

"SOCO report shows that whoever it was wore gloves so there are no fingerprints at the scene. This includes Whikley's computer, tablet and hard drives. They have been given to IT forensics so they can break them down. Hopefully, if what Emma Curtis is saying is true, then Ian Whikley took photos of Oatley abusing; that'll give us links to people who knew him, and we can work back from there. IT have bumped this up to high priority so we're waiting on it."

"The other things round the house are being examined as well and we'll hopefully have something going into tomorrow."

"Curtis has also given a statement on this as well and has been recorded, but unless we find solid evidence of this it just reads like a fantasist's story. She has given out names of other people who could collaborate the story and we are talking to them now to try and hunt down some of them who want these two people dead. Granted, I know that this list will be longer than my arm, but we have every available resource given to us which will mean other forces questioning people further afield."

"I just want to thank you all for your hard work so far and the hours left to come. I know conditions in the investigation aren't exactly what we wanted, especially from the media point of view, I can only ask that you let us deal with the press and you guys deal with the facts. Now, your DIs will have the lowdown for all your individual investigations, so let's get out there and find the guy who did this."

The DIs took it in turns to show what progress, or lack of it was being made with the other investigations. Half-leads were coming up short and public tips were slowly not coming in. The media's highlights of who these people were possibly hindering that. Suddenly Ashley didn't feel so bad about not solving this sooner.

Ferrets' case had almost run into a dead end with regards to suspects along with Kettings' but the team dealing with Oatley was now going through all the people who had made claims about him, which was a list Ashley didn't envy. Their main promising link, which was the phone data taken from around Oatley's house, had drawn a blank. The number was activated an hour before and destroyed shortly after with the only location data at Oatley's house.

But even the questions being asked of the other detectives showed that there weren't that many leads left to go on. The murder of Whikley was almost a blessing in disguise as it had given them more leads to go on, but also brought the social circle down. Ashley just hoped that there wasn't another murder and that they could wrap this up quickly.

"So, what was your lead?" Murphy asked as they walked up.

"I was looking into my Limehouse theory," Ashley said. Murphy frowned.

"Ashley, you know you can't go off on your own like that."

"I know, but I found something." Murphy looked around but followed Ashley to her desk. She got out the folder and pulled out the report on Kettings and how he was sacked from his route because he kept on going to the Limehouse area.

"See, he was there, that's another link," Ashley said. "And with Emma's statement we could put Whikley there as well."

"Ashley, McArthur told you to drop it," Murphy said. "Come on, don't let the side down, we need everyone on this case."

"But what have we got so far?" Ashley asked.

"Ashley, listen to me. Nothing good ever happened to an officer that didn't obey orders," Murphy said. "We still need to try and find out if there was any contact between our killers and victims. That's what we have to do." He walked away from her.

Ashley angrily stuffed her findings into her bag, threw it under her desk and angrily went back to her keyboard to do as she was told.

She went through the inventories for the first three victims to see if any phones other than their mobiles and landlines had been discovered. She was also trying to keep an eye out for anything that could be used as a means of communication between parties or even as a tracker, but the inventories showed no similarities.

If they were communicating, her hunch about the computers was probably the right one. She checked the computer analysis for the three victims, wading through the computer jargon; she was looking at their social media profiles, or what there was of them. Ferrets had Facebook under an alias, Kettings had Twitter but only followed Bitcoin news channels and a couple of gaming sites.

Oatley didn't have any social media profiles, just one handled by a PR firm. Whikley on the other hand had business ones but no personal one as far as she could see.

Ashley was struggling to think how else they could have spoken unless through phone. She was going back over phone records saved on her computer but there weren't any numbers that matched.

Ashley picked her phone up and rang Aaron.

"Hey Ash."

"How did you know it was me?" Ashley asked.

"You're the only one who calls me directly."

"That's sad."

"Very. Now what is it you need?"

"Is there anyway of comparing our three victim's computers to see if they had any programmes that are the same?" Ashley asked.

"We can do that, might take a couple of hours. Do you want victim four as well?" He asked.

"If you can, great," Ashley said. "I'm at my desk so can you phone the results through?"

"Will do, speak to you soon." Ashley put the phone down. Now came the waiting game.

Chapter 74

Killing Paedophiles should be in the Olympics at this rate. #goforgold
   Whoever's doing this is fully justified in doing so #changemymind
   @GMP I pay my taxes, I want you to spend mine not looking for this
person.

The office settled down with people going out to find leads, but people were coming back with disappointed faces and crossing lines of enquiry off the boards, and giving things for Sarandon to log for alibis. With each new arrival more bad news followed.

The media was giving them a hammering as well, with some going as far to say that the police wanted the killer on the streets.

By now it was getting traction on Twitter and Facebook on an international scale; that there was a potential serial killer around Manchester and to avoid the area altogether.

"How the fuck is City supposed to sign anyone when there's a killer around?" Armstrong asked. It was affecting all walks of life.

Ashley was busy looking back through telephone records to see if any one of the victims had called the same number.

Ashley's desk phone went off, she could see that it was IT from the display. This was it, the whole investigation hinged on this one phone call. Ashley looked around briefly at her colleagues who were all hard at work, unaware of what was about to happen.

Ashley picked the phone up.

"DC Fenway."

"Hi, it's Bill." The voice sounded tired and full of dread. He didn't want to make this call as much as Ashley didn't want to receive it. Ashley knew then.

"We've finished the deep analysis of Ian Whikley's computer," he said. "We didn't find any material on the machine that we did with the other three." Ashley closed her eyes.

"What about his hard drives?" Ashley asked.

"They were archives of his photography work," Bill said. "I'm sorry."

"Nothing, nothing at all we can use?"

"Not on this computer," Bill said. "I'll send my analysis up."

"What about that other thing I asked you about?" Ashley asked.

"Whikley didn't have a link to the dark web and none of his social media profiles, like the others, showed that he was talking to anyone for anything other than business," Bill said.

"Was there anything similar on their computers at all? The same programmes, apps?"

"Apart from all the standard apps, calculator, word, and games, nothing," Bill told her. There was a thick silence from the other end of the phone. Ashley was finding it hard to find the words.

"Are you OK?" Ashley snapped back to reality.

"Yeah, yeah, we'll be fine. Thank you." Ashley put the phone down and took a deep breath, the feeling of dread rushing through her. More so wondering how she was going to break this to the rest of the team.

"IT just got back." They all turned around.

"And?" Ashley shook her head, and everyone let out a large sigh with some people swearing and kicking furniture in anger.

McArthur looked down at the floor and then at Ashley. She could only offer a blank expression that must have looked like defeat. McArthur looked down at the floor and thought for a moment.

"Everyone, everyone, listen to me." The room fell silent. "This has been a long few days. I want you all to go home, get a good night's sleep, come back tomorrow with some fresh ideas and minds." He looked around. "Go, you've all done well."

Some people didn't need asking twice, while others were a little slow. But McArthur was right, the last few days had been intense, and non-stop, everyone needed some respite; her included.

"Come on Fenway, that means you too," he said, walking over.

"I know," Ashley said dejectedly, getting to her feet. "I'll see you in the morning."

"Bright and early," he said with a smile and walking away, leaving Ashley to grab her bag and leave as well.

Chapter 75

Ashley got in her car; she closed the door, let out a sigh and fell forward into her hands that were already on the steering wheel. She was mentally preparing herself for the deflating car journey home. They couldn't have just hit another dead end. Now they were hoping that the killer killed again so they had something new to go on. Ashley pulled out of the carpark and started her drive home.

That was always the problem with serial killers, because they were smart enough to evade capture, they usually were good at not leaving any evidence. You had to wait for them to slip up and make a mistake.

As Ashley navigated her way through the concrete jungle, the radio presenter was prattling on about how this murderer, whoever they were was performing a public service by taking them off the street. The more this propaganda was being shoved down her throat, the more Ashley was beginning to believe it. Ashley turned into the carpark of her apartment complex. The day was slowly catching up with her. She decided not to go to MMA tonight.

After getting through the most secure building in Manchester and taking the stairs, not least being stuck in the world's slowest lift, Ashley opened her front door and flicked the lights on in her apartment. Ashley walked to her wall, she took the black marker pen and crossed out the leads that went to another dead end.

Ashley threw her bag onto her desk chair, sat down on the sofa and turned the TV on to the evening news.

She went into her bedroom and changed into some jeans and a long-sleeved top. From her bedroom she could hear that the government had performed a U-turn on a policy that was more important than a serial killer. But because he was killing paedophiles it was OK. As Ashley kept telling herself, they were people too, and they deserved justice. Ashley walked straight to the kitchen to get herself some wine and a smoothie.

When she walked back, she saw the tail end of the news. She leaned on the door frame looking at a feel-good piece about mothers and daughters. She hadn't spoken to her mum in a while. Ashley picked her phone up and rang home. As it rang, she sat down on the sofa, and brought her feet up under her knees and muted the TV.

"Hello?" Ashley smiled at how her mum put on a posher voice when she answered the phone. It was something she realised when she moved away.

"Hey mum, it's me," Ashley replied, trying to sound upbeat.

"Ashley dear?" Her mum almost sounded confused. "Well this is a turn up for the books, you phoning me."

"I know mum," Ashley said, rubbing the bridge of her nose. "But you are the one who said that I should call more often."

"I know I did, but it takes all the king's horses for you to answer your phone," her mum said.

"I've been busy with work over the last couple of weeks."

"You're not working that paedophile hunter, are you?" Her mum asked nervously. Here comes the lecture about how working for the police was too dangerous. She gulped some wine in preparation.

"Yeah, I am."

"Ashley, you know how dangerous —"

"I know it's dangerous," Ashley said, rubbing her bruised ribs. "But it's what I like to do."

"OK, OK," her Mum said, not wanting an argument as much as Ashley. "How are things with you?"

"Fine," Ashley said, pulling up her shirt to check her ribs, which were quite bruised.

"How's the hockey going?" Her mum asked, trying to sound cheerful.

"We're doing OK," Ashley said, reaching over for her moisturiser. "We have a big game next week though. How's the farm?"

"Oh, you know, just ticking over," her mum said. "Your father thinks we can land a new contract with another dairy."

"That sounds great," Ashley said. She rubbed the moisturiser into her skin, which made her wince.

"Are you OK?"

"I'm fine, just a hockey injury," Ashley replied. "Just rubbing some moisturiser onto it."

"Well I'm glad something I taught you sunk in," her mum said. Ashley smiled.

"Have you spoken to your brother at all?"

"He's too busy having fun at uni. I didn't call home that much while I was away."

"Well me and your sister are worried about him. Abs thinks that he could be getting into trouble."

"I told him if he got into trouble that he should call me. Doing the big sister thing."

"Well, Abs said that to him too."

"That would be sound advice if she had actually gone," Ashley said, pulling down her top.

"Ashley," her Mum said, warningly. "Less of that." Ashley smiled to herself.

"Your sister was talking about going back to college to do a course in something, she hasn't decided what to do yet."

"And are you going to make her phone home too?" Ashley asked. Her mum let out an exasperated laugh.

"You're wicked you are sometimes." They shared a mutual laugh.

"How is work Ashley?" Ashley swallowed.

"It's… OK," she said, choosing her words carefully. "This case is quite taxing."

"Do you have any leads?" Her mum asked. Ashley ran a hand through her hair, careful not to give anything away.

"A couple. But it's quite difficult doing this under the public's scrutiny."

"We've heard about it," her mum said. "Ashley, just promise me you're being careful. You can be quite… impulsive."

"I'm fine mum," Ashley said, quietly. "It's just difficult, it seems like half the population doesn't want us to do our job."

447

"Maybe you could let them take a couple more out." Ashley slumped. It was just like talking to the TV she thought.

"Well if you endorse the murders of certain people, where does it end?" Ashley said annoyed. "People need to see that the law works. We can't have vigilantes running amok branding out justice where they think they need to."

"Ashley, these people are the lowest of the low," her mum said. "When you have children, you'll know how despicable they are."

"Some of them had families themselves," Ashley reasoned." They deserve justice too."

"As do their victims."

"Can we talk about something else?" Ashley asked, scratching her head. "I kinda called to get away from that today."

"Well, I have news on the wedding." Why did Ashley open her mouth?

"Anyway, do you remember Tatton Hall?" Her mum taking her silence as a cue to continue. "The one your sister wanted for the reception?" Ashley rolled her eyes but, in a way, she did ask for it. She picked up her smoothie.

"Yeah, what about it?" She gulped her smoothie.

"Well she's got it now for the twenty first of June," Her mum said, excitedly. Ashley frowned. That was quick, only a couple of weeks ago there was no chance of getting the hall. "Isn't that great?"

Terrific, thought Ashley. She got up and looked at the board with all the evidence on it. "How did that come about?" She asked, her eyes scanning all the pieces of information.

"Well," her mum changed to her busy body tone. "Do you remember Abbey's friend Sarah who works there?" Ashley answered with a small sound, nodding her head to the conversation. Her mind though looking at their four victims, what was it that linked them personally, apart from their taste? The TV was showing a soap that the name escaped her.

"Well the couple who had booked it have split up, according to Sarah, the bride was telling her she caught the groom with his trousers down in some bath house." Ashley ohhed and ahhed where appropriate as her mum went into detail about this man's infidelity. Her train of thought though was on why these men, after being inactive on the abusing front for so long would somehow now decide that they should be killed in such a brutal way.

"So, Sarah phoned Abs up telling her this and said that although there was another wedding on standby, she could get us first refusal for the twenty-first." Ashley frowned.

"What's the catch?" Ashley asked. Her police intuition telling her nothing this good ever came without a price to pay.

"Well, we paid a bit extra too, but Sarah said that she needed to keep it hush hush from her boss. I tell you what Ashley, an offer like that is too good to refuse." Ashley frowned. Too good to refuse... She stared out into space.

Too good to refuse. An offer that the hotel couldn't refuse... or her parents couldn't refuse because it was there in front of them. A little extra money on the side to guarantee it... why was she thinking about this so much?

What if instead of being tailed and hunted down they were asked to come. What if they invited the killer round... what if they had been given an offer they couldn't turn down... or not wanted to turn down?

They would think that they were somewhere safe, a person coming to their house.

Ashley breathed.

It would explain why there was no forced entry.

That they were all found in a place that they considered safe.

The synapses in her brain shot off with that one phrase. All the jumbled-up pieces and questions were now starting to fit together; her stomach fluttering with the feeling of success. Ashley seemed to see the wall in some sort of vertigo motion.

Why had she not seen it earlier?

"So, we had to rearrange the caterer," her Mum had paused. "Ashley? Ashley love? Are you still there?" Ashley though had picked up her pen and was writing something down, making the finer points to her theory in her mind.

"Ashley?" Shit, her mum was still talking.

"You said that Sarah told you the extra money was to keep it from her manager," Ashley said. "What if the manager was in on it?"

"What? Ashley what are you —"

"The manager would have given it to the other couple but knew through Sarah how much Abbey wanted it. So much that..." Ashley trailed off. Of course, how could she have been so blind.

"Ashley?"

"If you really wanted something... if you were truly desperate, if something fell into your lap like that, you would grab the opportunity. You wouldn't think it through."

"Well, me and your father did think it through, thank you very much."

"No mum, don't you see? The reason there was no forced entry is because they were expecting someone. They weren't hunted down, they were approached. They were approached by the killer, their trust was gained, and that's why they were invited in; because they had something that our victims wanted, and they were too dumb to think it through." Ashley held the phone against her ear with her shoulder. She had pulled out her notebook and started to jot down her theory, her mind going a mile a minute.

"So... are you saying we've been fleeced?" Her Mum asked.

"No, of course not, anything for Abs, right," Ashley said, really wanting to get her off the phone. "Listen, I have to go but I'll speak to you soon, I promise, love you. Bye." Before her Mum could get a word in, she had ended the call.

Ashley was looking at the board, breathing deeply with the information in her mind. They weren't taken, they weren't stalked like everyone else thought, they were drawn in; they were offered something so good they couldn't turn it down.

"They were offered the chance to abuse another child," Ashley whispered. This though brought up other questions. The main one, how did they arrange this? They searched the social medias and found nothing, but there was something there, she could feel it.

Ashley jogged to her desk chair and picked her coat up as well as her satchel. She dialled Aaron's number on her phone.

"Ashley?"

"What are you doing tonight?" Ashley asked, locking her door and walking through the building.

"Uhm, I was just about to go home for the night."

"Scrap that, we're having dinner, I'm buying," Ashley said, as she walked out into the streets. "Do you prefer Chinese or Indian?"

"Uhm… Chinese."

"Wrong, I know a great Indian place, I'll convert you." Ashley crossed over, thanking a car that had slowed down.

"What, at my place or?"

"No, at the office," Ashley said. "I'll get dinner, I want you to set up our victim's computers again."

"Ashley, we didn't find anything."

"We were looking in the wrong place," Ashley told him. "Set them up and I'll explain when I get there. Now what do you want?"

"I'll just have a korma." Ashley stopped on the pavement, pulling a face.

"I'll pretend you never said that," she said, continuing to walk.

Chapter 76

The computer lab was dark when Ashley walked in. The corridor in front of her was only lit up partially from the lift light. Ashley walked towards Aaron's desk; on the floor beside it were the four victim's computers with Aaron beside them on his own. He was busy clicking away with his headphones on.

"Dinner is served," Ashley said, placing the bag of food on the desk. She instantly went to the computers. Aaron paused whatever he was doing and looked up at her.

"Hello to you too."

"Hi," Ashley replied slowly, her attention going to the other computers. "I got you a biryani, I couldn't bring myself to ask for a korma." Ashley didn't look up. She took her coat off and sat on one of the chairs by the computers.

"Thanks," Aaron said, helping himself. "So, are you going to tell me your theory or are you going to keep me in suspense?"

"They were hunted down," Ashley said. "But not in the conventional sense." Aaron raised his eyebrow.

"Does DCI McArthur know about this theory yet?"

"No, but I want solid proof before I go to him with it," Ashley said. "Because all their theories have drawn blanks and mine ridiculed."

"And what is this theory?" Aaron asked. Ashley pulled one of the computers towards her.

"They were drawn in," Ashley said. "The killer gained their trust. Then they were presented with an offer they couldn't refuse," she said, typing in the password to one of the computers.

"And that was?"

"The opportunity to abuse a child again," Ashley said. She went to Gordan Ferrets' computer and pulled up his internet search engine.

"That's why there was no forced entry on any of them. The killer was expected to come. I still think our killer was at Limehouse and they knew exactly what it was our victims wanted. They're picking off the people who abused them."

"Surely the others would have got wind after the first one?" Aaron said.

"It's like an itch," Ashley replied, frowning. "It doesn't go away until you scratch it. For the likes of Ferrets, Kettings and Whikley it had been so long that they didn't think it through when the chance came up. Oatley was so arrogant he thought he wouldn't be caught. If we had a list of people at Limehouse they all abused it would be so much easier."

"That's going to be like finding a needle in a haystack," Aaron said, taking a bite of his curry. Ashley ran her hands through her hair.

"Yeah, it is," Ashley agreed. "But if we can find how they were lured it will make it a hell of a lot easier."

"And this is why you needed my help?" Aaron asked.

"Computers is more your thing," Ashley conceded.

"We tried all the social medias. Nothing came up," Aaron said, pushing his glasses up his nose.

"What about dark web chatrooms?"

"The websites bounce through different servers and IPs," Aaron explained. "And then their accounts are encrypted with passwords which someone would know if we tried to break into them. Besides, DCI McArthur hasn't authorised it."

"They were communicating with our killer somehow," Ashley mused. "There must be some sort of encrypted messenger they used."

"Facebook and Twitter showed nothing."

"Hardly any of them were on Facebook and Twitter," Ashley sighed. "Is there anything else on their computers that would generate chat at all?" Aaron shook his head.

"As I said, all the social medias came back clean. They were old; maybe they used old school methods?"

"Our killer isn't old school," Ashley said, bringing up the menu bar on Ferrets' computer. "Maybe there was something planted on their computers?" Ashley sighed at the thought of having to go through computer repair shops. Ashley looked over at Aaron's screen. He had been playing on a game before Ashley came in. It was still streaming what looked like a battle with loads of people talking, she could hear the voices coming from Aaron's headphones.

"What are you playing on?" Ashley asked, taking a bite. Aaron made a sound through a mouthful of food and Ashley pointed to his screen.

"Oh, it's an online game," he said. "It's called Fortnite. Do you play?"

"Not a gamer," Ashley said, through a mouthful of food. She watched as the game finished. It went to a lobby screen where people were still talking. On the side though, there was a message box. Ashley frowned. She put her fork back in the container and got up from her seat and walked over to his computer and looked at it.

"What about this?" She asked pointing to the messages.

"People can talk across the game," Aaron said. "Normally it's just twelve-year olds telling everyone how they've shagged your mum."

"Nice," Ashley said lightly, while looking at some of the messages. Ashley pressed on one of the people talking and it opened another box.

"What's this?"

"It's a direct message," Aaron explained. "So, you can reply to the twelve-year olds." What if they had communication via this or something similar? Ashley thought. Ashley pushed herself back to the laptops. Something Bill had said to her earlier was racing in her thoughts.

"Apart from all the standard apps, calculator, word, and games."

"Games…" Ashley whispered to herself. Joyce Kettings said Stan like playing on games.

"What is it?"

"Joyce Kettings complained to me about her son playing on a game," Ashley said. "She said he would spend his nights playing on something." Ashley brought up the start menu and started to look through the menu.

Aaron pulled up the inventory on Kettings' computer on his own and looked through what programmes they found. Most of it was to help crack the complex algorithms to mine Bitcoin, but Aaron was looking through them.

"Here's one," he said. "Overwatch, it's like Fortnite and has direct messaging too," Aaron turned around to Ashley. "Popular with teenagers."

Ashley typed the name in, and it brought up a programme. Ashley clicked on it and it brought up a black screen with the name Overwatch. It faded into a menu screen which brought up a log in page.

"Do you have anything for this?" Ashley asked. Aaron shook his head.

"No, but we can find something." He ushered Ashley out of the way and minimised the game. With a few clicks he retrieved the password.

"How did you do that?" Ashley asked.

"Trade secret," Aaron said with a smile. He brought the game up, entered the password and was let into the menu page.

"Can we see who he's been messaging?" Ashley asked impatiently. Aaron again fiddled with the keyboard and brought up a notepad document.

"You need to start a game to log in. I've bypassed the data privacy protocol to extract this, otherwise your killer might see us logging in."

"Good point," Ashley agreed, looking back at the screen. "How many people has he talked to?"

"Hard to say," Aaron said. "There could be hundreds of people, some of it's nonsense, the others might be a link."

"So, we need something that links all of them," Ashley said, thoughtfully. Ashley got to her feet and started to go through all the links she made with the four victims.

"There's a network, a web of paedophiles that operated in Manchester. Ferrets was an ex-scout whose past was creeping up on him, but he only downloaded the porn, probably from Kettings." Aaron nodded his head with an uncertain look.

"That would make sense. And it links two of your victims together, but where does Oatley and Whikley fit into it?" Ashley looked down at the computers.

"Oatley owned the building the New Agers leased," Ashley said, getting out her Limehouse folder. She brought up an online article about Will Oatley. "He owned lots of property in and around the Manchester area, one of them was this place." The next article Ashley got out was of an old, dilapidated building.

"Limehouse," Ashley said. "An old stately home the Oatley's owned after it fell into disrepair, in the seventies and eighties it was rented to a cult."

"A cult?" Aaron said, leaning down to look at the article.

"The New Agers. They were led by a self-proclaimed new wave of Christianity," Ashley explained. "They believed in simple living, living off the land and stuff like that. On the outside anyway."

"It's a religious sect, it doesn't sound like a cult," Aaron countered.

"How about signing over all your money to them and being bullied and conditioned to obey a series of strict and insane rules?"

"That sounds more like a cult," Aaron conceded. "Why weren't they ever shut down?"

"Because people joined of their own free will," Ashley said.

"Why?"

"The sixties were a wave of new love and rebellion against traditional values," Ashley explained. "Imagine going to a place where they still held those values. Likeminded people who were against all the new age propaganda."

"I still don't see why they would do that?"

"Well, neither do I," Ashley replied. "So, I did some research into it. The cult received numerous grants and donations to carry out 'Agriculture projects'." Aaron walked round to the back of her chair.

"Who from?"

"The city council, church groups, and business associations," Ashley said, as she shook her head. "But not one thing about them producing anything of substance."

"So not a centre of agriculture?"

Ashley pulled out the old case reports.

"It was a private club where people paid a fee to rape the kids on site. There must have been a culture of fear which made them go along with it."

"Numerous people made claims of systematic abuse against them," Ashley explained. "Children at the time saying that they were sold off to be abused by the highest bidder. I would bet my future mortgage on these donations being payments to Dennis Thompson, the cult leader, so they could abuse the kids at that home." Aaron picked up the accountancy report.

"These all come from reputable people," he said, flicking through it. "Shit. Ashley, this could be huge…" Ashley nodded.

"OK, that's Oatley linked to this cult, what about the others?" Ashley reached into her bag, pulled out a photocopy of the Manchester Evening news and handed it to him. On it was an article that Ashley had highlighted about Ferrets' Sports Academy.

"That's Gordon Ferrets," Aaron said, pointing to a younger Gordon Ferrets who was smiling with Thompson and Oatley, with a group of children by Limehouse. The article was about Ferrets' academy that was providing sports training to the cult. A simple feel-good piece that had gone unnoticed.

"Right, two of four."

"Three," Ashley said. She turned her head and saw Aaron looking at her puzzled. Ashley smiled to herself.

"I missed it at first," she said. "Look who took the photo." Aaron looked down and saw the name of the photographer.

"Son of a bitch." Aaron muttered under his breath.

"Kettings had one of the gowns the children are wearing in his wardrobe. He made some prostitutes wear it. It was taken from the scene, probably by the killer."

"Ashley, this means —"

"This means that they are connected but we don't know by who," Ashley said. "Thompson is dead so it's not about loose ends. And there are so many cases of child abuse from there that if we went looking for them, they'll fall back into the shadows."

"So, is this it then?" Aaron asked. "We just stop and let them carry on."

"No, of course not," Ashley said. "I don't think we have the conventional serial killer."

"What's a conventional serial killer?" Aaron asked, sitting opposite her. Ashley looked up from the computer.

"Most serial killers go to great lengths, so they don't get caught." Ashley had a bite of her curry. "They have high IQs; they are meticulous and thoughtful."

"This one sounds like the others." Ashley shook her head and swallowed her food.

"Think about it. Serial killers never want the bodies to be found, otherwise people would be onto them," Ashley explained. "But our killer wanted them to be found." Aaron quirked an eyebrow. Ashley leaned forward and held one finger up.

"Gordon Ferrets was found at a hotel, he lived alone so he needed luring out so someone would find him. A maid perhaps?" Aaron was about to speak when Ashley held up another finger.

"Stan Kettings, he was found in his home by a burglar who was tipped off that it was going to be empty, so he would be found." Ashley held her third finger up.

"Will Oatley, was killed while his wife was away on holiday. She came back and found him the day after he died, that's not coincidence. She was meant to find him."

"OK, and Whikley? Aaron said.

"He was found by a bride who wanted her wedding photos, the bride said that he was recommended to her, the killer wanted her to find him…" Ashley got back to her feet and started to pace.

"Try… Limehouse," Ashley said, pointing at the notepad document. "If our killer wants to be found there would be a mark, and that's the only one."

"OK, give me a sec." Aaron went around all the computers.

"What are you doing?" Ashley asked.

"Searching for games in these computers," he said, typing away. "OK, every one of them has Overwatch." He was starting to go to each one with such speed it was almost a blur.

"Right." He went over to his own computer and brought up four different notepads on screen and another with a black screen. He started to type into the black screen.

"What are you doing now?"

"Coding that name," Aaron explained. "Limehouse." He coded around the word and pressed enter. A loading bar came up.

"Right, in a minute. We'll see if that name comes up," Aaron said with a triumphant smile, eating his curry.

"Thanks," Ashley said. "I'd have no idea how to do all this."

"Don't mention it. Here we go." The loading bar stopped.

"Right…" Aaron looked at the report.

"There is mention of Limehouse." Aaron scrolled down the report. He highlighted a few things. "It looks like they were all in contact with a… Limehouse Babe?"

"What?" Ashley walked round the back of Aaron's chair. Highlighted on the screen were conversations with a player called Limehouse Babe.

"Can you isolate their conversations with this person?" She asked.

"Yeah."

"Good, send them to me," Ashley said, making her way to the computer. Aaron mumbled something while he isolated the conversations and sent them over to her. Ashley opened the transcripts, the first one she opened was for Stan Kettings.

Kettleone1
OK, I got the game, now can we talk about your proposition?

Limehouse Babe
All in good time. Are you sure you want to go through with this?

Kettleone1
Yes, I am, how much money are we talking?

"That was it," Ashley said, as the green message board came up. She searched for Limehouse Babe and the conversations came up.

Ashley scrolled down the conversations. There was more groomer / victim material; the further it went down the lewder the conversations became. It made Ashley's skin crawl to think that someone could speak to another person like this. Then, a picture came up. Ashley scrolled past, not wanting to look at whatever was on screen.

The conversation started to talk about meeting up. Ashley sat up more from her ever-growing slouching position.

Kettleone1
We can meet at my house. It'll be free.

Limehouse Babe
Good, I'll see that everything is arranged.

Kettleone1
Are we still on?

Limehouse Babe

Absolutely.

Kettleone1

OK, my address is Fawkes Road in Salford, come next Saturday.

Ashley stopped, that lined up the murder perfectly. Well at least they knew this Limehouse Babe was connected to their killer; could maybe even be the killer. Ashley went back to the notepad transcripts for all three and searched for Overwatch. (She needed to learn that coding trick of Aaron's.) The search confirmed her hunch that this Limehouse Babe had told them to use the Overwatch private message to talk.

"Right, you check Ferrets' and Oatley's computer for Overwatch," she said. Ashley gave him two because with his superior computer knowledge he would be able to check faster. "I'll check Whikley's."

"OK, what are we looking for?"

"We're looking for them talking about meeting up, where and when if possible and the dates to make sure they match up." Ashley logged into Whikley's Overwatch. She found the conversation with Limehouse Babe and started to go through it too.

It started off the same, being approached by this Limehouse Babe to discuss a transaction, which Ashley correctly assumed was the buying of a child for abuse, judging by the messages.

She wasn't surprised to see Whikley boasting about his photography business and asking if it was all right if he took photos, which this Limehouse Babe agreed to; not that it mattered, there was no child. The last messages were after the day Will Oatley died. He had cancelled the deal and said it was too risky. Surprisingly, this Limehouse Babe said OK and that it was fine. They must have had a backup plan in case this happened.

Something clicked in her head. Whikley didn't have any indecent photos of children on his computer or hard drives.

"Is this everything?" Ashley asked.

"Everything that was found."

"What about his laptop?"

"Just his portfolio," Aaron said, walking round to it. "Like all the others there was nothing on the social medias." Ashley nodded and sat down, her body buzzing off the adrenaline of a case moving forward quickly. It was just like the first time she experienced it. She took a deep breath; who the hell got a kick out of something like this?

"Do you think I'm crazy?" Ashley asked. She blinked and looked over at Aaron. Aaron made a surprised sound, with a mouth full of food.

"Crazy?" He laughed nervously. "Why, why would anyone think you were crazy?" Ashley looked down at the computers before her.

"What sane person comes up with these sorts of theories in their head?" Ashley said, looking down at the evidence.

"Well... it's your job, isn't it?" Aaron said. "To piece this all together." Ashley nodded.

"And now I have," she said. She laughed to herself. "Playing a game of spot the difference and hide and seek all rolled into one."

"Maybe you should go home and sleep. We don't have anything more; maybe they'll listen to you in the morning," Aaron offered. Ashley shook her head and got to her feet.

"Thanks for this," Ashley said, pointing to all the computers.

"Where are you going?" Aaron asked, walking to her.

"To Whikley's house," Ashley said. "I'm missing something. I know I am." She went to walk away but Aaron grabbed the cuff of her arm.

"No, stay for a little longer," he said. "We can go through this. You shouldn't go hurdling headfirst into this." Ashley breathed out.

"You don't even know what you're looking for." Ashley nodded and smiled lightly.

"You're a good friend Aaron," she said. "But this is the part where you let me go," she said, looking down at her arm. Aaron gingerly let go of her coat.

"I'll speak to you soon." Ashley walked to the lift and got inside. She turned around just as the door closed. The last thing she saw was Aaron looking down at the floor. Ashley leaned back on the back of the lift and closed her eyes.

"Smooth, Ashley."

Chapter 77

Ashley pulled up outside the home of Ian Whikley; the officers outside, were having a laugh and a joke with each other. Ashley got out the car and walked up towards them.

"Sorry miss," one of them said, walking towards her. "This is an active crime scene. You can't be here." Ashley reached into her inside pocket and showed them her ID.

"DC Fenway. Major Crimes," she said, putting her ID away. "I want to have a look around."

"I thought your lot already had a look around," one of them said. "Something the great almighty department missed?" The two officers laughed. Ashley looked down and half smiled to herself.

"Look, I've had a busy day. If you two are done measuring dicks, I'll go through now." One of them shook his head.

"Your guys shook it top to bottom. I'm not sure what else you can find."

"New lead," Ashley said, walking past them.

"I hope you're not squeamish. There's a bit of blood in there." Ashley stopped at the top of the stairs leading up to the house.

"I'm used to the sight of blood."

"Whoa, way too much info." Ashley shook her head and pushed the door open.

"She's kinda hot you know. For a DC."

"For a DC?"

"Well, remember that frumpy one that used to come around."

"Smelled like tuna?"

"Yeah, her." The other looked back at the house.

"Any girl's an improvement on that."

Ashley turned on the torch on her phone; the power was shut off. Ashley was in the entrance hall with everything out of place from the search. Ashley moved around the ground floor; the rooms were filled with photos from his portfolio, landscapes in strange lights and angles, very abstract. Ashley knew a few people from her uni days who would love this.

She walked through the hallway and looked at a chest of drawers which had its contents thrown out. Ashley looked at a series of photographs on the top of it. They were of Whikley at various tourist spots. One though was of a girl, looked no older than sixteen, who was looking away from the camera, taken off guard. His niece perhaps? Ashley picked it up and looked behind it, nothing. She placed it down and carried on.

She reached the bedroom. The body was removed, and the bed stripped clean to be tested but the blood was stained onto the mattress. Ashley opened the file and looked at the photos from the scene.

Ian Whikley, 58 years old, ex-journalist and part time photographer. Killed the same way as the previous three victims, tied down to a bed with their throats slashed. Ashley consulted the autopsy report, killed in the same way with a sharp object, but was tortured first. Ashley walked to the bed and pulled out a photo of the knots that were made to tie him down.

The same as the first three victims. Ashley started to pace, her footsteps echoing around the silent room.

Four men, all from different backgrounds, all from different walks of life, and no connection to one another other than Limehouse and this Limehouse Babe. They were all tied to a bed and had their throat slashed.

Why did the killer want this body to be found now? Ashley looked around the room, if there was something to be found, it was here. Ashley walked round to the bookcases, running her hands over the joints and openings, trying to feel something that was out of place.

After that proved fruitless, she lifted the mattress off the bed. After running her hand over the surfaces again she felt nothing.

Checking behind pictures on the wall, checking the walls. Nothing. Ashley grunted and ran her hands through her hair. There was a reason why she was here, she was seeing the pattern but not sure what she was looking for.

Maybe this was a mistake; she was tired, it had been a long day, she wasn't thinking straight. Maybe if she looked over what she'd done tomorrow it would make more sense.

Ashley walked forward but stumbled slightly on the ground. Ashley swore and flashed her torch down at her foot. The toes of her boot were higher than the heel. Ashley closed the file and placed it down on the bed. She kneeled and looked at the floorboard which was raised more than the other two beside it.

It took Ashley back to her bedroom at the family home; she had one loose floorboard which she would hide things under that she didn't want her family finding. Ashley ran her finger across the side of the raised floorboard and held her finger to the light. No dust, it was regularly opened.

Ashley tried to pull the board up, but it didn't budge. Ashley shone her torch up the floorboard and saw that it was being held down by the bed. Ashley could even see the marks from where the bed had been moved. Ashley pushed the bed with her shoulder.

With a groan it reluctantly moved. Ashley got her phone out again and shone it on the board. She stepped down on one end of the board which made the other shoot up. Ashley kicked it over and got back down on her knees to see what was inside.

It took a second for her eyes to adjust but for a second all she could see was the dust. Ashley breathed out in frustration and looked down when a glint from her torch caught her eye. Ashley looked up and ran her torch across the hole and saw it again. Ashley pulled out a glove and picked up a portable hard drive. Ashley turned it over in her hand.

Ashley got to her feet and looked at the hard drive.

"Now what, are you?"

Chapter 78

This zigzagging across Manchester wasn't good for her health; it was nearly eleven by the time she got back to the office, Aaron now long gone from the lab. Ashley let herself into the office, sat down at her desk and turned on her computer and desk lamp, impatiently tapping the desk with her fingers while waiting for it to load.

She looked down at the hard drive, half wondering if she was making the right decision to look at it now and not wait for the morning. But after going through the trouble of adding it to the log she wanted to see what was on it.

When her computer finally opened Ashley connected the hard drive, waiting for it to load on her screen. While she waited, she saw that she had an e-mail. It was Ian Whikley's harassment case. Ashley sent it to the printer.

Ashley opened the file explorer and saw the hard drive. Ashley dragged it over to a file scanner on her desktop to see if there were any viruses on it.

The scan showed that it was clean, with over five hundred thousand images and videos on the drive. Ashley went back to it and opened it up with the folder icons cascading down the screen. Ashley suddenly got an uneasy feeling in her stomach. This man was probably a paedophile... who knows what she was about to look at.

Ashley ran a hand through her hair and looked down at the screen. What if the key to solving this case was hidden inside these photos?

Ashley wasn't sure where to start first. There were likely to be hundreds of children in these pictures. She decided to go with the name of one she knew was there. Lisa.

The file explorer showed up multiple folders with Lisa in them. Ashley clicked on the first one.

She wasn't sure how long she had been sitting there but she finally mustered the courage to open the first picture, which was of a blonde girl in a bedroom.

The picture was in the grainy colour of the time, and clearly scanned. Ashley looked at the girl. She was between twelve and fourteen and slim, but she was in stockings, bra and knickers, something no child should be in. She looked shy and scared out of her mind. Her eyes looked like they had seen too much for a young life like hers.

"Christ," Ashley said, leaning forward onto the desk. This certainly wasn't on any of the hard drives they found with Whikley.

Ashley pressed to view the next one which was of the same girl but from behind. Ashley pressed 'next', which was of her looking down at her feet. Ashley started to go through the photos, the first few were of her posing for the camera, although it looked obvious that she was doing it under duress and direction.

The next one was of this girl being kissed by a man who was much too old for her. Was this really what the killer wanted her to find? Were they trying to taunt her now, live what the victims of Limehouse went through as well? No, that could never compare.

As Ashley went further into the photos, they became more and more perverse, with not just one man with this girl. Her eyes much more fearful and her body language was of desperation and the resignation with all these other men kissing and touching her.

Ashley rubbed her eyes. She felt tired and going through this wasn't the best idea. Maybe she should give it to IT to sort through tomorrow. Ashley clicked along to the next photo and froze. She leaned forward on the desk. The face was younger, but she could see it.

Will Oatley.

Ashley leaned back in her chair. The photo of Oatley clear as day with this poor girl. Ashley clicked through a few more and saw another face she knew.

Gordon Ferrets.

Ashley swore and ran a hand over her face. She clicked through a few more and saw another face. A young Stan Kettings. Ashley looked down at the keyboard, not really wanting to carry on. She swallowed hard and clicked the next one. After a couple more clicks, she saw Ian

Whikley getting involved as well. Ashley was trying her best to keep track of all the people in the shot, trying her best not to look at the pained look on the poor girl's face. She knew from the faces she recognised that there were at least three men.

Ashley couldn't look through any more and walked away from her screen to the large windows that looked down on Manchester City Centre.

This was it, this was what the killer wanted her to find, to prove to the world they did what they did. Ashley rubbed the bridge of her nose, trying to figure out how all of this made sense. Ashley frowned. So that was Lisa Strachan.

Ashley got her notepad and wrote down to take the hard drive to IT and see if they could identify siblings that stayed at Limehouse. Just as Ashley finished writing the note down, her old theory came back to her.

Everyone had assumed that this was a man killing these people. The angle of the knife, the force was all consistent with a man according to the coroner; what if her original idea was correct?

What if this was a woman killing them? The evidence was against it, but it was possible; but still unlikely given the balance of probability.

Ashley pulled out her notebook. She flipped the pages back to the notes she took on the Ferrets murder about the crime scene. Most of them were about the crime scene and the blood spatter. Ashley looked at the next page which was of the interviews she had conducted.

The first one was with Mr Cowan who was angry and abrasive from the start. Further down Ashley had described him as delusional because he thought the murderer was after him. The next ones were Dora Sanchez and Glenn Young, they seemed like a lifetime ago now.

There was a few more on the floor that talked about the voyeur coming up to that room but nothing that stood out to Ashley as being the woman she was after. Ashley walked over to the board that had been cleared earlier in the day and got her pen and scribbled down 'The Woman' in the centre, with the murder victims down the sides of the board.

Ashley linked up how the murder victims were connected by Limehouse, and she added the head of the snake, Thompson, who was found murdered in nearly identical circumstances. Even though McArthur refused to link him with the deaths, she did.

They were connected to Limehouse and Ashley bet that it was someone at the house; whether it was the girl on the film, she was at the centre of this. Ashley finished drawing the lines and took a step back, looking at the links.

What if this was it? What if there wasn't going to be any more killings? What if she was meant to find all this so the killings were more justified than they already were? What if this was another dead end? Ashley groaned and sat down at the edge of her desk. Whikley's harassment case.

Ashley walked over to the printer and brought it back to her desk to look over it.

"Jesus." The claim had been put in by the mother of a girl who was on work experience at The Manchester Evening News. Citing inappropriate behaviour from him and unwanted sexual advances towards a minor. He was let go from the paper quietly with a payoff. Ashley couldn't believe it. Why was this confidential?

The more she looked at the evidence the more the lines blurred. Ashley sat back down at her computer. She minimised the photo gallery and opened Google. She laid out all the links between the others and Limehouse and stared at them one at a time.

Ferrets Sports Academy. Ashley brought up his Company House filings and looked through the annual returns; the only person listed as a director was Ferrets himself. It was registered at his home address at the time and that he got a lot of grant money coming into it from the city, as well as the two Manchester clubs. Ashley added sticky notes to what might be a connecting fact and moved on.

Stan Kettings. A postman who got fired, ran his own IT business and become a Bitcoin enthusiast. Ashley checked over his financials which again showed nothing out of the ordinary. Ashley checked the letter his mum gave her about his dismissal, nothing that really stood out to her; he was dismissed for hoarding mail and delivering mail outside his jurisdiction.

Will Oatley. He was the one with the biggest pile of evidence on the count that he had the biggest money trail. Ashley was looking through all the lawyer papers and Companies House filings which seemed to just repeat in her mind.

Ian Whikley. The journalist and photographer, who looked like a sex pest as well; a perfect foil for them all. Ashley was skimming at a file of lawyer's letters when she threw it down on the desk and ran a hand through her hair.

"Go home," Ashley told herself. She started to gather up the files. "You need some sleep because nothing's…" Ashley shook her head. "Matching…". She could not be that stupid.

Gordon & Spencer LLP

Attorneys at Law

There were two pieces of paper on her desk with the same name. Gordon Ferrets Sports Academy annual report and Ian Whikley's defence on his harassment case.

Ashley picked up the two pieces of paper and slammed them down on the desk next to her. The two names matched up perfectly. Ashley was breathing deeply. She walked back over to her desk and started to route through the mountain of paperwork. Now she'd seen that name, it was everywhere.

Gordon & Spencer was the lawyer for Gordon Ferrets Academy, they were also Ian Whikley's lawyers in his harassment case. Ashley was looking through Oatley Developments plc annual reports and saw it there in black and white.

Attorneys.

Gordon & Spencer LLP.

Ashley let out a breathless laugh. She scampered over to Ketting's file. She had seen that name. She picked up the letter about his expulsion from the postal service. His attorney, Gordon & Spencer LLP.

Ashley walked over to the files on Limehouse, brought them over to her desk and got them out. She pulled out the leasing contract. Ashley sat on her desk and went through the contract. Attorney, Gordon & Spencer LLP.

Ashley smiled to herself but then shook her head. For all the answers she had, now there were more questions. Ashley sat down in her seat and cradled her head in her hands.

Sometimes, she was too smart for her own good. Ashley opened Google and typed 'Gordon & Spencer'. Ashley clicked the first result, which was their company website. The front page was of James Gordon and Nick Spencer shaking hands and laughing for the camera. Ashley looked at the fancy name and the 'Established in 1969'.

Ashley clicked on a section of lawyers which went in a hierarchy format. Gordon and Spencer on the top with partners and associates below them. Ashley was clicking through the partners which gave a brief description about them. Almost all of them worked after the Limehouse scandal. Ashley was about to close it in anger when she saw something at the bottom of the page.

Past lawyers.

Ashley opened it; most of the lawyers were old and retired. Their profiles going on about how much service and good they did. They might be involved but they weren't in the same age range as the other victims; if they were related, they had to be in the same age bracket. Maybe there was someone working there at the time.

Well there wasn't anything Ashley could do now, without going down to their offices. She would do that in the morning. Ashley looked up and saw another name across from the retirees. Ashley clicked on it and brought up Deputy Mayor Harold Donaldson.

Ashley frowned. She knew he was previously a lawyer. She didn't know that he worked for this firm. She knew that face; it looked familiar, and not from the TV. Ashley leaned back in her chair. What if she knew the name of the lawyer who represented these people, it could fall into place?

Joyce Kettings. Ashley pulled her phone out and instantly rang Joyce's number. It was only when the phone started ringing that Ashley realised what time it was. Before she could end it, Joyce answered.

"Hello." Well, she was in for it now.

"Hello, Mrs Kettings it's DC Ashley Fenway, how are you?"

"Well, I'm all right detective," she said. "Just… just thinking how big and lonely this house is now." Ashley closed her eyes.

"I'm surprised you're up this late, I was going to leave you a message."

"I've always been a bit of a night owl," she said. "What can I do for you detective?"

"I'm sorry to bring this up but I was just looking through your son's dismissal from the Royal Mail and I was wondering who represented him?"

"Oh, uh… I know that it was a friend of his," she said. "Apparently, he owed him a favour, he came for dinner. Oh, what was his name?" Ashley was tapping her foot impatiently.

"Uhm, Harold," she said. "Yeah, such a nice boy, he did all he could for my Stan but…"

"Harold… as in Harold Donaldson?" Ashley asked, not quiet believing it herself.

"Yes, that was his name!" She said. "He was such a nice boy. He sent some flowers after Stan passed away." Ashley was staring out into space.

"Ms Fenway?" Ashley walked to the lease agreement for Limehouse and started to look through it.

"Ms Fenway, are you all right?"

"Fine," Ashley said, absentmindedly. "Listen… thanks for taking my call Mrs Kettings. I'll speak to you soon."

"OK, goodnight detective."

"Goodnight." Ashley ended the call and went back to the lease agreement. Through all the legal mumbo jumbo she found the section for signing the document over.

The attorney that signed.

"Donaldson…" Ashley whispered.

She started to go back through all the documents she had previously been poring over. The names she was looking for were now everywhere. Harold Donaldson was the presiding lawyer over Limehouse's abuse claims, he was also the lawyer who defended Kettings on his dismissal, he was the one who sorted out Limehouse's charity status. She looked at the original court case against the New Agers, the one with Lisa Strachan. The lawyer, Harold Donaldson.

Ashley was now searching him on Google. Most of the results were his mayoral at engagements, his interviews on Manchester and some about the old cases he worked. Ashley was mentally kicking herself at

471

how stupid she had been. She was looking at an old photo of him when he graduated law school from Gordon and Spencer's website.

Ashley got up from her seat, trying to figure out what this all meant, while she hung up all these links on the board. She took a step back and admired her handy work, but something was still amiss. She should have found this link a long time ago but why was Gordon & Spencer and Donaldson so important… now?

Ashley looked over at the computer screen, more so at the minimised photo gallery. Ashley walked slowly to the screen and sat down in her chair. Her hand gingerly hovered over the icon. She pressed it and the photo she had last looked at came up. She clicked through a few more, until she found the one she was meant to find.

"Oh fuck!"

Chapter 79

"Come on, pick up. Pick up!" Ashley muttered over her blue tooth. She took a sharp corner towards Harold Donaldson's house. The photos proved that he too was involved in the paedophile ring at Limehouse. He was the man that made it all go away.

Since he was involved, he was probably on the killer's hit list as well. She was on her way over to his house to either try and warn him and arrest him or find his corpse like the other victims. She was currently trying to also call DCI McArthur to tell him what she learned.

"Come, on!" Ashley shouted, turning her car again.

"McArthur," he said, tiredly.

"Sir, it's Fenway."

"Fenway? Why are you phoning me at… close to midnight? Do you have no concept of time?" He asked.

"Sorry Sir, but this information is time sensitive," Ashley said. "I've found our next potential victim."

"What?" He was more alert now. "What you mean? We hit another dead end?"

"I had an idea," Ashley said. "Long and short of it, our killer lured the victims to their deaths with the promise of abusing another child." She made another turn.

"They were all talking to this one person on that online game that's been on the news, Overwatch, their name was Limehouse Babe."

"Limehouse? That sounds familiar," McArthur said. Ashley rolled her eyes.

"It's the house I told you about!" She replied irritably. "The one that was at the centre of those abuse scandals!"

"Yes, yes, you did bring it up," McArthur said. "So, what did you find?"

"I did some more digging into it and linked our victims to this house. Whoever's killing these paedophiles is linked to it."

"Great, we'll get a list of names in the morning," McArthur said.

"Not soon enough," Ashley stressed. "Making those links I found another man linked to it all." She took a deep breath.

"Harold Donaldson." McArthur was silent from the other end of the phone.

"Ashley, are you serious?"

"Before you say anything, I have the proof on my desk," she said. "He was linked to all of them and was abusing children as well."

"How do you know this?" McArthur asked.

"I had another look round Whikley's place and found another hard drive with photos of a girl being abused by all of our victims *and* Donaldson," Ashley said, braking sharply at a deserted junction. The lights had turned red. She could hear McArthur pacing.

"So, he could be the next target?" He asked.

"Or the next body," Ashley replied.

"Ashley, Donaldson is one of Manchester's favourite people right now," McArthur said. "This has to be watertight or we're both back to walking the beat." The lights turned green and Ashley drove off.

"Sir, it's in black and white what this man is. No amount of lawyering is going to be able to get him out of this. If we get his laptop, we should be able to trace back conversations as well. He's organising to abuse another child through the gaming messages like all the others." McArthur paused.

"This is a risky gambit."

"I know, Sir," she said. "But right now, it's the only lead we have; I'll be damned if I'll let it go through my fingers now."

"Where are you?"

"On my way to his house."

"I'll call it in and have some cars sent there to meet you. Don't go in without back up, do you hear me?" Ashley paused.

"Fenway."

"Yes, Sir," she said, knowing she wouldn't do anything of the sort.

"Right, I'll swing by the office first and see what you put together. I'm trusting you on this, so bring him in so we can question him."

"Will do, Sir," Ashley said, ending the call.

Chapter 80

Ashley pulled up outside Donaldson's house. Being a lawyer and deputy mayor had been good to him. It looked like a large farmhouse with bright brickwork and a large iron gate at the front.

Ashley pulled up and got out of the car. She opened the boot and pulled out a taser, checking that it had its charge. Ashley walked over to the iron gate and looked in the drive. There was only one car in the drive. Surely, he and his wife had two cars? Ashley looked up at the top floor and saw a light on in the house with the curtains drawn.

Ashley looked through the bars, thinking about what McArthur said about waiting for backup. Ashley looked up at the drawn curtains. What if something was going on in there right now?

Ashley made her mind up, she walked to the wall. There must be some sort of security system at the front. Ashley cursed under her breath. She grabbed the gate and shook it, trying to get some attention from it. Ashley tried to pull it and it gave a little. Ashley looked down at the end and saw that it had given away.

She could fit through that. Ashley got her foot through and went to push through. It was tight, but... Ashley took her coat off and sucked her stomach in. She pushed and fell through the gap onto the drive. Ashley groaned, breathing deeply. She picked herself up and wormed her other leg through. Ashley got to her feet, pulled her coat back on, jogged up to the front door and gently tried it. Locked.

Ashley looked up at the windows to see if any of them were open. Nothing. She jogged around to the back of the house which was as well-lit up as the front. There was a swimming pool on the patio and a large garden with a small football pitch on it. Ashley though was looking up at the windows which were all closed. Ashley crept over to a set of patio doors. She leaned against the wall and peered inside.

It looked like the kitchen and dining room, which was partly lighted from a light in the entrance hall. Ashley went to look round further when she saw someone coming. Ashley leaned back up against the wall. What if that was Donaldson, or the killer, or someone else? Ashley breathed deeply, held her breath and looked around.

She was looking into a large dining room with an oak table and chairs, which were just visible in the darkness. Ashley looked beyond the room to what looked like the entrance hall. Ashley tried to look round into the kitchen but there wasn't anyone there. As she went to move, she saw a shadow coming down the stairs.

Ashley shot back round. She couldn't hear the person but could see their shadow because of the light. It looked like they had gone into the kitchen. The light turned off.

Ashley watched the shadow go into the dining room and stop. She dared her luck and looked around the corner.

"Damn."

She knew that face. She leaned back around the corner, blinking to make sure the light wasn't playing tricks on her. She looked back round.

Kate Marsh was in the dining room inspecting a blade in the light, but she had blonde hair not brown. Maybe she was wearing a wig… or maybe she had been blonde all along. Something snapped in Ashley's head.

"I have a twelve-year-old in there."

The blonde woman from the Cambrian, at the end of the hall.

That's what she had said to Ashley at The Cambrian; she had been there as well. She hadn't recognised her with her blonde hair. It all made sense; that's why Kate had seemed so familiar when Ashley had gone to her house and seen her with blonde hair in that picture at her house.

Ashley had bloody interviewed her. She'd interviewed her twice!

Ashley took a deep breath to gather her thoughts; this made sense now. Kate must have been at Limehouse while Ferrets was there. All that bullshit about moving on was just an act.

Ashley looked back through the patio door. Kate was walking towards the entrance hall. Now was her chance.

Ashley pulled the door back, walked into the dining room and closed the door as quietly as she could. Ashley walked through the dining room and into the dark, living room to the staircase in the large entrance hall.

Ashley tested the step which thankfully wasn't creaky. Her years of sneaking in back home were finally paying dividends as she walked up the staircase.

She got to the landing, her heart thundering in her ears, feeling as if it wanted to run out and leave her behind. Ashley could hear voices from one side of the house. Ashley turned her head to one of the long corridors going to the right of the house. The sound was coming through the door, so was muffled. She couldn't hear what they were saying.

Ashley walked forward slowly, not wanting to give herself away with heavy footsteps. As she got closer, she could hear the voices a little more clearly.

"Who are you? What do you want?" Donaldson.

"Huh, I guess guys and lawyers really don't remember all the people they've screwed," Kate retorted.

Ashley inched herself closer to the door. When she was close enough Ashley stood in front of it and took another deep breath. Preparing herself for whatever lay beyond that door.

Ashley pulled her taser out and kicked the door down which broke in one kick.

"POLICE! HANDS IN THE AIR!" Ashley shouted.

Donaldson was tied up on the bed like the others. Kate was standing beside him with the knife on his chest. Donaldson though was spluttering.

"Thank god officer, this crazy bitch was going to kill me!"

"I wouldn't call her that," Ashley said. Her stare fixed on Kate. "She's still the one with the knife."

"Besides, I know what you are, and I have the proof. You're going away for a long time."

"You." She pointed at Kate with her taser. "Get away from him."

Kate looked furiously at Ashley.

"You're going to put the knife down and come with me." Kate smiled.

"You remember me now, don't you?" Kate said.

"I remember. Maybe you should have come clean then."

"And miss out on all this?" Kate said, with a smile. "Getting my revenge."

"That sounds like admittance of guilt," Ashley shot back. "But... I found what you left behind."

"Left behind?" Kate said round a disbelieving laugh. "What are you talking about?"

"The pictures, the hard drive. You wanted to be found," Ashley said. Kate looked perplexed.

"You really don't know anything, do you?" Kate said, shaking her head. "I didn't want you to find anything. I was looking for those damn pictures myself!" Ashley frowned.

"What? Then..."

"I was his muse, you, stupid bitch," she said. "I was the one who always seemed to be the centre of his attention." She shook her head. "He used to take 'special photos' of me for him and his friends. I'm not surprised he kept them to himself. You didn't honestly think I wanted my body to be viewed by more perverts, did you?" Ashley shook her head. Kate looked down. "You've seen them then."

"Yes."

"And that's what led you to him," she said, pointing the knife at Donaldson. "You saw him in the pictures."

"Officer, whatever she's saying she's lying!"

"Shut, up!" Ashley said at him. "I saw him in the photos, but I followed the paper trail to him. They all used him as a lawyer to cover it up. The photos just confirmed why he did it." Kate laughed to herself lightly.

"You're a clever one," she said. "I didn't even think about that." Kate nodded. "So, you saw what they did to me?" She said, a slight crack in her voice.

"Yes."

"Then you know why I'm doing this then," she said, pulling the knife out and pointing it at him. "You know why I did it to all of them." Ashley didn't say anything, not wanting to emphasise or condone right away.

"I'm really sorry for all you've gone through," Ashley said.

"I don't need your pity!" She spat back. "I want revenge, justice!"

"Look, you can still have that and finish this amicably," Ashley said. "Just, put the knife down, come with me, and we can —"

"We can what? Let the system go through due process?" She laughed humourlessly. "I've been let down by the system before." Kate looked down at Donaldson.

"I have this son of a bitch to thank for that," she said. "So no, this has gone too far for due process to get all the credit."

"You don't mean that." Kate smiled, a small curl at the side of her mouth.

"That's the thing," she said, with a slight smile. "I do."

She slashed Donaldson across the chest and jumped over the bed, with the knife from the kitchen raised in her hand. Ashley got her arm across her to stop Kate from stabbing her. The force however sent her back onto the windowsill. Ashley hit her lower arm on it; she grunted and fell to one knee while Kate went to jab at her. Ashley deflected the blow onto the sill, but she felt a searing pain in her left arm which made her scream.

Kate had now got up, satisfied that she'd hurt Ashley sufficiently and ran off.

Ashley forced herself to her feet, holstered her taser and made for the door.

"Officer, are you going to get me out of here?" Ashley looked back over her shoulder at Donaldson, who had a scandalous look on his face.

"You'll live. Police should be here in a moment," Ashley panted, she bolted from the room with Donaldson shouting after her. Ashley ran down the stairs to the entrance where she heard a car door slam. Ashley ran to the front door and opened it out into the night where she saw the Range Rover in the drive shoot off through the open gates.

Ashley grunted and ran over towards the open gate to her own car, which she got into and drove off after her. She could already see blues and twos coming up to the house. Ashley pressed on the police radio.

"This is DC Ashley Fenway! 1701. I am in hot pursuit of a suspect's vehicle in a residential area, does anyone copy!" Marsh overtook the car in front. Ashley banged on her blues and twos.

"This is dispatch, DC Fenway, what's the suspect driving?"

"It's a white Range Rover Evoque sport!" Ashley said, driving past a car that had pulled over.

"License plate?"

"Hotel, Victor, Six, Seven, Alpha, Indigo, Golf."

"Copy that. Where is the suspect heading?"

"Suspects heading—" Ashley swerved out of the way of an oncoming car.

"Suspects heading south through Didsbury heading towards Kenworthy Woods.

"Copy that, help is en route."

"Copy."

Ashley pressed the button on the steering wheel that brought up her contacts.

"DCI McArthur!" She shouted, as her tyres screeched. The central console on the car showed the blue phone and blue dots going in circles. Ashley took the corner at the end of the road sharply and sped off.

"Fenway, how did Donaldson's house go?"

"She's on the run!" Ashley said.

"What?" McArthur said confused. "She?"

"Yes, it's a woman. Big fucking shock!" Ashley said, trying to keep the Range Rover in her eyesight. "I couldn't wait for back up."

"Ashley."

"Listen!" Ashley shouted. "She was about to murder him, I had to go in!"

"Right, not important."

"It was Kate Marsh!" Ashley shouted. "She's the person behind it all, get a unit to her house to cut her off!"

"Yes, Fenway, what about Donaldson?" McArthur asked, not sure what was going on.

"He's tied up."

"Figuratively?"

"Literally," Ashley said, running a red light to blaring car horns. "And the woman is on the run!"

"Wait, are you chasing her?"

"Right now!" Ashley said, taking a roundabout short and going onto the dual carriageway.

"Right, Parland is en-route to the house, I'm calling in support for you. Don't let her out of your sight."

"Yes, Sir," Ashley said, ending the call and speeding off after her. The Range Rover was weaving in and out of traffic on the carriageway. Ashley did the same, zigzagging through the cars as well. The Range Rover cut across the two lanes and went up the turn off.

"Dammit." Ashley did the same to more horn-blaring and followed the Range Rover down a pitch-black country road. Ashley put the BMW in sport mode, instantly felt the power in the engine and put her foot down to eat up the distance. The Range Rover began to build up more speed.

The Range Rover took another sharp turn which made Ashley do the same thing. In the distance Ashley could see a level crossing. Just as she noticed it the barriers started going down.

"No, no, don't do it. Don't even think about it," Ashley said to herself. Just as the barrier went down the Range Rover narrowly went under it and did the same on the other side, spinning out of control. Ashley braked hard and skidded across the road. Ashley reversed the steering, the tyres screeched to a halt and span so she was facing the wrong way, just as a coal train came down the tracks. Ashley breathed deeply and got out of her car.

The train that sounded like it was thundering was only slowly making its way across the tracks. Ashley walked forward, the blue light of the blues and twos lighting the way in front of her. She leaned forward on the barrier. She looked up through the gaps of the cars and saw the white Range Rover start up again and drive off up the road.

Ashley radioed dispatch, told them where she was and that Marsh had got away.

She had lost her. She had to phone McArthur. Ashley picked her phone out of her pocket and dialled him.

"Ashley?"

"I lost her," Ashley said. "She jumped over a level crossing." There was a pause. Ashley was thinking that he was going to shout at her for losing her.

"I'm sorry," she said.

"For what? Fenway, you've blown this case wide open."

"For not following her."

"And saving me the trouble of scraping you off the train tracks. Fenway, you did good, we have Donaldson by the short and curlies and we have him in custody. We can regroup and go again." Ashley nodded and made her way to her car.

"I don't even know where I am?" Ashley said, sitting in her car looking round. "And I might have jumped a couple of red lights."

"We'll worry about that later," McArthur said. "Look, go home now, there's not much else we can do. You can help with the questioning of Donaldson tomorrow and we'll try and extract some info from him. She won't hide for long. See you in the morning."

"Yeah, goodnight," Ashley said round a yawn, the night catching up with her. She placed her phone down and winced, she looked down at her arm which was starting to feel numb. Great, she sprained it. Ashley walked to the boot of her car and got out the first aid kit as well as her road atlas. She sat in the car, turned on the internal light and fashioned herself a wrist support out of tubular bandage. After clenching her fist to test it she checked the road atlas because 'You can't rely on your phone all the time,' her dad used to say.

Ashley looked at the last road she knew she was on and tried to work her way back from there. She followed the road up to the roundabout and down the country lane, scanning for a turn off as well as a level crossing. Finally, the two intersected and that's where she was.

Ashley was planning a route back in her head. As strange as it sounded the shortest way was to go over the level crossing and double back on herself. Heck, she might even get a trace as to where Kate went.

Ashley consulted the map and looked at the road ahead. She would have had to take the route Ashley was planning and either join the main road and go back to Manchester, or maybe go up further into the countryside. Ashley followed the road up into the countryside and saw the road connected at Limehurst.

Ashley frowned. Limehurst, that wasn't far away from the shell of Limehouse. Ashley leaned back into her car seat. This couldn't be a coincidence. Ashley started her car and turned in the road, so she was facing the now deserted level crossing and revved the engine before driving off into the night.

Chapter 81

Normally Ashley would drive a little faster down these sort of country roads, but right now she was driving at nearly thirty trying to get a glimpse of a white Range Rover. Ashley knew she was getting close to Limehouse. If Kate still had any sense left, she would have dumped the car with it being stolen and too hot to handle.

But all Ashley could think about was how she let Kate slip away from her. If the press got wind of that it would be a PR disaster, letting her slip through their fingertips so easily. It might have been the tiredness, but all Ashley could think about was that it was still her fault, even though McArthur said that it wasn't.

Ashley just hoped that Kate would try and come back to finish Donaldson off so they could get a second attempt.

Ashley continued her drive towards Limehouse but found it more difficult in the darkness.

Ashley saw its towers in the distance first and slowed down. She drove past the gates which were open, and in the drive, was a battered Range Rover. Ashley drove on a little longer and pulled into a layby. Ashley wanted the element of surprise, so she was going to walk back. Ashley phoned McArthur.

"I thought I told you to go home," he said.

"I was. I found her again."

"You did."

"Oh yeah."

"Where?" Ashley took a deep breath.

"Limehouse."

"You're shitting me," McArthur said. "You're sure?"

"I can see the car she stole in the drive of Limehouse," Ashley explained. "I'm going to go in there right now before you send the cavalry up here."

"No, no, Fenway, no."

"You can't talk me out of this," Ashley said. "If she sees the blues and twos she bolts, and we never find her again. If I can at least keep her talking you can surround her."

"Come with the cavalry, keep it quiet, that's what you're saying," McArthur said.

"It's as good an idea as any," Ashley replied.

He sighed. "The overtime bill's going to be horrendous."

"You have to break a few eggs to make an omelette," Ashley said, getting out of the car and opening the boot.

"This one would feed the five thousand," McArthur replied, as Ashley got out a box of zip ties. She got a few out and put them in her pocket.

"You might just have to do that too," Ashley said, closing the boot and starting to walk back down the road. "You know what coppers are like on an empty stomach." McArthur went quiet.

"If anything happens, phone me," he said. "And be careful. She's not afraid to kill."

"I'll be fine." Ashley ended the call, put her hands in her jacket pocket, walked to the open gate and gently pushed it open. She stepped into the entrance drive and looked up at the manor house which looked decrepit in the darkness. The lack of light giving it an eerie feel that it shouldn't be disturbed.

Ashley walked over to the Range Rover and saw the damage. She pulled the driver door open quietly and inspected the seat. No blood but a thin layer of sweat on the leather seats. Ashley left the door open and walked up to the front door of the house, which was partially open.

Ashley placed her hand on it and opened it to a large creaking sound that reverberated around the deserted entrance hall.

"Really," Ashley muttered to herself. She looked up at the grand staircase at the centre of the hall, wondering what it must have looked to people coming in at the time. It must have been a grand, old house for other like-minded people. A fresh challenge, a new start. Ashley pulled out some zip ties and zipped the doors together. If Kate was going to try and get out, she would have to make a noise.

Ashley remained quiet, trying to hear any sounds which might give this woman away. But the house betrayed nothing. Ashley knew she was at a disadvantage coming onto her turf; Kate knew the best places to hide.

Ashley walked up the staircase which creaked with every one of her steps. Ashley pulled a frustrated face as she made her way up. She got to the top where the open space landing went in a U shape around, with two corridors at either end which led to other parts of the house.

Ashley went with her gut and turned left. She had gone right in Donaldson's house. Ashley pulled out her taser and walked down the corridor which still had some of its grand architecture but was stained green by years of neglect and decay. Ashley pulled her phone out and turned the torch on so she could at least see where she was going.

Ashley walked past one of the room's doors, that were exposed. She heard the clocking of a shot gun. Ashley dived across as the shell shattered the top of the door frame. The splinters of wood flying down onto the floor as Ashley scrambled up to the wall.

"Fucking hell!" She breathed.

Ashley took a couple of deep breaths to calm herself, but her heart was beating wildly in her chest. The silence was thick, both knowing their game of hide and seek was over. Ashley looked up at the top of the door frame which had a large hole in the top with lots of little splinters of wood becoming clearer from the clearing of smoke.

"It's all right."

Ashley's head turned towards the door. Kate's voice was as calm as it had been in the house. Ashley waited to hear if she was about to talk again.

"All right?" Ashley shouted. "You almost shot me!"

"There are only two shells," Kate said, calmly. "One's already in the door, and the other is meant for something else." Ashley pulled her phone out, opened the camera and set it to a selfie setting, (the only time it was useful in her eyes) and gingerly placed it around the corner. From the screen she could see Kate sitting cross legged on a metal bed with a sawn-off shotgun resting at the base of her chin looking out the window.

This was not how Ashley wanted this to go down. There were far too many variables to consider now that this woman had a weapon and she didn't. Ashley pulled her phone back.

"Are you sure you're not going to put the other one in me?" Ashley asked.

"No," Kate said. "This was always how this was supposed to end. Even with the new beginning I was still going to end it all here."

"New beginning?" Ashley asked.

"Kate Marsh isn't my real name," she said. "I changed it after I escaped this place. I wanted a new start. It was the first thing I changed."

"So, what is your name?" Ashley asked.

"Lisa," she said, finally. "My name is Lisa Strachan." That name, the woman who made the complaint against the New Agers originally, and possibly the name that Stan called out when he was with prostitutes. The woman in the photos.

"Can I come in and talk to you?" Ashley asked. "No tricks, just talk, a conversation."

"Why do you want to talk?" She asked. "What can we possibly talk about?"

"I want to know why," Ashley said.

"You have the evidence, you know why," Lisa said. Ashley closed her eyes.

"I need some more details," Ashley said. "I have the bare bones. I need some more meat on it. I thought you were leaving me clues but you weren't." Lisa said nothing. She needed a different approach.

"You need to tell me what happened."

"There's a note in here that explains all that," Lisa said. Bingo.

"It would be better if you told me," Ashley said.

"And why's that?"

"Suicide notes can be dismissed at trial," Ashley explained. "But if you have that and the word of a police officer, then Donaldson will certainly go away." Ashley heard a whimper.

"He's not dead then?"

"Ambulance came afterwards," Ashley told her. "He's on his way to hospital now." There was another silence.

"You should have let him die," Lisa said. "If you only knew the things he did to me, you would watch him bleed out and smile."

"Well he's not," Ashley said. "And since you've decided that the other shell is for you, you need to make sure he's not going to get away with it."

"You should have let him die. Problem solved."

"But he's not dead," Ashley said. "And the only way we're going to make sure he never gets out and never does this again is to get the facts from the horse's mouth." Lisa went silent, all Ashley could hear from the room was the slight concealment of a whimper.

"Do you have a pen and paper?" She asked. Ashley breathed easier.

"Better," Ashley said, putting her phone out into the room. "This has a tape recorder on it. We'll be able to talk about what happened. No jury will dismiss this." Lisa didn't say anything.

"So, what do you say? Can we talk this over?"

"So *now* the police want to talk," Lisa said, shaking her head at the irony. "Why should I talk to you? From what I've seen and heard, people think I have the right idea about what to do with these bastards."

"Some of those men have families," Ashley said. "What about them having justice?" Lisa laughed loudly. A cold laugh that was still full of humour.

"Justice!?" She asked. "What about my justice! What about all the things that happened to me! Where's my justice for that!" She panted heavily. "I'll tell you where it is, in the slit throats of those bastards! That's my justice because the law decided that my word was worth jack shit! So, don't talk to me about justice! I've seen and experienced what happens to us, the victims. You just want us to crawl back into the woodwork and get over it! Well, some of us never get over it! You can never just, get over it! All we want is for the system to give us justice so we can try and get on with our lives, but we can't even get that! So, where's my justice? Huh? Where is my justice?"

She's right, Ashley said to herself. The system wasn't the most favourable to victims; this was just a story of one woman pushed to the very edge who needed closure on the unspeakable crimes committed against her. And she was right about the consensus on her actions. People admired her for taking the law into her own hands and were supporting her; but she was in the wrong to. It made her think back to Emma Curtis, two people moulded by tragedy but had gone to two such different extremes, and that's what made it hard. How can you reason with someone's actions when the whole world thinks they're right?

"I'm sorry for what happened to you, I really am," Ashley said. "And I can't turn back the clock to make all this right, but if you talk to me you can still at least get justice from Donaldson."

"So just like that, I should believe in the system now?" Lisa said round a laugh.

"Since he's still alive that's your only option," Ashley said. Lisa didn't say anything for a while, Ashley was praying that the shotgun didn't go off, waiting for a response.

"OK," Lisa said, softly. "Come in." Ashley pulled her phone back and holstered her taser. She breathed deeply and went into the room. Lisa's eyes following her like a hawk the entire time. Ashley saw a metal chair in the corner, dragged it over to the middle of the room and sat down. Lisa shuffled on the bed and took her finger off the trigger.

"Right," Ashley said. "I'll put this on, what you have to do is explain who you are and that you're doing this of your own free will. Is that OK?" Lisa nodded.

"OK." Ashley pointed her phone at Lisa and pressed record. She pointed at Lisa as her cue to go.

"My name is Lisa Strachan," she said. "I want the world to know, that I'm doing this of my own free will, and am not doing so under any duress." She swallowed. "I want Harold Donaldson to pay for his crimes and this is the only way I can do that now."

"My name is DC Ashley Fenway with the Manchester Major Crimes unit, seeing this recording."

Lisa looked up at Ashley to ask her a question.

"When did this all start?" Ashley asked. Lisa smiled while closing her eyes and nodded.

"Simple really," she said. "My parents bought me and my brother here in the summer of seventy-nine. They both weren't right in the head. They gave up our house and savings to come and live here as part of the 'New Agers'." Lisa's voice dripped with contempt.

"I was old enough to know that this was wrong and that I didn't want to do it." She looked round the room with a nostalgic look.

"And this is where we stayed," she said. "My parents had the bed while me and my brother slept on the floor. Children were meant to be seen and not heard round here. And willing to do what any adult told them to. Discipline was everything to them. One foot out of line and you were beaten to within an inch of your life." Ashley nodded.

"So, they made a culture of fear?" She asked. Lisa nodded. "When did the abuse start?" Lisa took her hand off the gun and pointed down to the bed.

"Here," she said. "What the New Agers didn't put in their pamphlet was that it encouraged inbreeding. Parents were encouraged to engage in relations with their children as a means of keeping the family close together."

"How old were you?"

"Ten," she said. "During the day we would work out in the fields as a way of earning our meals. At night... well, you can guess what happened to all of us." Ashley nodded.

"What about Donaldson and the others?" Ashley asked. "When did that start?" Lisa composed herself.

"When we worked out in the fields some of us were chosen to help the cult elders with 'special projects'. Of course, with the threat of a beating if we didn't obey, we did everything they told us to." Lisa's eyes and stare hardened. The ghosts of her past playing before her eyes as a broken tragedy. She looked down.

"They knew people through the underground paedophile network in Manchester; they hosted rape parties here for anyone who paid big money for the privilege. That's how I met them; they would video me and take photographs of me for..." She trailed off.

"You know what, I don't know," Lisa paused. "I never thought to ask."

"Donaldson was one who took a particular liking to me," Lisa explained. "He would pay extra for me and him to have one on one sessions with that pervert Whikley taking the photos of us." Ashley nodded.

"Thompson said that I was the biggest money maker in that house. Apparently, they liked my hair." She looked up at a loose bang.

"Strange really what they choose to focus on."

"What about the others?" Ashley asked. "Why them?"

"They, along with Donaldson, were their own little gang," Lisa explained. "Ferrets used to come in and give us sports training but was really there to see little girls and boys in tight clothes get sweaty. Kettings was the postman who would always leer at us when he came to deliver the huge wads of cash to the house. He was also responsible for delivering what we made to other paedophiles in the area. With his job it wasn't suspicious at all and they used to pay him with his pick of who he wanted."

"Oatley?"

"The landlord came in and strutted around like he owned the place. He would rape me in this room and brag to my family while he did it." The painful memory flashed before her again.

"Out of all of them he changed the least," she said. "He was still a cocky bastard, bragging about how he was still abusing kids even now. He struggled the most," Lisa said, narrowing her eyes slightly. "But in the end..."

"And Whikley? You said you were his muse." Lisa nodded.

"He met me at an orgy," Lisa explained. "He wasn't abusing, he was taking pictures for the rest of them. He told me that he wasn't like the rest. He told me that he could take me away from here." Lisa looked down at the bed.

"At the time I thought he was different. But in the end, he was just like the rest of them. Manipulating me for their own twisted gains." She breathed out. "Instead of abusing me in a group he had me all to himself and his camera." Lisa looked back at Ashley.

"That's what kills you in places like this. The hope. The hope of a better life.

"That's why I wanted to find those pictures, to start afresh. It felt like he was still holding them over me after all those years."

"He kept one of you in his house," Ashley said, now knowing who that girl in the photo was.

"Dick," Lisa said, shaking her head. "Even all these years later and he still thought I was his."

"What did you want to do with those pictures?" Ashley asked.

"I wanted them to destroy them. I looked all over his house and found nothing. Where did you find them?"

"In a floorboard under his bed," Ashley said. Lisa nodded.

"Good place to hide."

"You said back at the house that Donaldson had stopped you getting justice before," Ashley said. "What did you mean by that?"

"When I was sixteen, I left, got all my stuff and bolted in the night," Lisa explained; she breathed out.

"I left my brother in here," she said, looking round the room. "But... I had to get out, I couldn't stand it anymore, I didn't care where I went, I just left."

"Where did you go?"

"I slept rough for a couple of weeks," she explained. "I had to do what I had to, to survive." Lisa shuddered at the memory. "Then I was taken in by an abused women's shelter. I told them my story and they started proceedings against the New Agers."

"And Donaldson was their lawyer," Ashley finished. Lisa looked over at her and nodded.

"It went to trial. They thought my testimony was enough, but that bastard fucked me over; told the magistrates that I was some crack addicted whore who was making up a story for the money.

"Had to do what I had to, to survive." Ashley bowed her head, barely able to believe that someone had gone through such a life.

"He fucked me over in more ways than one," Lisa said. "That's why I wanted to get him last. So, I knew that I would be able to go through with it; not have the first-time nerves."

"When did the killing start?" Ashley asked. What was the point of beating round the bush?

"By accident," Lisa said. "After the court case I became half of what Donaldson said I was." She looked over at Ashley who quirked an eyebrow.

"A whore," she clarified. "It was all I knew what to do, well, that and farming, and there were no farmers taking on girls."

"My family would have," Ashley said. Lisa looked over at her. "My parents own a farm," she clarified.

"Really?" Lisa asked. Genuinely curious. "What kind?"

"Dairy," Ashley said with a smile. "We also keep other animals as well and sell hay in the summer." Lisa smiled.

"That was the dream," Lisa said, looking out the window at the darkness. "To leave this all behind and live on a farm where I could go out in the fields and just walk amongst the corn." She smiled sadly.

"But, one day I had a request from a client that one of the other girls usually dealt with, but she was in the slammer. He wanted someone young-looking; not uncommon. Anyway, I went to this guy's house and when he opened the door, I couldn't believe who it was."

"Thompson." Lisa nodded. She frowned slightly.

"Even all these years later I…" Her anger was getting the better of her. "I thought when he opened that door, I thought he would at least… recognise me," Lisa said, shaking her head. "Remember my face, or at least see the likeness." She laughed a little. "But he didn't. I thought of nothing else for years, about how he abused and wronged me, took everything away from me." Lisa breathed deeply to compose herself.

"And I was literally nothing to him," she said, looking down. "He never gave me another thought after all those years, not wondered what happened to his star attraction, his money maker." Lisa shook her head.

"I was frozen, but he invited me in." She shuddered at the thought. "I didn't know what else to do, I needed the money." Ashley nodded.

"He took me into the kitchen and bragged about how he was a big shot somebody at some company," Lisa explained. "As soon as I walked in, I saw the knife block. I just wanted to grab one and hurt him, tell him all the things that were in my head."

"He was found in the bedroom." Lisa nodded.

"After he finished bragging about how great he was, he led me upstairs," Lisa explained. "I'd taken a knife from the kitchen and hid it in my purse; I wasn't sure what I was going to do with it, but I just wanted something to defend myself with."

"So, you went upstairs."

"He took me in the bedroom and wanted me to wear one of those stupid gown things they used to make us wear up at the house." Lisa shook her head. "I swore that when I left that house, I would never wear it again. It just brought back all those painful nights being raped by them: Thompson, my father, the other kids in the house. It made me angry that my life had been reduced to this; about to screw the man who made my life hell, again, after vowing not to, because I didn't have a choice." Lisa breathed deeply to regain some composure.

"I went into the bathroom to put it on and slipped the knife up my sleeve." She looked down.

"I felt it then."

"Felt what?" Ashley asked.

"That urge…" Lisa said, looking back up at the window. "That urge to right the wrongs that were done to me."

"And that resulted in killing him?" Ashley asked. Lisa laughed to herself.

"You've never had something really bad done to you, have you?" Lisa said, looking over at Ashley. "You've not had someone change your life simply for their sick, twisted needs."

"No, I haven't," Ashley admitted.

"If you're ever unfortunate enough to experience that, you'll have an urge inside you for revenge," she said, looking back outside. "Logic and reason are the first virtues to walk out the door, it seems the only logical option. And at that time and that place, killing him was the only logical option, because I knew what a monster he was. If I had run away, he would have known something was up, and he might have recognised me. He used to keep girls as his personal slaves for weeks on end in the house, myself included. At least there I knew it would end, but out in the real world I couldn't take that chance.

"When I walked out, he was laid down on his bed, like he was some sort of god that needed to be worshiped." Lisa went quiet.

"Was he expecting it?" Ashley asked, trying to break the silence. She paused.

"No," Lisa replied. "I don't think he was." Another silence.

"Were you?" Lisa thought for a moment.

"No, it just… happened." Ashley could see Lisa replaying all that had happened in her mind.

"We walked into the bedroom and he turned to face me, then… I just saw red and attacked him. I slashed him across the neck with the knife." She mimicked the motion slowly with her hand.

"I remember watching him struggle for air while all the blood came out," she explained. "It was almost like he was suffocating the way he heaved. I thought I would feel guilt, remorse, something." Lisa paused for a moment to compose herself.

"But then I leaned down to talk to him, as his skin turned white, and the life was slowly leaving his eyes. And I told him the thing he always used to tell me during our sessions," Lisa smiled to herself.

"Here comes the money shot," she said softly. She breathed out.

"I like to think he knew then," she said. "Just a little spark in his eyes before the life left them; they went wide, more fearful than they already were. Then he knew his sins had finally caught up with him." Lisa went quiet again.

"I think he thought he was above dying," she said, finally. "He probably thought that he would somehow survive. That he was too good to be taken away." She laughed softly to herself.

"He got his comeuppance."

"What did you do with the weapon?"

"I scrubbed it down along with every other one in that block," Lisa said. "I changed back into my clothes and left. I thought that the police would try and at least figure out who did it, but they saw him for what he was too. I'm not even sure how long it was before he was discovered but it got me thinking."

"About who else there was."

"There are thousands of paedophiles and rapists in this country," Lisa said. "They're always where you least expect to find them but they're there. But also, the disdain there is for people like them; the police or the public wouldn't care if they all died tomorrow. But I knew the ones I wanted to see in the ground."

"If it was so easy, why such a long gap?" Ashley asked.

"Application is more difficult than identifying," Lisa said. "I located all of them, I watched them, studied their routines."

"For all those years?"

"No," Lisa said. "I tried various methods to try and lure them. I even tried to kidnap Ferrets at one point." Ashley thought back to the complaint that Ferrets had made about someone trying to kidnap him.

"Did that include Ferrets' civil case?" Ashley asked. "He wouldn't have been able to have assaulted you under the Kate Marsh alias," Ashley continued. "Your statement to it said that he assaulted you after a night of underage drinking." Lisa laughed.

"I lied," she said. "At that point I still thought that the system could help me. I found out through a mutual friend. All I did was make up the story and they all believed me, even the lawyer who was supposed to check it found proof of it somehow."

"So, they just added you on?" Ashley asked.

"Who was going to call me a liar? It would have compromised the entire case," Lisa explained. "In the end Donaldson got him off and my faith in the system was broken. I tried other things as well, but no matter what I tried I couldn't get close enough to them like I did Thompson," she said. "Over the years I lost track of what they were all doing," she admitted.

"So how did you do it?"

"I was working at The Jasmines Glass." Jasmines Glass was a notorious gentleman's club in Manchester which was run by the Tunnicliffe family, who were the biggest crime family in the north west. When Ashley first joined the Police, she was approached by an 'Agent' of the Glass who asked if she wanted to earn some extra money on the side. One swift kick to the balls later he got his answer, but she always treated the place with trepidation.

"As what?"

"A stripper," Lisa said. "I was able to charge more for my body that way, and I got to choose who touched me." Lisa looked over at Ashley who was still recording her.

"That's when I had my idea."

"Which was?"

"I didn't have anything that they wanted," Lisa said. "So, I created a scenario that even they would have trouble refusing. An agent that had children to abuse on a whim, almost like how Thompson was with us. Anyone like them would jump at the chance."

"What about your daughter?" Ashley asked.

"She's not aware of it," Lisa said.

"Is her father aware of it?"

"Her father doesn't want anything to do with her," Lisa explained. "He's high up in the Manchester underworld. In return for not claiming child support, I asked for a favour when the time was right."

"You wanted information on Ferrets and co," Ashley finished. Lisa nodded.

"And it worked. He gave me their addresses, what they did and used some computer stuff to show me what those bastards were still up to."

"Why use the game?" Ashley asked.

"That was my daughter's doing," Lisa said. "She was using it when one of those creeps was on it and tried to contact her."

"Kettings?" She nodded.

"It seemed like a good idea to arrange meetings on it because no one would think to look on there." It made sense Ashley thought, and it had worked.

"So, I started talking to them, tell them about who I was and the willing participants. The benefits of bringing them to a secure location just to get close to them."

"Gave them an offer that was too good to be true," Ashley said. Lisa nodded.

"After the fall of Limehouse I'd be betting that they didn't have the chance to abuse another child so readily. Turns out I was right; they were more than willing."

"Ferrets was found at a hotel while the rest were found at home, why was that?" Ashley asked. "Ferrets had his own home?"

"The hotel was his idea," Lisa said. "He said that he didn't want his neighbours to be suspicious because of the rumours about him. Smart idea. It would be more difficult for me, but I worked around it." Ashley nodded.

"And evade me," she said. "I told my DI that the killer should stay at the hotel. We were too busy looking at people who left."

"Because killers don't want to stick around after a crime," Lisa said, with a smile. "Staying put was the right choice."

"This might shock you, but the coroner thought we were looking for a man," Ashley said. Lisa laughed.

"Christ, were you in the right place at the right time?" She asked. "Sneaking round Donaldson's place." Ashley smiled to herself.

"I found Ian Whikley's private collection of you," Ashley said. "I didn't know it was you, but it showed Donaldson as well. I thought it would be best to get him into protective custody since I guessed you were after him next."

"And you backed it up with your... paper trail," Lisa finished. She nodded. "You are very smart."

"Thanks," Ashley said. "You are too if I'm honest. Is that everything?" Lisa nodded. Ashley turned the recording off.

"Not smart enough or I'd never have been caught," Lisa said. In the distance the sounds of sirens became more audible causing both women to look back at the door.

"I guess this is the end of the line," Lisa said, now looking out the window. She shuffled on the bed and readied the gun.

"Wait!" Ashley said, getting up with an outstretched arm.

"There's no use trying to talk me out of it," Lisa said. "I knew it would end like this. There's no other way it could end."

"There is."

"I'm a murderer," Lisa said with disdain. "All I have to look forward to is a life in prison now. They'll take Tammy away from me as well; that might not be a bad thing, she'll end up having a better life," Lisa paused. "And I'll no longer have the thirst for revenge."

Was that all she lived her life for; revenge? Rather than trying to turn her life around and make it better she was so consumed with revenge that she had now lost everything. Even her daughter. It was almost as if she didn't care anymore. It made Ashley pity her in a sense. She wasn't the person Ashley thought she was.

"So, what are you waiting for?" Ashley asked.

"The sunrise," Lisa said. "It's a small thing, but it's the one thing that I used to enjoy here. I just wanted to see it one last time." Ashley looked up at the window and saw the first rays of morning coming up.

"But your story only scratches the surface of what happened at Limehouse," Ashley implored. "What about all the other kids who

497

suffered abuse here, who lost their innocence too. You can help them find the justice you lost." Lisa was quiet, it was difficult to know what she was thinking. Ashley was afraid that she would just hear a gunshot ring out. She could also hear the police in the house.

"It can't end like this," Ashley said. "You could do so much more. People will listen to you."

"They won't," Lisa said, shaking her head. "I spent years trying to make people see what went on and they didn't want to know. They just wanted it buried along with the rest of us. No one wanted to listen to us."

"Who better to scare them then?" Ashley said. Lisa laughed and shook her head.

"Nice try. Someone else can, you have the story." Ashley looked down at the phone; it wasn't enough though. They had pictures but none that could place people in the here and now. Ashley breathed deeply. She needed to distract her to get the gun away.

"Do you want to hear a joke?" Ashley asked. Lisa looked over at her.

"A joke?"

"Yeah, a joke."

"Well they do say go out with a laugh," Lisa said, thoughtfully. "Go on." Ashley breathed deeply.

"Why are female serial killers so hard to catch?" Ashley asked. Lisa smirked to herself but thought for a moment.

"OK, why?"

"Because they know how to clean blood off every surface." Ashley wasn't sure if it was in good taste or faith, but Lisa was silent for a moment.

Lisa started to chuckle. Ashley could see her shoulder bouncing slightly. Then she started to laugh heartily, as did Ashley. They both looked at one another and continued to laugh as the sun started to come up. Ashley while still laughing, saw her chance.

She reached over and took the gun out of Lisa's hand and threw it across the room, while Lisa continued to laugh.

"Good move," Lisa chuckled. "Good move." Lisa sniffed and Ashley could see tears around her eyes. Ashley sat down on the bed and put her arm around Lisa who started to cry. They stayed silent for a while as the sun came up over the trees and laid sunlight down on the overgrown gardens.

"Ashley!" Ashley could hear McArthur's voice coming up the stairs. "Ashley are you OK?"

"I'm fine," she said. "You can come in." McArthur came in slowly and looked down at the shotgun. He looked over at Ashley and Lisa sitting on the bed looking up at the sunrise. He looked behind him and nodded and two uniform officers came into the room.

"Is it time to go?" Lisa asked. Ashley placed a reassuring hand on her leg.

"Yeah, it's time to go." Lisa breathed out, got to her feet and placed her hands behind her back. Ashley got her handcuffs out.

"Lisa Strachan, I'm arresting you for the murder of Dennis Thompson, Gordon Ferrets, Stanley Kettings, William Oatley and Ian Whikley. You do not have to say anything, but it may harm your defence if you do not mention when questioned, something which you later rely on in court. Anything you do say may be given in evidence. Do you understand?"

"I do," she said, as Ashley tightened the cuffs. Two uniformed officers took her and led her out of the room.

"Thank you," Lisa said, before she exited the room.

"For what?" Ashley asked.

"Listening," Lisa said, looking down. The officers led her out of the room while Ashley breathed deeply.

"Are you OK?" McArthur asked.

"I need a hot shower and a nap," Ashley said, running a hand through her hair. "Ow." She looked down at her arm.

"I think we need to get you to an ambulance; there's one outside," he said. "Then we need to talk about this." Ashley nodded and looked out the window at the sunrise.

Chapter 82

Ashley felt like she'd seen this scene before. She was sat in the back of an ambulance while looking at a building she hoped would burn down. The sun was rising over the spires of the house which lit up the mossy, green brickwork in a strange hue.

Word had spread through the night about what happened at Donaldson's house and subsequently here as well. There was now a large pool of reporters and news vans parked along the road. They were already at the house when Lisa was escorted out. Ashley could hear the jostling from inside and the questions they were asking her. It just made Ashley feel sorrier for her.

"Ow." Ashley looked at the paramedic who was touching her arm. "Could you please be a little more careful?"

"I think you've broken your arm," the paramedic said, looking at the bruised skin.

"Think, or know?" Ashley said rubbing her head, wanting nothing more than to just crawl into bed and stay there.

"I think you'll have to go in for an x-ray. How did you do it?"

"I fell over," Ashley replied. "Are you sure I need to go? I drove up here."

"Probably on adrenaline," the paramedic said. "Your boss said you winced when you moved and you're feeling pain."

"But it might not be broken?" Ashley asked.

"We won't know until you get an x-ray." Ashley didn't reply. "Right, well. Let's get you off then." Just as he finished McArthur came back from briefing the press. He walked towards her and stood next to her. He nodded at the paramedic to give them a minute.

"This seems vaguely familiar," he said.

"I was thinking that," Ashley agreed. "They think I've broken it," Ashley said, holding up her arm.

"x-rays?"

"The shower and nap are going to have to wait." She looked over at the pool of reporters who were stood by the gates. "What do they think?"

"Who cares?" McArthur said. "They'll probably say it's a travesty she was caught too soon. They don't know she was planning to stop."

"What about Donaldson?" Ashley asked.

"He's at the station sweating his bollocks off," McArthur said, with a small smile. "That stuff you left is enough to convict him. I've got Parland and Armstrong going through it now to make the case." Ashley nodded. It was a hollow victory in a sense. There wasn't a winner, only losers.

"What did you talk about?" McArthur asked. Ashley shook her head, took her phone out of her pocket and looked down at it.

"You might want to take the videos off this as well," she said. "What we talked about is on there." McArthur nodded. It was obvious to him that Ashley didn't want to talk there.

"Go get your arm sorted out," he told her. "First thing tomorrow, you need to come in for a debrief." Ashley nodded. McArthur sat down next to her.

"We failed them," Ashley said, looking up at the house. "She told me everything, she told the authorities everything and we all did nothing. We just wanted them all to forget and get on with their lives." They were both silent.

"She's right in a way." They both looked at each other. "Where was her justice for all the things that happened to her?"

"You know what, she probably was right," McArthur agreed. That surprised Ashley; he always seemed so above it. "That's the difficulty with this job sometimes. We can empathise too much with a criminal's cause and forget what the lines are." Ashley nodded. "You've seen the media. They think she should be knighted but we both know the slippery slope that leads to." Ashley nodded again.

"But we are the ones that reinforce those lines," McArthur said. "It seems harsh now knowing all she went through, but we have to consider

501

the families who want justice too. Two wrongs have never made a right. At the end of the day, she's a murderer."

"Half of the families think they're better off dead," Ashley said.

"That's why we're here. We can't rectify the mistakes of the past, but we can get justice for the here and the now," McArthur told her. "You going to come in tomorrow and help us wrap this up?" Ashley nodded.

"I need you to get my car too," she said, pulling out her keys and handing them to him.

"Where did you leave it?"

"In a layby down there," Ashley said, pointing down the road.

"Are we finally ready to go?" The paramedic asked. McArthur nodded and got to his feet while Ashley sat down on the bed. She looked up as McArthur closed the door.

***

Ashley got back home with her arm in a well-bandaged support and a little woozy from the painkillers she'd been given. It turned out she cracked her radius and was still able to play hockey. She clumsily opened her front door and let herself in.

She locked the door and leaned on it. She was tired; sleep deprived. Her stomach growled. And she was hungry.

"The vigilante killer known as the Manchester Maiden has been apprehended today after being cornered by police at the old, abandoned Limehouse manor which resulted in a tense stand-off."

"Hardly cornered," Ashley said, pushing herself off the door.

"It follows on when earlier in the evening a member of Manchester's new Major Crimes team foiled a suspected attack on Deputy Mayor Harold Donaldson at his home."

"DCI Donald McArthur, leading the case, stressed that they were still making enquiries and that a full statement would be made tomorrow after they had questioned Donaldson. Our northern affairs correspondent Jackie Quigley has more." Ashley walked across the living room to the back corner where her room was.

Ashley stripped to her knickers and a vest and sat down on the bed after closing the door. Ashley closed her curtains and laid down. The events of the last twelve hours or so running through her mind. She put her phone on charge and pulled the duvet round her, with Lisa Strachan's words going through her head like a twisted lullaby.

"Where is my justice?"

***

Lisa Strachan, my hero #notallheroswearcapes

Well done @GMP for finding who killed those monsters.

I was hoping they'd let her kill under supervision #winsomelosesome

The poor woman is as much a victim if not more so than the people she killed #prayforlisa

Hard to feel anything other than sympathy for Lisa Strachan after hearing her story. #prayforlisa.

All the millennials bleating on about sympathy, the woman is a killer and deserves the book to be thrown at her #shoveyoursympathy

Is this new @GMP Major Crimes Unit coming good? #devilsadvocate

After a few hours of restless sleep Ashley was woken by the buzzing of her phone. Ashley contemplated turning over and leaving it, but it might have been work. She reached over with her good arm to her bedside table and looked at her phone.

It was her mum. She sighed. Best get it over and done with now.

"Hi mum," Ashley said, turning over.

"Ashley are you OK?" She asked hurriedly. "I saw what happened on the news."

"Mum, I'm fine," Ashley tried to say.

"They said someone stopped that mad woman from killing the Mayor."

"Deputy Mayor."

"That he was bound and gagged!"

"Just bound." Though she would have liked to have gagged him.

"I mean after you rushed off the phone yesterday."

"I was in a rush."

"And that someone was taken to hospital."

"Yeah, that was me," Ashley said. Her mum breathed heavily down the other end of the phone.

"Honestly love, sometimes I can't deal with the stress." She was silent for a moment. "Are you hurt?"

"I cracked my radius," Ashley said. "Other than that, I'm fine. Save for a couple of hours sleep."

"Was that what you were doing?" She asked.

"Yeah, what time is it anyway?"

"Just after six. Jesus Ashley I've been worried sick."

"I meant to phone," Ashley said, sitting up in bed. "But everything happened so fast it passed my mind. I wanted to have a shower, but I've not been able to do that either."

"You caught her though." Ashley paused. Suddenly the memories of what happened becoming more vivid.

"Yeah, we caught her," Ashley said quietly, she could tell her mum had picked up on it.

"You don't seem very happy love?"

Ashley sighed. "It's one of those cases where no one wins mum," Ashley said. "I'm just really tired."

"Maybe you should come home for a few days," her mum said. That was a nice thought, go back to the farm, help her dad milk the cows and take Libby for a walk. But more than likely she would be dragged into helping her sister with her wedding plans.

"I still need to tie up stuff here," Ashley said. "Plus, I need something to eat and I can't be arsed cooking."

"Well I'm glad you're all right," she said. "Let me know if you change your mind about coming."

"I will mum. Love you."

"I love you too. Speak to you on Thursday. Bye."

"Bye." Ashley ended the call, leaned back on her pillows and checked how many missed calls she had; five off her mum along with a few texts, even a couple from Dan. Even though she felt like she could sleep for hours she forced herself out of bed. She put some short shorts on and walked into the living room where the radio was still playing, and the sun was slowly setting over the dock.

Ashley opened up Deliveroo and looked at the options, not wanting to think about how much time at the gym this would cost her. After ordering she sat down on her sofa and turned the TV on which was showing the tail end of the local weather, which meant the national news was going to start in a moment.

Out of the corner of her eye Ashley saw her board of the theory she had put together. Ashley walked over to it and looked at all the links she had made. Some had been right, others hilariously wrong now she looked back on it. She moved the board closer to the TV and started to rearrange the full picture as the news began to start.

'Office crisis in Manchester as the Deputy Mayor is caught up in the Manchester Maiden scandal.' The TV cut to a police van being driven away from his house with the paparazzi trying to photograph him. 'The deputy mayor has found himself at the mercy of the vigilante killer prowling Manchester as police finally apprehend the vigilante killer after she is caught fleeing his house, where she was caught at the original house of horrors.' The TV cut to Lisa Strachan's mugshot. Ashley noted that she was still a good-looking woman but there were noticeable lines on her face. 'Also, tonight.'

'A descendant of Limehouse. Others come out to speak about the abuse they suffered at the same place as the Manchester Maiden and why was nothing done before?' The screen cut to a man who was in his living room telling a reporter how bad it was.

"You have no idea," Ashley said to herself. Ashley wrote Harold Donaldson's name on the board and wrote down the links he had with the other four. To her surprise they were dedicating a lot of time to Lisa's capture; it must have captured the nation. Or maybe they were going to talk about the pros and cons of what her capture meant. Ashley stopped working on the board and sat down on the sofa to watch.

'Manchester Police have today apprehended the vigilante killer, dubbed the Manchester Maiden, after a tense stand-off with police. The killer, now known to be ex-stripper and prostitute Lisa Strachan was cornered in Limehouse Manor where she used to be part of a sect cult in the early eighties. It comes after she was caught almost murdering a fifth man, Manchester Deputy Mayor Harold Donaldson at his home, which has raised concerns over his position considering the rumours as to why her previous victims were killed. Our serious crime correspondent Tom Mellor has more.'

The TV cut to outside Limehouse as Lisa was taken into the back of a police van with the press trying to photograph her.

'Trying to end it where it all began, that seems to be the message coming out of all this today after police caught The Manchester Maiden.' It cut to Lisa Strachan's mugshot.

'Lisa Strachan was part of the religious group the New Agers when they occupied this house in the 1980s before running away to plan and extract her revenge on the men she murdered. She was only caught when an officer arrived at Deputy Mayor Donaldson's house in the middle of the night. The reason why is not being divulged from the Manchester Major Crimes team but the officer in question thwarted an attempt on the Deputy Mayor's life by Strachan; it's then reported that they chased Strachan up to here: Limehouse.'

The camera now showed the dilapidated manor house as it had been this morning. It cut to the reporter who was standing outside.

'It was here that Strachan was in a tense stand-off with the officer who chased her here, even when she was armed.'

'Police will not say what was said, nor will they say how the Deputy Mayor is involved. Head of the Investigation DCI Donald McArthur spoke to us earlier.' The camera panned to McArthur who was standing outside the gates.

"We still have a few lines of enquiry that we have to wrap up and I'm not comfortable with divulging information when we do not have the full picture yet. We will be questioning Harold Donaldson in connection to this investigation, but we will not have a clearer picture of this until tomorrow when we will be issuing a full statement on what has gone on. I'd also like to praise my team's heroism and professionalism in dealing with this difficult case. I can confirm that one of my officers has gone to hospital as a precaution, as a result of an attack by the suspect. Thank you, speak to you tomorrow."

The camera cut back to Mellor who was standing outside Limehouse.

"We have had a statement from the Manchester Mayor's office who tell us that they will not comment on this until the police have concluded their enquiries; but it does leave a large cloud over the Deputy Mayor considering that the other Maiden Murder victims were paedophiles."

The camera cut back to the anchor, who was looking down at an iPad, but then looked up at the camera.

"Surprised that someone didn't snap sooner. That's the verdict of other children abused by the same men at the centre of the Maiden Murders. Limehouse and the New Agers who resided there were dogged by abuse claims for years but nothing was ever done. Men and women abused as children by the men killed by Lisa Strachan had tried for years to get justice; it's only recently come to light that Strachan herself was part of a failed lawsuit against them years before. So, was this what tipped Strachan over the edge?"

"She was the victim of a failed system," Ashley said to herself, while getting up and walking to the board to finish, half listening to the dubbed-over voices of people who had experienced the same as Lisa. Though, as the news went on Ashley wondered what the people thought about Lisa now.

The camera panned back to the anchor who talked about how many businesses had links to Limehouse in the past and who else might have been caught up in it.

"How deep does this go?" Ashley wrote on the board. She took a step back. There would probably be quite a few people in Manchester watching the news nervously.

The intercom buzzed. Finally, food.

Ashley walked over to the intercom. "Hello?"

"Hi, Deliveroo for a Ms Fenway?"

"Yep, I'll buzz you in." Ashley pressed the button to unlock the door, walked back to the bedroom and got her purse out. By the time she made her way back and laid out her coffee table they were knocking on the door.

Ashley opened the door to the delivery boy was no older than eighteen. His eyes had gone wide with shock. Ashley was to slow to realise why.

"Uhm... Pizza Hut and a McDonald's milkshake."

"Thanks, I'm starving," Ashley said, getting the money out. When she looked back the delivery boy was looking at her legs. Ashley frowned.

"The transaction's up here," she said. He blushed furiously and blurted out an apology but was now staring at her chest.

"Try again," Ashley said, a little impatiently. He looked up at her face, mumbled another apology and handed her the food.

"Thanks," Ashley said, handing over the money. "Tips in there too, and one for the road, girls always know when you're looking at our tits. Night." Before he could say another word, she closed the door. The smell of her pizza making her less irritable.

She sat down on the sofa, pulled the coffee table closer to her and checked her phone to see the texts. Most of them were from her mum, one from her brother and two from Dan.

Matty: *Hey sis, seen the news, you weren't caught up in that were you?*

Dan: *Just seen the news, hope you're all right, do you want me to come over?*

Ashley unlocked her phone and opened WhatsApp. She quickly replied to her brother telling him that she was caught up in it and that she would call him later, all while having a slice of pizza. She turned her attention to Dan.

Just seen the news, hope you're all right, do you want me to come over?

No, it's ok, I feel really tired, so I'd be shit company anyway. Come around tomorrow though?

Ashley sent it off, placing her phone on the sofa and bringing up her sister's Netflix so she could find something to watch. After much deliberation she decided on *The Lincoln Lawyer*; as she was about to press play her phone vibrated. Ashley picked it up.

I finish at 10, late enough?

Ashley laughed to herself.

Perfect, fancy a sleepover?

Read my mind.

Great, I got Deliveroo and a film on, so I'll see you tomorrow.

Couldn't you wait till tomorrow?
I don't fancy that avocado salad you made last time.
It was amazing and you'd be lucky if I make that for you again.
Besides, the whole reason you're coming around tomorrow
is that I'm having this tonight.
Fine.

Didn't want to deal with your hangry arse anyway.

Ashley sent back a laughing emoji, sat back into the sofa and threw her phone away. She pressed play on the remote. She looked around her apartment and wondered what Lisa Strachan's home was like. But her mind wandered to what was being said on the TV about her maybe being unhinged. Nothing could be further from the truth.

Chapter 83

So Donaldson was a nonce to? What the fuck is in the water in Manchester? #sticktobottledstuffguys

Manchester supposedly the new northern powerhouse who has more corrupt officials than any other city. #goodstartboys

Can @GMP come out and tell me who else in Manchester has been touching kids up? #youleaveoasisalone

No wonder Lisa Strachan couldn't get justice. #rottenfromleaftoroot

I hope Donaldson has his soap thrown on the shower floor for the rest of his life.

Ashley now wished she'd turned her alarm off last night. She winced when she turned it off, she realised that she did it with her broken arm. Ashley turned on her back, cradled it and stared at the ceiling. Today was going to be another long day but at least this case was on its last legs.

Ashley thought about going back to sleep but before she knew what she was doing, she was already pulling her gym gear on and brushing her hair. She wrapped her arm up in the support and walked into the kitchen, opened the fridge, got a smoothie and walked to the window where she could look over the city.

Even with the benefit of a full night's sleep she felt tired mentally, but she wanted to get in early to make sure that they painted the right picture of Lisa for the media. She downed the rest of her smoothie and went back to the bedroom.

With her packed bag Ashley put the radio on while making up her lunch for the day ahead. Ashley rubbed her eyes and turned on the radio, which was playing a soothing tune, which died into the news.

"Good morning, this is the half six news on BBC Radio Two." Ashley was filling up her protein shake from the tub in the kitchen.

The news made a passing remark on the Maiden case while going on about something in government. Ashley popped the top on her bottle and went to grab her car keys.

"Oh yeah." It was at the station. Ashley put her bag over her shoulder and tightened the strap. Nice day to run to the gym.

Cardio.

Legs.

Core.

More cardio.

Normally this would be the time Ashley went on the bag but since she couldn't exercise her arm, she was doing a light jog on the treadmill while listening to her music; trying to block out what Lisa had said to her yesterday and what the news had said about her last night.

She slowed the treadmill down to a walking pace and looked up at the TV with the news on which had Lisa's mug shot on. Ashley took her headphones out and listened to two panellists who had been discussing it yesterday.

"This woman is the victim of a system that prioritises fat cats' interests and keeping their noses clean from their dirty dealings. Well, now they've been found out and I think this woman should walk free if she helps put all the other monsters in the system in jail."

"Yes, I agree she is a victim, but she broke the law. Murder is a life sentence no matter what the courts say. She'll have to live with the fact that she killed those men in cold blood. It's like the petition to absolve the suffragettes of their crimes. Yes, they did it for a noble cause, but they still committed crimes while doing so. The law does not care about cause when a crime has been committed."

"So, are you suggesting that she should be put away? The woman killed four paedophiles; scum on society. A large majority of the public would rather she was on the streets than these slimy abominations. To be honest, if there were more people like her then maybe what happened in Rochdale might never have happened."

"If you advocate the murders of one group, where does it end? I have sympathy for her, I really do, as does most of the public. But we cannot have people taking the law into their own hands as Ms Strachan has done, or any little misdemeanour could be skewered into a 'blameless murder'. The book has to be thrown at her to stop this happening again."

Ashley stopped the treadmill and got off; now it was like watching her conversation with her mum. After showering and changing Ashley walked to the City Tower with her hands in her jacket pockets looking at the world go by around her.

As she walked up to the entrance, she could see the media already gathered around outside. Ashley shook her head. As if people did this for a living.

As she moved closer some of the reporters clocked her and came towards her.

"Detective, is there any word if you're charging Deputy Mayor Donaldson?" One asked.

"What about Lisa Strachan?"

"Come on guys, haven't you got Z List celebs to take snaps of?" Ashley asked, as she walked through.

"Not as juicy as a serial killer, love" one of them said while taking a photo of her.

"We want answers!" another shouted.

"And you'll get them!" Ashley shouted back, as they started to form a barrier between her and the door into the building.

"But I have a broken arm, unless the rest of you want to join me in that then I suggest that you back off and let me through." She held up her arm to show them. They grumbled and moved aside.

"Thank you," Ashley said, walking through. "Press conference will be later." Ashley made her way into the forecourt and saw her car parked up. Well at least that made it back in one piece, she thought.

***

When Ashley got into the office it looked like a bomb had hit it. There was lots of paperwork strewn all over the place with various boards on the links between the victims and Strachan. Ashley walked over to her desk and turned her computer on, the thought of having to write up what happened becoming more and more unappealing.

While the computer loaded Ashley looked through the work they had done yesterday, flicking through the files they had compiled on each murder. She was even marginally impressed that Armstrong had been able to compile all the links she had found last night. She smirked to herself, she really wanted to see his face, when he realised she'd blown the case wide open.

Ashley walked over to the board which showed Lisa Strachan / Kate Marsh. Ashley looked at the evidence that had been gathered so far. Her house had been searched and they found the gown from Stan Kettings' wardrobe along with three burner phones which had Lisa's and the victim's DNA on them.

Ashley though still felt a twinge of guilt. She had interviewed Strachan earlier in the investigation and hadn't picked up on anything; scrap that she had interviewed her twice, once at the hotel and again at her house.

"Stupid, stupid, stupid," Ashley said, unable to see what she had missed.

She looked over at the computer analysis which said that she had contacted the victims through Facebook and Twitter. She had made the offer to them on their platform and they talked details over the direct message function in games, so it didn't leave a trail.

Ashley nodded, impressed at the forethought. Then the correspondence between Lisa, the victims and a few more people were easy to find when they knew what they were looking for; probably Aaron told them what they were looking for. It was all there; times, dates and locations, even the message from Whikley cancelling the rendezvous.

All wrapped up with Strachan's confession, the bow that held it all together. All in all, a good day for everybody.

Ashley logged into the computer and started to type up her statement. About an hour later McArthur came in.

"Ah, Fenway, good. Have you had a chance look over the conviction files?" He asked, walking towards her.

"Yes Sir, all the correct links are there," Ashley said. "I'm writing up my statement now."

"DNA should be back at some point to so that should be enough," McArthur said, now sitting on the edge of her desk. "How's the arm?"

"Cracked radius," Ashley said, as she leaned back on the seat and raised her arm. "How's Lisa, has she said anything?"

"Not a word," McArthur told her. "Doesn't even want a lawyer. Said everything she wanted to say, she said to you. And thanks to your recording we have her confession."

"What do the CPS want to do?" Ashley asked.

"They want her tried and have the whole library thrown at her. They feel she's made us lot look very stupid." Ashley shook her head.

"No," she said, getting up. "She's a victim too."

"Fenway, it's out of our hands now," McArthur said. "We've done our job and got the evidence for the CPS." He sighed and ran a hand through his hair.

"I watched the video and it does make harrowing viewing."

"Which is why we need to protect her. Try and convince them it's… diminished responsibility of some sort."

"Fenway, it's not feasible," McArthur said. "She planned the whole thing out. It doesn't matter which way you spin this; she's going down for a while."

"I hate it as much as you do," McArthur said, before Ashley could reply. "But I have my orders from up high too." Ashley frowned.

"What did they say?"

"They want the unit to have a big win. A corrupt paedophilic Deputy Mayor and a vigilante serial killer is up there as the biggest scores you can find around here. Especially with all that's happened with Rochdale recently and maybe the potential to catch more."

"But —"

"But sometimes Ashley, we have to look at the bigger picture. Who knows who else was involved with this? This might open up a whole new can of worms."

There was an odd finality in his voice which told Ashley that this was it.

"CPS should be here in a few minutes. They want to go through the evidence with you." Ashley nodded.

"Yes Sir," she said, going back to her computer. McArthur got up and walked to his office, leaving Ashley to ponder how unfair the system could be; but if the CPS had to talk to her, maybe she could plead her case directly to them.

Ashley finished typing up her report and read through it before printing it off. As she was at the printer more people from her unit started to come into the office.

"Hey Ashley, good collar," Murphy said, coming into the office. "Don't appreciate having to shift through all this though," he said, pointing at the papers.

"Well someone had to do it," Ashley said, separating pages on her statement into the different files. "I don't think you lot would want to deal with this?" Ashley said holding up her arm.

"Well done."

"How did Armstrong take it?"

"Like someone had told him he had to kick puppies," Ashley smirked.

"Good," she said, filing her statement into the files.

"How's the arm?"

"Cracked radius," Ashley said, showing him the support. "Nothing to serious."

"Have you been hearing what the press has been saying about it?" Ashley nodded to the TV.

"Yeah, me and the wife had a healthy debate about it this morning," he said, placing his coat on the back of his chair. "Turns out we should have let her go through with killing Donaldson."

"Funnily enough, my mum said the same thing," Ashley replied.

"I saw your video," Murphy said. "It made me feel really sorry for her. I thought we were dealing with a cold-blooded killer."

"I guess we are in a way," Ashley said. "She murdered them without a second thought."

"You know what I mean," Murphy said. "I thought it would be some sicko who lived in his parents' spare room." The TV showed Lisa's mugshot again. "You spoke to her. Did you think she had it in her?"

Now Ashley thought about it she didn't think Lisa had it in her at all. Then again did any killer think they had it in them? What Lisa said to her about someone hurting you to the point of killing them was now preying on Ashley's mind. Her train of thought was cut off when Armstrong came in.

"No. I didn't. But she did." Armstrong looked at Ashley and Murphy and looked at the TV.

"I'm sick of seeing her face," he said, sitting down.

"It's big news," Murphy said.

"Well done on the cases," Ashley said, patting them. Armstrong looked at her surprised.

"I thought you couldn't give out complements," he said, feigning shock.

"Only when you deserve it. So, what did I miss yesterday?"

"A shit storm," Armstrong said. "It was all-hands on deck in here yesterday."

"What about Donaldson's computer?" Ashley asked.

"Came back yesterday, he was the same. We told his wife and she suggested we keep him in protective custody." Made sense Ashley thought. Parland came in.

"How is he?"

"Trying to make a deal," Murphy said. "Upon high are considering it." Answering Ashley's next question.

"If he gets off, I'll hand my notice in," Parland said. Just as he finished McArthur came through.

"Right, come on round. I want to brief you lot first and then the rest of them," McArthur said, pointing outside.

"I think we can all give DC Fenway a round of applause for blowing this case wide open." The rest of them gave a small clap.

"Good work, it gives the department a big win, but we still have work to do regarding Donaldson. I'm letting the gremlins finish his phone and bank records since they started on them yesterday and besides Ashley, you'll have to talk to the CPS later today which I will be sitting in on. Armstrong and Parland I want you to carry on questioning him, Murphy I want you to go talk to his remaining associates, see if they knew anything about what he was doing. Plus, we have a conference for eleven this morning as well, so I'll be with PR after the CPS have finished with Fenway. Go on."

The rest of the team set off, but McArthur came to her desk.

"While we're waiting for the CPS, I want you to put together a list of people connected to this Limehouse place so we can track them down."

"Yes, Sir."

"When the suits get here can you bring them into my office. Not sure how long I'll be, have to brief upon high." Ashley nodded.

While everyone else got on with what they were doing Ashley was starting to go back over the paperwork for Limehouse to try and see who else was linked with this place.

Ashley looked up from her desk and saw two people from the CPS coming in; well she could hear them before seeing them they were that loud. How did she know they were CPS? Only lawyers wore suits in a place like this. They were both men, late twenties, early thirties with suits and briefcases. They walked up to McArthur's office and tried it.

"He's popped out," Ashley said. "Should be back in five minutes."

"That's all right, we need to speak to him and this guy." Ashley frowned and turned in her seat.

"Who?"

"Ash Fenway," the other one said, looking at a piece of paper.

"I'm Ash Fenway." Both looked up at her, the expression on their face telling Ashley that they didn't quite believe it.

"You?"

"In the flesh," Ashley said, getting up from her chair. She walked to McArthur's office and let her and the CPS in.

"DC Ashley Fenway." She put emphasis on her first name, only her friends called her Ash. She showed them into the office and sat down in one of the chairs across from McArthur. For all their talking beforehand both men were quiet now. Were they worried that they had offended her or were they too scared to speak to her? Maybe the support on her arm was the thing intimidating them.

One of them went to speak but thought against it. Was she really that off-putting? Thankfully she was saved by McArthur coming in. Instantly both men were in their comfort zone, walking over, shaking hands and making small talk. Their names were John Dayton and Simon Bromley.

"So, as you know, we have recommended provisionally to charge Lisa Strachan with five counts of murder and one of unlawful

517

imprisonment and attempted murder," Dayton said. "It might seem a bit harsh, but this is a complex case."

"Indeed," Bromley said, taking over. "She's decided not to have a psych evaluation and has said she won't contest with a claim of diminished responsibility. Also, the thing with Harold Donaldson is a bit of a tasty side dish too."

"Where do we stand on that, considering the evidence we gave you yesterday?" McArthur asked.

"He's a paedo and he'll go down for that," Dayton said. "Strachan has already said she'll testify against him but he's looking to make a deal that would implicate other people in this, and he says the Rochdale scandal."

"You buying it?" Ashley asked.

"We have to hear what he has to say," Bromley said, evenly. "If it means getting more people like him off the streets, then yes. This could be the domino that sends it all tumbling down."

"What am I doing here?" Ashley asked. "Why did you need me here?"

"We want to catch up with you to make sure that all the evidence you obtained was legal," Dayton clarified.

"All legal and in the public domain if you know where to look," Ashley said. "I assume you've looked through the case notes?"

"We have," Bromley said, looking at the new copy Ashley gave him. "We just need your statement confirming your version of events." Ashley pointed out where it was, and both started to look through it.

"You've painted her as a very sympathetic character," Dayton said with a frown.

"She is," Ashley said, as though it was obvious.

"She's a killer," Dayton replied flatly.

"And a killer has motive, as motive goes it's very compelling," Ashley said. "The public seem to be behind it."

"It's a good job the public doesn't know what's good for it," Bromley said, not looking up from his copy of Ashley's statement. "Really they should be afraid of her."

"Only the people who have something to hide are afraid of her," Ashley shot back. "People like Donaldson." McArthur tried to hide his smile while Dayton looked on amazed at her.

"The bottom line, DC Fenway, is that at the end of the day the public should be afraid of us."

"She shouldn't be afraid of us. The public shouldn't be afraid of us. Only the bad guys should be afraid of us," Ashley said, her heart breaking at the words. "She's a victim. She needs our understanding."

"Gordon Ferrets, Stan Kettings, Will Oatley and Ian Whikley, are victims too," Bromley replied.

"They are now. Before that they had escaped the system."

"Maybe they were victims of abuse too," Bromley said. "We don't know. But that's the problem of looking at every case differently. Most of the time we just have to look at the bare bones and go from there."

"Would they have got the same amount of help she will?"

"As a woman she'd probably get more," Dayton said. "She should have the best shrink her majesty's prison service has to offer," Dayton said, closing the file and getting up. "Thank you for your time DC Fenway, DCI McArthur." Dayton and Bromley walked out.

"What pricks," Ashley said after they closed the door; part of her hoped that they had heard her.

"I told you," McArthur said, looking at his watch. "I have the press conference in twenty minutes."

Chapter 84

The chatter of the national and semi-international press filled the room. In the old days there would be tape recorders on the front desk along with a multitude of fuzzy microphones. Now, there were only a couple of microphones and an array of iPhones, with the recorders ready to run.

The air of impatience was thick as the police hadn't been forthcoming with details about the case after the arrest of Harold Donaldson. It was either a good or bad move depending on who you were.

Details were drip-fed enough for rolling coverage but not enough to establish the full picture. This was the first serial killer caught in the UK this decade, and with the possibility of a documentary or TV series in the offing people wanted the details.

The door opened into the press room. All chatter died and was replaced by the clicks of cameras as McArthur came into the room along with Delany, Glen Mayer and DCS Cartwright.

"Boss looks good on TV, doesn't he?" Armstrong said. "I reckon they'll have George Clooney put on a Scottish accent for him." The team where watching the press conference from the office.

"Who do you reckon they'll have for me?" Murphy asked.

"That black guy from Star Wars?" Armstrong replied.

"Samuel L?"

"No, John, what's his name?"

"Boyega?" One of the other DC's offered.

"Yeah, him." Murphy nodded.

"I'll take that." Ashley had Jeffery Wright down to play Murphy.

"Obviously Leo Di Caprio would play yours truly and take the Oscar home for it. Daniel Day Lewis would fill Parland's boots."

"Hey! I'm not that old."

"OK, how about Mark Hamill?"

"Ha, ha," Parland deadpanned. "I thought myself more like Christian Bale."

"Yeah, if he was grey," Armstrong said.

"And I reckon if Margot Robbie dyed her hair brown, she could play Fenway." A few of the guys in the room nodded their approval. Ashley approved inwardly.

"Hope she likes doing her own stunts," Ashley said, holding up her support and not tearing her eyes away from the screen.

"Shut up, it's starting."

"Ladies and gentleman of the press." It was Mayer talking. "I can confirm that Lisa Strachan, also dubbed by you as the Manchester Maiden was captured and apprehended in the early hours of yesterday morning. Of course, with the complex nature of the case we have been reluctant to talk to you without first having everything watertight. First and foremost, I would like to congratulate DCI McArthur and his team for bringing this to a swift conclusion, despite intense pressure from all corners of the media."

"Hey, we got a mention," Armstrong interjected.

"Shut up."

The reins had now been passed to DCI McArthur.

"Thank you," he said, albeit a little uncomfortably. "To start I can confirm that the one officer taken to hospital after yesterday's event has been discharged and is fine. I can confirm that after talks with the CPS we are charging Lisa Strachan and both she and her attorney have been informed of this." There was lots of scribbling on paper and a few murmurs.

"She is being remanded in custody until a transfer later today to a secure location, which will not be shared with the public given the level of interest.

"Again, I would like to thank my team for their time and effort in this case and for bringing it to a swift conclusion."

"I know that you're all tetchy so I will answer a couple of questions." The room erupted into a swirl of noise and badgering. McArthur pointed at one.

"DCI McArthur, can you confirm what you have charged Ms Strachan with?"

"Due to legal reasons we can't tell you what we have charged her with," McArthur said. "Rest assured though you will all be told in time." He pointed to the next one.

"What sort of precedent does this send to other wannabe vigilantes?"

"Not to," McArthur said, bluntly. "Lisa Strachan has been caught and will feel the full weight of the law." Before he could move on the reporter cut in.

"But DCI McArthur, numerous polls have shown that the public are in support of Ms Strachan's actions."

"What bollocks," Parland said, loudly.

"Should there be some sort of leniency for her case?"

"It's not us that dish out the sentences, Ms?"

"De Luna. The Guardian."

"Well, Miss De Luna, the police only gather the evidence, it's the CPS who will try for the sentence based on the evidence we've given them. As for leniency in her case, that would set a dangerous precedent. I think you forget that she murdered five people in cold blood and almost killed a sixth. Would you want that someone living next door to you?"

"If it was Lisa Strachan I would."

"What a smug bitch," Ashley said.

"Yeah, she's a wound a bit too tightly," Armstrong said.

"Not one of your exes, is she?"

"I want to know if the police are piggybacking on this poor woman's plight to help justify the huge vanity project which is the Major Crimes Unit." McArthur narrowed his eyes at her.

"The fact that you insinuate such a thing makes me think that you're not worth the paper your name is printed on," McArthur said.

"The fact that you would use this woman so flippantly to try and provoke a reaction is despicable to say the least."

McArthur stopped. He looked down at the table. Ashley had a sinking feeling that he was going to stop it there.

"The thing is that looking over this case has shown us that Miss Strachan is a victim in this too," McArthur said, in a measured voice.

"She's a victim too?" McArthur nodded and Ashley smiled.

"Not that we condone what she has done, far from it, but like the public we too are sympathetic with her story. She was let down by everyone, us included and the only way she thought she could regain some sort of control was to carry out these acts. Although we can't get her justice for the other five deceased, we are putting together the case against another one of her abusers."

"Can you say who?"

"No, not at this time," McArthur said. "We don't want her to rot in prison, ideally; we don't want that for anyone. We want her to get the help she needs, and in time maybe she will see that what she did was wrong and be able to integrate back into society.

"Thank you all for your time."

There was a strong silence in both rooms at what McArthur had said. Ashley was smiling to herself and was the first to get up from her seat, taking her empty mug with her.

Ashley made herself a tea and him a coffee and waited for McArthur in the press waiting room. Hopefully what she had said to him had sunk through, or maybe he always thought that Lisa was a victim. A couple of minutes later he came through.

"Fenway, brilliant." he said, taking his cup. "I thought you didn't make other people drinks."

"I thought you might need one," Ashley replied.

"Bloody right there," he said, walking past her.

"Scottish?" He asked.

"Scottish?"

"Scotch."

"Sir, it's half eleven in the morning."

"I'll take that as a no."

"Yeah, it's a no," Ashley said. "Well I think we just showed to them why we need a Major Crimes Unit." MacArthur laughed.

"I'm glad I didn't take my boss's advice," he said. "He said you were going to be trouble."

"Still time to prove him right," Ashley retorted.

"Maybe, but I knew when I saw your file that you had to be on this team."

"I had to?"

"I know DCI McCallum," he said. "We were in training together. When I saw you had a personal recommendation from him, I knew you would be a good fit."

"I didn't know that," Ashley said, off guard.

"I'd like to know how you got it."

"His recommendation?" McArthur nodded. Ashley smiled.

"I impressed him."

"With what?"

"You're the detective. You figure it out." McArthur nodded.

"Fine, I will," he said. "I'm feeling generous so you can all have a weekend off. Tell the rest of the team."

"I could do with one," Ashley said. "Thanks, Sir."

Chapter 85

"The fact that this woman has been let down so badly, not only by the police and the state, but by us as well, the public; the consequences of this whole thing have been... sad, in a way."

"I couldn't agree more. The world has progressed more in the last thirty years but unfortunately not quick enough for the likes of Lisa Strachan, and the hundreds of people that have been subjected to abuse like hers. We can only hope that they find the strength to come forward."

"The Mayor of Manchester has had to come out and defend himself over his appointment of Harold Donaldson as his deputy. Mike Buchannan has been silent over the allegations that Mr Donaldson is a serial paedophile who has been sucked into the Limehouse Scandal. The Mayor said that he had no comments at this time. It comes after he earlier had to defend his links to Will Oatley after revelations of his private life was made public."

Ashley turned the news off. As pleased as she was that she had solved a murder case she was sick of the names that had plagued her for the last two weeks.

She had been able to complete her washing, clean the apartment and get the food shopping done; a proper one at that, not just a day at a time shop.

Ashley looked down at her phone which was lying flat on her stomach. She turned it over and saw the messages from the hockey group chat which were full of excitement for Sunday's match. But the one she was interested in was at the top.

Dan: *Finish at half ten, can't wait to see you.*

It was adorned with a purple devil emoji after it. Ashley slipped her phone into the pocket of her sweatpants and got up from the sofa. She went to her bathroom, brushed her teeth and her hair and tied it up in a loose ponytail for an easy pull that would let her hair fall (Dan liked that for some reason). Her phone vibrated in her pocket.

She pulled it out; she would hate it if Dan cancelled. Thankfully it was only Dave.

"Hey."

"Hey, heard you had a busy couple of days."

"Yeah, I did," Ashley said, looking at her arm. "How's Metro?"

"Boring," Dave replied. "Finally, been able to get a conviction on the serial wife beater."

"Good. Did you get her to talk?"

"He hit one of the kids and that was the straw that broke the camel's back," Dave explained. "CPS were happy; he'll be before the magistrates in a few days."

"Good, cycle looks broken then," Ashley said.

"They're like weeds Ash, once one gets pulled up there's always another one to take their place." He was right, much as Ashley hated it.

"Makes you wonder why we do it?"

"You should have seen her face when she saw that he was going away," Dave said. "That's why I do it." If only Ashley had that to hold onto. Like she said to her mum, there were no winners in this case. Only losers.

"How about you?"

"Talking to the CPS about the murder; bunch of pricks they were," Ashley said. "They said that Lisa Strachan deserves the book thrown at her." Ashley sighed and shook her head.

"You know, I was so focused on trying to catch a serial killer that I didn't even think about why she would want to do what she did."

"Not even when you knew they were nonces?" Ashley sighed.

"It didn't even occur to me then," she said. "You hear about these hunters, I thought maybe one of them took it too far."

"There's still time for that. I followed your case. You were fortunate that you found her when you did, or you may not have."

"Yeah, I suppose we were," Ashley said.

"Too late to tell you that you get days like this."

"Yeah, I know," Ashley said, though none of those days had hit her quite as hard as this.

"Well I'm cleaning the pond out tomorrow; what are you doing to unwind?" A twinge of guilt ran through her stomach.

"I have a friend coming over tonight and then I've got hockey on over the weekend," Ashley said quietly, just wanting to get off the phone.

"OK, I'll speak to you soon, unless you muscle in on our territory again." Ashley smiled.

"Not my remit," she said. "Take care Dave, see you soon." Ashley hung up, sat back down on the sofa and looked up at the ceiling. At least Dan was coming around, she could shut her mind off for a bit at least; but her stomach was now twisting anxiously at the thought.

Ashley went to the kitchen to try and keep herself busy. She turned the radio down a little and poured a couple of glasses of wine, a knot forming in her stomach as she poured. There was a knock on the door. She always paused before this and asked herself if it was still a good idea.

"It's open!" Ashley shouted, taking a sip. The door opened.

"Brrr. It's fucking Baltic out there. Do you have a drink handy?" Ashley lifted her hand out and shook the half-filled glass.

"Go sit down, I'll be with you in a minute. Something to eat?"

"No thanks. Maybe a bit later."

"Lucky for you I went to the shops," Ashley said, walking to the living room where Danielle was leaning on the back of the sofa taking her scarf and coat off. When she took them off, Ashley handed Danielle's wine to her and stood in front of her, taking a measured sip. Danielle huffed and ran her hands through her hair, her gaze going to Ashley and smiling.

"You good?"

"Very good," Ashley said, taking another sip. "How was work?"

"Urgh, boring as hell," Danielle said, leaning over and picking her glass up. "We had a gig on, and these two metal heads were trying to flirt with me."

"Trying being the operative word." Danielle nodded.

"Honestly I have never been drier than speaking to them. Constantly asking why I don't have tattoos and making some joke about a needle." She took a deep breath. "Annoying." She smiled. "Not as busy as yours though." Ashley shrugged.

"It's the day job. Bet your dad's happy you don't want to be a cop, right?"

"Still goes on at me getting a career, I want to do journalism but he's against that as well." Danielle took another sip of wine and her gaze went down to Ashley's arm.

"What have you done?" Ashley looked down at it too.

"Oh, yeah, I broke it," Ashley said. "Well, cracked. Should be right as rain in a couple of weeks."

"So, when I asked if you were all right and you said yes this was what? An oversight?"

"If it hurt, I would have told you," Ashley said. "But I'm fine, I'm just... I'm just tired." She finished.

"Exhausting week?"

"Exhausting couple of weeks," Ashley said, taking another sip. "It's days like this I wonder why I didn't stick to being a shrink."

"Because you like chasing and tackling guys?" Danielle offered.

"Look who I'm asking," Ashley said, looking down at her glass.

"Yeah..." Danielle bit her lip. Ashley's eyes flickered up and saw Danielle's gaze wandering to her lips, her own gaze now raking over Danielle, the tight work t-shirt she was wearing complimenting her body very well.

It had been a long week. Ashley downed the rest of her drink and kissed her. Danielle responded by kissing Ashley back, leaning into her body and running her hands up Ashley's back to her shoulders and locking them behind Ashley's neck; her strawberry lip gloss, a welcome taste after a long day.

"Keen?" Danielle asked, teasingly as she pulled back.

"It's been a long week," Ashley replied. Danielle moved some stray hair behind Ashley's ear and took her hand.

"Let me help you forget it." Danielle led her wordlessly to Ashley's room. Danielle opened the door, let herself in and made herself comfortable on the bed. She looked back at Ashley who was still at the mouth of her own room, the guilty knot in her stomach telling her to stop this now.

"Are you just gonna stand there?" Ashley looked up and saw Danielle laid out on her bed, her jeans and t-shirt long discarded, and after the week Ashley had it was the most inviting scene she could wish for.

That was the reason she kept on coming back to doing this. Ashley smiled, the knot untightening and disappearing. She pulled her vest over her head, took her hair out of its ponytail and walked towards her.

Say I'm not a sinner but you make me a liar!
I like the games we play,
When you're inside my veins,
No, a little good don't stop the devil.
Don't Stop the Devil.
Dead Posey.